To Nicky and Simon

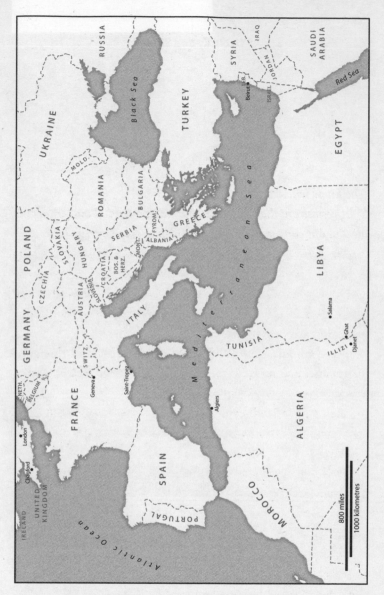

She knew where to go.

A restaurant that was quiet, but not too quiet. Loud enough to drown out conversation; quiet enough to catch every word.

She didn't want his voice to fade, carefully, at just the wrong moment. Expensive gaps between tables helped.

Floors could be traps. She looked for carpets. Floorboards at a stretch. Tiles echoed. Walls could be troublesome, too. Wooden panelling was best, or tapestries.

She eliminated sprawling table decorations, and discarded live music. She usually, but not always, avoided hotels. Rooms upstairs could shift the mood.

She'd learned that expensive was best, because she paid and everyone – everyone – was distracted by a dozen oysters or a Château Lafite.

She'd had lunch here once before. Half enjoying the exquisite food, and half twitching at a raucous coffee machine.

She tipped well, so the waiters would respond immediately, next time.

This time.

And she had made it clear – but oh so politely – that she did not welcome intrusion. Nothing worse than an interruption – Coffee, more wine, the pudding menu? – when all you wanted was that strange sort of peace.

She had eaten in all the best restaurants in London. It surprised her, now, when someone thought it was a treat.

It had to be a place where nobody knew her. Although you could never be sure. It had happened. But she had seen off that danger. 'Casey? No, sorry . . . My name is Caroline. Caroline Eyre.' A half laugh. 'I look like a lot of people.'

And her friends, knowing what she did, would almost-guess and walk away. And her acquaintances would doubt, and amble off, half shaking their heads. 'I could have sworn . . .'

The light mattered, of course. Always the light.

Every time she walked into a room, now, she was aware of the light. Candles and lamps, windows and daylight. Because glare in her eyes could flare everything.

She dressed for the surroundings too. Always dark colours. Always expensive fabrics. Clothes that covered everything, but made a man want to strip her bare.

She had a generous clothing allowance. They knew it was worth it.

And she couldn't use her own clothes.

Because the smart suits and the black dresses, the neat shirts and the smart blazers, they would all be ripped apart.

And then, in a crooked attic in Holborn, they would be stitched back together.

But now, the suits and the dresses, the shirts and the coats, now they were different. Now they were – carefully, oh so carefully – embedded with the wires and the buttons, the eyes and the secrets.

And no one would ever see the blank, stark stare of the tiniest hidden camera.

1

The news editor was shouting at his team. Even the people who weren't in the firing line ambled over, because Ross in a rage was worth watching.

The people who were in the firing line quivered.

'You're all fucking useless,' he bellowed. He was waving a copy of *The Times*, which had the exclusive interview with the Home Office minister. 'We've been chasing this fucking story for fucking months. There are at least five of you covering this fucking patch and none of you could find a story in a bloody library.'

He hurled *The Times* to the back of the room, where it confettied the health editor.

'Fuck's sake, Ross.' The health editor jammed the BMA on hold and swung round. 'Your aim is about as good as your news sense.'

The Times was flung back across the room. The junior minister's handsome face smiled from the front page. He emanated calm intelligence, and cool ambition.

'Get the fucking political team on the line.'

The hapless secretary pushed buttons.

'Yes?' The political editor's voice echoed unwillingly down the line. The political team worked from the House of Commons, in a tiny eyrie just beneath Big Ben. The Burma Road, it is called, the corridor where all the papers have an office. In the heart of power, and far from the news editor's reach.

'Did it occur to you that just fucking maybe, we might be interested in the first major interview with eyes-on-the-prize Alexander twatting Kingsley?'

'We tried, Ross. You know we tried.'

'Well, why didn't we fucking get it? I thought you were meant to be bloody mates with him. You lot couldn't break a fucking window.'

'You pissed off Downing Street with that splash on pension numbers. They gave him to *The Times* instead.'

The splash had had the biggest headline on the London *Post*'s front page, the lead article designed to jerk readers away from their rivals. The splash haunted Ross's dreams.

'Fuck that.' A pause as he worked out how to return fire on Number Ten. 'It's still not fucking good enough.'

The political editor sensed weakness.

'Sarah just had a good readout from that Defence spad.'

The news editor wavered. If you could offer him tomorrow, you might survive today. The spad – the defence secretary's special adviser – might be worth a few seconds.

'She's got some great stuff on the new aircraft carrier,' the political editor ploughed on.

He had not risen to managing the London *Post*'s political coverage without seeing off the occasional sling and arrow over the years.

'Right. Right.' The news editor's nose quivered. 'But we've been behind three times this week and it's only fucking Tuesday ... So what did he say about delivery times?'

Ross listened for a bit longer.

'Fine. That will do for the front basement. And tell Downing Street that I don't believe in this revenge-served-cold crap. I think of it more as a fucking tasting menu. No, scrap that. Tell them I think of revenge as an all-you-can-eat fucking buffet.'

He slammed down the phone, but the crisis had passed.

Behind him, Casey kicked her heels against the crime correspondent's desk, and dislodged a pile of papers.

'Casey . . .' The crime correspondent dived after the pages.

'I'm bored,' she moaned, wandering off. 'Bored, bored, bored.'

Casey Benedict was one of the paper's investigations reporters. Probably their star, but no one would ever say that, not in a newsroom.

Now, Casey stamped across the *Post*'s offices, past the rows of desks. The London *Post* sat somewhere between *The Times* and the *Telegraph* politically, clinging on to its broadsheet reputation while duking it out with the tabloids online.

Under Ross's ravenous management, the *Post*'s news team prided itself on its aggression.

'Get the fuckers. Get them. I want them on their knees.'

They took on Fleet Street every day, looking for a fight. The public torn between horror at the tactics, and addiction to the words.

And always the race to be first. To win, win, win at all costs.

Casey had worked her way up through the ranks. She'd started as the news desk junior, making Ross's coffee.

'Half and half, granules and hot water.'

'That'll kill you.'

'I don't care.'

It astonished her, looking back, that she'd survived.

The paper's management was Darwinian, and she made it through by luck and desperation.

They tried to break her and, when they couldn't, they grudgingly put her to work. All over the country and then all over the world.

Afghanistan. Exhausted soldiers, and endless wars. The echoing siren wailing over a base in the middle of nowhere, after a contact somewhere out beyond the wire. The worst sound, that siren. Everyone waiting for the helicopter to race back to the base's makeshift hospital. And Casey waiting to tap out the desperate words, and give them a beauty that wasn't there.

Wrexham. A damp Mecca bingo hall. Waiting for the Prime Minister's wife to make a rousing speech to a few Welsh pensioners. The octogenarians all furious at having their endless game disrupted for even a moment; the wife, shy, embarrassed, wanting it all to be over. She got her wish, not long after.

Kazakhstan. A plane full of Brits slammed into a cold mountainside. T-shirts and shoes, sunglasses and paperbacks, splintered on the rocks. Trying, for a second, to imagine the sudden plunge. The chaos and the screams. Writing it up, and shoving it away.

Along with the tears and the anger, the disaster and the death knocks.

Casey was always there, translating it into words that churned through the subs and were up, online, blazing across the front pages. Bannering into breakfasts, and blaring into tea breaks. So people chattered at the water cooler about how awful it was, can you believe it, and joked about a headline as the kettle boiled.

At the age of twenty-eight, Casey never knew where she would spend the night. She kept changes of clothes – warm jackets and cool dresses – under her desk.

Tokyo. Jerusalem. Buenos Aires. DC.

On the Heathrow train before she had a moment to think. Scroll through her messages, and learn her target.

Shanghai. Vancouver. Frankfurt. Delhi.

There as the statues fell and crowds triumphed, or the earth shook and the bombs exploded.

Sydney. Baghdad. Cape Town. St Petersburg.

'I go wherever there is something interesting happening,' she said once to a friend. 'The extremes.'

And then she stopped, because how can you explain that if you are always there, flying in only when the joy is overwhelming and the colours are brightest and the grief is everything, how do you go back to everyday?

Then, one day, three years ago, Miranda Darcey arrived. From the *Daily Argus*, god of a thousand eyes, and deadly rival to the *Post*.

They eyed each other suspiciously. Casey was the newsroom's bright young thing. Miranda was an established star, poached at huge cost.

By the age of thirty-three, Miranda had been running the investigations team at the *Argus*, her stock particularly high after forcing a cabinet minister from soaring heights to sulky backbenches. A scalp, they called it, and Miranda had collected several.

Ross wanted an investigations team for the *Post*, to dig into the big stories that take days, weeks, months.

'In-depth,' an investigations correspondent will say.

'Slow,' the newsroom will bitch.

But Ross wanted the exclusives, the huge scoops that an investigations team could deliver.

They could have gone either way, Miranda and Casey.

Miranda had deliberate blonde curls and blue eyes that noticed every flicker. She moved in a cloud of Chanel N°5, and her cackle rang round the office. With glamour as armour, Miranda had an easy confidence and the right to pick and choose her new team. Casey glowered at first, competitive to the bone.

But their first story went well, better than anyone could have hoped. A chief executive resigning over a black hole in his blue chip. Reading an apology down the barrel to the *Ten O'Clock News*, as shareholders rioted.

Casey and Miranda watched the news bulletins roll, and then went and got drunk.

'Well done, Casey' – that glint of kindness.

'Any time.'

And the next day, laughing, they started sharing ideas and tricks.

Journalists live and die by ideas. Sharing, like anywhere, is trust.

But today, Casey was bored. They were working on a leak, a huge one. The sprawling data dump that happens as technology blazes forward, and defence only learns from attack.

Thousands of documents. Endless spidery pages stolen from some offshore accountancy firm. And slowly, agonisingly slowly, they were piecing together the paperwork for hundreds of companies.

British Virgin Islands companies, owned by Seychelles companies, owned by Panamanian foundations, owned by nominee directors, owned by the cousin of the bloodiest of dictators.

Eventually, it would be a story that would shake the bedrock of the City. But that story was months away. For now, Wynford Mortimer were, unknowingly, enjoying their last moments of offshore anonymity.

Journalists live off Mars Bars and bylines, coffee and adrenaline.

And Miranda, knowing her well enough to know that a bored Casey meant trouble, glanced up from her computer screen.

'Well, go and do something then.'

'But where? But what?' Casey sprawled forward over her desk.

'I don't care.' Miranda gave her the light gleam of a smile. 'Stop bloody jittering.'

Finally, the office emptied, Casey joining the flood. The evening stretched out. And then her phone chirped.

'Those guys you were after. They're here.'

2

Barmen go one of two ways, Casey realised early on. They either fell in love with the free drinks and the loud music, the pretty girls and the cheap drugs. Or they grew tired and angry. They grew bored of the drunken nights and wasted days. The champagne sprayed in the air and the girls scraped off the floor.

One too many my-dad-could-fucking-buy-you-creeps and they turned, looking for a way to lash back. And there was Casey, waiting with a sympathetic grin and a roll of her eyes. The barmen knew everything.

Jasper, the head doorman at Gigi's, loathed it so much that Casey thought he was close to abandoning the show altogether. But for now, every so often, he would drop her a quick message.

He was clever, Jasper. And she had told him exactly what she wanted.

'Cormium boys just walked in.'

Casey moped out of the *Post* for the tiny flat just off the Bethnal Green Road that didn't quite feel like home. Planning some half-hearted yoga, with Miranda's words ringing in her ears, trying to be interested in the boxset that everyone was talking about in the office.

Jasper's text about Cormium lifted her out of her bed.

One of the biggest commodity traders in the world, and yet almost no one had heard of Cormium.

Cormium filled the world's car, from a Venezuelan oil well. Cormium made the world's toast; wheat bought and sold before it was even planted, in some dusty field in Iowa. Cormium even poured the coffee, sharked off some scrappy farmer in Kenya and trucked halfway across Africa in hours.

People lived Cormium lives without ever knowing it.

And Cormium was also, Casey suspected, about to sign a deal for most of the oil in Libya.

Libya, beautiful, crumbling Libya, was trying to drag itself out of an endless civil war. Perched on the northern edge of Africa, with its bewildered new leadership – men who had never expected power in the first place – looking around for people who understood business. People who *knew*.

Cormium, based on the opposite side of the Mediterranean, in glitzy Monaco, was elbowing its way to the front of the queue, eyes on the prize.

The company had recently employed a former defence minister to charm for them. And he was good at it. Charm, politicians find, is a transferable skill set. Purely coincidentally, he insisted, the last government had worked closely with the Libyan rebels. Back when they were battling to overthrow the mad–bad dictator.

Purely coincidentally, British airstrikes had crushed the last lines of defence. The small war a triumph, the defence minister had pointed out at the time. Everyone a winner.

Of course, there had been complications since then. Those tottering countries were so very vulnerable. And swathes of the country were, well, frangible. But right now, there was a tender sort of peace.

And Casey had heard that the former defence minister was now the point person for Cormium's lengthy negotiations with Libya's precarious new government.

Those men in Gigi's, right now, might know all about that careful deal.

Black dress, high heels, hair blow-dried upside down in a hurry. In her black satin dress, Casey would disappear in Gigi's. She had the sort of face she could make up to exquisite, and fade to nothing. Delicate features could transform with a brush of mascara, or a glint of lipstick. Careless grey eyes sparkled at a flick of eyeshadow.

Casey glanced in the mirror, and was almost ready to go.

Vodka in the freezer. Just a quick shot, for the glint in her eye. You took the components of everyday, and twisted them.

Gigi's, down a small alley, just off Piccadilly, was the place for celebrating footballers and prowling girls.

The paparazzi crouched, scavenging the blurred smiles and sloppy fights.

There was a queue, always a queue, but Jasper nodded her in. Half Somali, with mournful eyes and a narrow jaw, he looked too fragile for the black leather jacket with the glittering diamante *Gigi's* on the back. But Casey had seen him hurl a fighting drunk out of Gigi's and knew that he won by not caring.

'Table Eight. You'll see them.' Quietly.

'Thanks, Jazz.'

'Always.'

He gave her a half-salute and faded away. Casey walked down the mirrored stairs, and into the punch of noise.

Gigi's was a maze of small tables and low sofas and ruthless hierarchies. A group of men would take a table for the night. When a table splashed out £10,000 for a bottle of vodka, the whole place came to a standstill. The club's theme tune boomed and a parade of girls, all sparklers and sparkling smiles, sashayed the bottle to the table. That parade happened again and again, all night long.

Some days, it made Casey laugh. A playpen for the lost boys. But not tonight.

Table 8 was in a booth near the dance floor. Casey strolled over.

'Oh God.' She tripped and fell, landing awkwardly on one of the sofas surrounding Table 8. 'I am so sorry.'

She had almost landed on one of the men. He turned in irritation, and Casey's smile lit up like a torch.

'I'm such an idiot. Oh God, my shoe is broken.' It wasn't, but he would never know. And if he did, he would never mention it. 'And I've spilled your drink. I'm so sorry. Let me get you another one.'

That was the password. It reminded him why they were there.

'Don't worry about it, babe. We've got loads. Here. Let's get you one. Champers, all right?'

And, limping gazelle, she was in.

Always wary, she watched him pouring the drink, ticking off what she knew about him. His suit, the shoes, the watch. Casey had seen his place in the table pecking order. Not the boss of the team. That was the guy in the middle, with the big laugh and the eye of the hostess. Not the office junior with the nervous smile, almost falling off the edge of the sofa.

They were all men, apart from the one beautiful girl, right next to the boss.

The girl had glossy dark hair and slanting green eyes, and was wearing a white dress, similar in style to Casey's. Ravishing, Casey noted. As Casey watched, the girl began laughing at a rambling anecdote from the boss, mirroring his body language.

Not the PA, definitely not. He didn't own her.

Not yet.

Casey forgot the girl and concentrated on the boss. Laughing at his own joke, he leaned back and snapped his fingers at the beautiful Nigerian hostess. The hostess was wearing pink satin hotpants with red braces. Just for a second, so that Casey was sure only she noticed, the hostess failed to hide her loathing.

Casey turned her attention to the man sitting beside her.

'I like your tie,' she said, and he preened.

She took the smallest sip of the drink and they talked for a while, and she knew he wouldn't remember a thing she said.

'I'm Brendan,' he said. 'Who are you?'

'Callie.' Because it was close enough to Casey to make her head turn if he said it. The first syllable, that was the key.

And soon she would ask, 'And what do you do then?'

Girls always asked. He knew it was to find out what lay behind the Savile Row suit and the Rolex.

But this one, it turned out, was really interested. Girls never were, not really. They'd ask for a bank statement, if they could, to speed things up. But this one asked clever questions, questions that showed she was actually listening.

And so Brendan became expansive. And the more he boasted, the more impressed she was.

She was just edging the conversation around to Libya when the boss stood up. The men looked up, like dogs when their leads were rattled.

'Oh. It's Oliver. We've got this … thing …'

And they were marched to the middle of the tiny dance floor for some complicated drinking game.

Casey leaned back against the ruby plush of the sofa. She had learned patience.

On the opposite side of the table, the girl in the white dress smiled at Casey, easily likable.

'I'm Amelie.' She reached out her hand.

'Callie. You've got a lovely tan.'

'Oh, thanks. Just back from Dubai. You having a fun evening?'

'Lovely, thanks. Do you know this lot well?' Casey asked.

'Kind of … But, you know, never put all your eggs in one basket case.'

Casey grinned back at the beautiful girl.

'Tell me about it.'

The first bars of the next song played.

'God, the music is dreadful in this place,' Amelie grinned. 'But I do love this song.'

'It's ridiculous,' said Casey. 'But me too.'

'So,' Amelie rolled her eyes at the cliché, 'what do you do?'

'Marketing,' said Casey, who felt she could hold her own in that field. 'You?'

'Same,' said Amelie. 'Where do you work?'

Casey did not want to get into a conversation with someone who actually worked in marketing.

'Oh.' She pretended a message had come through on her phone, making one-moment signs at Amelie.

'Just going to run to the bathroom,' said Amelie, standing up.

Casey tapped some notes to herself into her phone, smiling as she did so, because it would look like she was messaging a friend. She wasn't recording this evening, because nothing could fight the wall of music. There were rules about undercover recording too. Not that she always followed them.

Brief googling revealed that the group's alpha male was the chief executive of Cormium. Oliver Selby. Three years in post. Very rich; very tough. Pushed through a hostile takeover of one of Cormium's main rivals last year, against all odds. Recently divorced, for the second time. No wonder Amelie was laughing at his jokes.

Casey put her phone away and smiled vaguely at Brendan, out on the dance floor. There was a famous actor across the room, flanked by girls. Casey watched him idly.

Almost by accident, fiddling with her cocktail, she tuned in to the conversation in the booth behind her.

'He actually did that?'

'Yeah. Fucking crazy.'

'That is so fucking dark.'

At first, she was almost testing herself. Like when she read Ross's notes upside down on his desk, when she was bored in a meeting. Eavesdropping was one of her professional skills. Something to take pride in.

One was French, she thought. They weren't both French, because they wouldn't have been speaking English. The other one was American, Casey decided.

'He said you feel completely different afterwards,' said the American.

'I guess you would.'

'He always wanted to do it, he said.'

The music was blaring. Casey struggled to hear, losing words to delighted screams as a new song billowed.

'Still. It's too far, no?'

'I guess so. You'd have to be a good shot too. The place is near a camp ... For fuck's sake—'

'What?'

'I know. So you go to this camp, in the middle of fucking nowhere, and they give you a gun or something and you just shoot ... From a hilltop or whatever. At some poor fucker ...'

Casey jolted. Suddenly, glad she couldn't see them. Because that meant they couldn't see her, and for a second, just a second, her face dissolved to shock. She forced herself not to look round.

'To do that ... Sick ...'

'I know ... I said to him ...'

The music swallowed up their words. They must have leaned forward.

'Are you all right?' Amelie was back in her seat, eyes concerned. Casey hadn't seen her sit down. 'You look like you've seen a ghost.'

Casey's mind raced. 'I just saw an ex of mine, actually. Over there, with someone else. He always – I don't know – throws me. The one that got away, I suppose.'

'We've all,' Amelie grinned, 'got one of those.'

Brendan thudded back on to the seat next to Casey. He was considerably more drunk, she saw. Shots. He would tell her more, but know less.

'All right, babe?' He put his arm around her, sweaty from dancing.

Casey smiled automatically.

'Stephano is shit-faced,' one of the voices behind her was back, laughing now.

'Man, do you remember that time in New York? Crazy fucker.'

'That blonde is going to punch him out.'

The conversation had moved on and there was a third voice now.

'Got to run to the loo.' She stood up and smiled brightly at Brendan.

'Right, babe.' His eyes weren't quite focusing.

She edged away from the table, heading for the bar. She sat down on one of the bar stools, where Brendan couldn't see, as if she were resting her feet while searching for a friend.

Casually, she twirled the stool until she was looking at the group sitting behind Brendan. Phone out again, she snapped photographs of all the men sitting at the table.

'Help you, madam?'

It was Jasper. He must have come down to check she was all right.

'I'd love a vodka, Jasper,' she sparkled back. It would look so normal, a pretty girl flirting with a barman. Then her voice dropped. 'And can you tell me who that is at Table Nine?'

He glanced across at them, while she knocked back her shot.

'Important?'

'Yes.'

'Hang on.'

He sauntered away, while she fiddled with her shot glass.

Amelie walked past, effortlessly graceful. She gave Casey a glittery, flickery smile. In another time, another life, Casey thought, she and Amelie could have been friends.

'Here.' Jasper pushed a small piece of paper into her hand. 'It's the name from the tab. A Black Amex. All right, Amelie?'

'Hi, Jazz,' Amelie called back.

They always took a card when someone began ordering drinks. No one could walk out on a six-figure bar tab.

'You're a star, Jazz.'

'Don't know the name.' He rubbed his eyes as he thought. 'I know most of the guys who come in regularly. Not that one.'

She put a big tip down on the bar.

'You know I don't do it for that.'

'I know. But it's still there.'

He pocketed the money and smiled at her, disappearing off down the bar, looking for trouble.

Casey looked back towards Table 9. They had been joined by girls now, purposeful-looking girls. Casey knew her careful dance wouldn't stand a chance against the professionals.

She moved back towards the Cormium table. They were too far gone now, she decided. Brendan would never concentrate on work now.

Still. Maybe next time.

'I've got to run, Brendan.'

He blinked at her, remembering.

'Babe ...' He was groping around for her name.

'Maybe next time?' There was something in this. It was worth chasing.

'Yeah,' he brightened. 'We come most Thursdays. The boys.'

'See you then.' She put some promise into her smile.

'Take my number?' He was hopeful, and she accepted it, to a few desultory cheers.

And then she was off, swirling through the tables. Amelie waved a graceful goodbye, as Casey clutched her scrap of paper, reading the name again and again.

3

'Do you think it's fucking possible?' The head of news leaned back in his seat.

'Anything's fucking possible,' said Miranda. 'That much I know.'

'It would be ...' For once, words failed Dash Bishop.

The head of news is a step up from the news editor. News editors obsess over the list.

The list. The list. Always the list.

The list of the next wave of stories to be published, in just a few hours. The head of news, meanwhile, is meant to think long-term thoughts. Anything from the big Saturday interview to campaigns for the newspaper to battle. The head of news hosts breakfasts with fatcats, lunches with cabinet ministers and dines with film stars. Feeding back tips, while the newsroom beehives away.

Because their projects were long-term operations, Miranda and Casey reported to Dash.

Dash was quieter than Ross, more aloof; he watched more than he spoke.

'Unclubbable,' the political editor muttered once, not entirely approvingly.

The three of them were in Dash's office, a small room with broken blinds and no view. Dash ran his hands through his dark hair all day, so it stood up scruffily. He never wore his suit jacket and often lost his tie over the course of the day, dark eyes narrowed with concentration. He could be very funny, under his breath.

'I've got photographs of them.' Casey tapped at her laptop.

The three of them peered at the eight men. The light was low in Gigi's; the photographs blurry.

'Not your best effort,' said Miranda.

'Have we heard of this guy?' asked Dash. 'The guy with the Amex. Sebastian Azarola.'

'Hedge funds. He's from Argentina originally, but now splits his time between Geneva and London. Thirty-seven. Married. Two kids. Cyan Capital is based in the Cayman Islands, for tax purposes. But they all are – tax neutral and all that. It's had a belter of a few years. I would put his worth at two hundred million.'

Dash whistled. 'Sterling?'

Casey nodded. 'He was one of the founders of Cyan Capital.'

'It would be a bloody hedge-fund manager,' said Dash. 'They're all the same.'

'And what's he like?' Miranda asked.

'He's very low-profile,' Casey admitted. 'No interviews. No profiles. He married an Argentinian girl. They've made a few donations here and there. An art gallery. A couple of hospitals. Nothing political. Nothing to draw attention. I don't have a sense of him.'

She had pounded the databases before this meeting, the vast swamps of information the *Post* tapped every day. But this time they had given her numbers, not moods, not feelings.

'And these guys? Any ID?' Dash peered closer at the three men on the far left of the photograph.

'I think the one second from left is the one who knew about it all.' Casey pointed. 'But I'm not completely sure.'

They looked more closely at the men on the Cyan table. Azarola was in the middle of the group, the centre of attention.

The Cyan Capital website gave away almost nothing. A telephone number. An address near Green Park. A scramble of words about commitment to responsibility and careful calculations and not being responsible for anything on the site at all.

Casey had found only one picture of Azarola. It was on the *Forbes* site, as the magazine slavered over Cyan's returns. In that one, he was in a neat dark suit with an unremarkable tie. Dark hair and cool, calculating eyes. Hair thinning, waist spreading.

In the Gigi's photograph, the white shirt gaped sweatily, to show curls of dark hair and a thick gold chain. Azarola had a gold-braceleted arm round the neck of the man next to him, in what wasn't quite a hug.

'I can start asking around.'

'No,' Dash cut her off. 'Stay dark for now.'

'Sure.'

They were used to this, hunting silently in the shadows. There was always a point in an investigation when they broke cover. When their target finally knew they were coming for him. But that moment would be delayed as long as possible. Tracks could be covered, too easily.

'Do you think it's fucking possible?' Dash said again.

He stood up and stared across the *Post*'s offices.

In that bit of Victoria that some call Belgravia, the *Post* news-room looked like any other office. Messier, though. Newsrooms are never glamorous. The desks were grouped in rough sections. News. Business. Sport. Comment.

The fluffy sections – Culture, Books, Features, Mags – were a floor up, keeping themselves smartly separate from the ruffians on News. The glamour girls on fashion strolled up the stairs, watched appreciatively by the mostly male reporters.

Down here, piles of newspapers and files lay everywhere. The walls were dotted with huge framed pictures of the paper's best front pages. A royal wedding here. A new prime minister there. A bombed-out bus dominated the news desk.

Big screens showed constant rolling news. The sound was turned down, the focus not on the doe-eyed presenters, but the scrolling news along the bottom. When a big story broke, the volume would be cranked up. The chatter adding to the grow-ing cacophony, as reporters were dispatched and phone lines hammered.

The reporters themselves were scruffy, grumpy; Dorian Gray paintings of their own byline photographs.

'It could be possible. Maybe.'

'It could be,' he repeated. 'It doesn't even need to be Azarola. They could have been talking about anyone. You didn't hear them mention a name, did you?'

Dash was used to taking a punt. His skill was deciding where to deploy resources, when to push on. But it was also his job to pull reporters out of blind alleys. Cutting his losses.

'Kick the tyres,' Dash decided. 'I want to know everything about Azarola. Find out who those guys are, in the photo-graphs. Think about it. Think about the whole thing. There aren't that many places where you can just kill someone, and no one notices.'

'We know that people go to Thailand to rape four-year-olds,' Casey pointed out.

'And we all know what else you can find on the Internet,' added Miranda.

Miranda had posed as an eleven-year-old on the Internet once; the messages still shocked her awake at night.

'There were rumours about this sort of thing during the war in the old Yugoslavia, I remember. Sniper Alley. In Sarajevo, with rich men up in the hills.' Dash shrugged.

'You said one of them sounded disapproving?' Miranda had read the notes. Casey had typed up every detail before she had even left the club.

'Sick, he called it. He's the American.'

'Could be a way in,' said Dash. 'But be careful. I mean it. Dead reporters are a pain in the arse.'

'Charming.'

'How did it go with Cormium?' Dash asked. That was in the notes too.

'I was a bit distracted,' Casey admitted. 'I didn't get much. A foothold.'

'Nicky thinks they might be vulnerable to a takeover,' he said. 'She thinks they're a bit overstretched after last year, and Alphavivo might try and snap them up.'

Nicky was on the business desk. She dressed like a banker and read balance sheets as if they were trashy novels, and sometimes they were. She talked fluently about collateralised debt obligations and credit default swaps, PIK notes and senior credit. It unnerved Ross, and Nicky enjoyed unnerving Ross.

Alphavivo, the biggest commodities traders in the world, had not enjoyed Cormium appearing in their rear-view mirror, swallowing up the competition.

'I'll check in with her,' said Casey. 'I know where they hang out now, and when, so that's something.'

Dash glanced at the clock. 'Got to go.'

It was coming up to 4 p.m., the conference where the editor decided the front-page stories.

The conferences punctuated the day, like rocks in a river. Set times in a day of ducking and diving, as they alchemised the chaos into thousands of words and dozens of photographs, every single day.

Dash powered out of the office. Casey and Miranda strolled back to their desks.

Some of the male reporters watched them with interest. Miranda was wearing a very short blue PVC skirt.

'I used to wear grey polo necks and brown skirts, right down to my ankles,' Miranda had told Casey once. 'Because I wanted to be taken seriously as a journalist and all that. But then I realised that I was twenty-six and smoking hot, and so no one was ever going to take me seriously whatever I wore. So I offed a couple of cabinet ministers and wore whatever the fuck I wanted.'

Today, though, Miranda's thoughts were elsewhere.

Miranda and Casey had a small room, off to the side of the main office. They used it for making the calls that needed a silent background. Or the shadier documents. Or bouncing around ideas that couldn't be broadcast, not even in a newsroom.

Now they retreated there. Miranda leaned against her desk.

'I don't know about this, Casey ... It could be dangerous.'

Her concern, masked mostly, shimmered for a moment.

'It could be,' Casey agreed. 'But those Wynford documents are starting to drive me crazy.'

'And he didn't kill it.'

'No.'

Casey sat down at her computer.

'Where?' she said, almost to herself. 'A camp. A campsite.'

'They can't mean something like Glastonbury,' said Miranda. 'Or Burning Man.'

Casey thought of the thousands of colourful tents, sprawling across the desert acres. Faces giggling, bright flags fluttering in the wind. The music pounding, and a fire blazing into the sky.

'We'd know,' said Casey. 'It would be a huge story, if anything like that happened there. We hear if one person overdoses there.'

'A camping site? For holidays?' suggested Miranda. 'Camping always sounds hellish to me, but who knows?'

'Again,' said Casey. 'We would know about it. I'll do the checks, but I am sure we would have heard.'

Casey fiddled with the necklace around her neck, a little silver bird.

'How about' – she didn't want to say it – 'the shanty towns?'

The huge slums, bound around some of the biggest cities in the world. Cape Town, Nairobi, Mexico City, Dhaka, they all had their miles of shacks, built from anything to hand.

'Some of those shanty towns make their own laws,' said Casey.

'And if you think about gun crime in Rio,' Miranda said thoughtfully, 'there's almost two hundred shootings a week, I think, so would a few extra deaths be noticed in a favela?'

'They would,' Casey said, 'by the people around them.'

'But those people,' said Miranda, 'might not be heard.'

They sat in silence, for a moment.

'Oi, Case.' It was the paper's diarist at the door. 'Felix Lincombe snogging someone who isn't his wife in Gigi's last night. Is the source kosher?'

Felix Lincombe was currently Macbeth in the West End, burnishing his already stellar acting credentials ahead of next year's Oscar battle. The *Post* had given him a particularly dazzling review.

'Totally, Bill.'

'Wouldn't ask, only Legal want to know. They're a bit jumpy.'

The legal team at the *Post* were fearsome. They read through any article flagged as sensitive, and red-lined anything the reporters couldn't stand up.

'Tell them it's fine,' Casey said. 'I saw it with my own eyes. Snapped it too, though we'd better not mention that.'

'You were in Gigi's last night?' He laughed. 'When the hell do you sleep?'

He shambled off.

'You filed that?' Miranda asked.

'This morning. First thing.'

'Jesus, you never fucking stop.'

'It's a story,' Casey protested. 'A good one. The bad guys will never notice, and Jazz's lot will like the publicity. It'll look like it came from her, whoever the hell she is.'

Miranda rolled her eyes, and they got to work.

4

The foundations of an investigation take time. Casey began by trawling through the data. Companies House, Electoral Roll, Land Registry. Slowly, she learned how Cyan thought. She disentangled its successes, and its failures. There weren't many of the latter.

The spiderweb grew.

She needed the name of the American. That was her target. Forensically, she made a list of Azarola's associates, and then all his connections. It grew slowly, like a photograph coming to life in a bowlful of chemicals. Ghosts, rising.

On the big television screen above her head, a murder, on a street in Cobham. A husband battering his wife, they thought, and fleeing into the night. A neighbour was being interviewed, neat in her navy cardigan and surprised at herself for being on television. Casey didn't need to turn up the volume to know what she was saying.

Such a shock. You wouldn't think that sort of thing could happen here. Lovely family, you know. He always seemed so polite. You never can tell, can you? The woman shook her head, and the pearl drop earrings danced.

*

Her mind switched back to her investigation again.

That American could be a brother, a friend, a friend of a friend of a friend. But they probably worked together, because those are the easiest friendships for those City boys. It would be easy if she could show the photograph to someone in their postroom. Because the postroom always knew.

'Why do you want to know ...'

A shrug, a smile, a tenner.

'Oh, yeah, him ... That's ...'

But it was a risk, and she didn't take risks. Not until she had to. Then it might become a secret crush. A giggle, and a flick of the hair. I just want to drop off a card for him ...

'There's always someone doing the photocopying,' Miranda said to her early on.

There's always a weak link in the chain. Someone who cares less, someone who is paid less, someone who no one else notices. Ross spent a lot of time debriefing confused Bulgarian cleaners, because they emptied the bins at the *Post*, and could know it all if they cared.

But not this time.

She emailed a list of names to the picture editor. No questions asked, the photographs appeared. She stared at the blurry photograph of her American, and tried to fit the jigsaw together.

It was always hard to be sure.

Different angles. Different expressions. Different outfits.

She tested a few possibilities on Miranda.

'Look at his eyebrows,' Miranda shook her head. 'The way they curve up at the end. Not him.'

'Couldn't it be? A few years on. And a couple of stone. Smiling.'

'No.'

Casey glanced up. The network had dispatched their star anchor to the murder case. She looked otherworldly, stranded in a Cobham cul-de-sac. The red bob that hadn't changed for a decade glistened in the weak sun and she was nodding to an elderly neighbour.

Who are you? Tell me who you are.

The red bob nodded again. The wife filled the screen, blonde and smiling, and frozen for ever.

We only know snapshots.

Casey worked on.

'Him? With a bit of a tan. And longer hair.'

'Look at the angle from cheekbone to eye socket. No.'

You recognise a walk, Casey learned early on. The way someone tilts their head. A voice could tell her everything. Looking from a photograph to a person was like looking from a map to a mountainside. You learned to read them, but it could catch you out.

As she worked, Casey made careful notes, all the time. Partly because it was easy to forget stuff you thought you never could. Partly because, some day, Legal would crawl over every word. Investigations take days, weeks, months. She messaged Jasper.

'Let me know if Azarola comes back to the club. Priority one.'

'Will do. He's not a regular though. I asked around a bit. Carefully. Nothing.'

'Spread the net a bit? He might be in Geneva. Anyone from Cyan Capital, too. That's his fund.'

'Will try. Promise.'

'Star.'

That network of bar staff was vital. They gossip and compete, but they know who's been chucked out of the club just up the road for taking a swing at a barman, and which girls are dirty drunk and will be sick in the loos.

And there's the unofficial whisper, too, when the undercover police are trawling the clubs, on the hopeless pursuit of the endless drugs that swirl across the capital.

She went down to Gigi's on Saturday. Sulked across the room, at where the American should have been.

The Cobham neighbours got bored with the drama, and eventually the cameras moved on.

Carefully, dangerously, Casey started to wonder how she might get alongside them. Into the heart of the secret, wherever it was. In any investigation it could take months, getting to that final scene. She rarely just walked up to someone. A phone call out of the blue raises hackles. And that initial meeting would define everything. So Casey and Miranda would plot for hours, days, weeks.

The brush-by was one option. They'd done it a dozen ways to a hundred people.

Bumping into a target in a lift in Malta, 'Haven't I met you somewhere before? Don't I recognise you from something?' Handing over a business card, and walking away. His eyes following, as she broke the contact, so casual.

He was flattered to be recognised, anyway. And no newspaper would send a team to Malta when the introduction could be done in a London lunch break, would they … That would make no sense, would it?

So he relaxed abroad.

Or someone could recommend the target.

Gosh, I need someone who can get things done. A lobbyist, I suppose.

Oh, sure, I know a guy. Let me give you his number.

And the first contact would pause, and think – maybe quite slowly, so Casey needed an unfamiliar patience – that it would be helpful for the target to know who is sending business his way.

'Tell you what,' he'd say eventually. 'I'll email you both. Put you in touch. Yeah.'

'That's so helpful,' with just the right touch of gratitude.

You scratch my back . . .

And already she would have email addresses and business cards and a website. Maybe even a company.

And, of course, after that the first guy, consciously or not, needs her to be real. He can't have been the one to open the gates for the Trojan horse.

Dash peered into the investigations room. Casey and Miranda, heads close together, were deep in thought.

'Where?' he said. 'Where is this happening? Try working it backwards.'

Miranda looked up and smiled. Casey glowered at the interruption.

'I am,' Casey said. 'Always. Backwards and in heels.'

Miranda smiled again. She was eating a cupcake absent-mindedly. Casey, whippet slim, forgot to eat.

'It was just' – Dash pacified Casey now – 'a thought.'

He disappeared towards the news desk, and Casey bit the end of her pen. Where.

They hushed as the editor walked past their desks.

The Editor. As an American president is always awarded his definite article, so the Editor will also be known at his newspaper.

Andrew Salcombe had worked his way up through Fleet Street, each paper a stepping stone to the next. New to the *Post*, he was regarded with suspicion by his newsroom.

Casey watched him now. With red-gold hair and glasses, his pale skin looked bloodless. Bloodless and ruthless, she thought.

Salcombe was quiet compared with the *Post*'s last editor, whose laugh had clattered round the office as the paper went to press. Much lamented, the last editor used to wander round the office waving a polo stick around his head and exhorting his troops onwards into battle. A bottle of champagne arrived on a reporter's desk after an especial triumph.

But the last editor had departed three months ago, after some row with the newspaper's owners.

Salcombe had shown up within hours, suspiciously fast to some, the *Post* the latest stage of his seamless rise. Miranda thought Dash might have aspired to the editorship. A bit young though.

This editor listened in silence in conference, absorbing ideas and then the credit. A perfectionist, his allies called him. A control freak, said everyone else. Casey had heard the editor ripping into journalists, quietly vicious. The attacks had an edge of sadism that no one liked. The journalists were getting wary.

Dash had muttered something about budgets, too. The investigations team was expensive, Salcombe had pointed out.

Necessary? Huge legal risk on every story, too. Then the other papers ripped off three months' work in three minutes. And some of the readers didn't like the brutality.

'Bollocks,' snapped Ross.

Out of the corner of her eye, Casey occasionally caught the editor watching her, both watchful and indifferent. It made her feel uneasy. He looked at Casey now, pale eyes flickering, and she was a butterfly on a pin. Dash hadn't briefed him on her wild goose chase yet.

'I'm going to head out,' she muttered to Miranda, sliding towards the door.

Later, Casey sat outside Azarola's house. Knightsbridge. Stuccoed white frontage. Unarguable wealth. The sort of money that buys you anything.

Anything.

There was a park opposite, and she lay in the grass with an ice cream, invisible in a cotton skirt and pink flowery top. From there, she had been watching the Azarola family come and go. Nanny. Yoga teacher. Wife. Learning the routines. Learning the weaknesses.

Azarola was rarely there, she knew now. None of the faces marked possible in her file came or went. And Azarola disappeared for days at a time, and Casey couldn't know where he went.

Who are you? Tell me who you are.

'There's something very weird about sitting outside someone's house for hours at a time,' she said to Miranda, as she wrote up her notes back in the office.

'You have to worry if it stops being weird,' Miranda answered.

He never went back to Gigi's.

Days crawled past.

'You getting anywhere?' Dash paused at her desk.

'No,' Casey had to admit.

She hunched over her story, as if encircled by hyenas.

'It could all be nothing, Casey.'

And, of course, it could be nothing. It could be an urban myth – a friend of a friend of a friend. A boast that ran out of control. It could, so easily, be a drunken fool exaggerating a story to a credulous buddy.

She could – worst case – have misheard.

'It could be.'

'Miranda needs help on the Wynford Mortimer stuff,' said Dash. 'It's millions of documents. Plus I woke up in the middle of the night and just thought, it's complete and utter madness, isn't it? No one could actually do that. And, anyway, you'd need to see it happen to write that story, or no one would ever believe it.'

'You're probably right.'

'Well. Get on with it.' He was almost sympathetic.

Failure burned through Casey. She hadn't pulled the threads together. She hadn't worked it out. She'd fucked up.

Failure might be the only thing that could make Casey cry.

Miranda nodded at her.

'It was worth chasing, babe. It's what we do. It's not your fault.'

Dash and Miranda were being kind, she knew. Newsrooms could be far less forgiving.

'Fuck.' Casey kicked her wastepaper bin over. 'Fuck it.'

'You can't stand up every story. We know that.'

'Maybe we should just do a really aggressive front-up on Azarola? And bounce him?'

Legally, the *Post* had to go to people before it published stories. It was duty-bound to report fairly, which was the opportunity to give the other version of events.

Even if that was: 'No comment, or I'll call the police.'

Casey might also ambush someone, fire questions, watch their reactions as the worst of the allegations were slapped down in front of them. And sometimes, quite often, she broke through and got an admission, or a half-admission, or a denial of one aspect of the story, which might mean the rest was true.

Surprise could be exploited. The TV crews routinely chased people down the street.

'You can front him up, sure,' said Miranda. 'But I don't think you'll get anywhere. You don't have enough detail.'

Because if you say 'You killed someone', people can shrug it off. But if you have the details – 'It was Miss Scarlett in the drawing room, with a candlestick at 4 p.m. last Tuesday' – they pause, and think, how do they know that? And what else do they know?

Confronting, but without revealing your hand.

'It really is the last play, if I do that.' Casey's shoulders slumped. 'He doesn't look like he would scare. And you never know, something else might come in.'

'You never know.'

Casey sat at her desk. And she felt it. The flicker of rage.

All journalists have done something appalling, but they have to get up in the morning. They have to think, yes, OK, I can live with this. I can sleep at night.

They need to make their own rules, and stick to them.

'Just don't screw your friends over,' said Dash early on. 'You need your friends. There are six billion other sources out there.'

So Casey had her own code, and she couldn't let go.

A few minutes later, she sat up straight and clicked the file back open.

'What are you working on?' Miranda asked, barely glancing up.

'Wynford Mortimer,' came the reply.

A last check, in the mirror. For wires, and buttons that don't look like buttons.

They think it's vanity, women gazing at mirrors.

'Go for the jugular.'

'No.' She was twirling slowly, might have been dancing. 'Go for the ego.'

The street outside the office was crowded, lunchtime rush. Faces, so many faces. She slipped down the street, alone.

It wasn't far. Quicker to walk, even in these shoes. She could think, as she walked. Away from the chaos, and into the role.

She was never the arms dealer. Never the chief executive. Never the hero, nor the star.

This time would be no different.

She was the PA, the PR, the girl next door. Simpering and smiling, so he laughed without thinking. Sometimes she was the girlfriend, half-seen, then ignored. Brushed off but nicely, because she might report rudeness. She was there to be patronised. To have things explained, quite slowly.

'I don't exactly understand how it works ...' She had smiled again and again.

So often, she didn't quite understand first time. Not precisely. So very often.

And he would explain, again, only half concentrating on her. Politely flirtatious, but eyes fixed on the star. That out-of-work actor she'd dressed as a tycoon, only a few hours earlier.

She was the personal assistant, the executive assistant, the magician's assistant. Because no one notices the figures in black. Those backstage mice, safe in the dark, shifting the set so quietly.

Look like the innocent flower ...

'I know I am being hopeless,' she would smile, 'but what exactly is *lobbying*?'

And he would tell all the secrets to the tycoon's toy.

And as she walked away from the restaurant, her step would change from teeter to prowl. From tethered goat to cheetah.

She would cast off the pearls, eyes narrowed, head lifted.

'Fuck the patriarchy,' she would say, stripping off wires, and only half joking.

5

She roamed around the newsroom, irritating other journalists.

'Bill.' She washed up at the diarist's desk. 'You never ran that Felix Lincombe piece. Him in Gigi's, not with his wife.'

'Felix Lincombe.' Bill's face broke into a rueful smile. 'Ah, Felix Lincombe. Mr Lincombe turns out to be the Editor's brother.'

'You're kidding.' Casey got the giggles. 'Shit.'

'Lincombe, Salcombe.' Bill rounded his vowels. 'It's a stage name. Just down the road on the same Devon estuary, don't you know. Very upmarket. Family joke, apparently. Crap one, if you ask me.'

'They kept that quiet,' said Casey.

'Suits them both, doesn't it?'

'So we're not doing the story,' said Casey.

'We've decided to respect Mr Lincombe's right to privacy on this one,' Bill agreed. 'Thank you very much.'

'Sorry.' Casey was still laughing.

'Don't worry, petal.' Bill swished his notepad. 'It wasn't awkward at all.'

She watched the editor for a few minutes, seeing the suddenly familiar jawline, the tilt of the head, then stalked on.

*

Casey was asleep when the call came through.

'He's here. He's fucking here.' The words were drowned in a blast of music.

'Who is this?' Casey looked blearily at her phone. 0033. A French number.

'Sorry, babe. It's me, Jasper. I'm in France. Down south. St-Tropez.'

None of it was making sense to Casey.

'Came down for the weekend.' Jasper was clearly wide awake. 'Gigi's are hosting out on Pampelonne, off and on.'

Some of the clubs did that in the summer, Casey knew. Licensing their name, working the brand, sending off their staff on a jolly, in the hot pink hotpants and bright red braces.

'Nice,' she said weakly.

'Anyway,' Jasper humoured her. 'That Azarola guy is here. With a bunch of guys from Cyan. Might be a stag do or something. Don't know. But they've got a table booked for Saturday too. They're here for the weekend.'

'Jazz, you angel.'

'I don't know what you wanted him for.' He was pleased, she could hear it. 'But I figured you would want to know.'

'I do, Jasper. I really do.'

The music in the background blared louder.

'I gotta go.'

'I'll call you tomorrow. First thing. Talk to my boss, then call.'

'Not too early, sweetheart,' he warned. 'It'll be messy here. It's kicking off.'

'Promise not.'

The phone went dead.

Casey slumped back on her pillows.

'Call me as soon as you wake up,' she tapped out to Miranda. 'We need to pack.'

6

Fizzing, Casey bounded into the newsroom early the next morning.

'Where's Dash?' she asked Ross.

'Don't fucking know.' The news editor was glowering at the huge TV screens above his desk. He picked up the phone, tapping in the number for the *Post*'s reporter currently in the bunfight outside the Old Bailey.

'Get stuck in, Eric. I can see you dicking around at the back ... You're not even holding a fucking biro, you useless clown ... I can see you live on Sky. I'm fucking everywhere, OK? Get the fuck on with it.'

He slammed the phone back into the cradle.

'Could you ask Dash to drop into the investigations office when he gets in?' Casey said.

'Do I look like your fucking secretary?'

Casey grinned at Ross, which annoyed him even more.

When Casey was little, her aunt had owned a small black Scottish terrier. Endlessly combative, Tig would bite so hard on a stick that you could lift him up by it, very slowly, jaw locked. The dog would dangle in the air, eyes glinting, the growl a constant rumble.

With his short dark hair and glittery eyes, Ross reminded Casey of Tig. 'Remind me,' Ross was bawling to his deputy now. 'Who are we throwing to the lions today?'

Casey headed to her office. Minutes after Miranda had got in, Dash joined them there. He raised an eyebrow at the suitcases.

'I thought we'd dropped this.'

'Of course she hadn't,' said Miranda. 'You knew she wouldn't.'

'Miranda should approach him in the club.' Casey ignored Dash. 'Just get him talking and then float it in, very gently, at first. She can go harder later, if she needs to.'

'We might have to burn Miranda on this one,' Dash agreed.

If a target saw Miranda in one environment, she couldn't pop up anywhere else. If Miranda appeared in Pampelonne, she was branded. The human mind dislikes coincidence.

Miranda nodded. 'But Casey should be there too. In case.'

'Course', said Dash. 'I haven't told Salcombe'.

It worried Miranda, Dash's secrecy with the editor. She'd seen budgets slashed before.

'We could say it was research for the Wynford Mortimer story,' she suggested. Flexibility was still built into the investigations budget. 'In fact, we could doorstep that LPG trader as we go through Cannes.'

'Do it,' said Dash.

As soon as he had disappeared, Casey grabbed Cressida, the fashion editor.

'We need costumes.' Miranda batted her eyelashes.

'St-Tropez, this time of year?' Cressida said thoughtfully. 'Sure.'

Cressida led them into the fashion cupboard, the magical grotto seemingly filled with exquisite fashion assistants and endless enchanting clothes. The clothes, the jewellery, the shoes were called in and photographed on elegant beanpoles, wrapped up and sent back. Occasionally, they were diverted. Briefly.

The fashion team defended the cupboard like Custer's last stand.

'Drop, Miranda,' Cressida said sweetly, as Miranda picked up a Balenciaga handbag. Miranda and Casey could just fit into the sample sizes.

'Now ...' Cressida flicked through some racks. 'Odabash cover-ups ... Yes, to some Christopher Kane dresses ... Ooh, and some Anjuna would be nice. If I had some more time, I could have called in some Erdem. And if you lose any of this, I swear to god I'll set all their PRs on you.'

There had been an unfortunate incident with Casey and a Victoria Beckham dress a few months before. The only rose-pink one in the sample size, it had turned out. Cressida's mouth suggested this hadn't entirely been forgiven.

Waving their thanks, they headed for Holborn.

'Cameras hidden in floaty white dresses?' The camera wizard raised an eyebrow. 'I mean, like, how?'

'Oh, Sagah, I thought you worked miracles.'

The technology got better every year. When Casey was starting, a battery had failed, strapped into its black harness. It overheated, and burned, so slowly. And when she moved, it slipped against her skin. She never wavered, not for a moment. There was a scar, now, on her hip.

He sighed. 'Could you use a bag one?'

'That lot will see through a fake,' Casey pointed out. 'And Cressida will never let us chop up a Birkin.'

'Birkin?' asked the camera wizard, sweating through his nylon shirt.

'Keep trying,' said Miranda.

They were late, in the end, running for their flight. They always had their passports with them, instinctive as phone, keys, wallet. Casey had two, so she could leave one at an embassy. Both were almost full.

She never told anyone, of course, that she was scared. Not even Miranda.

Sometimes it didn't matter, the nerves. Most people would be nervous in front of the Business Secretary.

It didn't matter, that time when she choked over a few words. Balding and bespectacled, he thought that was normal. She learned, then, that she could mangle a few words.

'My mind's gone blank,' she giggled.

And that happens to everyone sometimes, doesn't it?

Even mistakes didn't matter. People are oddly polite.

That time, she was a mummy from Twickenham. With the gold ring – not a wedding ring – on her wedding-ring finger. Brown polo neck, and neat polished boots. A furry gilet, borrowed from somewhere. Fake fox fur, for suburban camouflage.

He never even looked at her. Not really, with her diamond ring that caught the light. Because in her invisible armour, this woman could never be a threat. In her unseeable armour, that saw it all.

Just a few wires, for Boadicea's sword.

Thou mayst be a queen, and check the world.

Precious little honey in the honeytrap, he'd sneered afterwards, furious and humiliated, lashing out.

And she'd smiled, when no one could see, and thought, I could bring you to your knees.

If I cared.

7

They stepped off the plane at Nice into air warm as a bath and then whipped west down the coast road. The mountains to the north, jagged orange rocks and green scrub, always looked too wild for the Côte d'Azur.

In Cannes, the oil trader was away, the Filipina maid said. She didn't know when he would be back. He was probably on his yacht, she hazarded, dot-to-dotting from Paxos to Hydra, from Santorini to Cephalonia.

Then they raced on, slowing only for the endless stop–start traffic into St-Tropez.

The travel department, possibly on purpose, had booked them into the cheapest hotel.

'Better than the cheapest hotel in Leicester,' said Miranda.

'Or Bratislava.'

'Christ, yes.'

Pampelonne stretches away to the south of St-Tropez, a long strip of bleached sand. Beach clubs, where the party starts at lunch and goes on all day, line the dunes. The billionaires' boats glittered along the coast. Millions of pounds-worth of yacht looked like bathtub toys. A helicopter was landing gingerly on the back of the largest.

'It must be so fucking irritating,' Casey said. 'You drop Germany's GDP on a super-yacht, then some oligarch pulls alongside and you look like their jet ski.'

They meandered down the beach, exploring.

Elegant tenders ferried groups to and fro. Golden girls skipped down piers that stuck out like exclamation marks. These girls were Bardot beautiful, with cats' eyes and witchy bitchy smiles.

Gigi's was halfway down Pampelonne beach, with furniture that looked like driftwood, but wasn't. Blue beribboned palm trees guarded the entrance. Palest azure muslin tenting kept the sun off bored faces.

'Girls!' Jasper shouted. 'My loves. You look ravishing.'

He kissed them on both cheeks, as he would any of the little mermaids coming in on the tide.

'How you doing, darling?' Miranda hugged him.

He waved them round the club. He didn't intro- duce them to the club's staff, to avoid friendly questions. Showing them around inserted them into the hierarchy. I'm giving them my time, it said. They're important. Keep them sweet.

'Want a table tomorrow night?' he asked. 'It's no bother.'

'That's lovely of you. But actually, it would be better if we could operate as free agents ...' said Miranda. 'We don't want them to see us together, necessarily.'

'Although if Miranda can't get into their table any other way, a fallback of a table close by would be good,' added Casey. 'But only if we get desperate.'

'You two would never get desperate,' said Jasper. He was looking round the club, positioning the Cyan party.

The Cyan team would expect a table at the heart of it all, close to the dance floor. The placement at Gigi's was as careful as in any Tudor court.

'There isn't really a quieter area, is there?' Miranda asked. 'It'll murder the recordings.'

Jasper grimaced. 'The DJ would lose his shit if I turned down the music. And I am not letting myself think about how much we are paying him for tomorrow night. I could kill one of the speakers near their table. Although if they complain ...'

'Of course,' said Miranda. 'Of course.'

'I need to top up my tan,' Casey laughed, looking at her arms.

'Take a sunlounger,' offered Jasper. 'I'll send over a bottle.'

He hadn't asked what they were chasing, Casey noticed. She wondered about his world, a world where it was easier not to know, and wiser not to ask.

They lay on the sunloungers. The Cyan crowd would only come in the evening.

'This is precisely what Ross worries we get up to the moment his back is turned,' said Casey, rubbing in sunscreen.

'The tan is camouflage.' Miranda flicked her hair. 'I'll get a manicure when we get back into St-Trop.'

'Do you reckon we should hire a boat for our arrival?' Casey was watching two glistening girls teeter down the rickety pier towards Gigi's.

'Ross would send out the business desk to assassinate us,' said Miranda. 'Nicky with a poisoned umbrella. And we'd probably sink it.'

'The *Screws* used to hire yachts and everything,' remembered Casey.

The *News of the World* – News of the Screws – had created whole worlds as their stage, much to Miranda's envy.

'One day, baby. One day.'

A smiling boy brought them glasses of cherries and strawberries and champagne. Miranda angled the parasol and lay back, watching, learning.

When they arrived the next night, the music was blasting down the beach. Flaming torches lit up the sand. A spotlight strobed miles into the sky. Miranda tagged in behind a large group. A few minutes later, Casey sauntered in.

Girls were already dancing on the tables, picking their way through bottles and kicking over glasses.

Miranda was wearing a floaty blue dress – slashed to indecency at the front – and a gold necklace.

A statement piece, *Vogue* would call that necklace. It glinted in the torchlight, intricate and beautiful, a breastplate for a battle. Right in the centre, a tiny camera was buried in the busy glitz. It filmed everything, tilted up to capture faces. Taped to the necklace, the wires ran round Miranda's neck and down her back, covered by a curtain of newly blow-dried hair. Underneath the silky blue dress, a battery pack clipped into a belt.

'I am a fucking genius,' the man in Holborn had announced, before sending them racing to Heathrow.

Now Miranda strutted into the club.

From across Gigi's, Casey could listen in to Miranda's conversation with a tiny transmitter. Directional microphones wouldn't pick up a thing through the wall of noise, so they had to use radios.

In a normal operation, Casey could listen in through headphones, because they were common enough to be invisible anywhere, but headphones would look odd in Gigi's pounding music, so instead Casey was running the recording through her phone. No one would ever notice a pretty girl chatting on a phone.

Now Miranda was sashaying through the club towards the Cyan table. Casey picked up her phone and held it, with a smile, to her ear.

'Oh, hey.' Miranda stopped next to the table. 'Sebastian Azarola, isn't it?'

Azarola looked up, and softened as he took in the gazelle-like legs.

'Hi, there ...'

'Didn't we meet at Ascot?' It was a guess, but a good one. The hedge-fund managers had stormed that citadel many years before. 'I was there with Tyler Walton.'

Tyler Walton's name was the secret handshake. The private-equity tycoon had dominated US boardrooms for years, building up a fortune measured in billions. Azarola would never deny a visit to Ascot with Walton.

'Oh, sure, Tyler,' said Azarola. 'How's he doing at the moment?'

'He's good,' said Miranda, who kept a close eye on the oblivious billionaire's activities, mainly through the *Post*'s business pages. 'Things got pretty tough over Canada Gold, but he seems happy with it now.'

'Yeah, Canada Gold got brutal.' Azarola nodded appreciatively.

'He was back and forth between Boston and Chicago all the time,' added Miranda, who monitored the flight-tracking websites for Walton's Learjet. 'Crazy busy.'

'I heard,' said Azarola.

'And, you know Tyler, he's totally obsessed with racing at the moment. Was Montana Blue running that day at Ascot?'

Azarola avoided the question by ushering her to a seat at the low-slung table. He didn't know Tyler Walton at all well, diagnosed Casey. But was keen to cover that up.

'Thank you.' Miranda accepted a glass of champagne. She leaned back carefully against a blue silk cushion, so no one could brush against the wires running down her back.

'So how are you?' she went on.

'I'm good, I'm good ...'

They chatted on. Her arrival time had been carefully calculated. Jasper had texted them when the Cyan group had arrived, and Casey and Miranda had arrived two hours later.

After two hours of vodka, Azarola was drunk.

He was smart though, Casey thought. There was a sophisticated mind there, even through the vodka. Both were doing a superb job of pretending to know Tyler Walton. For a second, Casey smiled at what the Chicago magnate would make of it all.

Casey sat down briefly on a stool, dodging a girl, spilling champagne on her shoes. Across the club, Jasper gave her an almost invisible wink. Miranda and Azarola chatted on. The group around the table ebbed and flowed. People danced and table-hopped, and Miranda stayed next to Azarola in a way that looked accidental.

Finally, just for a moment, they were alone at the table. Miranda poured them both shots of tequila, and they did them fast: salt, lemon, gasp.

'To tell you the truth.' Miranda's voice dropped. 'I haven't seen much of him since his trip to that camp.'

'What camp?' Azarola seemed interested.

'The camp,' Miranda said again. 'Where those people are …'

'Where?'

'The one where …' Miranda hesitated. 'The one where people … die.'

'They what?'

'Oh, I thought you were one of them …'

'One of who?'

'That group …'

He doesn't know anything about it, Casey thought. He was curious, but there was no distress in his body language, no tightening in the spine. His voice hadn't tautened, and it was the voice that always gave them away.

Miranda would keep going though, she thought. Because that was what Miranda did.

'It was all so fucking dark,' Miranda went on. 'That group of guys who are killing people there.'

'They what?' Azarola's voice was sudden ice.

'They shoot them … Out in …'

'They shoot …'

'Some girls think it's hot.' She almost made it flirtatious, but it didn't quite work.

'That is so fucked up …'

Azarola was getting angrier.

'You never did that sort of thing?' They were trained to ask the question they didn't want to ask.

'No.' Azarola was horrified. It was unfakeable that horror. 'Never.'

People don't use the word 'never' when they are lying, a Kroll investigator told Casey once. 'Never' is impossible to blur later.

'What sort of a sick fuck do you think I am?' Azarola's voice was rising. 'Is that what Walton gets off on?'

'Tyler?' Miranda covered her tracks. 'Totally not. God, no. It was this other guy I know ... It's so loud in here.'

'Who the fuck was it?' But Miranda was ready to disappear. He didn't have her name. He was drunk. She would be forgotten by the morning, hopefully.

'I have to get back to my friends.' She waved vaguely across the club. 'It's my friend's birthday ...'

She was on her feet, smiling blandly. Halfway across the club before he knew it.

'Get out of here, Casey.' Miranda knew Casey was still listening in. 'He doesn't know anything.'

Casey watched Miranda stride across the club, moving fast without hurrying. She was furious, Casey could see. Miranda hated to be mistaken.

Out of the corner of her eye, Casey saw a latecomer arriving at the Cyan table.

It was the guy on the left, she realised, at the club back in London. The American voice. The one who knew.

'Let's go, Casey.' Miranda's voice again. 'Azarola could lose his shit.'

Just one moment, thought Casey. Just one moment.

Their system only allowed Miranda to talk at her. The tiny radio earmikes weren't subtle enough for whispering in a club.

Casey started towards Azarola.

'Casey.' She heard the anger in Miranda's voice as she headed towards the Cyan table. 'I've told you. It's a bust. Let's go.'

But Casey was already at the table.

'Oh my God, *hi*,' she gave it six syllables. 'Patrick Lister!'

The American glanced around, trying to work out who she was shrieking at.

'Patrick!' She threw herself into his arms, kissing his cheek.

'Hi.' He didn't want to be rude, which was a good sign. 'I'm ... I'm not Patrick ...'

It was the right voice. That light American accent, fading at the end of a sentence.

'Shut up.' She gave it the full Valley Girl inflection. 'Shut up.' She took a step back and looked up at him through her eyelashes. 'Dude, this is like totally freaky. You're literally his twin.'

He laughed, because people always did. 'I don't have a twin. Only child.'

'No way. No way ... What's your name? You have got to be related ...'

'Adam.'

'Adam? Must be Lister though ... Has to be ... A cousin or shit.'

'Fraid not. Jefferson.'

'Adam Jefferson. Get outta here ... You must be from LA though ...'

'New York.'

'Shut up,' she repeated. 'Long way from home, down here in old St-Tropez.'

'Nah, we came down from Geneva for the weekend. I'm living there at the moment.'

'Geneva.' She rolled the word around her mouth. 'In Switzerland, right? You work there?'

'With these guys.' He gestured at the Cyan group.

'Awesome. And you're here for a few more days?'

'No.' He looked regretful. 'We split first thing tomorrow morning. Got to get back for work.'

'I have got to take a photograph to show my friends,' she squealed. 'They will totally die.'

He posed with fake reluctance, smiling for her shot.

'They will die,' she promised again.

Over his shoulder, she could see Azarola glowering. Not at her, especially, but his evening was ruined. He was looking for a fight.

'Well, Mister Adam Jefferson' – a pause to let him correct it, in case she had misheard – 'I had better go find my friends. But it was an absolute pleasure meeting you. And I am going to tell Patrick he has a ... Oh, what is that word? Dopp ...'

'Doppelgänger,' he supplied, and watched her go.

Miranda was in a taxi as Casey emerged, waving a goodbye across the club to Jasper.

'Well, that was a disaster,' said Miranda.

'It might not be,' said Casey. 'I found the American.'

'The one from Gigi's?'

'Exactly. I got his name. Based in Switzerland.'

They were always careful, speaking in front of a stranger. The taxi driver was swearing at the limos triple-parked outside the clubs, but you never knew.

'It doesn't feel like it's going to work,' said Miranda,

'We've found someone who definitely knows one way or another,' Casey pointed out. 'Now we can work out exactly how to go for him. Azarola was always going to be trickier. If it's someone who is just confirming, it's less tricky.'

'Azarola was completely and utterly horrified. He was furious.' Miranda's shoulders slumped. 'I feel like I fucked up.'

'You didn't,' Casey promised. 'He just didn't know anything. If anything, it was my fault. I should have found a way to eliminate Azarola earlier. But now we can find the American in Geneva and get everything out of him.'

'Dash might have had enough of it all,' said Miranda. She was loosening the wires carefully, so that the taxi driver couldn't notice. 'Geneva will cost more.'

'No.' Casey leaned forward. 'Dash loves this story. He can't give it up.'

'You must never do that, you know. Go back in, when I've called it.'

'No,' said Casey. 'I know. Sorry.'

They had several codes, for walking away. Two quick taps on the table meant abort, drop everything, urgent. You didn't stop to ask questions. You trusted that the other person would only hit the panic button *in extremis*. Sometimes, for them, the exit route was more important than the path in.

'It doesn't matter. And now we can spend tomorrow plotting on the beach,' said Miranda. 'Plage des Graniers is meant to be delightful.'

'And still be in the office by 9 a.m. on Monday.' They grinned at each other.

8

'Geneva?' Dash did not sound impressed. 'We sure this isn't a hiding to nothing?'

'It might be, Dash. It just might be.'

It was Monday morning. Behind the news executive, crumpled reporters were sneaking in late to their desks.

'And Azarola definitely didn't have a clue what you were talking about?'

'If he did, we're not going to crack him,' said Miranda. 'He'd be the best actor ever, even drunk.'

'Switzerland … No chance you two could do something based in London at some point?' Dash hadn't missed their tans. 'Somewhere on the Circle Line maybe? Although I suppose I should be grateful that this is your European season.'

Miranda rolled her eyes at him. Every November, she and Casey focused on financial skulduggery.

'Tax-haven time, is it?' Dash would bawl, as they set out their urgent need to travel to Bermuda. 'Which Caribbean paradise has grabbed your attention this time?'

'There has to be a way in,' Casey had said to Miranda, stretched out on the beach, raking her hands through her hair. 'How do they find each other in the first place?'

'Could be some sort of initiation ceremony,' suggested Miranda now. 'Some mad Bilderberg extension?'

The Bilderberg group, meeting up in five-star hotels around the world, attracted suspicion at the *Post*. Politicians, tycoons and those men from the shadows, they all flew to a discreet venue to mutter in corners. One day, Casey planned to be a chambermaid.

'We'd surely have heard of something,' said Casey. 'This lot would make Bilderberg look like Eurovision.'

'Spare me.'

'Maybe it's something you work your way up to,' said Casey. 'You go to some ridiculously exclusive game reserve to shoot the Big Five. And after you've nailed a lion, someone whispers in your ear about something even more specialised.'

'How about some neo-Nazi horror?' suggested Miranda. 'Ethnic cleansing before they even get on the boats?'

'I hope not,' said Casey. 'But it's happened before.'

They got back to work. Casey was already tracking Jefferson through school, through college, up the first rungs of the hedge-fund ladder.

'We could ask to borrow Toby.'

'What?' Casey glanced up. She was chewing a pencil to splinters, surrounded by coffee cups.

'Toby,' said Miranda. 'You know, to trawl through the darkest depths of the internet.'

'Of course.' Casey got to her feet.

Coming up to lunchtime, the office was accelerating through the day. A fire near Dover, a politician on the ropes over employment figures, a nasty rape in Lincolnshire, which might or might not involve migrants. Nothing unusual.

'Can I grab Toby?' Casey appeared at Dash's desk.

'Now? Toby's on the train down from York.'

'Of course.'

The Deputy Prime Minister travelled back down from his Hull constituency every Monday morning like clockwork, solidly ensconced in first class. The Deputy Prime Minister had a loud voice and a cowed special adviser. He was not an early riser. Toby, one of the junior reporters, solemnly boarded the same train, and travelled all the way down to London, making busy notes.

To the *Post*'s knowledge, there had been six separate leak inquiries into Toby's stories.

'Toby'll be in Euston by twelve forty-three,' said Dash. 'You can have him then.'

Toby lived in ironic T-shirts and skinny jeans, and played around in the dark web. If it was there, Toby – who thought in algorithms and played his keyboard like a Steinway – would find it.

Back from Euston, Toby's slightly squinting eyes and pallid face lit up at the idea.

'Usual rules apply,' said Miranda breezily. 'If you tell anyone, at all, ever, they will never find your body.'

'Sure,' agreed Toby easily.

There was a roar from the news desk. Ross had the boxing up on one of the big screens. The crowd screamed. Blood and sweat, and tears and pain. A bellow. Come on, my son. Come on. At her desk Casey went back to drawing up everything there was to know about Adam Jefferson. An analyst at Cyan Cap, he was less discreet than Azarola. LinkedIn, Twitter, Facebook, without enough understanding of the privacy settings. Analysts are junior in an industry which sprinkles titles like vice president and director.

In Geneva, there was a predictable girlfriend. Lulu. Slim, unexcitingly pretty, carefully groomed. Blonde hair, dark eyebrows. Slightly too thin lips, and slightly too much lipliner. Liked yoga; loved ballet flats; adored cats.

You could tell a man from the woman he lived with, thought Casey. The person they chose was a window to the soul.

The man who had chosen Lulu was a man she would be able to turn over.

9

A couple of days later, they flew to Geneva.

Casey always found Geneva stultifyingly dull. Curling round the southern end of the lake, the city felt like it was trying to impose civilisation on the towering mountains. It was a grey day when they arrived, the heavy clouds bellying over the hills. In the brisk wind, the lake was oyster, strewn with chips of silver, the jet fountain in its centre blowing in a metallic arc.

'Miserable place.' Miranda huddled deeper into her coat.

The Cyan offices were an ugly building near the river, softened by an ostentatious front entrance. The silver and marble hall was guarded by receptionists in cyan-blue suits. The office was flanked by shops, Rolex and Christian Louboutin. Clean streets; dirty money.

'This is not where I would choose to work,' said Casey.

They had found Jefferson's home address, a flat in one of Geneva's glossy suburbs. But they wanted to grab him between work and home. In a city notorious for its discretion, anyone would shy away from journalists near the office. Often, people don't mind talking, but they mind being seen to talk.

They also wanted to speak to him between home and Lulu. Lulu could fill the air with noise and emotion and justification. Away from home and office, he would be isolated. Sometimes, people can tell the whole world, but not their wife. And once someone was safely in their house, you could wait days for them to re-emerge.

One of the old hands at the *Post* used to knock on a door, looking innocent, 'I think someone's scratched your car, madam.'

And when they came out to inspect their untouched Audi, huffing and puffing, he might get fifty yards of questions back to the house.

After a couple of passes, Casey and Miranda waited in a café across the street. Red roses in a little vase on the table, endless coffees and an easy line of sight to the pillared entrance. They paid for each coffee as it came, which confused the smiling waitress, but it meant they could leave invisibly, in seconds.

The day wore on. They saw Azarola arrive and stay only a few minutes, his PA trailing him. It began to rain, and the pavement mushroomed umbrellas. As the car headlights grew brighter than the day, the more senior staff left. Only the worker bees lingered, battling to stay in the game.

At last the doorman doffed his cap to a slim figure.

'There he is,' Miranda said unnecessarily.

Tracking someone invisibly is harder than people realise. Commuters move fast, not glancing at signposts or consulting maps. Casey had followed people who barely looked up as they headed home: fifteen paces to the corner, eight strides across the platform, straight to a favourite seat, next to the window.

They fell in behind Adam, camouflaged by crowds and relieved when he turned for home. They had worked out his likely route, and it was easier to follow someone when you were anticipating their path.

Miranda dropped in about twenty feet behind him, Casey a few paces behind her.

Adam passed the manicured grass of the Jardin Anglais and crossed the bridge, turning right along the broad embankment, which was studded with tidy trees, clipped to stumps and a few leaves. The windows of the apartment blocks were empty blind eyes.

It was a cold day; the last few commuters scuttling along with their heads down, wishing for warmer coats. Adam was hurrying, occasionally pausing to prod at his phone. They waited until he was alone and then almost ran the last few steps, until they were inches behind him.

'Adam Jefferson,' said Miranda.

He turned, startled.

Miranda and Casey stood there, in matching dark coats. Bland briefcases, blank faces.

Even if he recognised Casey, there was no way of knowing who they were. And, like everyone, he had a secret. Everyone has a guilty secret. A careless email here; a whispered hint there. A gamble when he already knew the score. It could be anything.

Halfway between work and home, so they already knew far too much.

They let the silence hold.

'We know about the camp,' stated Miranda.

'Camp?' Bewilderment, and then the quickest flicker of something else. 'What camp?'

'Don't, Adam.' He flinched at his name.

'I don't know what you're talking about.'

'You do, and you're going to tell us,' said Miranda. 'We know what they do there.'

'I have no idea what you're talking about' – too quickly.

'Adam,' Miranda paused. 'They are killing people.'

'It wasn't me.' The shift to despair was so familiar. 'It was nothing to do with me, I swear.'

'People, Adam.' Another statement.

'But I've never been.' His voice taut, as if he couldn't quite breathe.

'People, Adam,' Miranda hissed. 'They kill people.'

'I said it was wrong. I told him so.'

'Wrong?' The wind whipped through the trees. 'Wrong?'

'I don't know anything.' He was edging towards defiance.

'You're going to tell us everything you know.'

'No!' It was instinctive. 'I won't.'

'We know everything about you, Adam,' Casey joined in. 'And you're going to tell us about this.'

'I can't.' He glanced around in panic. 'Who are you?'

'That doesn't matter,' said Miranda. 'We need to know who told you about killing them.'

'No.' His voice rising to a scream. 'You can't prove anything.'

And he was away, racing between the trees, slipping and sliding, running blindly towards home and safety and Lulu.

They watched him go, icy-faced, in case, even in his panic, he turned back for a second.

'Well.' Casey dug through her pockets, pressed pause on her recorder. 'He certainly knows something.'

They were waiting for him the next morning, as he left his flat, dropping into his stride and flanking him.

'I don't know anything,' he yelled, bringing the busy street to a halt. 'Leave me alone.'

He sprinted towards the lake, dodging through bewildered commuters.

'I don't think,' Miranda said thoughtfully, 'that we are going to be able to catch him.'

'He hadn't slept,' said Casey. 'He was grey. Gaunt.'

'He's going to get greyer.'

'Do we give him one more chance?'

'I don't think he fucking deserves one.' Miranda's mouth was set.

'You spoke to him.'

'Yes. Maybe.'

'We'll have to …'

'Yes.'

They never liked doing this, because you could never be sure about loyalties.

Miranda and Casey took a taxi to the Cyan office, back to the café opposite the grand pillars. The waitress welcomed them, ever more baffled.

'Coffee and cheque?' – and a professional smile.

They sipped cappuccinos, eyes never leaving Cyan's doors. Jefferson reeled in half an hour later, looking shell-shocked. He had lost his tie somewhere on the walk to work.

A few minutes later, Azarola's battleship-grey car appeared, the usual chauffeur.

'Go,' said Miranda.

Moving fast, they cut off Azarola before he reached the door.

'What the …' He looked them up and down, eyes narrowed.

The chauffeur leaped back out of the car. 'Ladies … Sorry, sir.'

'I recognise you.' But, for a second, he couldn't place Miranda, in her charcoal Armani suit.

'Gigi's.' And she watched the recognition flicker across his face.

'What do you want?'

'It would be better if we talked in your office. Sir.'

'Not until you tell me who you are.' He was used to making a dozen decisions in the time most men choose their coffee.

'It won't take long.' Miranda edged forward.

'Tell me who you are.' Azarola was used to being obeyed.

'Miranda Darcey from the London *Post*, and Casey Benedict.' They had decided not to play him any more. He would not enjoy being fooled once, they thought. Twice would be unforgivable.

'I don't talk to journalists.' The shutters came down.

'It's very important, Mr Azarola.'

'Get lost.'

He turned on his heel, striding towards the door. The receptionists were peering down the steps, flustered and nervous, unsure if they had got something wrong.

'It's about one of your competitors,' Casey said quietly.

He paused, just for a second.

'Which one?'

'Aurora Partners.' She hesitated just for a moment. Tyler Walton's operation.

He turned on his heel and came back towards them.

'I don't believe you.' He put his face close to hers. 'You're lying.'

'We're not going to go away though,' said Casey. 'You know we won't just leave.'

'What do you want?'

'It will take us five minutes to explain,' Miranda interjected smoothly. 'In your office.'

A lift went straight to his office. It was the size of a tennis court, and the view opened out over the lake, blown to ripples by the cold breeze. The walls were pale grey, and a Picasso hung beside the window. Six computer screens lit up his desk.

'Five minutes,' he said. 'No tapes. If you fuck me around, I will come after you for ever.'

Miranda nodded. 'Do you remember what we talked about in Gigi's?'

His face darkened. 'Of course I remember. Psycho stuff. No one does that shit.'

'We think someone did.'

'Walton?' He was incredulous.

'No,' Casey said hastily. 'We are very sorry about that. It was nothing to do with him.'

'What the fuck then?'

'We overheard one of your staff talking about it,' said Miranda. 'They seemed to know about it.'

'And you assumed they were talking about me.' He was outraged. 'Me?'

'There was nothing else to point to you,' Miranda said carefully. 'We assumed. Wrongly it turned out.'

'But we need to know who it was,' said Casey. 'We need to know who could do this.'

'You listen to my staff . . .' He trailed off, then the anger surged back. 'How? Where? Where did you do this?'

'It was only in Gigi's,' said Casey. 'The London one. Back in April. You were celebrating something and I overheard . . . I was sitting nearby.'

'Of course you were,' he snarled at her. 'Well, who was it? Who said this?'

'Adam Jefferson.'

'Adam?' He was shocked. 'Adam? I don't believe it. He's an analyst . . . He's no one.'

'He knows something,' said Miranda.

Casey took her recorder out of her handbag.

'I said no fucking tapes.'

Ignoring Azarola, she pressed a button. The recording was crystal clear.

'People, Adam. They kill people.'

'I said it was wrong.'

Casey stopped the tape.

'He knows, Mr Azarola.' Casey looked at him squarely. 'He knows.'

'People,' Miranda said again. 'In camps.'

Azarola blinked, just for a second. Then his mouth tightened.

'You will leave Cyan out of this.' It was an order.

'Completely,' Miranda promised. 'We will never connect Cyan to this story at all. If you can help us, we will never reveal your link to this investigation.'

He gave her a long hard stare, then turned to look out over the lake. The water glittered, silver on gunmetal. They couldn't see his face.

After a long minute, he turned to his desk, and pushed a button on his phone.

'Send Adam Jefferson up to my office. Now.'

It took Adam a long time to get to Azarola's office. They spent the minutes in silence. Azarola stared into space. Occasionally, his fists clenched.

There was a quiet knock and Adam slid in, like a lost schoolboy, his good looks crushed by terror. He crumbled as he saw Miranda and Casey there, standing by the window.

'What the actual fuck, Jefferson?' Azarola turned on him in a rage.

'They're lying.'

'I don't think they are.'

'I don't know anything.'

'I think we'll be the judge of that.' Miranda and Casey caught each other's eye at 'we'. Azarola was going to do their job.

'Please …'

'You are going to tell me every single fucking thing you know. Every single detail.'

'I can't.'

'You will, Adam. You will, or I will fire you. Then I will have your visa rescinded and you will be thrown out of this country. Then I will ensure that no one in this entire industry employs you ever again. Do you understand me, Adam?'

'I can't tell you.' It was a plea.

'Do you think this is a fucking joke, Adam? Do you think I won't destroy you?'

'I thought reporters protected their sources.' Adam turned to Miranda. He was begging now, almost in tears.

'You're not a fucking source, Adam,' said Miranda. 'Sources tell us things. Right now, you're absolutely nothing.'

'We can protect you.' Casey shifted to good cop. 'No one ever needs to know you've spoken to us.'

He turned to her, pilgrim to a cross.

'Tell us what you know and we can work with you,' she said, so softly.

'I ... I don't know ...'

'It's OK, Adam,' said Casey. 'We can look after you ...'

'I don't know much ... You promise?'

'I promise,' said Casey, although promises had stopped meaning anything a long time ago.

'It was this guy I know ... Milo Newbury ... I was in London for a bit before I moved here. I'd met him a few years back, when he was in New York to party. So when I was moving to Europe, I gave him a call. He can be fun. We got to be friends. He's always been, well, pretty wild. Drugs, obviously. Some pretty dark porn.' Adam winced at a memory. 'He was laughing about it.'

'Go on,' said Miranda.

'Anyway, we started hanging out quite a lot. About a year after I arrived, I got invited to this shooting thing. Pheasants. They chase them down to you, with dogs. Somewhere in Yorkshire ... It was raining, and freezing. Not very fun at all. Not like back home. Milo was there. We started chatting, between, what do they call them? Drives?'

'Something like that,' said Casey.

'And he said that it wasn't as good as the real thing. And I had no idea what he was talking about, I promise ... I never guessed. And then later ... He was drinking all day. Hip flask.

Whisky, I think. Later on, we were away from the others, and he said ...'

Adam's voice trailed away.

'Keep talking, Adam.' Azarola's voice was glacial.

'I was sort of kidding along with him,' Adam admitted. 'We were laughing in this sort of library room ... Playing pool. I made out like I was impressed. I asked him, what did he mean about the real thing. And he said there was this place you went, and it was like a proper safari, but ... but you shot people ...'

'Adam.' There was horror in Azarola's voice.

Behind Adam's back, Miranda made an abrupt gesture to keep him quiet.

'He said it was the most intense thing he had ever done. He said he felt completely different afterwards,' and Casey heard the echo of his voice, part-gloating, in the club.

Adam had laughed along, wondered after.

'Where was the camp?' Casey asked, to cover up her sudden contempt.

'I don't know.'

'And who,' Casey asked, the realisation rising like nausea. 'Who were the people?'

'I thought you knew,' Adam said, almost wonderingly. 'Refugees. They shoot at refugees.'

10

Casey had visited refugee camps all around the world. There are more refugee camps than anyone realises. Scattered across Africa, curving in a desperate arc around Syria. In Pakistan. In India. In Thailand. In Bangladesh.

Her first visit had been to Zaatari, just over the Syrian border in the northern edge of Jordan. People forget about refugee camps. They don't make the headlines. Casey had only been in Zaatari because of some grim milestone. Two million refugees, three million, four …

There are no people running for their lives in the refugee camps. No explosions. The children aren't starving. A refugee camp doesn't look like a tragedy.

But it is. *It is.*

As they arrive, people hit pause on their lives. All those thousands of lives, all paused. Waiting for something. Waiting to live.

That first day in Zaatari, to get orientated, Casey had been driven round the camp by her fixer. She and Khaled stared out of the window of the jeep, at the miles and miles of camp. The refugees stared back, sullen, bored. And angry.

In South Africa, there are guided tours of the townships, gazing at scruffy children, safe in the air-conditioning. Snapping cameras at people, like lions at Longleat.

In Zaatari, Casey was relieved to ditch the car.

Originally, the camp had set up in neat rows of tents, but soon people began to move the tents around: to family groups, village groups.

Ancient feuds. Old friendships. New sex. Astonishing how fast people rebuild the infrastructure of their lives. Mosques popped up. Market stalls opened. The main thoroughfare became – with stone-cold cynicism – the Champs Élysées.

And children, children, everywhere children.

Babies were born, miles from their homes. And the elderly died, so quietly, dreaming of those long-lost graveyards.

As they walked around, the next day, a woman, in the dusty veil, held up a tiny baby to Casey.

'Malak. She is Malak.'

The syllables were still new, and proud. Casey looked at the baby, wrapped in rags, with the green eyes of Syria. She was just a few weeks old. Khaled looked away.

'The average age of a refugee camp is twelve years,' the UNHCR worker said, almost casually.

And Casey thought of that baby growing, almost to adulthood, before she had a hope of living her life anywhere except that raggedy camp.

She is Malak.

Later, Casey watched more refugees arrive, struggling through the entrance. Sometimes they were picked up by the Jordanian border guards and dropped, weeping, at the gates. They would join the back of the queue, the long queue of arrivals. The whole family crying. Broken. Even the men, ground to desert dust.

They had held out, these people. Amidst the bombs, and the starvation, and the hunger, and the disappearances. Clinging on to what is ours. *Ours.* Our house. Our school. Our jobs. Our lives.

Until finally, something happened. A brother vanishing in the night. A neighbour's house blown to fragments. A last whispered warning. And finally, *finally*, they decide they have to leave.

Days of walking, away from the known. Goodbye and goodbye and goodbye. The terror of being stopped. Abandoning precious, most loved objects one by one. Until all they can carry is the children. And the children are all they have left. And a last sacrifice, to bribe past the border guards.

The queue, in the hot sun, weaved its way through the dusty shacks. And finally they were safe, for the first time in years. So they cried, there, in the hot blinding sun. And as they queued, her photographer snapped the pretty weeping children. Cameras in the face, right up close, so that, even then, they tried to smile. Although smiles weren't what the man wanted.

And as they moved up the queue, scraps of food and drink were handed out, and Casey watched them lift. It was like watching cut roses put in water.

By the time they reached the head of the queue, the mother would be clipping ears and wiping noses. The father, in his fake Armani jumper, would be trying to forget he had ever cried.

But they would never forget, any of them. And after struggling for days over a desert, people are grateful for a few weeks, a few days. Sometimes only a few hours.

Then they looked around, and realised they had been interned for the crime of being born in a country that had fallen apart. A crime, their birthplace.

Some of these Syrians had come from wealth, from education.

'We had rooms in the house we never even used,' a doctor said to Casey, shaking his head. He was living in a caravan, one room, his six children. 'I cannot imagine it now. I cannot imagine it.'

Casey left him sitting on his doorstep, looking out at nothing.

'If it can happen to us, it can happen to anyone,' he called after her. 'Never think this can never happen to you.'

But the refugees are supposed, if nothing else, to be safe.

Now Casey looked at Adam with horror. 'A refugee camp?' she asked. 'One of the refugee camps?'

Both Azarola and Miranda were shocked to silence.

'Adam ...' Azarola ran out of words. 'Oh, Adam.'

'Where' – Miranda took over – 'was the camp?'

'I don't know. He said it was a palace. This crazy house up in the middle of the hills. A huge white house with a golden roof. It's a kind of hotel, I guess ... He said it was amazingly luxurious, even by his standards. And then, a drive away, there's this camp.'

'How far away?'

'I don't know.'

'Do you know the name of the place?'

'No.'

'Of the refugee camp?'

'He didn't say.'

Newbury had been careful about that, at least.

'When did he go?'

'We talked about it in January,' Adam paused. 'I got the feeling that it was quite recent, then.'

'Did he say anything,' Miranda asked, 'about the person he shot?'

'No.' Adam winced. 'Milo said she. He didn't say anything else about it, but it was a woman. I'm sure ...'

'How?' Casey asked the key question. 'How did he know to go there?'

'He said it was some really shady guys.' Adam's anxiety rocketed back up. 'He said they were fucking crazy. He was scared of them. Deep down. You could see it.'

'How did they know him?'

'I don't know. He mentioned a guy called Charlie ... That's all I know ... He said that Charlie sorted it all ...'

Adam was crying, suddenly, shoulders shaking. Azarola eyed him with disdain.

'I hate that I didn't say anything,' said Adam. 'I should have done something ...'

'Do you think he could have been lying?'

Adam looked up, grey-faced. 'No. No. I don't think that he could have been lying. It felt' – Adam searched for the word – 'like he was confessing.'

The words fell into a silence.

I must confess, Casey thought. *I've all my lifetime played the fool till now.*

They went back and forwards, again and again, to see if the story changed.

It didn't change. Adam remembered a few more details, but the story didn't change.

'I guess we need to talk to Milo Newbury,' Casey said eventually.

Adam looked up. 'No, you can't.'

'Of course we must,' said Miranda. 'It's the next step.'

'You can't.'

'We have to, Adam,' said Casey.

'You don't understand.' His eyes were hollow now. 'Milo ... Milo is dead.'

11

'Bill!' Dash shouted across the office.

The newspaper's diarist scuttled across the newsroom.

'All right, poppet?' asked Bill, which was his standard opening for anyone from princess to postboy.

'Milo Newbury,' said Dash. 'Go.'

Bill screwed up his face for a moment.

'Met him a few times,' he started.

The hive mind of a newsroom can reach almost anyone. Worst case, someone will know someone who knows someone. Tap a room of journalists, and they know everything from mobile number to knicker colour for the Prime Minister to next year's Best Actress. Information flows like a river.

Bill scratched his forehead with his notepad, thinking.

'Popped up on that reality show. You know, that Chelsea one. Few years ago and only a few scenes.' Bill concentrated. 'Wasn't really his sort of thing. Heart not in it. Father's an art dealer. Conrad Newbury. Sir. Old school. Shop on Dover Street. They do chichi private views fairly regularly. There's a lot of money there. You'll see them at the Serpentine party. Art Basel. Good-looking boy. Dead, which I assume is why you're asking. Last month.'

'What was he like?'

'Clever,' said Bill with certainty, 'but arrogant. Pleased with himself, but one suspects that papa cast quite a long shadow. Knew all about the paintings, sure. Last saw him at their de Kooning opening. He was drunk. Too drunk. Papa was shooting him furious looks.'

'When was that?'

'November? Can check.'

'Get the picture editor to pull photos.'

'Sure. Anything else?'

'Put together a memo on everything there is to know about Newbury. No calls, just cuts.'

A cuts job was trawling through the archives, for the cuttings on a person.

'No problem.'

'And the people around him.'

'On it. Toodles, sweet pea,' Bill bounded back to the newsroom.

'Arthur,' Dash bawled.

The crime reporter was at the door in seconds.

'Boss?'

'Milo Newbury.'

'Died last month. We did a story.'

'And?'

'Fell out of the window of his flat. One of those tall houses in Pimlico. From the top floor. He landed on the railings below. Impaled. Very, very dead. Think they had a bit of a hassle getting him off the spikes.'

'Were there any questions about it?'

'There's an inquest. Open and adjourned. Can check when they're doing the whole thing. Won't be for a bit though. It was pointing towards suicide.'

'Why?' Casey was leaning against the wall.

'Windows aren't the right sort for falling out of,' said Arthur. 'One of the cops let me into the flat on the q.t. It's a sort of mansard arrangement. You would have to properly climb out, and there were ashtrays and so on in the flat, so it wasn't like he scrambled out to smoke or anything.'

'Could have been murder?' Miranda asked.

'Well.' Arthur blew out his cheeks and thought. 'There was no sign of forced entry. He was a big bloke too. Over six foot, played rugby, hard to push around. But then there wasn't a note either. He'd been drinking and there were drugs in the flat. Coke. Weed. Usual stuff, really.'

'State of mind?'

'I spoke to the girlfriend.' Arthur sounded slightly defensive. 'She said he'd been a mess recently. I think they might have broken up a bit before, to be honest, just she quite fancied being the distraught girlfriend. And she was a better quote as the current squeeze.'

'Parents?'

'Yes. Well, the father, anyway. Sir Conrad, himself. He sounded like he barely knew his son, from the way he was speaking of him. Said straight out that he hadn't seen him for months.'

'Odd,' said Dash. 'Did the police do the prints and all that?'

'Not sure,' Arthur admitted. 'I can go back to them. I know the detective who was on it that day. He's a bit bloody useless, if I'm honest. Can't see him getting to the bottom of anything.'

'Check in with them,' Dash decided. 'Just see if it's something they are considering. Don't make it a big deal.'

'Sure. Shall I do a bit more digging?'

'Not yet,' said Miranda.

'Like that, is it?' Arthur eyed her. Some of the specialists didn't like the investigations team on their turf.

'Yes,' said Dash. 'It is.'

'Sure.' Arthur rolled over. He would keep quiet, they knew. Journalists are surprisingly good at keeping secrets. Every day they see the consequences of a loose word here, a Chinese whisper there.

'That everything, boss?' asked Arthur. 'Just Ross wants six hundred words on that vanished teenager five minutes ago.'

Ross appeared at the door to Dash's office.

'Arthur, there's a murder, down in Catford. Could you shift on down there?' Ross paused, checked his phone. 'Unless it's black on black, Trident bollocks, in which case, stick with the vanished teenager and we'll take agency copy on the stabbing.'

'Ross!' Casey winced.

'You can shout all you want,' Ross shrugged at her. 'But I watch the metrics all day long, and I can see which articles people actually read. No one reads about bloody Trident deaths.'

He strode away, to pick off his prey from the news desk.

'That all then?' Arthur asked.

'Yes,' said Dash. 'But I want a memo on Newbury as soon as possible. Copy these two in.'

'No worries.' Arthur disappeared back into the newsroom.

Salcombe appeared at Dash's door. He usually stayed in a glass box at the far end of the room, with a view over the busy street one way and a wary PA the other. 'Doing anything interesting?'

'Just working out where we are on Wynford Mortimer,' Dash said smoothly.

They smiled politely at each other. Miranda and Casey admired the stained grey carpet.

'Can I get a readout of that soon,' said Salcombe, not quite making it a question.

'Of course.'

The editor glided away across the office, reporters turning like sunflowers to smile as he passed. Dash peered at his computer for a few seconds, and Casey and Miranda didn't ask the question.

The picture editor tapped on the doorframe.

'Pix from the de Kooning private view. Full set. Bill said you wanted them. Shout if you need anything else.'

You could see that Milo was drunk. His eyes weren't quite focused, his smile too big. Each photograph was captioned with the names of the people in the foreground. In one grouping he was grinning vacantly at a ravishing girl in an emerald dress. The girl was watching him ambivalently, while Sir Conrad Newbury eyed his son with barely concealed distaste.

In another photograph, of three ravishing blondes, Newbury was in the background. Unlit by a smile, he looked distressed, the camera catching a despair missed by the room.

'He's suntanned in these photographs,' said Casey thoughtfully.

'Yes,' said Miranda. 'He is.'

'Might be an all-year-round thing though, for someone like that,' Casey added. 'Skiing holidays, and all that.'

'Need to speak to the girlfriend, or whatever she was,' said Dash. 'And parents and so on.'

'I'll try the parents,' said Miranda.

'And I'll start here.' Casey picked up the photographs. 'Start here and work outwards. And find it.'

12

Miranda called the Newburys, and got nowhere.

'Same thing as he said to Bill,' she reported. 'Virtually no contact with his son. No idea about any trips. Phone down. Useless.'

Casey, meanwhile, listed the details that Adam had recalled. Carefully, she sketched them out in her mind. Not the flat deserts around Zaatari; there had to be hills. It would be in one of the more chaotic camps, too.

Along the Lebanese border, to the west of Syria, there are hundreds of unofficial camps. Where refugees scrambled over the hazy border, and collapsed in a ditch. Living under tents of scraps of plastic. Subsisting off handouts. Dying from forgotten diseases. The Bekaa Valley, where it scorches in summer and snows in the winter.

Every one of those scratching existences could be called a refugee camp. It could be anywhere up there.

'Lebanon,' said Casey. 'It has to be Lebanon.'

The Bekaa Valley. Casey kept coming back to it. That slice of Lebanon, up above the cacophony of Beirut, edged by Syria to the north and east.

When the world first heard of ISIS, in that summer of horror, it watched ineffectually as they raged east into Iraq and then flooded down the rivers. Down the Tigris and the Euphrates, almost all the way to a desperate Baghdad. And Isis meant to surge west, too, right across to the Mediterranean. That was the plan, for the rise of the caliphate. They wanted Iraq, but they wanted the Levant too, that whole swathe over to the Mediterranean.

But to reach the sea from Syria, they needed to blaze through the Bekaa Valley, that wide sweep of beauty. It's a delicate balance, peace in the Bekaa, and it always has been. With the Christians and the Druze, and the Shia and the Sunni, all living side by side.

And as Isis raged towards Lebanon, they were only just held at the border and the refugees had escaped into the Bekaa in their millions. The lucky ones, they were, if you could call it luck. And now the Syrians were waiting for their world to stop crumbling. Years, they might wait. For ever, maybe.

Casey examined it again. That beautiful wide valley, Lebanon's grain store was hemmed in on both sides by mountains. Refugees, Casey thought. Refugees. And mountains. And sightlines.

She analysed it again and again. It must be there that they go, she decided. Somewhere in the mountains that glower west over the Bekaa. It's the very top of the Great Rift Valley, the Bekaa. That long split in the world that runs all the way from Lebanon to Mozambique. That must be where they went, these people, Casey decided. To the beautiful tinderbox of the Bekaa Valley.

She thought for a bit, then picked up the phone.

He answered at the first ring.

'Darbyshire,' he snapped.

'George,' she said, and told him what she needed.

*

He was waiting as she came through the arrivals gate at Beirut airport, arms wide.

'The mountain,' he shouted, 'has come to Muhammad!'

'Take me up to the mountains,' she said.

'As they say in Cairo,' he grinned, 'yalla, bitches.'

Casey had met George Darbyshire in another airport, years before. She'd been marooned in Jakarta's sprawling airport for seventeen hours, because the *Post* had got her a cheap, long connection. And George was stuck there because he wasn't sure where he was going next, quite yet. She'd heard his voice, clipped and bored, and turned, almost in recognition. They'd got through most of a bottle of duty-free rum in the long easy hours, and nearly missed their flights.

They'd been friends at once, and stayed in touch haphazardly.

He was opaque about his past. A long time in special forces, she'd guessed. Still connected – deniably now – to the Foreign Office. In his early fifties, he stalked around the Middle East, on a series of vague tasks, directed by some nameless authority.

With greying hair clipped close to his head, blue eyes and an irrepressible energy, George Darbyshire knew everything and everyone. He answered Casey's questions, always: 'On deepest, darkest background, you. I don't exist, right?'

They drove into Beirut, that smashed-up, beautiful city, with George laughing as she flinched at the traffic.

'The Lebanese army'll give us a lift up to the camps tomorrow morning.' He dropped her off at her hotel. 'I'll pick you up at 6 a.m.'

At the army base outside Beirut, the Lebanese major greeted George with a slap on the back, and some quick Arabic backchat.

'*As-salaam alaikum*,' the major greeted Casey politely.

'*Wa-alaikum-salaam*,' she returned, as she had a thousand times.

Casey climbed into the helicopter and it swirled into the air. They soared over the mountains, and skimmed up the patchwork fields of the Bekaa Valley. Legs dangling, Casey gazed towards Syria as the helicopter hurtled north. Somewhere. Over there. Maybe. It was possible.

Those men could have travelled to Beirut so easily. Direct flights, and everything. Then they would find their way up the valley, past the cedars and the ancient Roman ruins of Bacchus and Jupiter and Venus. Scramble up into the hills, and find their place, high above one of the camps.

It could happen.

Casey looked across to Syria. It would take only an hour or so to drive to Homs from here, right into the heart of the nightmare. But the valley below looked so peaceful, and so beautiful, with the orchards rolling like smoke into the distance.

They landed in a cloud of dust, then drove down to the refugee camp, through the vineyards and the orchards, where the opium poppies fluttered, careless as pink silk.

As they rolled into the camp, Casey looked up at the brown hills to the east. It could be here. It could be here, very easily.

I am Malak.

Thousands of people existed here, right in the shadow of Syria. They'd made it to Lebanon, but only just. A few steps ahead of the war, the silver lining of a nightmare cloud. A small crowd of refugees watched Casey lethargically as she climbed out of the jeep.

They had lost everything.

These tents were patched, sagging in the sun. Here and there were a few buildings, ugly with breeze block. Smoke rose from a thousand cooking stoves. A man hopped past on crutches, one leg missing. He turned to look at Casey and she saw that he had lost an eye, too, a long time ago.

'There's not much,' George nodded, 'in the way of medical care up here. They die of medieval diseases.'

A scattering of children had made kites out of tattered plastic bags. They ran down a path, screaming giggles, kites almost fluttering into the air.

Three of the children were playing with a wheelchair, one pushing, two riding solemnly.

Squaring her shoulders, Casey walked over to one woman. The Lebanese translator talked rapidly to her. She had four-year-old twins, three-year-old twins, a two-year-old, the translator explained, and a baby. She was pregnant again.

'I know,' said the woman's eyes, without any need for a translator. 'Oh, I know.'

Her left eye was bruised, and her headscarf grimy. She stood there, tugging at her abaya, lost among a few scraps of rubbish that might have been her possessions.

With the semaphore delay of a translator, Casey questioned the woman: had anyone been shot in the camp, were there any rumours, was there anything ...

No, the message came back. No. She hadn't heard of anything like that. She could imagine it though. She could imagine anything. There were guns everywhere in the camp anyway. They were needed, though, because there had been an attack over the border before; and everyone was scared.

They left her, shipwrecked among her children, without a backward glance.

Patiently, the small group worked their way round a small slice of the camp. No one had heard anything, not even a rumour.

They hesitated at a school, or an approximation of one.

'This will be washed away as soon as the rains come.' George frowned at the roof. 'It'll never last, this. It rains for days at a time up here, and everything gets wet. And then it stays wet for the whole rest of winter.'

Casey was watching a small girl dancing in the dust. She was twirling, a tiny ballerina pirouetting in the sunlight. They all stopped to watch, as she leaped and spun. Joyous as any child, just for a moment.

They clapped as she sank into a curtsy and grinned up at them, illuminated. Skinny, with a smile missing a front tooth. Dark hair that faded to gold where it was chopped into a rough fringe. She was wearing a frayed T-shirt with a smug cartoon cat, chucked into a charity box in Weybridge a long time ago.

For thereby some have entertained angels unawares, thought Casey.

'Yara,' said her mother, proud as any mother. 'Yara. My girl. Together.'

'The babies freeze up here in winter,' said George, suddenly angry. 'There's no clean water, no fuel for a fire, nothing ... So they die ... They die.'

'Lebanon is doing all it can,' persisted the translator. 'But there are so many.'

And there were. Millions and millions of refugees pouring into a tiny country, a country that struggled at the best of times.

A boy was standing nearby, Yara's brother, Casey guessed, in a tattered Manchester United shirt. Kicking a battered football, and limping from an old injury that had never been fixed.

About thirteen and he didn't like reporters, she could see. And why not be angry?

Because soon, too soon, this boy would be sent off, on that terrible modern odyssey. North towards Turkey, most probably, and then across that narrow sea to Greece.

Maybe he'd get to Europe, that precious, precarious dream.

Might die, though, of course. Might slip off any of the steps on that crumbling ladder. And never be heard of ever again. And, in the shadow of these mountains, this small family would wait for ever. First in hope, and then a slow-growing grief.

His mother, nervous of his anger, invited them into her tent. Yara's sticky little fingers tugged at Casey's. They had to bend double to get in, and then to fold like origami to sit down. There was old carpet on the floor, and a sharp smell of smoke.

The mother made tea, with Yara and all the others giggling. Other women scrambled into the tent, too, riveted by this new development.

Yara's doll had lost a leg. She was brushing the doll's woolly hair, so carefully, tying it back with a snippet of ribbon. Next to her, a toddler played with a green toy car, which was ending its journey here, somehow. No doors and no bonnet; thrown away in an instant, in a terrace in Wandsworth. Precious here, though. The eldest woman untied and retied her blue headscarf thoughtfully.

Yara's mother spoke rapidly.

'I thought we were leaving for only a few days,' said the translator. 'I would have brought more, if I had known.'

Casey handed out melted chocolate bars.

One woman, grey with sorrow, brought out a photograph with an art restorer's care. Three children, smiling at the camera.

'Bomb,' said Yara's mother. 'In Deraa. Burn. They burn. No one care.'

The woman looked down at the photograph.

'You ...' The mother was trying to make conversation with scraps of English, and gesturing to Casey and George. 'You ... Marry?'

'No,' roared George in horror. 'Absolutely not.'

They were all relieved to laugh.

'I' – Casey gestured in turn – 'I am not married at all. Never.'

And all the Syrian women put their heads to one side and sighed.

'It's ... So sad.'

'You,' said George happily, 'are being pitied by Syrian refugees.'

The little boy held out his green toy car to her, face smeared with chocolate. When Casey smiled at him, he ducked his head at his mother's skirt, then peered round at her, delighted. It was only when he moved that she realised he had lost both his legs.

'Asim.' The mother rubbed his face so he wriggled. 'Asim. What will become us?'

Through the tent opening, Casey could see the older boy outside, alone, listening to the laughter and wishing for a different life.

Yara trotted behind them when they left the tent, giggling in their wake. The little girl followed them all the way along the row of tents, trailing a tattered pink kite. A dirty Disney hair-band pulled back tangled hair, and her round face curved into a serious frown as she fought with her kite.

Just as Casey was turning to her, a helicopter whirred over-head and Yara screamed, huge eyes shot through with dark terror. In Syria, helicopters drop barrel bombs. Yara fled away down the path, kite abandoned, so that Casey's last glimpse was of a tiny child diving for cover, chased by a nightmare that would never let go.

They kept on though, George and Casey, round and round the camps for days. Asking the same questions again and again. But the refugees shook their heads. No. No. No.

'The thing is,' said George eventually, 'that if you wanted to kill someone round these parts, Isis could make it happen, quite easily. And you wouldn't have to shoot from a distance either. They'd let you do whatever you wanted. It'd be a job off their hands. Pour a bucket of petrol on someone and throw a match? Fine. Chainsaw a man in half? Easy. Chuck a man off an apartment block? Any day of the week. Have you ever seen someone being stoned to death? Never watch that. Never. They'd probably even edit a nice film together for you, if you asked nicely, just for the memories.'

'But could you get in and out? Of the areas they control?'

'If they wanted to get you back safely, no problem,' said George. 'It would have to be worth more than kidnapping you, but they'll do stuff for cash, cool as you like. And we know there are some fuckers smuggling stuff in and out all the time anyway. The oil gets out somehow, because it always bloody does. And you can pick up some very nice antiquities in Beirut, if you know where to look. From Palmyra and so on. There's always some arsehole with a route in and out of those places, no matter what's going on.'

'And do you think it's possible, that people are doing this?'

'Of course it's possible.' His voice was icy. 'Some people just like killing other people. They get a kick from it. Why do you think some men join the army, anyway? Some of them get a taste for death, too. A craving even, after a while. One of my boys, back in the day, he took himself off to Chechnya, of all places, in a bit of time off. We had to go in and get him back pretty sharpish.'

'Bread and circuses,' said Casey. '*Damnatio ad bestias*. People queued up to watch Christians and lions.'

'And think of the executions out in Saudi.' George lit a cigarette. 'Are they there to watch justice? Or just to watch somebody die?'

They looked across the camp. The refugees were queuing for bread. First, they would stand in that line for hours, and then they would queue for water.

'And then we wonder why they hate us,' said George quietly. 'And why they come with their bombs.'

'I can't see how anyone could do it,' muttered Casey. 'To people who've got nothing in the first place.'

'There is no such man,' quoted George. 'It is impossible.'

'I just can't understand it.'

'I think you do,' said George. 'That's the problem.'

He kept going though, escorting her for days around the refugee camps, scattered all across the valley. No one had heard about it. No one.

Miranda rang up, half-cross.

You coming home anytime soon?

I suppose I should.

Yeah. I'll order you, if that will help.

Not really.

Anything?

No.

George dropped her back to Beirut, jollying her as they drove down the road into the frisky old city.

'I'll keep my ear to the ground,' he promised. 'I'll ask around. If anything like that's going on anywhere in this region, I will find out.'

'Thanks, George. And maybe it's just not here. I hope it isn't, really. Maybe I'm looking in the wrong place.'

'You might be.' He was suddenly serious. 'Some of my boys, they were debriefing the girls trafficked up to Italy. What's going on down there in north Africa, it's horrific. A woman was talking about that drive across the Sahara. One girl kept crying and crying, and begging for water. After a bit, the traffickers got fed up. They stopped the truck. Kicked her out of the back. Drove on. She was just left there, in the middle of the desert. That's where I would go looking.'

'You're right,' said Casey. She stared at the racing traffic.

After he'd roared off into the distance, she walked along the beautiful corniche. She looked out at the blue sparkle of the Mediterranean, and thought about the refugees risking it all, in the boats that filled with water, and the life jackets that never worked. It's impossible, surely, that it's all the same sea.

The men were fishing out on the rocks. Casey watched for a few minutes more.

'The Sahara,' she thought. 'Libya.'

*

Back in the office, the satellite pictures of Libya showed endless burnt sand, and dark rocky outcrops here and there. Inky circles were crops, where the irrigation wheels turned ceaselessly. Roads knifed across the desert, between villages with names like incantations. She traced the roads, one by one, witch-whispering the words.

And then, there it was. Salama refugee camp, a scratchy patch of land not far from the long, blurry border with Algeria. Mountains curled around the camp to the south. To the west, there was a huge building. Ragged gardens sprawled around golden roofs.

Salama. Salama. Casey tried out the word as she zoomed in and out on the images. From above, the camp looked like all the others. Squares of roads, and chaos in between. It had grown up during a sudden crisis somewhere on the Gulf of Guinea. Driven by war and starvation and fear, thousands of people headed north, as they always do in Africa.

Bamako, Ségou, Gao, Tamanrasset. The old caravan trail.

Agadez. Dirkou. Al Qatrun. Sabha. That ancient path of desperation, up through Niger and Libya.

On foot, when every step hurts. In cars which overheat in the middle of the desert, and there are days and days to realise the water will run out. In trucks that run out of fuel, and people are left to die on the side of a road that no one ever wants to take.

But for a few, somewhere, just over the border from Niger into Libya, the surge had slowed. The flood of people pooled, and Salama was born.

Refugee camps are thrown together in a rush. They are designed to keep the cascade of humanity somewhere, anywhere, contained. And so they grow, a nightmare Babel. An overnight city.

Once it was there, Salama grew rapidly. They were fleeing Boko Haram, in the first wave. Then Somalis, escaping their endless horror. The Eritreans found their way too, in the end. Europe was the dream. Always the dream. But Salama was the staging post that became the life.

And hundreds of miles away, Casey zoomed in and out, thinking.

It took longer than she expected to track down an aid worker who had been to Salama and would talk about it. Usually, it took a couple of calls to find the right person, speed being one of her skills. She called old allies from the Zaatari camp, put the word out. But it took hours to find Logan, and still longer to convince him to talk.

There was Irish in his voice, and a tired patience.

'Gather you want to know about Salama.'

'Yes. Please.'

He explained, carefully, cautiously. That the camp had started its sprawl just as an enormous earthquake shattered the other side of the world. All the fund-raising and experts were diverted to photogenic orphans in Nepal, rather than yet more refugees. And in the absence of the bigger charities, and the more efficient NGOs, Salama grew chaotically.

You'll know there's the odd science to positioning a refugee camp, Logan went on laconically, which means someone, thousands of miles away, looking at a map and deciding the position of the camp. On sandy ground, which would degenerate to a tedious dust that would need to be washed out of a thousand cooking pots every single day. Or on the black rock, which would heat to a Dante inferno every summer. For Zaatari, someone had carefully chosen dust, rather than dark heat.

'We could hear the explosions at night there,' he said. 'They don't like that much. But we figured, if we got to the point where Syria was mortaring straight into Jordan, the camp would be the least of our worries.'

Places that are nice to live in, Logan pointed out lugubriously, tend to have people there already. And of course, refugee camps are there to assuage the host country. Because even in the most desperate parts of the world, the host country has to believe the refugees are going somewhere. The refugees, too, have to believe they are going somewhere. Even though some of the Palestinian camps, in Jordan, have been there since the fifties, and Zaatari is the country's fourth-largest city.

But no one was concentrating as Salama took root, Logan said, which is why it was in Libya, that painfully fragile state, in the first place. Salama was all a fuck-up. A huge fuck-up. I had to get out, in the end.

Casey took notes, made him laugh and then turned the conversation, quite abruptly.

'Were people ever shot in Salama?'

A silence. 'What do you mean?'

'I think you know what I mean.'

He waited.

'Were there ever,' Casey pushed him, 'unexplained gunshot injuries in Salama?'

'That camp was out of control,' said Logan. 'You'll know there's organised crime in many of those camps, anyway.'

'I know,' said Casey. He was calling from Dadaab, in the east of Kenya. A quarter of a million people, over the border from Somalia, and starvation a memory away. 'But I mean sniper injuries. I think you know what I am talking about.'

'There were child soldiers in Salama.' Logan's voice was quiet. 'Hundreds of them. Coming from countries where almost every woman has been raped, give or take. Do you know what it does to a country, when the women have been broken like that? That level of distress. An entire nation, traumatised.'

'I do know,' said Casey. 'A bit.'

'Yes,' said Logan. 'There were gunshot injuries in Salama.'

'Ones that would indicate sniper fire?'

'I'm not that sort of expert.' The line dropped out for a second. 'I don't know about ... Guns.'

He spat out the word.

'A sniper rifle would cause a catastrophic injury.' Casey was deliberately surgical. 'Not just a bullet hole. The body would be almost blown apart.'

The silence was so long that she thought she had lost him. She remembered one of the aid workers talking in Jordan: 'It's only the ones with faith who survive. It breaks everyone else. They have to believe there is a purpose, to it all. A reason. It's only those who truly believe who can bear it, in the end.'

And Logan sounded like he had lost his faith, a long time ago.

'There were' – his voice when it came again was almost a shock – 'There were injuries that maybe might have been caused by something bigger than a handgun. Now and again. Not that it happened often.'

'Did you report them?'

'Who were we meant to tell? We didn't have time to breathe, let alone try and get anything done. You don't know what it was like. It was dangerous, really dangerous, all of the time. We had to live in a special compound in the camp, and we couldn't travel around. The whole place was a nightmare. And it just went on and on, and never got better. No matter what we did.'

'I'm sorry,' said Casey. 'I am really sorry.'

'Everyone is sorry,' he said. 'Everyone is always sorry and sorry and sorry, and nothing ever changes. But yes, we saw injuries that didn't make sense. And they could have been caused by a sniper bullet. We talked about it, sure. But we didn't have any proof. We didn't have anything.'

'How often?'

'Maybe every few months? That we knew about. Not regular. I couldn't be sure.'

'Do you remember any dates?'

'No.' He hesitated. 'Hang on. I do remember one. The sixteenth of October last year. There was a woman, shot down by one of the shitty medical centres. They tried to save her, but there was nothing to be done. She was dead before she hit the floor. Her daughter was screaming and screaming, until her voice disappeared. A little girl, six or something. God knows what happened to her, alone in that camp.'

'How can you be sure of the date? Did you keep a diary?'

'No.' His voice was bleak. 'Why keep a diary when every day's the same? The sixteenth was my birthday.'

13

Arthur was right, thought Casey. Isabella Monroe was enjoying the drama.

They were in Bella's apartment, just off the Portobello Road in Notting Hill. Bella was wearing a flowing blue dress and too much eyeliner for someone who thought they might cry.

Casey had rung up to talk about the appalling hats that Isabella made. For Goodwood, for Ascot, for the Derby. Invited round to the pretty little shop, Casey at first let the words drift over her, nodding enthusiastically while wondering if it would be possible to fit a breton with a camera.

After twenty minutes of feathers and fascinators, Casey worked the conversation around to Milo. Bella was only too happy to talk.

'Milo and I had been together for eighteen months,' she began.

'It must be terrible for you,' said Casey. 'Such a shock.'

'It was,' Bella agreed. 'It was.'

'Would it upset you too much to talk me through it? I think it's such a fascinating story. We'd do a separate piece on your hats.'

'No.' Bella looked brave. 'That would be OK.'

'It's very strong of you,' said Casey obediently.

Bella had met Milo the Christmas before, at a party.

'At the McCarthys' house. You know the McCarthys. Maria and Simon. Everyone was there. Everyone.'

'Of course,' said Casey, thinking, not eighteen months then.

'He kissed me under the mistletoe at midnight. It was so romantic. Everyone said we were the perfect couple.'

The art lay in letting them tell their story.

'It was lovely at first,' Bella went on. 'We had such fun. I just remember being at Wimbledon, on Centre Court, crying with laughter. And then we went down to Mykonos for a couple of weeks. It was all perfect.'

'Where did you stay?'

'In a villa, with some friends. It was gorgeous.'

'So you weren't island hopping, backpacking?' Before the *Post*, Casey had spent a summer, once, bouncing from island to island round Greece. Lazy heat and blue blue water.

'Oh no,' Bella said. 'He never did the whole backpacking thing. He went to India on his gap year, I remember him talking about it. Said he spent one night in some utterly grim hostel, with cockroaches and horrible stains on the sheets. And then called his father and said he'd had quite enough of that, thank you. He'd always have cars waiting for us. And we stayed in the loveliest places.'

'And then what?'

'Then he changed,' said Bella. 'He went on holiday with some friends to Morocco. Six months ago or something. In about October, I think?'

'Which friends?' Casey, lightly.

'I'm not sure.' Bella frowned. 'It was a boys' thing. I wasn't allowed to go.'

'Stag party?'

'No,' said Bella. 'I thought that. And that there would be a fun wedding afterwards, and we could go to that together, but Milo said it wasn't a stag.'

'Did he say where he went in Morocco?'

'Essaouira?' Bella screwed up her face, concentrating. 'They went to do surfing there, I think. He'd been there before, a few years ago. He'd had a brilliant trip.'

'How long was he there for?'

'A week, I think. He was very brown when he got back.'

'And how was he changed when he got back?' asked Casey.

For a second, Bella's eyes filled with real tears.

'He was so different. In every way. Sometimes, he would be completely up, and so hectic and crazy. And other times, he would just slump. He was doing a lot more drugs. I mean, everyone would do the odd line here and there, but not much. And suddenly he was taking them for days and days and disappearing for nights. And he would get so angry. I never knew what was going to happen next ...'

'It must have been very hard for you.'

'I don't know what happened to him,' she said. 'It was that trip to Morocco, I am sure of it. He was completely all over the place after that.'

'Did he ever say what happened in Morocco?'

'No, he wouldn't talk about it at all.'

'And do you know who he went with?'

'I think there was someone called Charlie?' Bella hazarded. 'I don't think I ever met him.'

'Charlie.' Casey scribbled notes. 'Have the police asked you about it all?'

'Not really,' said Bella. 'I think they thought it was suicide.'

'Had he ever mentioned killing himself?'

'No,' said Bella. 'Never.'

'And what do you think? Deep down.'

'I don't know,' Bella said quietly. 'Sometimes, I think that I never really knew him at all.'

Casey wrote up the interview with Isabella on the train down to Exeter, looking out over fields of black and white cows. She put in a few hints of tragedy, but made Milo's death sound like a suicide. She didn't want her rivals getting interested. Then she filled the article with adjectives and filed it to the fashion desk, adding a quick note to Ross.

'Could you boot Fashion into publishing? I know she's not a name, but brownie points with Bella Monroe would be helpful. You never know. Not fussed about whose byline goes on, if that helps. In fact, probably best if it isn't mine.'

Articles were the easiest currency, for the *Post*.

Now she stared out of the train window, watching green fields slip past. Everyone has their Achilles heel, she had learned. Not always money. Often not money, surprisingly. But once you understand greed, you understand everything. And there is always a bait.

The big tabloids dangled ridiculous carrots, back in the day. Fame. Fortune. Power. And their props were a Rolex, a Ferrari, a yacht in Dubai.

Casey remembered one of the *Post*'s boys laughing over a Lamborghini, borrowed for a review in the driving section, and then used to turn over some soap star. The hacks promised the world and their prey fell over themselves. It felt oddly unsporting to Casey.

'*Timeo danaos*,' Miranda had grinned once.

The train slowed into the station, and Casey got a taxi out to the small village on the edge of Dartmoor.

The Newburys lived in Georgian perfection just outside Chagford. Early roses were coming into flower as the last few tulips collapsed in scarlet petals. The wisteria spilled across the front in Japanese beauty, so the house looked like it was wearing eyeshadow. House martins were building nests under the eaves. The moor soared away in the distance, up to the granite might of Kes Tor.

Casey knocked at the door. She could see the echoes of Milo in the man who opened the door. The clear blue eyes and the straight eyebrows. He was wearing a golf jumper, grey and blue diamonds.

'Sir Conrad?' she asked.

'Yes?'

'My name is Cassandra Benedict and I'm a reporter at the *Post*. I am very sorry to bother you, but could I possibly talk to you about your son?'

His face shuttered.

'I've told your newspaper once. No. Absolutely not.'

'Please ...'

'Please leave.'

The door closed firmly in her face. Not unusual. Casey retreated down the path. As she turned down the pretty lane towards the village, she caught a glimpse of a woman in the window. The woman looked as if she had forgotten how to smile.

Wandering around the village, Casey drifted into conversations, with the greengrocer and the baker, the postman and the woman at the Spar. It was a terrible shame. The funeral was the saddest day. Isabella couldn't stop crying. Such a pretty girl, she is. Lady N hollowed out with sadness. Sir Conrad was just playing golf all the time now, over outside Okehampton. He was never home. Nothing like that had ever happened in Chagford before. Their only child, can you believe it? A tragedy. London, you know. A real tragedy.

Casey bought a Cornish pasty from the bakery and waited, on a bench, in Chagford's pretty square. Eventually, a green Range Rover reversed out of the drive and disappeared in the direction of Okehampton.

A few minutes later, Lady Newbury came out of the house, carrying a trug and wearing gardening gloves. A snuffly pug followed closely.

She must have been beautiful, thought Casey, before her world splintered.

Casey walked to the garden gate, but stopped outside.

'Lady Newbury?'

There was a long pause.

'I'll leave whenever you want me to,' Casey promised.

The sparrows bickering on the bird table were the only sound. Casey waited, and very slowly Lady Newbury walked towards her. As she opened the gate, Casey saw that her hands were shaking.

Still in silence, they walked towards the house. Lady Newbury dropped the trug on the hall table, knocking some white roses to a shower of petals. In the library, without a word, Casey was pointed to a faded armchair. Lady Newbury disappeared towards the kitchen.

Casey looked around her. The room was lined with books, the spines a jumble of gold letters and battered favourites. A stag's head mourned above, and an antique Persian rug glowed with jewel-box colour. A delicate globe, of fragile beauty, sat on a Sheraton table. The room was immaculate; letters on the writing desk neatly stacked. There were photographs everywhere, in silver frames: Milo opening birthday presents, Milo on the rugby field, Milo playing polo.

The art was superb. A watercolour of Milo, Milo at his best, hung by the window.

Casey looked at it for a long time. The Newburys' golden boy, in a white shirt, open at the neck. He was laughing, lit up, happy.

'I've always loved that painting.' Casey turned at the voice. Lady Newbury was carrying a tray, with a blue and white teapot and a plate of shortbread. Her voice sounded rusty.

'It's beautiful,' said Casey.

'I don't know why you have come here, Miss ...'

'Benedict. Cassandra. I wanted to ask you about Milo. And how he died. I'm very sorry. Would you mind if ...'

'You can.' Her voice dried up for a second, and then went on. 'You can ask.'

'We think,' Casey said carefully, 'that something may have happened to Milo on a holiday a few months before he died.'

'The Morocco trip?'

'I spoke to Isabella Monroe,' said Casey. 'She said that he changed a lot after that trip.'

'Yes,' said Lady Newbury. 'I don't know what happened out in Morocco, but Isabella is most certainly right. Something changed.'

'Why do you say that?'

'He didn't come down here very much. He hadn't for a long time. All the mothers round here would get together and laugh about it. Our children running around in London, being silly, having a fine old time. We would only hear from them when they had run out of funds. But we thought it was fun for them. We thought it was a phase, and then they would be back...'

Casey gazed out of the window, to give her time. The rain was coming down now, dancing the tulips to rags.

'So he didn't come down often?'

'No. I last saw him when he was down for Christmas. He always came, for a few days. But this time, I was shocked. He'd lost a lot of weight, and he had terrible ... Well, mood swings I think you would call it. One minute, he couldn't stop talking, the next he was sulking like a teenager.'

'Did you ask him about it?'

'No ...' She hesitated for a long time. 'I'm the verger at the church, you know. I keep an eye on it. Organise the flower rota, make sure we have enough candles.'

One of the building blocks of English village life, thought Casey. The foundations, really.

'It's a beautiful church.' Casey had wandered around the churchyard, wasting time.

Milo's headstone – most beloved son – was carved white marble. Among the crooked old gravestones, covered in lichen, it stood out like a false tooth.

'I walked up there on Christmas Eve, just to check on it before Midnight Mass,' said Lady Newbury. 'I walked in, quietly. Not on purpose, I'm just quiet. My husband doesn't like ... fuss. And Milo was there ... Up by the altar. He was on his knees, and Milo was never religious. Never. I had to drag him along to church when he was little.'

'What was he saying?'

'I couldn't hear.' His mother's voice shook. 'But he was saying something. I froze.'

'And then?'

'The door slammed,' said Lady Newbury. 'In the wind. It was such a bang. And Milo jumped up. He was furious with me, shouting had I heard anything. I said I hadn't. I don't know why. I should have asked him what on earth was going on ... I should have asked him ... And I didn't ... It was so stupid of me. My son. My only son.'

She ran out of words then.

'Did you ever ask him about it?'

'No. It was Christmas the next day. My sister, and her family. And they all stayed until Boxing Day, and Milo went back to London that evening. And there just wasn't time. I tried to ask him about it, just on the phone a few times. But he wouldn't talk about it ... He would just hang up. So eventually, I stopped asking.'

'And then?'

'He died.' The words were stark in the gentle room. 'He died, and I'll never know now. My darling boy. My darling, darling boy.'

'Do you think that he jumped? I am so sorry to ask.'

'I don't know.' There was agony in every word. 'I just don't know. I don't know which is worse.'

The rain was pouring down now. Sir Conrad's golf would be washed away. Hopefully, he would head to the bar, but he might return.

'Lady Newbury ...' She paused. 'I know it is an odd question, but do you have Milo's passport?'

'His passport?' She was bewildered.

Casey nodded.

'I suppose so. It must be somewhere. Upstairs. Conrad handled his ... effects.'

Uncertainly, she went to the door. Her footsteps hesitated around the bedrooms above. A few minutes later she reappeared.

'Here.'

Casey examined it.

Laos. New York. Kenya. Barbados. The Seychelles.

Dozens of them, but finally, Casey found it, feeling the shiver go down her spine. The Tinkarine border crossing, in the south-west corner of Libya. Into Libya, over from Algeria. It was always astonishing how seriously chaotic states took their bureaucracy. As if insisting on a stamp could end the havoc.

'Would you mind if I made a list of the places he visited?'

'Of course not.' Lady Newbury was confused, but seemed untroubled.

Casey quickly noted down the times and places. She snapped a photograph of the Tinkarine stamp, and an Algerian one too. Last October, middle of the month. This passport had never been to Morocco.

'You've been generous with your time, Lady Newbury. Thank you so much.'

'I don't do much any more,' she said. 'Will you let me know if you find out anything about my son?'

My son.

I am Malak.

'Of course,' said Casey, because that was her job. Her brutal, agonising job. 'Of course I will let you know, if I can find out.'

Casey handed over her business card.

'I think it's the worst thing,' said Lady Newbury. 'The worst thing. Not knowing what happened to him.'

14

Casey left before Sir Conrad could return, meeting the taxi driver in the pretty village square. Lady Newbury watched her go, lost in an irreparable grief.

'He was clearly having problems after this October trip.' Casey called Miranda when she was safely at the station. 'Could have been struggling with guilt. Could have been having a meltdown with whoever organises this crap.'

'And he flew to Algeria, not Morocco?'

'Yes, exactly, and then crossed over at Tinkarine. They obviously don't trust Libyan airspace. Which is probably sensible given the number of lunatics who could be wandering around with surface-to-air missiles. Gaddafi's lot left weapon dumps all over that country, and no one knows where they are now. The SAS didn't get to some of them in time.'

'Who the fuck is this Charlie character Bella mentioned?'

Over the next week, they trawled every angle. Milo had no visible connection to anyone called Charlie who wasn't a PR girl or an estate agent.

Casey even pretended to be interested in buying a ten-million-pound mansion in Knightsbridge to check out one possible Charlie.

'Not him,' she sighed to Miranda on the phone later. 'Although it has huge potential for digging out an Olympic-sized swimming pool and cinema room in the basement. And I could hear the people in the garden next door doing some leisurely insider trading. I must mention it to Nicky.'

Casey let her eyes drift around the room. She was back in her sitting room, the tiny haven where she spent her occasional evenings off. She always meant to paint the walls something other than dull magnolia.

Tonight she was frustrated. Bella, thrilled by the flattering article about her hats, had dug under her bed and unearthed Milo's bank statements. He had withdrawn thousands in cash, but there were no transfers to anyone called Charlie.

'Could be drugs,' said Casey now. 'That would explain the cash withdrawals.'

Charlie; cocaine. Molly; MDMA. Dangerous when they became close friends.

'Bella did say he was doing a lot towards the end, didn't she?' said Miranda. 'Too much can make anyone a bit crazy. And paranoid. And all over the place.'

They thought about, but didn't mention, the *Post*'s defence editor. He had taken a pill just before the last Christmas lunch, and spent the party arguing with a pillar. Then he had a fight with himself behind a sofa. He'd been dispatched to rehab somewhere, after faxing death threats to Ross.

'He faxed them?' someone said. 'I didn't even know we still had a fucking fax. Jesus, that man spent far too long in Afghan.'

They sat in silence.

'Doesn't quite make sense though, does it?' said Miranda eventually. 'Going on holiday with drugs. Even if you're totally losing it, Algeria is the last place you'd go with drugs. They kick up a fuss over alcohol over there.'

Casey slumped down at her tiny dinner table. She examined her pot plant, a pretty purple flower bought one lazy Sunday morning in Columbia Road. It was dead. Very dead. The label a tiny tombstone.

'So what's the next step?' said Miranda. 'Wynford Mortimer is driving me to drink.'

'You were there already.'

There was a pause.

'The problem is that I think we know the next step,' said Casey. 'And we don't want to say it.'

'What is it?' asked Miranda, although she knew.

'The next step is obvious. Undercover.'

'Out there? It's total madness, Casey. We don't know where, or when, or who. The basic questions. We don't know what the rules are. And we're dealing with people who appear supremely unfussed about killing. It's close to suicide.'

Casey fiddled with the pot plant, pulling off the shrivelled leaves.

'We know where,' said Casey. 'And knowing the name Charlie could be enough.'

'In a country where people die,' added Miranda, 'all the time.'

'Yes,' agreed Casey.

Casey could hear Miranda's husband asking about dinner in the background.

'Just a minute.' Miranda's voice was impatient.

'I could go with a guy,' Casey said, in the end. 'Just be a couple of slightly dim backpackers. Hang out in the nearest town and see what happens.'

'Long shot,' said Miranda. 'And fucking dangerous. It's dangerous crossing a road in that country, let alone anything else.'

Casey poured a teacup of water over the purple flower. The water ran off the dry earth, splashing over the table.

'Shit. OK. Let me think.'

'I may have thought of something. Speak tomorrow.'

'You're not going to like this plan,' Miranda smiled at Casey the next morning.

Casey hadn't slept. She had spent the night playing war games in her head instead.

'You're probably right,' Casey agreed.

'You look terrible by the way.'

'I know,' Casey said equably.

'Ed.'

'Absolutely not.'

'He could do it,' said Miranda. 'And I can't think of anyone else.'

'Miranda,' said Casey. 'I can't.'

Even his name made her heart twist.

'Let's go and talk to Dash,' said Miranda.

'Fine,' said Casey, knowing it was a trap.

They sat down at the conference table. Dash steepled his fingers and waited for them to speak. Miranda presented the evidence, point by point.

'We're going to have to go in,' Miranda kept her voice steady. 'Through Algeria.'

'That would be insanity,' said Dash.

'It would be such an important story,' said Miranda, light in her eyes. 'The very best. It's worth a risk.'

'More importantly,' interrupted Casey, 'we can't let this carry on. We know ... We think we know that somewhere out there, refugees are being hunted like animals ...'

The conference room fell into silence.

'You'd actually go there?' asked Dash. 'And see whatever they do ... Legally, I don't know if ...'

'We could work it out on the ground.' Miranda was at her most persuasive. 'We might be able to crack it out there, before even going out to the camp. If they told us enough.'

Behind Dash's back, Casey raised an eyebrow at Miranda.

'What' – Dash was wary – 'is the plan?'

'We go in,' Miranda said smoothly. 'We find a guy who can go in alongside Casey. They join up with the group – whoever they are – in Algeria, and tag along on the way to Libya. Then we find out where they go, and what they do.'

Dash dropped his head and peered at them through the bars of his fingers.

'You're insane.'

'A little bit,' agreed Casey.

Dash spun his chair round and stared out of the window.

'I don't like this idea,' he said, almost to himself. 'Not at all.'

But he wanted it, they could tell.

'Dash' – Miranda told him what he wanted to hear – 'there isn't any other way. We could never run this story based on a few anecdotes. You know that.'

He spun his chair back round. 'So who do you have in mind? To go in with Casey.'

Casting was always difficult. Back at the *News of the World*, the Fake Sheikh used to spend days selecting the team around him, for just the right impression.

Miranda opened her mouth.

'Nathan Hill,' Casey cut across.

'Nathan?' Dash raised his eyebrows.

Nathan was one of the staff photographers at the *Post*. Tall and blond, he hugely enjoyed telling girls about his exploits as a war photographer. Casey had heard about his camera zoom being shot off in Aleppo several times. As a chat-up line, it never failed, he insisted.

'It's that mix of creativity and bravery, sweetheart,' he'd explain. 'Gets them every time.'

'Nathan would be fine,' said Casey. 'He's tough, and he's had his back to the wall a hundred times. He thinks quickly. And he wouldn't panic.'

'Too much ego,' said Miranda. 'It would have to be you running this, making the decisions. And – no matter what Nathan claims – there would be a split second before he obeyed an order from a woman. You know what he's like.'

'He'd get the job done though,' objected Casey.

She'd watched Nathan prowl towards a wounded soldier, ducking in and out of doorways, sliding over crumbling wreckage, seeing the whole world through a frame. Nathan always got his shot.

'Risky,' said Dash. 'He's too wild.'

'Dave?' suggested Casey.

A tough private detective, Dave Accardi tracked cheating employees and vanishing creditors. He specialised in errant husbands, approached out of the blue, by a knowing blonde in a hotel bar who laughed at all his jokes. The divorce payouts quadrupled when the wives called in Dave.

Before the game was shut down, the *Post* had occasionally used private detectives. Accardi could magic a phone bill from thin air, or know a bit more than he should about a bank account. Charming and understated, he cost a fortune and was worth every penny. The dark arts, it used to be called, and Accardi knew them all.

'Dave's sharp,' agreed Miranda. 'And there isn't much he hasn't done before.'

But Dash was wincing.

'I think Dave got a bit cute on the Ashton case,' he said. 'I heard the police are taking an interest in him at the moment.'

'I'd forgotten about that,' admitted Miranda.

Bobby Ashton, top scorer in the Premier League, had been splashed across the tabloids a few months earlier. He'd been snapped coming out of a hotel in the far reaches of Aberdeenshire with not one, but three hookers. His press man, who'd come up the hard way at the *Sun*, went over Ashton's Lamborghini inch by inch, and when he found the tracker he'd called in the police and got an injunction.

'Smart,' everyone agreed, crossly. And because of the fast work of his poacher turned gamekeeper, Bobby Ashton was still shifting cereal bars and football shirts by the million.

'Not Dave then.' Dash shook his head.

'One of the actors?' Miranda suggested. 'One of the ones we've used before. Or we could even give the editor's brother a decent part for once.'

'Can't see Felix Lincombe,' Dash said, 'coping with snipers in the Sahara.'

There was a long pause.

'Ed,' said Miranda, eventually. 'It's got to be him.'

Dash knew Ed. Had sent him out to Tahrir Square with one of their reporters. Back when women were dragged away by a hundred hands, and violated a thousand screaming times. 'He could do it.'

'Not Ed,' said Casey, and felt Dash's eyes on her.

'He'd be good,' said Miranda. 'He taught himself a bit of Arabic, too, while he was out in Iraq.'

'Give me a bit of time.' Casey stood up. 'I'll think of someone.' She walked out of the conference room.

'You're not there yet, anyway.' Dash looked at Miranda. 'I need more detail. It's too shaky. Too many holes. You're going to have to find more before I let you go anywhere.'

Miranda waved it away. 'We'll find something.'

One of her phones went. She looked at it.

'Give me a moment, Dash? It's an estate agent trying to flog Casey a mega-mansion.'

'And you're her PA now?' He laughed at her.

'Well, after all, Dash,' she smirked at him. 'Who doesn't enjoy a bit of role play?' She pushed a button. 'Hugo, darling. She's decided to go with the Trevor Square one, I'm afraid . . .'

15

Back in the investigations room, Casey dropped her head into her hands. Just for a moment. She had met Ed years ago, when he was a Royal Marine, hunting pirates out in the Indian Ocean. Casey had been sent there just for a few days, boarding the ship from some scruffy port in Oman, and heading for the wild Somali coastline.

I'm Ed.

Casey.

And she just knew. Ed. He had kissed her once. Just once. At the top of Primrose Hill. They had met, just once, when he got back to England. His tour had come to an end, weeks after Casey had flown home from the Seychelles.

'What the fuck are you doing in the Seychelles?' Ross had asked, when she finally got off the boat, legs quivering at dry land. 'I thought you were flying back from Oman.'

'The pirates are going to prison here.' She was watching the Somalis look up in wonder at the wild orange flowers, the neat little houses.

'Casey, I've had hacks turn up in the wrong place before, but never the wrong fucking hemisphere.'

Now, Casey remembered when Ed had called. 'My tour is finished. I just thought you might want to know. I am back.'

By then, they were writing to each other, enchanted letters. She had fallen deeper with every word. He made her smile, and wonder, and hope. And she scribbled back, this is who I am, tell me who I love.

It was odd seeing him not in uniform for the first time. She had only ever seen him in that khaki camouflage, that hotch-potch of green. She had wondered if it was the uniform. She had never been into them before, like some girls were. But maybe it was just the uniform.

It wasn't the uniform.

They smiled at each other, on an anonymous train platform, crowds bustling past.

'Hello' sounded so oddly polite, when she could see the rest of her life, quite suddenly.

'Hello,' he said. 'Hello.'

They walked the streets of London, not quite daring to go to her home, to where it would be real, or not.

It started to rain when they were near the zoo in Regent's Park. 'When I was younger, I used to go to the top of Primrose Hill when there was a thunderstorm,' said Casey. 'You could see lightning exploding over London.'

'Let's go up there now,' said Ed.

So they did, running through the rain, dodging the London plane trees, He had to pull her up the last bit, giggling, out of breath. Then they looked out across the rooftops of London, as the storm erupted overhead. The park smelled green.

'It's not very clever standing on the top of a hill in a thunder-storm,' said Ed.

'Never mind that.' Casey pointed towards Westminster. 'I think that's the *Post* building.'

He kissed her then, just for a moment, and she kissed him back, knowing happiness.

But suddenly, from nowhere, he was pulling away. 'I can't. I'm sorry, Casey. I'm so sorry.'

He looked at her again, just for a second, and then turned and ran away, away down the hill, slipping and sliding in the mud.

There had been references when they were on the ship, just oblique ones. Iraq. Afghanistan. The Marines, in at the worst. Again and again. The blood and the terror. The agony and the silence. There had been too many tours, too close together. Six months away, too many times. No time to remember how to laugh.

'We were in this field of maize,' he started once. They were drinking tea in the officers' mess, whiling away time. 'And I suddenly realised there were too many of them. Taliban. And I had to cover the others, my men, so they could get out. I had to stay behind. In this endless field of maize. And I just thought, "I'm going to die. I am going to die now." It felt so simple suddenly. I don't know ... I still don't know how I got out ...'

His voice had trailed off.

'Go on,' said Casey gently.

'No.' He got up and walked away, leaving his tea steaming on the side.

She had looked up his battles, when she got home. Working out where his troops had been, and when, during those unwinnable wars. Calculating the deaths and the amputations and the pain, as if careful research, proper notes, could make sense of it all.

After he had run away, there were desperate telephone calls.

'We can make this better.'

'No, Casey. I can't ... I can't do this to you ... I can't make this your life too.'

'Ed. Please. *Please*.'

She'd never chased anyone, Casey. Always been the one to run away. But she had tried then.

He had left the Marines, at least. Gone into private security.

She got him working with one of the television crews, who needed someone to keep their cameras and presenters out of trouble.

'He's so smart,' one of the presenters had chirruped to Casey afterwards. 'He just gets things, straight away. And, man, we got in some tight spots out there.'

That was how Miranda got to know Ed too, after bumping into him on a jaunt to some explosion in Palestine. They had stayed friends, Casey knew. But Casey didn't ask about him. She could never ask about him.

Miranda walked into the office. She was eating a sandwich, and chucked a brownie at Casey.

'Got you that.' It was their standard peace offering. 'Dash doesn't think we're there yet. We need something more.'

'I can't work with Ed.'

'He's clever,' said Miranda. 'He thinks fast. And he might be able to keep you alive.'

'No,' said Casey. 'Not Ed. I can't. And you're letting Dash pretend we can do this without being involved ... And you know we can't.'

'If you want to do this, and I know you do, it's going to have to be Ed. I think Dash will let you go out there with him, and I can't think of anyone else.'

Casey got up abruptly.

Miranda was talking about something. Casey moved clumsily; swayed out of their office, headed for the door. Unable to see where she was going, sudden tears, she bumped into John – John, the office bully, who couldn't look a woman under the age of forty straight in the eye.

'Careful, Casey.' John looked at her more closely and sighed. 'Oh dear, girlie problems?'

'Fuck off, you twat.'

And Miranda, watching her stumble off, knew she would never be able to stay away.

16

Casey was running round the park. Round and round. And every time she thought she might stop, she found she couldn't.

She didn't fall in love easily, Casey. It was easier, always easier, to run away. And not many men could keep up.

Round and round and round.

Hyde Park was at its most green, almost unbearably lush. The grass had both the promise of spring and the beauty of summer. There were ducklings on the Serpentine, with anxious parents.

Round and round and round and round.

It was her phone, finally, that broke the spell.

'Casey?' The voice was unsure, uncertain.

'Lady Newbury?' Casey found that she could hardly breathe.

'I've come up to London,' said Lady Newbury. 'I've got to visit the flat. I suddenly decided I had to, someday, so I might as well get on with it. I thought that you might be interested to come along.'

'I am,' said Casey, without having to think.

'I'm going there now.'

'I'll meet you there. Pimlico, wasn't it? I'll be twenty minutes.'

Lady Newbury told her the address and Casey started to run. The pain began again. She ran faster.

*

Charlwood Street was a pretty road on the Pimlico grid. Lady Newbury was standing outside one of the white stucco houses, looking up at the top-floor flat. There was a gap in the railings, like a missing tooth. For a second, Casey wondered how Lady Newbury could bear it.

'This was where I lived before I was married,' Lady Newbury said, almost speaking to herself. 'I was happy here.'

'Sorry about ...' Casey gestured at her running clothes.

'You must think it odd that I asked you here,' Lady Newbury carried on. 'I suppose I could have asked one of my friends, instead.'

But she couldn't stand it, Casey understood. She wanted someone who would witness, but not grieve; commemorate without reminiscing.

A friend, bringing flowers and sympathy, shortbread and normality, that would be unbearable.

'I do know,' said Casey. 'It isn't unusual.'

The hallway had a colourless carpet and knocked-about paint. Lady Newbury climbed the stairs slowly, as if to Bluebeard's chamber. On each floor, the ceiling was lower. Just under the roof, the flat was airless, stifling. There were two bedrooms and a kitchen knocked into the sitting room. The eaves nibbled away at the headspace.

The police had searched the sitting room and put every-thing back, slightly skewed. The table wasn't where it normally sat, according to the bumps in the carpet. The paintings were slightly off kilter.

'I've meant to do it up for years,' said Lady Newbury. 'But he had parties for his friends, you know. I thought I would do it one day.'

Just as at the house in Chagford, the art was of a magical quality. Casey didn't know much about paintings, but even she could see the incandescence in the still life above the fireplace.

Silver photograph frames dotted the flat. On bookshelves, on a chest of drawers, on the windowsill. The Newburys framed everything in silver.

'I don't know why I came. I suppose it was more so that I had been,' said Lady Newbury. 'So that it wasn't ahead of me any more. I can't imagine that there is any chance that we would find anything the police had missed.'

She sat down on a grey chenille sofa, as if exhausted.

'I suppose you're right,' said Casey.

'It's terribly stuffy,' said Lady Newbury. 'Could you open the ...'

They both looked at the window. Casey moved towards it, hesitated for a moment and then pushed it open.

She saw what Arthur had meant. Milo could not have fallen by mistake. The window was too high up the wall, with a sort of parapet beyond. He must have climbed out and then slipped, or jumped. There were no scratches on the paint, Casey saw, no scuffs. Milo couldn't have been forced out. Not a murder, then.

Casey glanced back at Lady Newbury. She was staring hopelessly at the wall, just next to the front door.

A painting was missing there, Casey saw. The brass picture hook empty, a square of wallpaper unfaded.

'Conrad said it was missing.' Lady Newbury looked destroyed. 'He warned me, at least.'

Conrad, Milo's father, Casey remembered. The art dealer.

'Was it nice?' asked Casey.

Lady Newbury almost smiled. 'It was a Renoir drawing. Stunning,' she said. 'The insurers are kicking up a fuss because they say we don't know when it went missing. And we don't, really. I suppose Milo could have sold it at any time, for whatever reason.'

'But it could have been stolen, too,' Casey thought out loud, 'at any time.'

Casey moved into the bedroom. It didn't look as if the police had searched in here. There wasn't the sense of slight shift. Lady Newbury's influence was clear in here. Heavy chintz curtains fell to the ground, and the furniture was mahogany. There was a striped armchair in one corner, with a matching footstool. The footstool crouched like a faithful dog. Casey opened a cupboard door. Dozens of beautiful shirts; ties in neat rows; dark Italian suits.

'Do you mind if I look around?' she shouted through.

There was a pause.

'Please do,' the words echoed back.

On a dressing table were silver-backed hairbrushes, and another of the silver photograph frames. This one held several smaller photographs.

At the bottom of the cupboard, among a confusion of shoes, there was a folded *gandoura*, the long white tunic worn in north-east Africa. Casey picked at the yellow embroidery for a second. Flecks of sand still stuck to a pair of walking boots.

As she jerked out the tunic, one of the silver frames clinked to the floor. Casey picked it up. It was a large one, several photographs trapped under the glass. She peered at it. Artistic pictures of a desert. An oasis and some dunes and a long line of camels, silhouetted against the sky. A glass of champagne, close-up, and what looked like a private jet blurred behind. A black jeep. In one of the photographs, Milo was squinting into the sun, smiling. He was sunburned. Behind him, golden sand billowed in the relentless waves of the desert.

Sometimes, Casey thought, you just knew.

She photographed the photograph, holding her phone carefully, so the glass didn't flare light.

Then she carried the silver frame into the sitting room.

'Have you seen this photograph before?' she asked.

'Oh …' Lady Newbury's face crumpled. 'Oh, doesn't he look lovely?'

Casey realised that she had barely glanced at Milo. He did look happy in the photograph, she thought. A shadow lay across the sand in front of him; the man taking the photograph.

'When do you think that photograph was taken?' asked Casey. 'Could you tell from Milo's haircut, or anything?'

Lady Newbury concentrated on the photograph, for a moment, stroking her son's face with her finger.

'It must have been taken since last summer,' she said at last. 'I gave him … I gave him that shirt for his birthday … Last August …'

A tear splashed on to the frame.

'I am so terribly sorry,' said Casey, because she was. She always was.

'He looks so happy, doesn't he?'

'He does,' said Casey. 'He does.'

'It must have been such a lovely holiday.'

17

Casey was in a better mood as she headed back to the office. She bumped into Ross as she walked through the entrance. He was clutching a Pret A Manger bag, and humming the *Dambusters* theme tune.

'You really should try and eat lunch before 3 p.m. one day,' said Casey wisely.

'You really should try and get the paper off stone on time with only these jokers to hand,' said Ross. 'Lunch is the least of my fucking problems.'

Off stone, the moment a paper was approved for printing. The whole day centred on that second.

Casey and Ross walked up the escalator into the newsroom. No one ever stood on the escalator. The door to one of the tiny offices off the main newsroom was closed, with a chair wedged under the handle. Ross looked with interest through the door's glass panels.

'Why's the home affairs editor locked in a cupboard?' he asked the room.

'He tried to punch the Whitehall correspondent,' said the deputy news editor, not looking up.

'Jesus,' said Ross, looking at the portly Whitehall correspondent, who was lolling against the news desk. 'How the fuck did he miss?'

The deputy news editor shrugged; he was concentrating on the list.

'What was the fight over?' Casey asked.

'He called him a byline bandit,' the deputy news editor gesticulated vaguely.

'He *is* a byline bandit,' said Casey.

Ross looked through the glass panels again. The home affairs editor had his feet up on the desk and was eating an apple. He flicked a V-sign at Ross.

Two signs were stuck to the glass panels. One said 'I'm watching porn' and the other said 'The phone's connected to a sex chatline, in Australia'.

Australia was underlined three times.

'Thing is,' said Ross, reading the list over the deputy news editor's shoulder, 'we do really need that page lead on home-grown terrorism and he probably won't do it until we let him out.'

'Drop home-grown terror down page,' said the deputy news editor helpfully. 'Then you can leave him in there another half-hour. He can do a down page in twenty minutes.'

'Fine,' said Ross.

Casey sighed. Still in her running kit, she really needed to go down to the slightly unsavoury showers in the *Post*'s basement.

'Come have a look, Casey.' Laura, one of the senior opinion writers, was drooling over a photograph of a white sand beach. 'Doesn't it look heavenly?'

Laura wrote clever articles about women enjoying sex, and therefore got 400 rape threats a day. Casey liked her. She wandered over, admired the picture.

Under the beach, in swirling blue writing, was the promise: All you could ever want.

'Glorious,' said Casey. 'You doing it for travel?'

'Yup,' Laura winked.

Journalists get a lot of free holidays, which is why the travel section tends to have a rather more flattering tone compared with the rest of the paper. Complementary has a homophone.

'I'm going cycling along the Danube this summer,' interjected the slightly pompous chief opinion writer. 'Stopping in Salzburg for *Der Rosenkavalier*.'

'To each their own,' grinned Casey.

'I can't make up my mind,' Laura went on. She clicked on a photograph of Machu Picchu. 'There are so many things I want to do, so many things I want to see.'

'We are so lucky,' the chief opinion writer carried on, 'to live at a time when it's so easy to visit almost anywhere.'

'I've always wished that I had spent more time in Syria straight after university,' said Alice, one desk along, who wrote opinion pieces about the Middle East and therefore got even more abuse than Laura. 'Because you wonder if you will go again, during our lifetimes. And that makes you think about worlds that are getting bigger and smaller, all at the same time ...'

Casey sensed a lengthy dissertation coming on. It was easy to get bogged down by the comment desk. She turned towards the investigations office.

'Miranda, I've been thinking ...'

She stopped, abruptly, all words forgotten. Ed was leaning against the wall.

'Hello, Casey.'

She couldn't breathe. He was walking towards her, as if that were a normal thing to do. He held out his hand, and it felt impossible.

'Miranda's been filling me in,' said Ed. 'It sounds …'

But Casey was whirling around, electric speed, and racing across the office.

She bolted down the escalators, and was out in the street. Running again, and now every step was an agony. Ed had followed her for the first few paces. He could have caught her easily, but even in a newsroom that looked odd. So he hesitated, and stopped. She could hear him, just for a second, calling her name.

How could Miranda have brought him in? Just like that. How could she? Was the story the only thing that ever mattered to Miranda?

Casey reached the park.

Round and round and round.

The sun was dropping now; the magical sloping light of an English evening.

Round and round and round.

Her phone went. Miranda. It went again. And again.

'Don't make me triangulate your phone,' the text bleeped in. 'Because I can and I will.'

It rang once more, and Casey was just about to clear it when she saw the name. Adam Jefferson. The terrified boy in Geneva.

'Adam?' Casey staggered to a halt. The world reeled.

'Casey. Hello.'

'How are you, Adam?'

'I'm good, I'm good … The thing is,' he went on. 'I thought you would want to know. This woman called Jessica Miller turned up. I think that was her name, anyway.'

Even through her exhaustion, Casey felt the name fizz down her spine.

Jessica Miller had taken over Miranda's job at the *Argus*, stepping up to run their investigations team. She was their main rival.

'What did you tell her, Adam?' Casey just managed to keep the urgency out of her voice.

'Nothing,' he said. 'You told me not to say anything about this to anyone. And I haven't. I promise I haven't. Not a word.'

'So what did she say, exactly?'

'I don't remember quite,' he said. 'She did ask if Milo had ever said anything about a trip to Africa. And asked if I had heard how he died. I just shrugged.'

'Well done, Adam.' Casey wondered if he had been at all convincing.

'Then I pretended to freak out about talking to a journalist,' Adam went on. 'Said that my boss hated the press, and would go mad if I spoke to her any more, and got away. I wasn't surprised this time, like I was by you, and that helped. She left me her cell number, just in case, she said.'

'OK. Good.'

So often, Casey felt like a counsellor; so often out of her depth. In the face of human misery and terror, rage and despair. But she listened. She listened. It was all she could do. After Adam had fled Azarola's office, back in Geneva, they'd all sat together on the long tan sofas. Azarola had looked at the vase of lilies on the table as if he had never seen them before.

'Thank you,' Miranda had said. 'I don't think he would have spoken if you hadn't scared the shit out him.'

'My grandmother went to Argentina from Europe.' Azarola had stared straight ahead. 'She lived in Austria before the war.

She was Jewish. Her mother escaped, with two daughters. Over the border, somehow. They never said how. They could never even speak about it. But her father went to a camp. Disappeared. They never knew what happened to him.'

He'd got up and walked across to the window. Looked out, over the lake, to the mountains of Switzerland.

'My grandmother was a refugee,' said Azarola.

Now, as Adam carried on, Casey watched the park darken around her.

When the telephone call was over, she hurried towards the office. It was a race, now. A race to a death.

Casey rushed back up the escalators. Ed and Miranda were still in the office, as she had known they would be.

'OK.' She walked into the investigations room. 'OK.'

Miranda slipped out of the room, muttering about a cup of tea.

'I'm sorry,' said Ed awkwardly. 'I thought Miranda had discussed it with you. I should have guessed she would just — '

'It doesn't matter.' Casey was aware, suddenly, of her running clothes and flushed face. She dropped into the scruffy armchair in the corner of the room.

'We've been discussing the options,' said Ed.

Miranda reappeared, juggling three cups of tea with burned fingers.

'The Algerian stamp in Milo's passport is smudged,' Miranda began. There was no hint of apology. For a moment, Casey tried to remember if Miranda had ever apologised. 'So we can see when he crossed into Libya, but you can't see the date he landed in Algeria, or which airport. It's a bit of a bugger.'

She caught a glimpse of Casey's stony face.

'I said I'd talk to the lawyers about last week's minor fuck-up,' said Miranda quickly. 'Back in a bit.'

Clutching her tea, she vanished from the office. Silence descended.

Moving to her desk, Casey saw that the map was centred on southern Algeria. To the south, she could see its straight-line border with Niger.

A straight line on a map in Africa means the border was drawn with a ruler thousands of miles away. And just like among the peach orchards of the Bekaa, the local population is often indifferent to that line. The straighter the line on the map, the more blurred it is on the ground. And when you don't care about ruler-drawn borders, smuggling is just transport. Where once it was long caravans of camels and gold, now it is pickups and drugs and weapons.

And people, of course. Still a commodity, to be shifted thousands of miles, through the endless desert dust.

'Let's look at the airfields down there,' said Casey. 'There should be quite a few. Some of them are still the Second World War ones. They built them all across north Africa.'

She pulled up a list. Tindouf. Béchar. Touggourt. In Salah.

'They're most likely to have flown into southern Algeria.' Casey concentrated. 'And then they'd have driven to the crossing towards Ghat, just inside Libya.'

She stared at the map. 'We could start with Illizi.' Casey included Ed grudgingly. 'It's one of the bigger towns in the south, over the border from Libya.'

She fidgeted for a moment longer, aware of Ed watching her, then found a description of Illizi. 'There's a big national park nearby. The Tassili n'Ajjer ...' She stumbled over the words. 'So that tourists wouldn't look quite so odd, travelling through there. They'd look a bit weird, but it's not impossible.'

'But how do we know it's Illizi?' he asked. 'And even if that is where they are flying, what do we do?'

'Let me think,' she said, impatient with herself.

Casey was used to taking this scrap of information here, and swirling it into that little detail there. A clue here, the key to that lock there. A loose thread here, changing the whole tapestry.

Planes, she remembered, can be hunted, just like everything else.

It was the CIA, oddly, who learned that the hard way. Back when morality was being redrawn, in the aftermath of 9/11, America began shifting suspects around the world. Men with bags over their heads were transferred through a Gordian knot of jurisdictions, ending up in countries where torture was a starting point. Extraordinary rendition, they called it. Ghost flights transited around the world, stopping off at black sites, specks on the map where the prisons have no names and the prisoners have no future.

But, despite all that secrecy, the planes, with their big clear tail numbers, could not be hidden. Plane spotters and databases and civil aviation authorities – almost accidentally – provided the pieces of the jigsaw puzzle.

There was N379P, a Gulfstream V, which flew from Indonesia to Egypt, from Jordan to Afghanistan.

And N313P, a Boeing 737, which went from Thailand to Diego Garcia, from Poland to Guantánamo.

Or N85VM, a Gulfstream IV, flying from Morocco to Romania, from Dubai to Afghanistan.

And piece by piece, journalists fitted the jigsaw together.

Now Casey tapped her keyboard.

'We can look up the Illizi flights,' she explained. 'On the days before and after Milo crossed into Libya. There won't be too many planes going in and out of somewhere like Illizi.'

The endless scrolling tail numbers came up.

'What are you looking for?' asked Ed.

'I don't know yet.' She waved him away, still cross. 'I'll know when I see it.'

She made a list of all the planes that had flown in and out of the airport, in the weeks before and after Milo's passport crossed to Tinkarine.

'Not there.' He crossed out the words. 'Not Illizi.'

Casey stared at the map again.

'Djanet,' she muttered. 'Just over the border from Ghat. The road goes straight through. And it's only a bit smaller than Illizi.'

'But what if he flew commercial?' asked Ed. 'What if . . .'

She barely heard him, deep in her treasure hunt. 'The pattern . . .' She was talking to herself. 'There has to be a pattern.'

'And what if he just didn't fly to Djanet either?'

That snapped her attention: 'We'll just keep looking.' Coldly polite. 'Airport after airport. We look for as long as it takes.'

The office quietened around them. She carried on research-ing Algeria, and its long, brutal border with Libya.

And then, quite suddenly, she stopped.

'There.' She pointed. 'X587J.'

He smiled at her, enjoying her confidence.

'How do you know?'

She swung the screen around, showing him the photo-graph. A marketing shot of a plane coasting through a cloud dreamscape, its tail number designed to be visible through clouds. The Bombardier Global. A private jet that can carry up to a dozen people in secretive white glamour.

'That Bombardier has been flying in and out of Djanet on a regular basis,' said Casey. 'Not too often, maybe once or twice a month. But enough. The rest of the time, it does ordinary charters, flying all over the world. But it always heads back to Djanet. That's the plane they're using. I just know it.'

The Bombardier Global can stay in the air for thirteen hours, Ed read out from beneath the photograph. It can fly almost anywhere.

'Where does it come and go from? On the flights to Djanet?' he asked.

'London, Paris, Los Angeles,' said Casey. 'It doesn't seem to matter. The pattern is that it flies someone in, say from Berlin, and then picks them up four or five days later to take them back to Germany. Then there's a slightly erratic number of days until the next round trip. There isn't an overlap, and I suppose there wouldn't be, for this sort of thing.'

'In that case, these people,' Ed diagnosed, 'probably don't actually want to meet out in Algeria.'

'Probably not an initiation ceremony then.' Casey rubbed her forehead. 'Miranda and I thought it might be.'

They smiled at each other, united briefly by success.

'Milo had a photograph of a champagne glass in his flat,' said Casey, taking out her phone. 'It looks like the interior of that Bombardier.'

Ed studied her photograph.

'It's the same seating layout.'

'The next question' – Casey focused back in – 'is who the hell does that plane belong to?'

Together, they trawled the Internet. But nothing came up. The plane had been built a few years earlier, then sold into anonymity. In the end, Casey leaned back in her chair, and stared at the ceiling.

'If I tell you about something, can you promise you won't say anything about it to anyone else?'

'I promise,' he said easily.

'I mean it. I should ask you sign an NDA, I suppose, at the very least,' she said. 'But it all takes time, and I am not sure how much time we have.'

Journalists throw around NDAs – non-disclosure agreements – like confetti. And ignore them when it suits.

'It's fine,' said Ed. 'You can trust me.'

And Casey knew, deep down, that she could.

So she told him about Wynford Mortimer, the huge dump of leaked accountancy files, that was the strictest secret, known to only a few people at the *Post*.

'We could put X587J into the Wynford Mortimer database,' said Casey, 'and just see what comes up. It might be nothing.'

She fired up the Wynford Mortimer files. Eleven million documents stored on a server. Held offshore, ironically enough, just in case.

Once she was in, the minutes ticked past.

An hour later, Miranda peered round the door of the room.

Casey was too excited to stay angry. 'I think I've worked out how Milo was flown down to Algeria.'

Bit by bit, she walked Miranda through her calculations. The assumptions are always the dangerous part. The lawyers snarled at any hint of 'I assumed'.

'So who owns the plane?' Miranda asked at the end.

'I found the sales contract,' said Casey. 'It was sent through to Wynford Mortimer to be signed off by the nominee directors. It's owned by a British Virgin Islands company, something called Mostgrave Limited.'

The BVI registration was almost completely meaningless, they knew. The small dot in the Caribbean was home to an endless series of letterbox companies, with no office or staff actually present. The nominee directors would sign a sales contract on behalf of the owners, with no more than the quickest of glances. It was quite normal to own the most expensive toys – the jets and the yachts – through offshore companies.

'And who owns Mostgrave?' Miranda asked.

'It's issued shares,' said Casey. 'Ten per cent of those are owned by a man called Joshua Charlton. Milo's Charlie, possibly. He apparently lives in a PO Box in Jersey. The others are owned by yet another BVI company, Marakata Green Limited.'

'Mostgrave. Mostgrave. Mass grave? And who are Marakata Green?'

'We don't know,' said Casey. 'They're not managed by Wynford Mortimer, so we haven't got that data.'

And even if they could get the shareholders of Marakata Green, the beneficial owners – the actual owners of the other 90 per cent of X587J – could be ten companies away, buried behind layers and layers of paperwork.

'Who is this Joshua Charlton character then?' Miranda tracked back.

'Could be almost anyone,' said Casey. 'No one obvious on Google. There are dozens of Joshua Charltons. Hundreds, even. I haven't got stuck into that Jersey PO Box yet, but I will. There might be something there.'

The cleaners were starting to clean around the *Post*'s offices. It was the usual sign they had stayed too late. The night editor, in a pool of light, was the only figure at the news desk. He was watching the wires, the endless stream of information that cascaded carelessly around the world, day and night.

'So what's the plan?' asked Ed. 'Roughly.'

'Quite simple so far,' said Miranda. 'We go in, we meet up with one of the parties going into Libya, somehow. Then you and Casey go to wherever they go. And find out what they do, and record the conversations, and ...'

She trailed off.

'And get the hell out of there,' Ed filled in.

Miranda's eyes met Casey's over his shoulder, in a split second of silence.

'Yes,' said Miranda. 'Then you get the hell out of there.'

'I got something else too.' Casey pulled out her phone and sent the photograph of Milo in the desert to Miranda's computer screen.

'I'm sure that this was taken during the trip to Libya last October,' she said. 'Milo's mother says she gave him that shirt last August. She's going to check receipts. If you look at all the photographs of Milo in his last six months, he was never that tanned again.'

All three of them examined the photograph. Even blown up on the screen, there were no clues from the rolling dunes behind Milo.

Casey sighed. 'Nothing. And what's worse is that I think that Jessica Miller is on the case.'

Miranda's head jerked up.

'Jessie?' said Miranda, eyes sharpening. 'Why? How could she possibly know?'

Casey explained about the call to Adam, trembling in Geneva.

'Fuck,' said Miranda. 'Fuck. Right, well, I am not being scooped by Jessie bloody Miller.'

'We're doing our best,' Ed laughed at her. 'And as long as they're stopped from doing this . . .'

He caught Miranda's eye, and went quiet.

'We've got to be first,' said Miranda. '*First*. Now, let's put together a proper plan. We've got to be ready to go.'

18

By the next morning, they had built a proposal for Dash. It had been plotted out, in their little room, for hours.

Dash listened to Casey and Miranda, eyes narrowed. He fiddled with his penknife, which he did when he was thinking.

'I still don't feel you have enough,' he said eventually. 'What do you have, really? A rumour overheard in a club. A plane going to and fro. Some company names you can't unpick. A couple of passport stamps. The girlfriend saying he'd changed, whatever the hell that means. A suicide that could still be a stumble. An aid worker who saw some injuries that came from a high-velocity bullet, in a country where you can't move without tripping over a gun. You've only got one real source. It all comes from Milo, and from beyond the grave, at that. It's sketchy.'

Double-source everything, he'd told Casey once. We only know snapshots. One perspective is half blind. You've got to double-source.

'Adam wasn't lying,' Casey began. 'Milo had souvenirs from that trip. Photographs. Clothes. He was there. And the fact that he's dead ...'

'He could have just been losing it towards the end,' said Dash. 'For any number of reasons. It could all be nonsense.'

'It could.' Miranda gave what might have been a toreador flourish. 'But we can see it all on the ground out in Africa. The camp is there, you know. Some fucking huge palace is there with the golden roofs, just as Milo described. Why would some hedge-fund grunt have made that up? Why would some art buff have a passport stamp for Libya?'

'But you're assuming—'

'It could all be coincidence,' said Casey. 'Sure. But we have to chase it.'

'There may have been some big art collection down there,' Dash theorised. 'Some dictator's magpie hoard. You know how they do it. Milo could have gone down there to value it, and things got out of hand one night. It could have been a one-off.'

'Well, why wouldn't he have told his father about the art collection?'

'Pride. Might have wanted to present it as a done deal. Or maybe he just needed a secret from his father.'

It was always like this. Archaeologists gazing at a buried emerald, a chip of pottery, the long-lost sparkle of some battered coin. And guessing what it might mean, all of it. They pieced it together from the fragments left behind. A sharpened flint could mean a cook or a doctor, a hunter or a game.

Or a murder.

They picked them up, those scraps and those shards, and built their own story. And sometimes, it could be wrong.

Dash stared over their heads for a long time.

'You could all be killed, you know,' he said. 'If you're right. Seriously.'

'We know that,' said Miranda.

'I'd probably deny sending you out there in the first place,' he said. 'Because by then you'd be history, and so what? You'd be a tragic news-in-brief. Even I know this is a bit close to the line.'

'Anecdotal stuff on something like this would never get past the lawyers,' said Miranda.

'Only seeing' – Casey's voice was quiet – 'is believing.'

'The Editor would say no, if I asked,' Dash admitted. 'He keeps talking about cost-cutting and search optimisation. He doesn't want this sort of thing. Not any more.'

'Well,' said Casey cheerfully, 'you could always point out that if we disappear, there's a cost saving right there.'

'Be serious,' said Dash. 'For once. It would have to be off the books, all this. I could never get it signed off, at the moment. The lawyers would faint. I'd have to magic the budgets around it.'

'Fine,' said Miranda, because they'd done it before. 'Need to know only. And almost nobody does.'

Dash walked to his window. Outside, June was Novembering, people dashing through the rain, and hiding in doorways.

'Has Toby found anything?' Dash asked. 'In his bag of inter-net tricks?'

'Nothing,' said Miranda. 'He can't if there isn't anything to find.'

There was a silence.

'You know what they call the bit at the very top of Everest?' asked Dash. 'The death zone. Your body starts shutting down, as soon as you get up there, because there's so little air. You've got to summit and get down before it kills you, just being up there. And if something goes wrong, there's not a lot anyone can do, even if they wanted to. Everyone is already operating at their limit. You can't fly a helicopter up there; the air is too thin for that. It'll be the same for you out there in Libya. The British army won't come in after you. They won't risk a dozen soldiers when you've chosen this madness, all by yourself. I don't know anyone insane enough to send in after you. You would be on your own.'

'Jessie Miller's on the case,' said Miranda. 'We can't let her beat us to this.'

'No,' agreed Dash, flint in his voice.

'Let's ask Ross,' said Casey abruptly.

'You only want to ask Ross because he'll say yes to anything.' Dash eyed her.

'Probably,' Casey shrugged. 'But because he says yes to anything, if he actually says no, then we know it's too far.'

Dash called Ross into the room, and told him in a few words.

Ross nodded, professionally inscrutable, then grinned.

'I wondered what you idiots were up to.'

Ross snapped his fingers for a few seconds, thinking for a minute. Then shouted out into the office: 'Robert.'

The chief reporter glanced up from his screen, walked over.

Rob was the heart of the newsroom when the huge stories broke. When terrorism exploded, or a Royal was born, or a prime minister fell, he was at the centre of it all. Safe pair of hands, Ross would say approvingly: high praise indeed.

'Bianca Angelo,' said Ross. 'That girl who came in last sum mer.'

'She was a tricky one,' Rob remembered slowly. 'You were on holiday, Dash, or I'd have come to you.'

'Sure,' Dash nodded.

'She was a ring-in.' Rob meant the dozens of calls that came into the news desk every day, each one panned for gold. 'We chatted. Gorgeous girl. She met me at the Costa round the corner.'

Bizarre, the conversations they'd all had in that Costa, thought Casey. Life, death and brown envelopes sliding over the table, under the venti-latte babble.

'She was very nervous,' said Rob. 'They're always nervous, but you know … It stood out. She was an air hostess, working on a private jet. She said she was scared, properly scared. That they were doing something on trips to Algeria. Something terrible.'

He was mimicking her voice unconsciously as he thought back, a light London accent.

'Did she say what they were doing?'

'She said she'd heard one of them on the plane. An Australian, talking about a manhunt. Killing someone, out in the desert. For fun. He was laughing about it.'

Rob frowned, trying to remember.

'Anything else?' Casey asked.

'She was going to tell me more,' said Rob. 'The next time. And then she disappeared.'

'We chased her up,' said Ross. 'Couldn't find a Bianca Angelo anywhere. Rob said she was wearing a brunette wig, and a ton of make-up when she came in. Could have been a fake name, and a burner phone too. Fuck knows.'

'It was the level of fear,' said Rob. 'Memorable, really.'

'Did she say what plane it was?' Casey asked.

'No. Just that it was one of the very top-end jets. She poured the drinks and handed out the nuts.'

There's always someone doing the photocopying, thought Casey.

'Was she Italian?' she asked aloud. 'That name.'

'I asked her about it, for something to chat about. She said no. Always loved Italy, though. Rome, Florence, all that.'

'She ask for money?' Miranda's clipped tones.

'No,' Rob shrugged. 'She wanted protection.'

'But you couldn't stand it up.' Dash's voice wasn't accusatory.

'There was very little to go on,' Rob said. 'And it was so unlikely, to be honest. Maybe I could have done more, but it was right before the Pearce inquiry, and that had me tied me up for weeks. Why?' He rolled his eyes. 'Have I missed something?'

'Don't worry about it,' said Dash.

'I should have done more,' said Rob. But things slipped past, every day. And Rob caught more than most.

'It doesn't matter.'

Rob stood up, and walked back to tomorrow's story.

There was a long silence.

'It's real,' said Miranda. 'It has to be.'

'Fucking brilliant story,' said Ross.

'We've got to get out there,' said Casey. 'You know that.'

Dash stared into the distance for a long time. 'I suppose you do.'

'We'll need a point person in the office,' said Miranda, as if she had always expected him to agree. 'We're going to need someone to do the backup stuff from here, and they need to be fucking good. And they'll need to keep their mouth shut.'

'Who's free at the moment?' Dash turned to Ross.

The two men surveyed the newsroom.

'Julie?' Dash suggested.

'Christ, no,' said Ross. 'Totally useless. We only keep her because no one else can get the photocopier to do anything.'

'They need to be in the office for basically the next two weeks straight, and they need to be fucking good. And if they leak a single word, I'll sack them on the spot.'

'Hessa,' said Ross. 'Although she's flat-out already.'

'I like her,' said Miranda. 'She's sharp.'

Casey was fiddling with Dash's penknife, thinking ahead.

'Send her in,' said Dash, and then to Casey, 'Keep that, for luck.'

Hessa, a tiny girl with a pink scarf around her neck, was at the door in seconds. Clever eyes peered at them.

'Hessa,' said Miranda. 'I'm going to take you through a few things ...'

19

Ed and Casey flew first to Algiers. The Algerian police and their spies were notorious, even in northern Africa. Undercover, the usual cry of 'sahafi, sahafi' – journalist, journalist – wouldn't be a pass. They would be lucky, the local stringer warned, to escape the attention of the police on their trek south. Hemmed in by chaos – with Libya to the east, Mali to the south – the Algerian police crunched down on anything suspicious.

So Ed and Casey flew first to Algiers, and then the short stretch down to the oven heat of Illizi. The last hop south was in a small propeller plane that turned Ed green. A stoned taxi driver took them into the town of Illizi.

All around the road from the airport, the desert spread out, still and flat, and impossibly vast, baking under a relentless sun. Here and there, huge rock formations stabbed the sky. Battered signposts in Arabic pointed away down vanishing dirt tracks.

'It would be easy to disappear out here,' said Casey. 'Too easy.'

'Like the *Lady Be Good*,' said Ed. At her blank look, he went on, 'An American bomber that crashed over in Libya, right in the middle of the Second World War. They were flying back from a raid on Italy, and they got lost in the night, and thought that the desert was sea. Nine of them on board, parachutes floating down into the desert. And then they tried to walk out, but none of them made it. Not one. One of them got hundreds of miles, before dying, out there, all on his own. There are bits of the Sahara where no one returns.'

Casey looked out over the desert, thinking of those lives snapped like threads, and shuddered. The taxi driver muttered something in Arabic.

Ed went back to his book. They had decided he should be hunting cave paintings, as part of his cover. There are many caves, down there, on the edge of the desert. And deep into their darkness, man had crept, so carefully. I am here, I am here.

As they drove, Casey tried to push away Bianca Angelo. Bianca Angelo, the girl who loved Florence and Siena and Rome. Bianca. Bianca ... White? It was a guess, at first. And Casey had called the recruitment agencies, one by one.

Ringing from HMRC: naughty, but people always rushed to help.

We've got a glitch in our systems. A girl working as an air hostess, on private jets, I think. The surname's White? One of her first names is Angela or Angelina or something like that. It's hard to make out. Appreciate your help. Just for our records, you know.

And eventually heard the silence. Do you mean Natalie? Natalie Angela White? But Nat, she ... The growing suspicion. Why do you need to know, who are you, what do you want? She'd put the phone down then.

It hadn't taken long, after that. Pretty little air hostess, face smashed to pulp. Found two days after she'd met Rob in that

Costa, Casey worked out bleakly. At the bottom of a watery ditch, in a featureless patch of countryside. A hopeless appeal for information, the parents crying under a photograph of big blue eyes and rosebud lips. Blonde, it turned out, under the wig. A detective admitting he was shocked by the level of violence, and glancing down at his hands for a second. Dental records, they'd needed, to be sure.

No leads, the police admitted, a week later. Not a single one. Justice for Natalie was forgotten in a month.

Casey hadn't told the others about Bianca Angelo.

Not even Ed.

They had decided to fly to Illizi, the last town to the north of the national park. Rather than straight to Djanet, where they could stumble across the rattlesnake at any time.

They would need a few days to acclimatise, very slightly, to this wild north African world.

And X587J had been to Djanet just a few days ago, to fly someone back to Milan. If it followed its normal pattern, it wouldn't be back for several days. Right now, the Bombardier was sitting on the tarmac in Hong Kong and Hessa was monitoring it, hour by hour.

They had agreed to bump into Miranda somewhere in Illizi. Meet by coincidence, and gang up as Westerners do. The town was small and dusty, and the locals looked at them in bewilderment. But they collided with Miranda, so casually, in a café. Chatted over a guidebook, pointed out the recommendations and smiled.

Miranda had tied her blonde hair up under the long scarf that turns women into ghosts. Casey, too, disappeared into a long, baggy dress, covering everything from neck to ankle. But still they stood out.

Ed supervised the purchase of two of the battered Toyota Hiluxes, the pickups that rove all over Africa. Cheap, endlessly reliable and easy to fix when they finally conk out, the Hilux shifts everyone from farmer to warlord. Plus they are Japanese, and therefore slightly less hated than the American equivalent.

They went on a test drive, shifting through the gears, and slamming on the brakes. Casey thought about the last time she had been in a Hilux, her body armour pushed against the door because it might stop a bullet. She never wore it, if she could avoid it. It's heavier than people realise, body armour, and it was never designed for women.

They hadn't brought it anyway, this time.

A couple of days later, they were ready to drive south, in convoy. Algeria is huge. Ten times the size of France, which colonised this patch of Africa, bloodily, in the nineteenth century. The journey took hours, jolting over rough patches and sweating in the sun.

They saw just two cars in a hundred miles.

They stopped for lunch, near some of the strangest rock formations, a petrified madness of orange on orange, spiking into the blue.

'Where did you two meet?' Miranda asked abruptly. She was tucking away the last of the *kesra*, the Algerian flatbread she liked so much.

'You know where.' Casey batted away the fat flies that survived somehow. 'When I was on board the *Apollo*.'

'No,' said Miranda. 'Where are you going to *tell* them you met?'

Ed got it, 'We have to have the same story.'

It worked best when almost everything was true, and Casey knew all the details of Miranda's life. They only ever changed the minimum.

'My mother died in a car accident' was true for both Casey and 'Carrie'. Both Miranda and 'Anna' were married to Toms. Both Toms never did the washing-up and always forgot anniversaries. It was so easy to share the joke of a forgotten birthday. Wedding rings went on and off, depending on the situation. Casey's wasn't real, but it was gold. Bought in a junk shop, sometimes she wondered who had worn it before.

When Casey left a meeting, she would note down the lies and read them again before the next meeting. The truth usually stayed the truth.

Like any actor, she watched people. Actors study reactions to secrets and shocks, and joy and despair. And Casey did the same.

She had learned, quite precisely, how to change the mood. A scientist adding a chemical drop to change the colour blue to pink, pink to blue. She leveraged her likeability, she thought once. And she did it quite deliberately. A laugh here, a pause there. Sometimes even a half-wink. She could change the mood from giggles to seriousness in a blink. From bored impatience to delicious conspiracy without even thinking about it. Now, sometimes, she did it almost by accident.

They walked back down to the cars, parked in the shade where the empty road wrapped around a low red cliff.

'Favourite colour,' recited Miranda. 'Favourite food, favourite holiday, favourite song. And annoying habits, of course. You two have to learn your lines.'

'And where do we live?' wondered Ed. 'And what do we do?'

'Right.' Miranda winced at the oven waft of her car. 'And you'd better know it all, by the time we get to Djanet.'

'She's right, you know.' Casey climbed into the passenger seat. 'We will have to rehearse all those funny little things about each other. And we've never really spoken about anything like that.'

'Just about pirates, and kidnappers.'

Not in the letters, she thought. Not in the letters.

Ed drove down the road, trailing dust, and waiting for her to speak. She stole looks at him, sideways. He was always so calm, she thought, and watchful.

She'd watched him, once, as a fight flared on the *Apollo*. Cabin fever was real. Ed read his book, as the voices got louder and meaner. She knew he was listening, ready to step in with a ruthless speed, if needed. But the argument died away, and Ed turned a page, and they never even knew he was there.

Casey rolled down her window.

'It will be odd' – she straightened her back – 'if we don't know enough about each other. They help, those bits and pieces of truth.'

'I know,' said Ed.

'OK.' Casey looked at him. 'You first.'

Cigarette burns were dotted all over her seat, and she was tugging fretfully at the padding, picking it out, shred by shred.

'Why me?' he asked.

'Because I need to practise telling the truth.'

She heard him take a breath.

Normal, he called his childhood, because doesn't everyone think their childhood is normal?

A small village, somewhere in the Home Counties. An old vicarage. Pillars and iron gates, too nice for the vicar, nowadays. Rolling green fields all around, and conkers in autumn. Mum made cakes and fixed things, because it's a waste otherwise. A sensible village school, then the smart local. University, as expected.

'And why the Marines?'

'My father,' he gestured. 'And my older brother too. It was a big deal, to both of them. My father loved it all. He never really got over leaving the Navy. And my brother, he's still in it. Climbing the ladder. One of their stars.'

'Happy?'

'I think so. I don't know that he would tell me if he wasn't. I don't know how he would find the words.'

'And you liked the Marines?'

'I liked being part of something,' he said. 'Friendship is a building block there, to make it all possible. And it's a challenge, but designed so you can succeed. But the war ... Too many ... Not just the deaths, and the injuries ... It was more than that. No one came back the same ...'

He stopped.

'No,' she decided. 'The Marines are too easy to check. You can't risk someone knowing someone knowing someone. We'll have to come up with something else, for you. A different story.'

He looked sideways at her, almost amused, watching as her long dark hair whipped into knots. She usually scraped it back, tied it into an unforgiving bun. Pulled it away from a face of angles, taut across the cheekbones, with a few freckles in the sun.

Casey glanced across at him, and caught him looking at her now. And they smiled, in that moment of recognition.

'You lie to get to the truth,' he said.

'Sometimes I lie just to practise,' she said. 'And it's only real when it's on the front page.'

'OK,' he said. 'Tell me about you instead, for now.'

She began, fiddling with her safety belt.

'I grew up in London. All very normal, you know. It was just me, though. No brothers or sisters. And I always wanted a sister.'

She stopped, flicking over the stories she was leaving out. Casey only knew how to ask questions.

'It's easier to be mysterious, I find,' Miranda had laughed once. And it was, when lies were easier than truth.

The silence drifted on, and she wished she hadn't spoken. It seemed endless, this road. The horizon receding like a rainbow, in a sky that had forgotten to rain.

Casey stared out of the window, remembering the childhood she had almost discarded, beneath all those layers of lies.

She wondered, now, whether he watched over her. Looked out for her name, flaunted on the page.

Yes, that name.

And she met his grey eyes, every day, in the mirror.

She wondered if he ever felt pride.

Or fear.

Her existence, a threat. I can make your life a lie.

Or maybe he never even cared at all.

20

Ed reached over for the map, and she was back in the red desert, the sun burning the air.

'Not much further now,' he reassured. 'Friends. Who are your friends?'

Casey put on smiles like a dress in the morning, and sparkled for a thousand acquaintances. Few friends, though. None, really. She kept them all in the same orbit. Not too close. Never too close. Miranda was the only one who understood, in the end.

'I had a lot of friends at university,' she said, over the grumble of the Hilux.

And that was almost true. She'd learned to blend in at university, escaping her mother and the flat, and the memories. She had giggled and danced and cried with the best of them. And it was only more recently that the wise ones had stopped, and wondered, did we ever know you at all? Because you're so visible, as a journalist. Everyone knows your game. Or the version of it seen in the paper.

'It was a struggle to buy my flat,' she said. 'But I wanted somewhere that was just mine. And I was lucky.'

Thinking: I wasn't lucky. I worked and worked, so very hard. And it was after my mother died, and I couldn't bear her flat and her memories and her secrets.

'Boyfriend in London?'

'They,' she said, 'won't need to know about that.'

There were, of course, sometimes. But when there were so many versions of her, she never knew the one they loved. They fell for the glamour, and the danger, and the beauty, and the mask. I miss you, she would say. On the phone, because she could only say it a thousand miles and a war zone away.

I'll see you on Wednesday, won't I? She would hear the hope in his voice, and despise it, quite suddenly. And Wednesday would come, and she'd fly to Islamabad instead.

She'd tried to make it work, once, properly. He was in finance, a bank just off Green Park. Deals that didn't matter, one way or the other. Millions, a toy.

A kind man, who liked to hold her hand. A nice family, with a mother who balanced cushions on corners. And a gentle smile, so that she tried to care about the things he loved. The car. The house. The holidays.

Trapped, once, on an all-inclusive fortnight in Antigua. Country club and club sandwiches. Peering over the barbed wire at people laughing, down the road, outside. Pacing around the swimming pool.

Happy? he'd ask.

Oh yes. A lie.

He'd forgive, again and again.

'You don't understand.' One night, she was wailing, couldn't stop.

'I know I don't.' He was so patient. 'But I love you. I do love you. Believe me.'

And she turned away.

'You deserve to be loved,' he'd said once, side by side in the dark.

'I don't know how.' A whisper.

In the morning, she ignored those deliberate words as if they'd never existed. And let them drift into the quiet, as all words do.

Do you have to go? In the grey misty morning, late for a flight.

Yes. Meaning no.

Because no one made her go.

And didn't say: when you hold my hand, I feel like a fox in a snare. And when you get on top of me in the night, I howl in my mind.

She'd broken it, quite deliberately, in the end. Smashing it, like a favourite vase, and crying over the pieces. Cheating, because it was the only way to kill it, for ever. He was married now. Gone. A blonde, her opposite, in every way. The pastel version, in a terrace in Wandsworth, fully extended.

She pried into their lives, once, from an electronic distance. Invisibly invading. Two children, dull names. A boy and a girl.

That could have been me.

Could it?

No.

She watched them, pastel at parties, occasionally. Lives overlapping, ever so slightly. Housewife: she screamed the insult in her head. And wished it could be enough. Wondered, with spite: do you ever fuck, now?

If I had a hundred lives – she meant it kindly – I'd have spent one of them with you.

You're following a rainbow, he said. And no one ever reaches the end of the rainbow.

You're the one who wanted gold.

No, he said. I wanted you.

The car hit a bump, and skidded. Ed straightened it out.

'Parents?'

'No.'

She let the silence grow.

'We're not very good at this,' Ed said, after a while.

'I'm better,' she said carefully, 'at making friends when I fake it.'

And I can seduce anyone unless I care, she didn't say.

'I know,' he said.

Ed steered around a rusty oil drum lying in the middle of the road.

'Do you find it hard?' he asked. 'Being someone else?'

'It's easier,' she said, 'than being me.'

'Tell me about Miranda,' he said, letting her off. 'She can be the friend I talk about. We'll call her, I don't know ... Jasmine.'

'Miranda grew up somewhere in Hampshire,' and Casey could talk easily, at once. 'She had it all, you know, the pony and the tennis lessons, and the hair straighteners and the violin teacher.'

'Unlike you?' Ed suggested.

'But it wasn't enough for her, all that. She used to laugh and say that she'd been swapped at birth, but that isn't funny, when you think about it. She would leave her Fisher Price radio to record, after bedtime, to find out what her parents said when she'd gone to sleep.' Casey laughed, then hardened. 'I think there were endless loops of lies in her house. Her mother on pills, and her father sleeping with the secretary.'

Meeting Miranda had made her glad she hadn't shattered those lives, on that high street, one lazy Sunday.

'You're none of you easy, are you?'

'No,' said Casey honestly. 'We're searching for something, all the time. And we never know why.'

'Do you both think the same way, you and Miranda?'

'No,' said Casey, half smiling. 'We always say that she wants to know what people did, and I want to know why they did it. But we're outsiders, we have that much in common.'

'I don't think of you as an outsider.'

'That's all part of the act,' she said. 'Miranda called it a form of self-inflicted schizophrenia, once.'

Another silence. Casey remembered that she'd wished once that she could see the layers of a human being, like an archaeological dig. Here a good year, a happy year. That would be a kind lover, or a glossy summer. There, a dark layer. A death, maybe, of a friend. Scab-like. Black almost. Leaked down – or would it be up? – over several layers.

A buried emerald, a chip of pottery, the long-lost sparkle of some battered coin. And guessing, really, what it might mean, all of it.

Or if your skin could show what you'd been. A scar for every sorrow, and a burn for a broken heart.

Casey shook her head, and tried to think of secrets she could tell Ed. Secrets that would be enough.

'I love dancing,' she said, in the end. 'Sometimes, I go to a club all on my own, just to dance. My favourite colour is silver. My cleaner is called Tania, and she probably knows more about me than anyone else in the world, and she doesn't care, not even a bit. I'm a terrible cook. I tried to cook beef bourguignon once, and it was so disgusting that I had to give it to the neighbour's dog. I don't know my neighbours' name. I would love my own dog, too, but I never know when I will next be home.'

And then she ran out of throwaway facts to share.

'Let's say that I work in PR,' she almost snapped. 'Because I can lie about that all day long. We'll have to sit down and work out your job, because that will be complicated. And we might need different options. And we live in my flat, in east London, but neither of us thinks we'll last for ever. We met in a bar; love across a crowded room and all that. And we don't know when we're going home, because we're looking for something, and we'll never know what it is.'

'My favourite colour,' Ed tried, 'is blue.'

'I think,' she said, 'we'll have to make it up as we go along.'

21

Djanet was ugly and crowded, and surrounded by crumbling beige hills. As they drove into the town, the call to prayer was echoing through the streets.

The oasis, coffee brown, was fringed with dusty palm trees, a precarious toehold in the wilderness. They booked into a small hotel, set around a peaceful courtyard. It took ten minutes to see Djanet. They explored every street and then there was nothing more to do, other than wait.

In her early days, Casey enjoyed the hours outside houses. Houses famous for fifteen minutes, as she gossiped with her opposite number at the *Telegraph*. You learned the value of patience. Journalists learn to wait, and watch. They learn to wait on a doorstep. For hacks, doorstep is a verb.

Ross liked sending out his reporters to doorstep in the rain, because he had decided people were 20 per cent more likely to let the reporter in when they looked like a drowned rat. This ploy did not endear him to his newsroom. After the education correspondent went down with a nasty case of pneumonia, human resources killed the strategy. Even now, Ross was outraged.

*

In the quiet courtyard, Casey lay in a hammock slung between two scrubby trees. She spent hours staring at the map of Libya. The map looked very empty.

'*Hic sunt dracones*,' whispered Casey.

'What?' Miranda looked up from her book.

'Here be dragons,' said Casey. 'They wrote it on the edge of a globe, in olden times, when they'd reached the end of the known world.'

'Here be dragons,' Miranda repeated. 'Well, let's hope not.'

Casey compulsively checked her equipment again.

There were a few tourists in Djanet, at least, so the three of them blended in, just about. A couple of Germans were off to hike through the park. Some French archaeologists had flown down to immortalise the cave paintings, buried deep up in the hills. Mystical drawings of dancing men, swimming men, dying men.

Every tourist in Djanet was ignoring embassy guidance. There had been terrorist attacks in southern Algeria before, several of them. But the memories had faded just enough for a few determined explorers to make the trek.

At her desk in London, Hessa tracked the Bombardier as it cruised around the world. From Hong Kong it flew to Sydney, from Sydney to Jakarta, and then on to Singapore. A few hours later it appeared in Shanghai. Every time the jet left an airport, their nerves tightened, wondering where it would turn.

In Djanet, Casey lay sleepless on her bed, worrying about their plan. They needed luck, too much luck, and she didn't like relying on luck.

It was Miranda who snapped at them. Casey was avoiding Ed. Eating breakfast before he woke up, and escaping to her room after lunch with one of the strong, sweet Arabic coffees. Ed was polite and thoughtful, just as he had always been, carrying bags and holding doors. But he was distant, too, disappearing into a book as he sat down.

'I'm sorry, you two,' said Miranda, as they sat stiffly in the courtyard, under the shade of a soaring pink bougainvillea, 'but you're going to have to sort it out.'

They looked up, both instinctively wary.

'If you're going to pass as a couple, you can't be like this,' Miranda went on. 'I mean it. You won't get away with it.'

'We'll be fine when we have to be,' said Casey. She couldn't look at Ed and wondered if she was blushing.

'I'm sure you will be,' said Miranda. 'But we don't know yet what Ed is like in this sort of situation, and we're throwing him in at the deep end anyway.'

'I'll be fine,' Ed broke in.

'I don't know that you will be,' said Miranda. 'And if you fuck up, you're both dead. I mean it. I can't let you go in if you can't ask Casey to pass the salt.'

'It's not that bad,' Casey protested.

'It is,' Miranda said. 'Plus they're going to have to *want* to have you both around. You know how it is. You're going to have to be fun, and, quite frankly, right now the pair of you are making even me feel uncomfortable.'

'Maybe' – and Casey hated even to make it a possibility – 'maybe you should go in with Ed. And I'll stay behind.'

'You two know each other better,' said Miranda. 'Ed and I have no shared history. I would be flying blind. Plus I don't think that Tom would love the idea of me cavorting around with a gorgeous Marine.'

Ed ducked his head.

'You're just worrying because we're here, and waiting and waiting,' said Casey. 'We'll be fine once we get going.'

'I can't rely on that,' said Miranda. 'I was awake in the middle of the night thinking about sending someone with PTSD into this situation. It suddenly seems mad.'

Casey and Ed both went still. Post-traumatic stress disorder, the waking nightmares, the shattering mind. For a second, they all watched the bougainvillea petals spiralling in the wind.

'Fine,' said Ed. 'We will work at this.'

And even as he said it, with the echo of some marriage-counselling session, Casey felt the edges of her mouth lift.

'Better,' said Miranda. 'Right. I am going to go for a walk around sodding Djanet. You two find a way of making this work.'

She threw a scarf around her head, and swept out of the courtyard.

In one corner of the courtyard there was a wooden swing seat, padded with faded green cushions.

'Maybe,' Ed gestured, 'we should try sitting over there.'

They sat side by side, awkward as dolls.

'Maybe we should just try and talk,' suggested Casey.

'Great,' said Ed, too quickly.

A long silence followed. Someone further down the street was smoking a shisha, sweet apple smoke drifting in the breeze. Casey stared at the tiled walls of the courtyard, blue and white, corkscrewing curls and lacy stars. Her eyes followed the pattern all the way along the wall.

'Stop looking at the tiles,' said Ed.

'I can't help it,' said Casey. And then, all in a rush, 'How is it? The—'

'It's getting better,' interrupted Ed. 'I promise you I wouldn't be here if I couldn't handle it.'

'That's wonderful,' said Casey. 'Really wonderful.'

'They helped, as much as they could,' said Ed. 'I think it's just going to take time. You struggle with odd things, things you'd never expect.'

'But you're enjoying the work, with the news crews?'

'I am,' he told her. 'And I know you helped with getting that job, so thank you.'

'It was nothing.'

Casey was watching the tiles again, the pattern twisting in her mind.

'Is there someone …' Casey started and broke off. 'Sorry. I know I shouldn't ask. But I just need …'

'And you've never been great at unanswered questions.' Ed smiled at her. 'That much, I remember.'

'I'm just going to wonder until I know. I'm sorry.'

'It's OK.' He paused. 'There was someone for a bit. She was very sweet, very gentle.'

Casey felt jealousy burn through her.

'I moved on too,' she said.

'It didn't work,' Ed went on. 'I can't be that person to anyone right now. I don't know why … I just can't.'

'Well' – Casey made her voice brisk – 'I hope you work it out eventually.'

The silence lengthened. A skinny black cat, with hungry eyes and patchy fur, prowled across the courtyard.

'I'll look like that cat if I live here too long,' said Ed. 'That lunch was abysmal.'

It wasn't much of a joke, but Casey smiled. They sat, side by side, watching the cat stalk a pink petal across the courtyard.

Ed put his arm around her. Casey jumped up, knocking her book to the ground.

'You can't do that,' said Ed. 'You can't flinch when I touch you.'

'I know.' Casey clapped her hands over her eyes. 'I know. Sorry.'

They stared at each other, under the swirl of flowers.

'I'm going to have to touch you,' said Ed. 'I'm going to have to touch you and hug you and kiss you. That's just how it is.'

'I know,' Casey said. 'I know it's acting, OK? Love's young dream, and all that. And it's just for a few days.'

'Acting,' said Ed. 'It's just acting. You do this all the time.'

'Not this, exactly, but something like it.' Casey clenched her fists, nails deep into her palms. 'Kiss me now, Ed. We've got to just get it out of the way.'

For a second, they both laughed.

'I know it's ridiculous,' said Ed. He stepped towards her, moving slowly. Very carefully, he put his arms around her, brushing her hair back from her face.

He kissed her then, in the shady courtyard, watched by the disapproving cat. Gently at first, then harder, drawing her body to his, pulling her in.

And Casey kissed him back, her hands winding around his neck, closing her eyes until he was everything and there was nothing else.

From the entrance came the sound of clapping.

'That,' said Miranda, 'looks a lot more like it.'

22

They waited for days, with that odd combination of nerves and boredom. Casey and Ed practised meeting eyes and holding hands, curling up on the old swing seat in the evening light. She got used to his body against her, rock-solid and oddly gentle.

Occasionally, Casey wondered if her heart would break.

It wasn't real, any of it. Sometimes she watched as his eyes went blank, and he disappeared to somewhere else, a million miles away.

'Come back, Ed' – she would tap his elbow – 'Stay with me.'

And he would remember to smile and joke, stroking her face with a perfectly careless familiarity.

They read endless books and tried to sleep at night. Miranda, incapable of inaction, always tried to learn more Arabic on journeys, chanting school phrases at the elderly woman who ran the hotel.

'Am I making any sense, Ed?'

'Frankly, no.'

Ed tried to jog in the blazing heat, and returned brick-red and exhausted.

And then Miranda's phone bleeped.

'It's Hessa,' she said. 'The Bombardier has just landed at Tiska.'

They all went silent. Tiska was the scruffy little airport twenty miles south of Djanet.

'Where has it arrived from?' asked Casey.

'London,' said Miranda. 'It flew out of Northolt this morning.'

There was that pause, the quiet before the storm.

'OK.' Ed was the first to break the spell. 'We're ready. Let's go.'

They got lucky, at first.

Leaving the Bombardier gleaming on the runway, the shiny black pickup whisked out of Tiska and north towards Djanet. Not east, out along the scorched road that led directly to Libya. Just in case, Ed and Casey were waiting on the eastern road to Libya, stranded by a carefully disabled Hilux, and hoping that their plight, as a couple of pretty Western tourists, would be enough to convince the speeding car to stop.

'I'm just not convinced it will work,' Casey had said nervously. 'From all we know about these people, compassion may not be their thing. They'll go straight past us.'

'We just have to hope,' said Miranda. 'Shortest skirt and sweetest wave. But I do think they will go straight up to Djanet for a night, at least. It's ten hours' drive to anywhere in Libya, and they'll want to do that border crossing in the light.'

'They won't want to do any of that road in the dark,' said Ed. 'There'll be bandits out there.'

'Maybe they'll get a helicopter.'

'Milo wouldn't have had that stamp in his passport, if they'd gone by helicopter.'

'Fuck it,' said Casey. 'Fuck. If you don't spot them, how am I going to know who to aim for? Fuck.'

She always got tense before an operation.

'There aren't enough of us out here to make it easy,' agreed Miranda, who was used to calming her down. 'But you guys have to be out on that road, in case they go straight towards Ghat. We have to keep that route covered. I'll do the town. Don't worry.'

'We need more people,' said Casey. 'This team is far too fucking small. It's ridiculous. We can't cover all the options.'

'It will be OK,' Ed interrupted. 'Apart from our little place, there isn't really anywhere else for them to stay in Djanet, except that one hotel. We know the Germans are staying there, and the French, and we've seen them already. It isn't a huge place. We'll have to listen for English voices and work it out from there.'

'Just because they came in from London doesn't mean they're English,' Casey pointed out sulkily. 'And it only works if they go to that hotel.'

'It's OK, Casey.' Miranda was soothing. 'We've got lots of chances to get this right. Dash isn't expecting it to work straight off. Just take it slowly.'

Instead of taking the road to Libya, the Land Cruiser rolled into Djanet. As Miranda watched from the square, the black pickup drove under a green-tiled archway and straight into the courtyard of the Palais. A dark-haired man was driving, a pale man beside him. The dark-haired man was smiling, pointing, knowing.

Miranda gave them ten minutes, and followed. After the heat of the square, it was cool in the reception of the Riad Palais.

Miranda booked a room, using her married name. The bellboy was obsequious.

Now she untidied the room, and headed to the roof terrace. From there, the view stretched all around, scrappy rooftops ignoring the sun. There were only two tables up here, and a ragged umbrella. It wouldn't do. It would only work if they came up here for the view, and he might not care for the roof-tops of Djanet.

Miranda prowled around the hotel. As usual, the rooms were set around an interior courtyard, providing a breath of shade. There was an alcove at one end of the covered walk, with a couple of benches, padded with cushions. On a low table stood a beautiful chess set, ebony and ivory. Miranda sprawled gracefully, book out.

The dark-haired man came out of his room, and shouted a few words. A muffled reply, negative. He laughed and dis-appeared towards the street. Miranda didn't look up, didn't meet his eyes. Not him, she calculated. Not him. But now she knew which room to watch.

She stood up. The courtyard was empty. She dragged the bench a couple of feet to the right, flicked an imaginary speck from the cushions and settled back down. Now she had a direct line of sight to his room.

Miranda had waited for hours for the right prey. Now she relaxed, smiling blandly as the hotel staff trotted here and there. She gestured for a glass of water and a man brought it, ice bobbing, with a bow. And finally, the door cracked open. A man looked out. Dark red hair, and it suited him. Tall, and used to being obeyed. He stretched, and looked around, and there was Miranda.

A glance, a long one. She held his eye, so it was almost a promise. She'd been here before. So many times. And so had he, she knew already.

'Would you ever fuck someone for a story?' Miranda had asked Casey once.

'No!' It was always fun to shock Casey, who considered herself so unshockable. 'Never. You?'

'Not unless I wanted to anyway. And now not at all, I suppose. But, once upon a time ...'

An anonymous hotel room, in some desperate dot on the map. Grey walls and white sheets, soft laughter and gasping pleasure.

Just for one night.

Brought together, like this, he'd laugh.

Meant to be, he'd say.

Just for one night.

She remembered the dance, now.

This is what I want. This. That. Now. Again.

I'll tell you half of my secrets, but not my name. The words, but not the code. My story, but not its end.

And in the morning, the world spins on, and the kaleidoscope turns again.

A kiss goodbye, a long look and a smile. In another world ...

Turn, and laugh at the chance.

Maybe, she'd think. Maybe. Probably not.

She could see him now, thinking careless thoughts. And she smiled back, half promising. Because a promise might be enough, and promises can always be broken.

He walked towards her, already familiar.

'Hi.' That smile. 'And what are you doing in a place like this?'

She told him she was a researcher, one of those words that can mean everything and nothing. And he didn't pry, because he didn't care.

They sat and chatted, laughing at nothing. The night was hours away. No rush. She drifted questions at him, knowing he would lie, now more than ever. But there would be clues.

He said his name was Olly. And she thought it probably was, because he hesitated for a second.

They had spent hours deciding how to bait this trap. Milo came from the world of Cézanne and Monet, but Miranda thought they might come from anywhere, these men. They couldn't all come from the art world, surely. That world, too small. Too few targets.

And so now she talked in circles, drifting around his travels. Not what, but where. Aberdeen was freezing. Saudi, a hassle. And you never knew where you were with Iran.

Oil, thought Miranda. Gas.

She mentioned a visit to Kurdistan, and watched his eyes flicker.

'I met this amazing couple last night,' Miranda decided, in the end. 'He's looking at the cave art out here.'

'Cave art?'

'It's a thing, apparently.' She dismissed it with a laugh. 'Old drawings on the rock. But actually he's quite an interesting character, this guy. He's not just about cave art, whatever that is. He's got interests in oil too.'

She watched him shift, just so slightly.

'What sort of interests?'

'Not sure,' Miranda shrugged. 'But he was telling me all about some new find in Liberia last night, and it was just announced an hour ago. I got a Bloomberg alert. Should have bought shares, I suppose.'

They half laughed together.

'Useful guy to know,' he said.

'Right,' said Miranda. 'I looked up a piece in the *Post* about him. Ed Fitzwilliam.' She passed him her phone. The article was light on detail, carefully backdated on the system. No real reader would ever find it, in the Byzantine depths of the *Post* website. They had written several different articles, bait for whoever he might be.

This version of the story hinted at wealth, eccentricity, contacts.

'Interesting guy.' Oliver handed the phone back. 'You about for dinner?'

'I'm not.' And she watched his eyes glitter with frustration. 'I've got to meet someone. Tomorrow?'

'I think we'll have moved on by tomorrow.'

'Too bad.' She stretched lazily. 'Too bad.'

And a few minutes later, she slipped back to her room, with just a backwards glance.

23

In the evenings, as the sun burned out, Djanet's square filled gradually. One stall sold orange juice, another small cakes. A furious cobra, teeth ripped out, was tormented by a flute. A man with no legs and a horrible crust down one side of his face begged, agonisingly.

Small boys dodged through the crowd, kicking a football, bright bursts of energy, largely ignored.

'Hello, mister. Hello, mister,' they shouted at every tourist.

Casey and Ed sat at one table outside the coffee shop. All around them, men ate dates and smoked endless cigarettes.

You're Ed Fitzwilliam, the message came through. He's intrigued. And Ed pulled on the story like a cloak.

The Germans appeared, in sturdy walking boots, then the French. Casey fretted, but quietly. Then a figure appeared, on the other side of the square. The moment she saw him, Casey's nerves disappeared, the actress on her stage.

The man drew closer. He was tall, with the fox-red hair Miranda had described. There was a brutal confidence in his walk, even the pushiest Tuareg falling away as he strode past the stalls. This man was familiar, Casey thought. From somewhere. Somewhere ... Her brain ripped through a million faces, adrenalin speeding everything.

Oliver Selby, she realised. The Cormium boss. At Gigi's, that night, while she flirted with Brendan. Snapping his fingers at the hostess.

Would he recognise her? No, Casey was sure not. He might have seen her black satin dress that night, but never the girl inside. And he had been surrounded by his friends, acolytes, and drinking games and vodka. That girl, Amelie, coiled around him. It was safe, she was sure. It was safe.

She watched him for a moment, trying to assess how long he would stay in the square, how quickly she needed to pounce. There was no sign of the driver.

Almost as if she had willed it, he drew closer and closer. He was making for their café. There wasn't, in fact, anywhere else for him to sit in this square. And the Europeans were here, at these tables, and she'd thought that alone would draw him across.

Now she watched him out of the corner of her eye. On the table to her right, Casey had left some bags, piles of them, from the souk.

An ambush never looks like one. Once, in a hotel bar in Manchester, the *Post*'s team had filled almost every table in the room. They had done it gradually, over the hours. Each table filled swiftly as oblivious people finished their drinks and pottered away. And as the footballer swaggered into the busy room, thinking only of used fifties for some forgotten game, one couple stood up, all ready to leave.

'Have this one; we're just going.'

'Thanks, mate. Nice one.'

So the footballer sat down. Right in the middle of the hotel bar he'd chosen himself. And then talked for hours about how to fix the next game, and who would need a kickback, and – most fatally – how they'd done it before, again and again.

But here in Djanet, the team was tiny. As Selby walked up, Casey reached for the bags, head down, digging through for some embroidered leather sandals – look, darling, aren't these gorgeous?

And the waiter, in a long white *gandoura*, rushed to seat the new foreigner at the empty iron table next to theirs.

Selby looked at the menu, and the sprawls of Arabic.

'Beer.' He spoke slowly to the waiter. 'I want a beer.'

He became more abrupt. The waiter listened, head cocked to one side.

'Beer.' Selby was getting impatient. 'Get me a fucking beer.'

Laughing, charming, Casey turned to Selby. 'He won't be able to help. This bit of Algeria is basically dry. It's a fucking nightmare.'

There was an instant bond.

'Shit,' said Selby. 'I forgot. I just want a fucking beer.'

'These people, dude.' Ed joined in against the waiter. 'It's such a pointless rule.'

'Don't panic,' Casey said to Selby. 'We've found some booze. We've got loads back at our hotel.'

It hadn't taken long to track down the local moonshine, in a back street of Djanet, while they were waiting for the Bombardier to arrive. It was still possible to drink in some parts of the country, the attitude to alcohol yoyoing to and fro, depending on the politics of the time. In the small towns, it was always harder.

They had guessed that this visitor might want a drink that night. Might come looking for one, especially after being teased by Miranda.

'I would love a drink,' said Selby. 'Sometimes you just bloody need one.'

'Let's head off,' said Casey. 'I'm Carrie, by the way.'

She had planned to be Callie, again. But as he walked towards her, she decided to avoid the chance that the name might trigger a memory. Brendan might, just might, have been teased about a Callie, after that night in Gigi's. She hoped Ed would follow the change, would remember Carrie.

'Oliver,' said Selby, not giving his surname.

'Ed. Great to meet someone civilised out here. We've had it up to our fucking eyeballs with this town.'

'Oh, you're Ed ... I met a girl who knew you ...'

And just like that, it was double-sourced, and he would never wonder how. Three sources, really, with the article in the *Post*. Now he knew Ed was someone like him.

They had thrown some money to the unfortunate waiter and were walking towards their hotel.

'Our car broke down,' Casey explained. 'And it's taken for ever to get some new part. The moron mechanic keeps ordering the wrong thing.'

'Nightmare,' said Selby.

Ed let Oliver turn the conversation to oil, as they wandered through the streets. After spending days trawling through the cuttings organised by Hessa, Ed was able to drop more breadcrumbs. Within just a few minutes, Oliver was laughing that Miranda should have bought shares in Liberian oil, and Ed – glancing sideways – was agreeing.

They turned into the courtyard of Ed and Casey's hotel. The pink bougainvillea glowed in the dusk.

As soon as they were off the street, Ed turned to Casey, kissing her hard.

'They get so pissed off about that sort of thing here,' Ed moaned. 'All that stuff does my head in.'

They filled the courtyard with cigarette smoke and noise. Ed hooked up a cheap speaker that crackled out music.

It took a few hours to get Selby very drunk. The palm wine distilled to *lagmi*, a spirit with a vicious kick. Soon they got him laughing, drinking fast, filling his glass again and again. He was fifteen years older than them, somewhere in his early forties. But, out amongst the Algerian hills, away from all the usual gauges, it wouldn't take long to drift to familiarity.

Afterwards, Selby wouldn't have been able to say whose idea it was.

Casey didn't like this strategy. She had dismissed it the first time Miranda suggested it.

'That's just a stupid game,' Casey had said, back then.

'It'll work,' Miranda had persisted. 'People love to boast, you know that. And most games are just practice for war anyway.'

Take the pieces, thought Casey, and twist them. Be the stoned tourists, on some beach in Thailand, friends in minutes, forgotten next day.

Miranda had faced her: 'Do you have a better idea?'

Kicking at the dust, Casey couldn't think of another way.

'Well, then.' Miranda won.

And the game had worked before, here and there. The first secret hastens the second secret. A burst of honesty from one, and the other opens up like a flower.

The first time, it had been the chief executive of a pharmaceutical company who knew, *knew*, there was a problem with a contraceptive pill. A stroke here. A suicide there. The results coming in, but patchily. They were at a tedious convention, at the grim conference centre in Birmingham. They asked him where he got his tie, and spent an evening cackling in the bar at the Hyatt there. The sleek grey booth was their five-star castle, as the rain poured down out on Broad Street. I have never, have you ever? Drink, drink, drink.

The barman made the chief executive's drinks three times stronger than theirs and Casey never lost.

The next day, they went to the company fast, with a series of impossible questions. His hangover must have felt like a murky haze, with no way out.

That story ran under the health editor's byline. The chief executive never even realised they were journalists, the two of them. He must have thought that the two pretty girls had woken up with a crisis of conscience, turned whistleblower, run to the *Post*. Nine months later there was one of those population bounces, the statistical hiccup that happens when thousands of women come off the pill, in a panic.

'Better than being dead, though,' said Casey. 'Just about. Probably. I hope some of them are called Cassandra.'

As she rocked to and fro in the hammock, she remembered Selby on the dance floor of Gigi's, jeering as his army did shots. It could work.

In the candlelit courtyard, under the bougainvillea, Selby was eager to play the game. Because games from Gigi's would make Djanet feel safe, and he was so very far from home.

I have never, it starts, have you ever … Been to Paris. Ridden a horse. Had a threesome?

And if you have been to Paris, ridden a horse, had a threesome, you have to drink.

And you can't lie. You've got to tell the truth. Those are the rules.

Except, of course, you can lie. You can always lie. And sometimes you can't even remember the truth. It is the game that tourists play, when the television speaks Arabic and the locals shy away from the jokes.

Out here, Selby could forget about being the chief executive of Cormium. Keeping his secrets, he shied away from describing the company, his role. And that meant for the first time in a decade, he couldn't use shorthand to establish his status. Which might, briefly, give them the advantage.

'I have never,' Casey began slowly, 'have you ever, done a parachute jump?'

Ed drank, a gulp of the *lagmi*. They had made up some bottles earlier, diluting the cloudy white liquid with watery milk. You couldn't tell the difference, they were sure, especially in the flickering light of the candles.

The bottle nearest Selby was pure, ferociously so.

'Always wanted to do that,' said Selby. 'Haven't got round to it, yet. I have never, have you ever bungee-jumped?'

But no one had, so he lost that round. And that made it his turn to drink, again, more *lagmi*. Those are the rules. He drank more than he needed to. Nervous, diagnosed Casey. Stressed, even though he had chosen all this.

'I've done all the rest of it, dude.' Ed was flicking his hand back and forward through the candle flame. 'Base jumping, hang-gliding, even fucking wing-suits. Pushing the limits.'

'I have never, have you ever' – Casey gave a silly laugh – 'lost fifty grand on one poker hand.'

Ed drank.

'No way,' said Selby. 'On one fucking hand?'

'What else is it all for?' Ed shrugged. 'Makes you feel alive, right? And it's only fifty grand.'

And they watched Selby's perceptions of Ed shift, again, just slightly.

It would have helped to have Miranda there, Casey thought, too late. Someone for Selby to flirt with, to balance out the four. But it was too far in, and anyway, Miranda might be needed again at some point.

'I have never, have you ever, had sex in a car?' Casey was lying, but she wanted to change up the mood.

And Ed and Selby drank, clinking glasses, and catcalling in the dark.

The old woman, who had listened to Miranda's scrapings of Arabic, passed through the courtyard like a disapproving ghost.

Thank God, she couldn't understand what they were saying, thought Casey.

'I have never, have you ever fucked someone on a plane?' Selby asked.

Ed paused for effect but then drank, ostentatiously. Casey rolled her eyes and laughed – 'Bastard, when did you do that?' – as Selby high-fived him across the table.

Selby's glass was empty, and suddenly he was reaching across the table for the bottle next to Ed.

Casey smacked Ed, in mock outrage over the mile-high club, and swept the bottle away from Selby off the table.

'Oh, bugger,' she giggled at the smash of glass. 'I'll get another one.'

She was careful as she replaced the drinks, putting down another two bottles, one in easy reach of Selby. Selby could barely focus now, anyway, reaching for his new glass of *lagmi* with exaggerated care.

'I have never,' Casey said, 'have you ever, killed someone?'

The words dropped into a sudden silence.

Ed's eyes flashed for a second, and then he leaned back in his chair.

'No,' he said, 'but I've always wanted to. Out on the road here from In Ekker, you remember? About sixty miles out. We passed that guy, just walking along the road. And I thought, just for a second, that I could just accelerate. Kill him just like that. Who would ever know? And who, in this fucking country, would ever care? He's no one, that guy out there, with his shitty wheelbarrow.'

'That is so fucked up, Ed,' Casey grimaced at him. 'So dark.'

'Most things are fucked up when you think about them.'

'You couldn't do that.' She was almost flirting. 'You wouldn't.'

'I bet I could.'

'For me?' She smiled.

'For you.'

They waited for Selby to join in, but he was silent.

'Every man has thought about it,' said Ed. 'You must have thought about it, right?'

But Selby shook his head, firm through the alcohol, and poured another drink.

'Never have I ever,' he changed the subject, 'been arrested.'

And Ed had to drink, laugh, ramble: 'It was all a total misunderstanding. I can explain.'

And almost an hour passed, before they could try again, fly to the salmon.

'I have never, have you ever,' Casey said, 'killed an animal.'

Ed drank. 'Pheasants, sure. And on a stag weekend.' A shrug.

'You're kidding.' And was it real? Casey wondered. This story. 'A stag weekend?'

'We were all out in Cambodia, a few years ago,' Ed was laughing at the memory. 'We shot AKs, and all sorts, at some stray dogs out on a range. Just obliterated them.'

'Why?' Casey wrinkled her nose, 'would you want to do that?'

'The stag even took an RPG to a cow.' Ed grinned. 'It was brutal. You must have done something like that, Oliver?'

A pause. 'That sort of thing.'

'And we talked about it,' said Ed. 'Out in Cambodia, what it would be like to take the next step.'

Oliver was watching him, eyes half-closed.

'Well, no wonder,' Casey said, 'you were thinking about that man, and his wheelbarrow.'

'Why,' Selby looked up, the slur in his voice, 'didn't you do it? Out there, on the road.'

'It'd fuck up the car,' said Ed. 'Not that it isn't fucked already. I don't know. I almost wish I had. I guess I've always wondered about it. Always wanted to know what it felt like. Everyone has, right? It's being a man.'

But Selby shrugged, turned away. 'What else did you get up to in Cambodia?'

'That would be telling.' Ed became serious again. 'But you must have thought about it, right? Everyone has.'

'You boys,' said Casey. 'When you're small, even a twig is a gun. As soon as you can walk.'

'Do you remember that sniper in Washington?' said Ed. 'Killed seventeen people, I think. From his car. He had it all set up. I remember wondering what would that feel like? As if it was almost a logistical exercise.'

'But you wouldn't want to do it.' Oliver's eyes gleamed.

'I don't know,' said Ed. 'Maybe. *Maybe.*'

'Stop it,' said Casey. 'You'll freak Olly out. Stuck out here with us, in the middle of nowhere.'

'He won't,' said Selby. 'He won't.'

'Thousands of people are murdered every year,' said Ed. 'It's a human urge, and you can't deny it. Do you reckon you'd do it, Olly, if you had the chance? Take that shot?'

They let the pause lengthen; the laughter drying to silence.

'I don't know.' Oliver flinched away at last. 'No, of course not. Never.'

But there was a hesitation there, just for a second. And they covered the moment in smiles.

'It would be pretty awful though.' Casey gave her lazy smile.

'Turn you on?' Ed leaned forward, reaching for her, and she folded into him.

But Oliver stood up abruptly, jolted away from the table towards the arch. Casey couldn't bear it. Don't go, she willed. Stay. *Stay.*

She spoke to Ed, light as air, ignoring the figure prowling round the courtyard.

And Selby slowed, hesitated. A couple of seconds passed and she called out some question he could answer without thinking, and slowly, fish on a line, they edged him back in.

He sat down, lit a cigarette, and she breathed.

The conversation sprawled on.

For a while, Ed spoke about the cave drawings. I want to go all across the Sahara. Ticking them off, one by one. They're beautiful, you know? Course, you've got to be a bit careful out there, but whatever.

Chad next, he said. Tibesti. Then Ennedi.

Then it was back to oil. Ed hinting at a big find coming up in west Africa, flirting almost. Casey nudged the conversation here and there. Even through the alcohol, Selby was watching Ed, wanting his secrets. Ed found cigars in the room, and poured out more drinks.

And finally Casey pounced.

'So what the hell are you doing out here then?' She was friendly, chatty, couldn't bear for him to bolt.

'Exploring,' he shrugged. 'Same as you.'

'You're not.' She was watching him. 'You're out here for something else. It doesn't make sense, otherwise.'

'No,' he insisted. 'No.'

'There's something going on, though …'

And he looked at her, just for a second.

'Why?' There was a slur in his voice, but also something like pride. 'What do you think? Really.'

'I don't know!' Excitement and fun in her smile. 'A dare? A race?'

'Something mad, isn't it?' Ed leaned forward. 'I can tell.'

'Romance?' Casey gasped. 'How exciting?'

'A stag?' said Ed. 'You tying the knot?'

They were all laughing, that uncertain laughter, on the edge of frenzy.

'A business deal?' Casey gestured wildly round the court-yard. 'A treasure hunt?'

And Selby's laugh stopped.

'Something' – it was half-boast, half-confession – 'like that.'

'Some sort of hunt then,' Ed said slowly. 'Some sort of hunt.'

'A hunt,' Casey repeated. 'But what would you be hunting, out here? There isn't anything ...'

A mosquito buzzed round a candle.

'Go on,' persuaded Casey. 'There's no one out here for us to tell.'

'You can trust us,' said Ed. 'And we couldn't give a shit what you get up to anyway.'

Selby was leaning forward for the bottle, the liquid splashing on the table. 'Come on. Who's next?'

And this time, the silence ran on.

'That's why you're out here, isn't it?' said Ed, so slowly. 'You're out here for the kill.'

'But ...' Casey's voice trailed away.

'People.' Ed put awe into his voice. 'There are people. Out here.' He leaned back in his chair, raking his hand through his hair, waiting, an odd sort of smile on his face.

'I'm going to do it.' Selby couldn't stop himself. 'That is what I am here to do.'

They let the silence hang, so that for a second he couldn't know their reaction. Casey felt the horror flood her, the horror she had chased.

'No fucking way, dude.' Ed let excitement creep into his voice. 'That is fucking crazy.'

'What the ...' Casey found disbelief easy. 'No way. No way.'

Selby expanded with relief.

'How the fuck does that actually work?' asked Ed.

'There's this guy.' Selby was proud of himself now. 'You get flown out here, and he meets you at Tiska. And then we're going to travel out to Libya tomorrow. There's a place you go: you literally stand up on some rocks, with a sniper rifle. And you just fucking do it. You don't get caught, they promise. And then you get the fuck out of Libya. But who the fuck ever wants to come back to Libya, anyway?'

'That is the craziest thing I have ever heard,' said Casey. 'So fucking dark.'

They all grinned at each other, the secret a sudden pact.

'I want to do it,' Ed said suddenly.

'No way,' Casey snapped at him. 'No.'

'Oh, come on,' he said. 'It's a one-off. '

Selby leaned forward in his chair. 'I don't know if you can, mate. This guy I am travelling with, he's pretty hardcore. He's got his thing; I don't know if he'd let some people he's never met come along for the ride.'

'Would he care that much though? Really?' asked Ed. 'I can shoot. I know what I am doing with a rifle. Just me and . . . Carrie.'

He just managed it.

'It costs a fucking fortune, usually,' Selby couldn't resist boasting. 'The private jet I flew out on was insane. Off the hook.'

'We've got a lot of cash,' said Ed, suddenly serious. 'Fuck, I so want to do it. Can't you tell him we're cool?'

'I guess I can ask.' Selby looked worried abruptly. 'Shit, I hope he's not fucked off that I told you. You're meant to keep it a secret. Obviously. You mustn't tell anyone. Promise.'

'You're paying him, buddy,' Casey pointed out. 'You're in charge.'

'It's your call,' Ed insisted.

'Don't let him push you around. Your party.' Casey pushed it home. 'You get to hand out the invites.'

'Yeah.' Oliver's voice blurred. 'Yeah.'

Casey poured them all another drink, suddenly needing one. The last shot finished Selby.

'Sleep in the hammock, dude,' said Ed, hauling him up with an easy strength. They threw a thin blanket over him, and he passed out in seconds.

'We may be on,' Casey texted Miranda. 'But stay away tonight. He's sleeping in the courtyard.'

'No probs,' Miranda messaged back. 'Well done.'

Casey blew out the candles, the courtyard plunging into sudden darkness.

For a second, neither of them could speak.

'I don't think he'll notice if we sleep in our own rooms,' said Casey.

'I don't think he would notice if we slept in his hammock,' said Ed.

'Well done,' Casey whispered into the dark. 'You did brilliantly.'

'Let's see what tomorrow brings,' he whispered back.

She went into her room, closing the door quietly behind her, leaning against it for a second. Flopping on the bed, she closed her eyes and thought about Ed. Because she had seen his eyes flash, at the moment she asked the question. *Have you killed …*

They had flown all the way here, just to ask that one question.

And she knew that, just for a second, he had struggled.

24

They woke up early, Ed and Casey, not wanting Selby to leave the courtyard unseen. But they let him sleep, calculating that the driver would worry when he found his charge missing. You could achieve a lot, with relief.

The old woman brought them breakfast, mouth twisted with disapproval. She swept up the broken glass, muttering under her breath. They had to ignore her, eating their breakfast under the pink blossom.

Selby groaned awake, the purple hammock rocking as he tried to orientate himself.

'Morning.' Casey was chirpy, bringing him a fresh orange juice. 'Ed is so excited about the trip.'

They had decided that Ed would have the hangover, in sympathy: 'Mate, I feel appalling. How are you? I've got some ibuprofen, somewhere.'

'I'll look for it.' Casey could be so sweet.

Selby sat up, hazily. He didn't look much like the chief executive of Cormium, that morning.

'Do you want to give your pal a call?' Ed went on. 'I can tell him the way.'

They hustled him into calling his driver, shouting out directions in the background.

It took only minutes for the black Land Cruiser to turn into the courtyard. The man's eyes glittered with annoyance as he erupted from the car. He was tall, even taller than Casey had realised, with huge shoulders. Despite his size, there was precision in every motion. You've served in an army, Casey thought. The military edge was there, indefinable.

'Oliver, we needed to move out this morning. Early.' His voice was a jumble of accents.

He was wearing ancient jeans and a black vest. There was a large tattoo on his arm.

'Yeah, you said.' Even hungover, even in a fleapit of a Djanet motel, Selby would not apologise.

'We need to get going.'

This man could be charming, Casey sensed, but the charm had been switched off today. And Selby didn't like it.

'I've told what's-her-name to get us some coffee,' said Casey brightly.

'We need to go,' the man interrupted. 'We don't have time.'

'I want a fucking coffee,' said Selby.

'Your trip sounds intense, man.' Ed got up from the swing seat and moved towards the hammock.

'The trip …' The man's voice broke off.

'Your trip out to Libya. Sounds pretty wild, what you get up to out there.'

The man spun towards Selby. 'You told them?' There was real fury in his voice.

Selby lashed back instinctively. 'It's fucking fine. They wanted to come. It's cool.'

'You can't be—'

'We've got money,' Ed broke in. 'We're happy to pay.'

'No way,' said the man. 'That's not how it fucking works.'

'I don't see why not.' Casey's voice was an icicle in the dust of the courtyard. 'We already know what you're doing. And Ed's happy to pay whatever it costs.'

'I've got twenty thousand bucks on me,' said Ed. 'It's easy.'

'And I want them to come,' Selby said flatly.

'Whatever he's told you, it's bullshit. Who the fuck are you, anyway? What the fuck are you doing in Djanet?'

'Do you need to know?' Ed's voice was diamond-hard. 'I'm Ed and she's Carrie, and I really don't think you need to know anything else.'

For a moment, the man watched them, cat and mouse. Casey forced a grin on to her face.

'I'm Carrie.' She walked forward briskly, holding out her hand.

'Josh.' Oliver completed the introduction so carelessly that Casey saw real rage in the man's eyes.

He was Joshua Charlton, Casey thought. Almost certainly. Or at least that was his name at the moment. Ten per cent of Mostgrave. They had got that bit right, at least.

He shook her hand without wanting to, and spoke over her shoulder.

'We need to go. The roads are risky at night.'

'I'll need to pick up my stuff from the hotel,' whined Selby. 'I haven't packed.'

'The mechanic dropped off our car this morning,' said Casey. 'We're packed up, all ready to go. Amina was expecting us to leave today anyway.'

They took the silence that met this for a sort of assent. They drank the coffee fast, and moved towards the black pickup.

They didn't see the knife coming. One second they were walking towards the cars; the next, Selby was up against the wall, Charlton's knife panther-fast to his neck.

'You don't tell anyone,' he whispered. Casey could see the blade, right up against Selby's jugular. She felt all the air flood out of her body. 'Do you hear me, Oliver? You never tell anyone again. Or you will be killed. I promise you. If you ever tell anyone again, I swear to God, you will fucking die.'

Selby couldn't speak, couldn't breathe. A trickle of blood ran down his neck.

'Do you fucking understand?' Charlton spat. 'Never ever again.'

'Yes,' Selby found the words. 'I won't ... I won't tell anyone.'

Charlton dropped him, wheezing, to the ground.

He turned to Casey and Ed.

'Fuck off, the pair of you. And don't you ever say a word to anyone, or you'll regret it for ever.'

They watched as the man spun the black pickup in a rage, missing Amina's flowerpots by inches.

Selby sat beside him in the passenger seat, almost sulking.

Ed and Casey lolled carelessly in the hammock. But as soon as the car had turned the corner, Casey was on her phone.

'Delay Selby,' she messaged Hessa. 'You've got maybe half an hour. Probably less. Follow the plan.'

Genie from a bottle, Miranda appeared.

'We didn't turn him,' said Casey. 'But we may still be able to.'

'Ed,' said Miranda. 'Get to the Palais. Keep an eye on them. Keep them there, if you possibly can.'

'Should I box in his car?'

'No,' Miranda decided. 'Not unless you absolutely have to. We don't want anything that can connect us to the delay. It's got to look completely coincidental.'

Ed was gone, racing through the tangled streets.

'Right,' said Miranda. 'They know what to do back in London. They'll be fine.'

Miranda had plotted it all the night before, as soon as Selby's name was mentioned, priming the glossy business editor.

Nicky had almost laughed. But she would do it, they knew. She could stall Selby for hours.

Back in London, Nicky's first call was to Cormium's head of press.

'Just wondering if you could comment on this rumour that Alphavivo has its sights on Cormium?'

There would be a long pause, as the head of press rippled through the options.

It was well known that Alphavivo, the biggest commodity traders in the world, had not enjoyed Cormium appearing in their rear-view mirrors. Everyone knew that. But they wouldn't try and take over Cormium ... Would they?

They might though, the head of press thought. The maths was there, just about. It would be a punchy move, but bold moves were working for Cormium, and it could be the only play left for Alphavivo.

And there was bad blood between the Cormium management and Alphavivo. Selby had worked at Alphavivo, before jumping to Cormium. Alphavivo regarded Cormium as up-starts, and Selby had done everything to irritate them, like a wasp at a picnic.

All that meant that there wasn't a back channel between the two companies, and no one could pick up the phone and wipe away the rumour.

'I've not heard.' Cormium's head of press tried to dismiss it.

'I think you need to check.' Nicky knew people called her the Ice Queen, didn't care. 'Our sources are pretty clear.'

'I'll get back to you.'

At the same time, James, one of the boys on the business desk, was messaging his opposite number at *The Times*, a buddy from his trainee days.

'Mate, I'm getting it in the neck over this Alphavivo take-over … You heard anything about it? I didn't think they'd go for Cormium.'

'Whaat? Shit. No.'

The Times would be the second call into the Cormium press office. That would really unsettle them.

Hessa steeled herself. She picked up the phone.

'Oh, hey there.' She sounded as seductive as she knew how. 'It's Callie. I don't know if you remember me … ? We met at Gigi's a little while ago.'

'Callie.' Brendan knew her at once. Casey had given Hessa his number, and Hessa sneaked out of the dusty courtyard and down the road to role play over the phone.

'I'd broken my shoe.' Hessa laughed softly. 'You were so generous that evening.'

'That was a big night.' Brendan was smiling at the memory. 'But you ran away.'

'Cinderella,' said Hessa. 'I had to work the next day ... And actually, that's why I was calling ... Did I mention I worked at BPC? It's one of the hedge funds off Dover Street.'

They had made up a random collection of initials. It didn't matter. Dozens of them operated in Mayfair, behind brushed silver nameplates and a scattering of letters.

'Right.' He sounded deflated that it was about work, so she tried a giggle.

'We just heard a rumour that Cormium was being taken over by Alphavivo. I thought I would just see if you'd heard anything ...'

'Alphavivo?' There was shock in his voice. 'No, I hadn't ...'

But he stopped. Not knowing about the machinations of his own company revealed too much.

That call would be insider trading, of course. It happened every day.

'We could even snap up a few thousand Cormium shares,' Miranda had pointed out cheerfully. 'Get the market moving. The share price will spike if the City decides Cormium's about to be snapped up. We could make enough to cover the story costs.'

'No,' said Dash firmly, because in the past journalists had been a bit too clever about tipping shares, and ended up in jail.

'Oh, you hadn't heard?' Hessa sounded disappointed. 'I just thought you might know ... Oh, shit. I've got to run to a meeting. But talk soon, right, Brendan?'

'Right.' She could hear the cogs turning.

The *Post*'s business journalists were checking in with their usual sources. You heard anything ... Suppose it would make sense ... Thought you might be doing some of the analytics for

Alpha ... Cormium a bit overstretched after they snapped up that ... Guess Alphavivo must have seen an opportunity ... And it would be the last time they could ...

Nicky hadn't told them it was a trick. James especially needed putting in his place. It would do him no harm to spend the day chasing his tail. Nicky glowered at him across the desk, and he redoubled his efforts.

Then the share price began to move.

Alphavivo would never shut down the story, because it made them sparkle. And Cormium couldn't, because they didn't know where it had begun.

Selby, in his room in the Palais a thousand miles from anywhere, had a hundred phone calls crashing in, as Cormium pretended not to panic.

So Josh, hammering on his bedroom door, was told, 'I can't fucking go anywhere right now. No, I'm not messing you around. I fucking promise. I know about the light, on that road. I know. But I just can't leave this hotel for now. I could lose my company. Honestly.'

And Josh, both annoyed and pacified, stalked off to ramble around Djanet.

Back at their courtyard, Casey and Miranda were thinking aloud.

'There's a tattoo on his arm of a black eagle ... A military insignia. Must be,' Casey said. 'And there was a sticker of the South Africa flag on his car ...' She was searching frantically, the hotel's wifi creaking. 'There.' She stopped. 'It was that one. From the old Parachute Brigade in South Africa. He must have been involved with them. Or the new regiment, in some way. There must be a way ...'

She was scrolling again, Miranda pacing the floor in frustration.

'There.' Casey pointed, at one Josh Charlton out of hundreds of Joshua Charltons around the world. This one had served, just a few years ago, in the South African army. 'His name is on someone's old fund-raising page. No photo, but it must be him. And he must know some of the guys in 44 Para out there.'

Miranda was already on the phone.

'Aisling' – that was the *Post*'s smart Africa correspondent, based out of Johannesburg. 'Can you start sending me a list of as many men as possible who've ever served in 44 Parachute Regiment. Or connected to it in some way. Drop everything else – I'll tell Dash – and just keep the names coming.'

'Sure,' said Aisling, and the phone went dead.

Within minutes, the names started snapping in. From cuttings, from memory, from countless helpful sources.

'What did you make of Selby?' Casey was scrolling through search results. 'What's he like?'

'Tough. Cold. He wants the nameless girl in a silvery hotel room,' said Miranda. 'Not reality.'

'Maybe that's how they all want this death,' Casey said. 'Pre-packaged, rolls of meat, supermarket cold. They don't want to see the abattoir.'

'How about him?' Miranda pointed. 'Killed in a car crash, two years ago.'

'Married,' sighed Casey.

'Or this guy,' Miranda said, 'blown up in Afghanistan.'

'No,' Casey winced.

'No,' agreed Miranda, 'not unless we have to.'

And then another name appeared, and they both knew.

'Him,' said Miranda. 'He's absolutely perfect.'

Casey walked to the café in the square. She pulled out a novel and ordered a mint tea. A donkey meandered past, ribs nagged to bloody sores by huge panniers. A boy scolded it on, and Casey flinched, and looked away.

It seemed like hours before she saw the dark-haired man appear, at the far end of the square. Before he'd seen her, she was on her phone, deep in a half-sided conversation that, eventually, he would overhear.

'For God's sake,' she grumbled, when he was close, 'I can't believe how slack everyone at Wynford Mortimer is getting. You used to be so much more efficient. It's so fucking irritating.'

She cut off the call, half-recognised him and grimaced.

'The stupid accountants are being so bloody disorganised,' and she laughed at herself. 'I could scream.'

Let him come to you, she thought. It's all got to come from him this time.

'They're usually quite good, I thought, Wynford Mortimer.' He was friendlier now, because he was bored and she was minding her own business and they had something in common.

'Do you use them?' She put a note of surprise in her voice, because why would someone in a café in Djanet use expensive Panama accountants?

'Sometimes.' And now he had hesitated so long by her table that she almost had to gesture, sit down, help yourself.

'It's Ed's offshore accounts, really.' She poured tea. 'But I always end up organising him.'

She smiled at him, the smile that no one could resist. He didn't quite smile back, but he nodded to the waiter, who whisked across with some of the little biscuits.

'I didn't mean to be rude this morning,' he said. 'It's complicated.'

'Don't worry.' She flicked it away with her hand. 'It's good for Ed, having someone say no to him. Spoilt little rich boy.'

But her smile took the sting out of the words.

'That idiot Oliver wasn't meant to talk to anyone,' said Josh. 'The bloody fool. And now he's got some work crisis, so we're delayed again.'

'People should know,' Casey said, 'how to keep secrets.'

They sat there, for a moment, in friendly agreement.

Then Casey almost spoke, and hesitated. Josh looked up.

'It's nothing,' she said. 'Just your tattoo.'

She pointed to the iron eagle, black on his arm. Josh looked down at it, flexing his bicep almost without thinking.

'It's just ...' Her voice was sad. 'I used to go out with Ethan Newell.'

His head jerked at the name, and there was the sympathetic pause.

It had taken Miranda only a few minutes to check. 'I'm so sorry to bother you, Mrs Newell, like this, out of the blue. But I'm just writing an article about people in ... your son's situation. And I was wondering if you had a few minutes to tell me what it is like ... For the family ... I saw your campaign.'

A casual few moments, listening to the tears.

Then, 'It must be so dreadful for you, Mrs Newell ... I'm so sorry. And is there anyone else I could speak to about Ethan? A wife ... Or a girlfriend? Oh, there were always lots of girls ... He sounds quite the character, Mrs Newell ...'

Casey looked across the table in the dusty square in Djanet, and let her eyes fill with tears.

'I'm sorry,' said Josh. 'What happened to Ethan ... It was ...'

He rubbed his tattoo almost unconsciously.

'Did you know him well?'

'Not that well,' said Josh. 'I left a while back ... But he was such a great guy.'

And if Ethan had other girls, Josh would never mention it to a girl weeping in Djanet.

'He was just so fun and exciting.' Casey let her voice choke. 'And so gorgeous, of course. And what happened to him ...'

'It could' – Josh patted her hand awkwardly – 'happen to any of us.'

Except, of course, it couldn't. It could never happen to just anyone.

It had been a funny sort of coup, that one. Launched by a raggle-taggle of gamblers and daredevils. Funded by a charming rogue, and the prodigal son of some careless politician. Spurred on by some shady characters from nobody quite knew where.

They'd flown in, with their rocket launchers and AKs, pausing only to refuel one last time before the assault on that tiny country, that speck right on the edge of Africa. A speck with oil though, so much oil. And a dictator so vicious it could almost be a liberation.

Except that it wasn't. Not quite.

As they landed, on that potholed runway in the middle of Zimbabwe, they were surrounded. By searchlights and soldiers and the sudden gasping realisation that it wasn't going to be all right. Not this time. And not ever.

For a second, Casey imagined sitting on that ghostly plane. The rows of mercenaries, gathered from the darkest places, blinking in the sudden light of a torch.

They'd been dragged off the plane, and paraded in shackles. Hauled to a show trial, and condemned for an endless number of years. And now Ethan was rotting, as far as anyone knew, in a rat-infested prison somewhere, nowhere. Buried uncheckably deep, in the loneliest of cells. Alive, they thought, probably.

Josh would never be able to check who Ethan knew, or didn't.

The politician's son had been all right, of course, and the charming rogue. The money was always all right. But Ethan and his men were lost for ever.

'It was on and off, the two of us,' Casey went on, just in case. 'But I loved him. I really did.'

'He was a good guy, Ethan,' said Josh. 'It must have been fucking terrible for you, and his whole family, all that business.'

'I don't think he'll ever get out.' Casey blotted away a tear. 'I think about him every day.'

'I wish we could have done more,' said Josh. 'For one of our guys. But it was so fucked up, all of it.'

'I know people tried,' said Casey. 'His mother's still trying to get him out.'

'Poor old girl,' said Josh. 'And our government never lifted a finger for him, of course, with their stupid mercenary laws.'

He looked at her, as she had known he would, almost protective. She was one of them; and she'd loved one of them.

'You don't think it's bad, do you?' Casey asked tentatively. 'Me moving on with Ed? I waited for years, you know. Waited and waited. We don't even know if he is alive any more.'

'Not at all,' Josh reassured her. 'It was a shit situation, and you've got to live. Somehow.'

'Thank you.' She smiled up at him. 'It means so much to hear you say that.'

He smiled at her, enjoying the power of his forgiveness.

'It's lovely spending time with someone who knew Ethan.' She fiddled with her teacup. 'Tell me some stories about him. I love to hear them.'

So he told her stories about their lives, in South Africa. And she filed them away, all of them, for use someday.

She watched him, as he sat there, checking every person who came into the square, drawn to movement. Reading their eyes and their clothes, their walk and their gestures. With flickers of restless energy, he stared at the Algerians, who were oblivious to the tall white man at the café table. Even as he was talking, he was always moving, twitching a foot, stirring the tea, shredding a napkin.

And when he ran out of stories about Ethan, she asked him about Libya. Just carelessly, so he didn't even notice that he was talking about it.

'I'd love to see it,' she said, in the end. 'Libya sounds so incredible.'

'It's a shame ...' he started, but she waved him away.

'Don't worry about it. I understand completely. It's your thing.'

She looked around for the waiter, with a wave big enough to be seen by Ed all the way across the square, in a gloomy alley where he would never be noticed.

'Don't worry about it at all,' she said. 'And besides, Ed wants to head out there at some point anyway. You've given him some crazy ideas.'

'It might be …' He stopped. 'It would be dangerous for just the two of you out there … You mustn't …'

'We'll see.' She was careless. 'We'd be fine, I'm sure. And I've seen Ed shoot. He's good, it's not just talk. Oh, look, there he is now. I was wondering where he'd got to.'

And by now Josh was friendly enough to wave as Ed crossed the square.

'Please don't mention Ethan to him,' Casey whispered urgently. 'Ed doesn't like hearing about Ethan.'

So now they had a secret, Casey and Josh, and he wouldn't be asking her about Ethan again.

'We're friends now.' Casey introduced Josh to Ed.

'Sorry about not letting you come along,' said Josh. 'It's just tricky … and anyway, I'm sure Oliver was bullshitting about what it is.'

Ed waved it away too: 'Couldn't matter less, dude. We'll find our own fun. We always do, somehow.'

They sat and chatted, the waiter bringing them chopped-up fruit, and more tea. Josh was joking now, and they laughed back, as they stretched in the sun.

'Did Oliver say how long he would be?' asked Ed, in the end, as the sun dipped to the rooftops.

'I hope we'll be able to leave tomorrow morning,' said Josh. 'Be annoying if we can't, but guess I'll have to wait for that paycheck.'

He watched as she laughed, and she thought: it would be a mistake to underestimate you. And still, he didn't offer. And there was no way to ask.

They wandered to get some dinner, in the cool of the Palais. Selby appeared for a moment.

'Good to see you guys. It's sorting itself out,' he said. 'Just some stupid rumour that sent my company haywire. Pain in the arse, but it's going to be fine, thank fuck. Tomorrow morning? Yeah, Josh, don't worry. That should be fine.'

He grabbed food, spun back towards his room.

Their talk was idle. Above Josh's head, a gecko was creeping along the wall. Step and pause, and step and pause. Insects flickered around the light, hypnotised.

There must be a way through the maze, thought Casey. Find it.

'Christ, there is nothing to do in this town.' Josh leaned back in his seat. 'Never been stuck here for two nights.'

Above Josh's head, the gecko pounced, faster than she could see, scattering the drunken flutter. Only a moment, and then the insects were back. The gecko chewed slowly.

'Won't be a moment.' Casey stood up.

Miranda had given her Selby's room number. Casey paused for a moment, actress in the wings. The knock echoed.

He was genial, as he opened the door, amiable even. Almost confused, behind the polish. A man and a woman in a hotel room, that only meant one thing. And women found him attractive, she remembered, from that night in Gigi's.

She could see he had been working at a small plywood desk. The Berber rug was littered with clothes, and his laptop glowed mutely. The air was stale.

Casey closed the door, and leaned against it for a second. She let the silence shiver. He waited, the questions floating up from the dark.

'Oliver ...' The syllables dropped like stones into an icy pool. 'Oliver ... Selby.'

The surname stunned him. His spine went rigid.

'Don't even think about it.' She shut it down. 'They know I'm here. They know you're here, too.'

A long pause, and she watched calculations snap through his head.

'Who?' The word was ragged.

'It doesn't matter.' She swept it away. 'You are going to get us on the journey to Libya. Do you understand?'

A glimmer of understanding.

'But he won't let you,' said Selby. 'He's very clear about it.'

'I know that.' Casey never looked away. 'And I don't give a fuck. Because if you don't get Ed and me on that trip, I am going to destroy you. I know who you are, and I know what you do, and I know enough to prove it to anyone.'

'But I can't.' Selby's voice was empty. 'There isn't a way.'

'There is always a way' – Casey punched out the words – 'And you'll find it, because you have to.'

'He doesn't want you there. He said there was no fucking way. He was furious, this morning, after we drove off. I thought he would scrap the whole thing, even me going.'

'I don't care.'

'But I haven't even done anything yet.' Selby looked almost petulant, like a spoiled child faced with an outing rained off. 'You trapped me, with your stupid games, didn't you?' he spat. 'That was all a fucking scam. And I can't bloody do it anyway.'

'I don't care what you have to do,' Casey said. 'You'll do it.'

'I can't.'

'You will. You'll beg, if you have to.'

'Blackmailing bitch.'

'Yes.'

The silence filled the room.

'And don't even consider taking us out there, just to kill us out in the desert,' said Casey. 'There's someone who knows already, back in London, and if we disappear . . .'

'Are you a fucking journalist?'

'No.' The lie was easy. 'I work for a very rich man, and he heard about Josh and his operation. He sent me here to find out about it.'

He half-believed her, only because he was desperate to believe.

'Why don't you just tell Josh then? He might go for it anyway, if you give him enough money.'

'He doesn't trust me,' she snapped. 'He trusts you though, fuck knows why. And you are going to use that.'

'But I don't know how.'

'You're an intelligent man,' she said. 'Work it out. For starters, you're going to delay us in Djanet for another night. It'll give us more time.'

And more time for Selby to think of an escape too, she thought. But she would take that risk.

The laptop flashed a message, and Selby glanced away for a moment.

'Make this happen,' said Casey. 'Or I will ruin you.'

He stared at her. Casey met his eyes without a flicker. The seconds ticked by.

'All right.' Selby crossed over. 'All right.'

'Good,' said Casey. 'I knew you would see sense.'

'But who are you?'

He watched her contemptuous smile. 'I'll never tell you.' She was turning away. 'Just do this, and you'll never hear from me again. I promise you. Do this, and I will disappear.'

25

As she rejoined the others, she signalled to Ed. All done. Let's go. Now. They said goodnight to Josh, with the amiable shrugs that could have been a friendship or a farewell. Might be around tomorrow. Yeah, cool. See you.

In the morning, Casey and Ed ambled round the souk. The day ticked past, painfully slow. There was no sign of Josh or Selby. Miranda kept watch on the hotel, but the black pickup never moved.

In the still of the afternoon, Casey slipped into the Palais and knocked on Selby's door. He opened it as if he'd been waiting.

'I can't think of a way.' The words rushed out. 'It's not going to work.'

He was scratching his scalp as he talked, twitching with nerves.

'It has to.'

'I spoke to him last night. I said you seemed like a fun pair. Would be a laugh to have you along. He said it was out of the question, and that it all had to be agreed far in advance.'

'Well, you'll have to change that.'

'I can't.'

'You will.'

'But what if I can't? You won't—'

'What does he like?' She changed direction. 'What is he interested in?'

'I don't know,' Selby was impatient. 'I barely know the man.'

It wasn't Charlton, she thought, behind it all. There was someone else, deeper in the shadows.

'What did you talk about after we left last night? What did you do?'

'We played poker.' Selby winced. 'He knows what he's doing there too.'

A gambler, then.

'Did he take a lot off you?'

'Nothing I can't afford to lose. And I'll get it back.'

'Is he the sort to go back on a bet?'

A pause. 'Probably not.'

Amar Opening. Steinitz Countergambit. Alekhine's Defence.

'Tell Josh,' she said, 'that you asked us to join you for dinner.'

Later that evening, after dinner, they moved to the padded sofas in the half-darkness of the covered terrace. Selby sprawled across a bench meant for two. A waiter was standing nearby, head bowed over a notepad. He was young and awkward, dropping his pen and apologising, sorry, mister. Isa, he'd bobbed his head to Casey earlier. My name is Isa.

Josh was reaching for a pack of cards.

'You should play Ed at chess,' Casey said lazily to Josh. 'Though I bet he'd hammer you.'

'You reckon?' Josh's drawl.

'I know,' she smiled.

'You haven't seen me play.'

'Sometimes' – she met his eye – 'you just know.'

'Go on, Josh,' jeered Selby. 'If you dare, of course.'

Casey moved to the low table, where the chess set shone.

'Ten grand if you win,' Ed joined in. 'And ten grand if I beat you. But you also take me to Libya.'

Josh paused, then smiled. 'You won't win.'

And, in the flicker of the candlelight, they shook hands.

Earlier, she'd primed Ed. K is for King, Q is Queen …

Now, Ed and Josh faced each other, on padded benches. Opposite Selby, Casey pulled up a recliner for herself, picking up an abandoned novel. She was almost at the head of their table.

Josh held out both hands, in fists.

'Left,' said Ed, and that was the white pawn.

'Ever been to Rio?' Casey asked Josh. 'For the carnival. I was reading an article about it this morning.'

And as she spoke, she held the book with one hand, four fingers visible. First letter of her sentence, four across, E4.

And Ed moved a pawn, two steps forward.

'Only once.' Josh never hesitated. A pawn, two steps also. 'Not during the carnival.'

The Sicilian Defence. So Josh knew this game. Even after all this, it might end in defeat.

It couldn't.

'Could we go soon?' Casey pleaded, hiding one finger. 'Or Mexico. Day of the Dead. Such fun, all that.'

Ed shifted a pawn one square.

'Whenever you want,' Ed smiled at her.

'Next year, maybe,' she said, not moving her hand.

N, gracelessly, for the knight that leapt across the board. Dragon Variation, the ballet step.

Here be dragons.

Black on white, the game went on. Isa brought the shisha, smiling, with its clouds of smoke. Selby jabbed at his phone. And Casey tried to remember everything she had known, once upon a time.

The Cyclops, the Minotaur, the treasure hunt, hide and seek.

The pieces fell away, one by one. A knight cut down here, a bishop defrocked there.

High up the wall, the gecko was back, scavenging the light-drunk insects.

And Josh would know, by now, that he might be beaten by this unknown opponent.

But any pawn can be a queen. 'Do get on with it,' Casey yawned, holding the book with both hands, as a rook sliced down a knight.

Josh flicked her a glance, as his king twisted into check. Ed leaned back in his seat, triumphant.

'I don't get beaten often,' said Josh.

'It's not my game,' she answered.

There was a long silence, as she fiddled with the pieces. Josh was staring across the table.

'No,' he smiled, so that Casey almost misheard. 'You couldn't do it.'

And, just for a second, she saw Ed as he was: ruthless, kind. Good, killer. She pushed the thought away.

'Of course he can do it,' she insisted.

'You can't back out now,' Selby chimed in. 'No way, Josh. You made a bet.'

'He couldn't do it,' Josh shrugged. 'Not out there. Not him. He'd freeze in the moment.'

And who was it, Casey wondered, who chose? Who was it, who knew? 'He'll be fine. He wants to do it.'

'I want to do it,' Ed insisted. 'You bloody lost, Josh.'

But Josh was spider-still, in his web.

'You can always tell,' he said. 'And you'd never do it. Not up there. Not looking down through those sights.'

The waiter, Isa, was clearing the table, half a courtyard away. Picking up glasses, with small, precise movements.

'I can do it,' Ed repeated. 'And you'll get your fucking money.'

'Don't be a prick, Josh.' Selby was losing his temper. The desperation showed like blood through a bandage. 'You made a deal, and I want them to fucking come.'

The silence tautened between the men.

'Fine,' shrugged Josh. 'Hit him.'

He gestured to Isa, stacking plates in the candlelight.

'What?' Casey played for time.

'You heard.' Josh pointed again. 'Your guy punches that boy across the yard. And then I'll know.'

'Why?' And Casey could hear the uncertainty in Ed's voice. 'Why the fuck would I do that?'

'Because,' Josh snarled, 'it shouldn't matter to you. If you want to do this, why the fuck would smacking that guy mean anything to you at all?'

Casey was watching Isa move the chairs back to their proper place, lifting them gently so they didn't scrape along the marble floor.

'I don't want to be arrested in fucking Djanet for decking a waiter,' Ed stumbled. 'Fuck knows what the prison is like here.'

'I know this hotel,' said Josh. 'No one will say a word.'

'And then you fucking promise, right, Josh?' said Selby. 'No more messing around. Because then we're all playing the same fucking game.'

A nod.

Isa was laying the next table now, placing heavy silver knives with butler precision.

Ed's eyes flickered to Casey. I can't. Please. I will not do this. You must. Casey was suddenly sure, with a crystal certainty. You *must*.

Ed was looking away.

'No fucking way.' But they were waiting.

'If you can't do this' – Josh's voice was almost a whisper – 'there is no way you can come.'

Casey imagined Isa's face crunching under Ed's fist, and the memory of blood on his hands. Isa, afterwards, with his bruised face, and irreparable sadness.

'Of course he can fucking do it.' Casey was out of her seat. She turned to Ed so that only he could see her eyes. 'He's going to do it.'

Ed's face was completely expressionless as he looked up at her. For a moment, Casey felt as if she might lift him with her eyes alone.

Josh and Selby were watching them both, hyena and carrion.

'Do it, Ed,' and the smile was only in her voice. 'Do it.'

Ed stood then, ignoring Casey's outstretched hand.

In unison, Josh and Selby were on their feet, an instant gang. Across the courtyard, Isa had taken a step back from his table. One last, careful check, oblivious to the wolf pack on his right.

Casey saw only a blur of movement. Ed took three running steps, and slammed into Isa. The punch caught Isa on the side of his jaw, an explosion of power that sent him falling in a crash of china and cutlery. Casey caught Isa's face in a fragment of light. He was rolling, trying to get away from the next blow, terrified. Ed stood over him, fists clenched, unrecognisable.

'Ed,' she breathed.

He was turning away, furious, stepping back from the crumpled boy on the ground. And there was a shout from the front desk, a man running, and skidding to a halt as he saw Josh in the shadows.

'Sir.'

In an instant, he was gesturing Isa away, leaving only a chaos of white tablecloth and broken glass. There were tear stains on Isa's face, patches of blood on his shirt.

Ed prowled back across to the table.

'Now.' He came right up to Josh's face. 'Now will you keep to your word?'

26

The birds were screaming in the Sahara dawn when Casey woke up the next morning. They were ready when Josh's black pickup paused outside their small hotel. Miranda had hugged them goodbye, and ducked out of sight.

'Be careful, Casey,' she had whispered.

'You know I can't be,' said Casey, almost laughing.

'He could be taking you,' Miranda said flatly, 'just to kill you. Away from Djanet. So no one ever knows.'

Bianca Angelo. Tell us, please. *Please*. What happened to our girl ...

'I know.'

The black pickup waited patiently while Ed went into the bank, putting some cash into a deposit box to get a key. There were no questions asked by the cashier, who grumbled something under his breath.

And then they were on the road out of Djanet, leaving the scruffy town behind, and turning east towards Libya.

The road burned ahead of them, already shimmering in the heat. The Sahara rolled away. An ocean of sand, dangerous as any sea.

Josh really shifted his black pickup, Casey noticed. Ed was having to floor it just to keep up.

He wasn't speaking to her. Had walked back to their hotel in silence, leaving the shattered table behind. Now, she felt his rage.

'I'm sorry,' she said again.

'No,' he said. 'You're not.'

'I am.'

'You'll tell this story,' said Ed. 'Maybe. And that won't be in it. You'll never say what I did, but I will know. I will always know. You don't know what it felt like, hitting that poor little bastard. Seeing him look up at me like that.'

'No.'

'I didn't know what you would do,' he said. 'I didn't know how fucking stupid you might be. I thought you might get us killed. Josh isn't fucking playing, Casey.'

His anger knifed at her, and she didn't know how to explain.

'It worked though,' she said. 'Miranda will apologise to Isa for us. She'll give him something. The *Post* will.'

'She won't tell him the truth though,' he said. 'He won't understand.'

'No.'

The windscreen was speckling flies.

'Don't you want to do more?' he said into the silence. 'Than this?'

Casey felt a shock of surprise.

'What else is there? We are ...' She struggled for the word, 'illuminating.'

'It's so destructive.' His voice was harsh. 'All the time. Don't you want to make things better? Not just snipe from the sidelines?'

She thought for a moment. 'But this is the only thing I can do. This is my part.'

'Maybe.'

They drove on.

'Please,' she said. 'Please don't be angry with me. We can't do this if you're angry with me.'

'I know,' he said. 'I know.'

And in an oddly tender gesture, he reached out and stroked the back of her head, clumsily, so that she felt her heart swell for a second.

A few miles out of city, the road forked to the left. Two pickups were parked there, four Tuareg men in each.

One of the Tuareg, cheekbones like a burned-out house, was leaning unsmiling against the car.

Josh stopped his car; Ed and Casey pulled up behind him.

After a few words with the Tuareg, Josh walked over to their car.

'Our bodyguards,' he gestured. 'They've come over the border to take us in. Our lot are the nastiest out here. We'll be fine.'

'I wondered' – Casey forced herself to laugh – 'how you moved in and out of here.'

'This lot don't want to know what we do,' Josh said. 'They don't give a fuck. They work for the highest bidder. Like so many people out here.'

Just for a second, Casey caught the eye of one of the men in the back of one of the pickups. His eyes burned black hatred, and she just concealed her shudder in time.

They drove on, the Tuareg falling in behind.

A few hours out of the desert town, Casey rang Hessa on the satellite phone. Hessa patched in Miranda.

'All fine so far,' said Casey. She was on speakerphone, so that if Josh looked back it would look like she was chatting to Ed. 'We're going to have to be careful with comms from now on, I think.'

'Dash wanted to know if it had all gone smoothly,' said Hessa.

'As smoothly as it could,' said Casey.

Casey had decided not to tell Miranda about Josh's knife, or the bodyguards. Dash would go into orbit.

'I still don't like it,' said Miranda. 'Anything could happen out there.'

'We knew that.' Casey sounded more confident than she felt. 'We knew it would be like this from the start. By the way, thanks for the information on Ethan, Hessa.'

Hessa had trawled for every detail on the mercenary, from birth certificate onwards.

'No worries,' said Hessa.

Casey paused. 'Hessa, tell us something funny about the office. We need something to make us laugh.'

'I can't think.' There was something cheering about Hessa's London accent. 'Oh, yes, Ross is having a fight with the head of news at the *Argus*. You know, that new woman they have running things over there, who's meant to be quite scary.'

'How come?' Miranda and Casey spoke at the same time.

'Well, there was that big demo, out by Heathrow. Protesters in trees and so on. Usual stuff. Anyway, we used a big photo of one of the hippies for our front page. Turns out it was the undercover reporter from the *Argus*. Jessica Miller.'

Hessa's voice got more confident as she chatted on.

'Jessie?' Miranda giggled. 'No way.'

Undercover reporters are careful not to be photographed. In a world where reporters are pushed to build their brand, the investigations team kept a low profile.

'She was all covered in mud, looking a bit bonkers,' Hessa went on cheerfully. 'They're not happy at all. Ross didn't help when he said that she was the only vaguely acceptable-looking person at the protest and that's why they'd used her pic. He didn't understand why their new editor went even more ballistic.'

They all laughed, a release of tension.

'You OK, Ed?' Hessa asked.

'I'm fine, thank you.' He seemed pleased that she'd asked.

Casey glanced sideways at him. 'Ed did a brilliant job.'

He smiled at her then, glancing sideways just for a second. Then his attention was back on the road.

It was a long drive to the border. The two cars curled through the mountains, the thin ribbon of tarmac stretching out endlessly.

They stopped occasionally, to stretch their legs. Ed looked out over the broken desert.

'It's beautiful,' said Casey. 'Don't you think?'

Camels had been here, leaving hoof prints like upside-down broken hearts. A brutal wind was blowing, a wind that might take the red dust all the way to Paris and London, Frankfurt and Rome.

'I suppose so.'

The cars moved on, hundreds of miles from Djanet now. There were no other cars out here, in the wilds. Casey leaned her head against the window, and closed her eyes.

*

She was almost asleep, dozing against the window when the brakes slammed on.

'Shit.' Ed's voice.

Casey looked up, and felt the ice in her spine.

Josh had pulled up, and was waving at them to stop. Deep drainage ditches ran along both sides of the road here, with no way past. In the mirror she could see the Tuareg, tight up to their bumper.

'Oh God.'

Dust settled around them. There was no way to outrun these people, not here. Josh stepped out of his car, and all Casey could see was his gun. She felt the world haze.

'Get out.' There was no smile on Josh's face now.

'What?' Selby was craning round, curious. 'Josh, no ...'

'This is nothing to fucking do with you, Oliver.'

And Selby was looking away, as an animal will sidle away from a carcass.

I am Malak.

'What?' Casey's voice was higher than usual. 'What the hell is this all about?'

Josh, the soldier, who moved like a panther. You fool, she thought, to die like this.

'Get out of the fucking car.'

The Tuareg were in a scrappy circle, guns hanging by their sides. One of them was chewing gum, contempt in every line.

'I don't understand,' Casey tried again. 'What is this all about?'

Josh came closer. His face was dirty, she noticed, dust had settled in the creases by his eyes. He lifted the gun. Man to executioner, in one move.

'Yes,' said Casey. 'I'll get out.'

They climbed out of the car, Ed's movements clumsy.

'Over there.'

Josh pointed them to the edge of the drainage ditch, six feet deep, where the earth was like blood.

It never looks like an ambush.

Crumpled bodies flickered through Casey's mind. This is how it ends: stumbling in the ruts of some forgotten road. The horror, the fear and the sudden agonising silence. Eyes unseeing, and silver flies flickering. A trickle of blood from the mouth.

A ditch, my grave. Just another death in Africa.

My world, she thought, you were so very beautiful.

'Who told you?' Josh was standing behind them. There was nothing before them, except baking red desert.

'I don't understand,' Casey blustered. A clod crumbled under her foot, and she lurched sideways, scrambling to steady herself.

'Yes,' he said. 'You do. I know it.'

'You're mad.'

'Why?' His voice was a blade. 'Why are you here? With all your stories.'

The sky quivered.

'Milo,' she said abruptly. 'Milo Newbury told me.'

'Milo?' He was disbelieving. 'Why the fuck would he tell you?'

'We grew up together.' The words were a rush. 'Near Chagford, in Devon.'

Near, not in, because that was harder to check.

'I've known him since we were kids,' she babbled. 'His mother knows my mother. Old friends. Way back. She's lovely, Lady N.'

Because Lady Newbury's manners meant she would smile, yes, of course, even if she had never heard the name.

'And why would he tell you?'

'He was down in the village, last Christmas.' Take the facts, twist them. 'I bumped into him coming out of the graveyard one night, and we got chatting, catching up. We went back to his house, just for a drink. It's beautiful, their place. With the paintings and all that.'

A ghost conversation. Professional liar. And she was back in that grim, splendid house, in front of the painting of a beautiful boy. The lost boy, and his old house.

'And he told you.'

'Yes,' she was turning around very slowly. 'And then I told Ed. After Christmas, when I was back in London. He wanted to know all about it. And then he got so fascinated.'

'And then Milo killed himself.' Ed was turning too. 'So we didn't know how to get out here.'

'He'd said Djanet.' Casey faced Josh now. 'I'd never heard of it. He had to show me on a globe. There's a lovely old one at their house. Under a stag's head, in the library.'

'And did he say how he got out here?'

She felt the nausea flooding, the quickening of the terror.

'No,' she said. 'I've no idea. We thought if we came out here, we would find it somehow. And we were planning a trip round Africa anyway.'

'Why didn't you say all that at first?'

'You know' – she spread her hands – 'Milo got fucked up towards the end. I didn't know how he had left it with you.'

A gust of wind blew across the desert floor.

'I know her.' It was Selby.

Josh's eyes flicked to him.

'I've known her for years, just knocking about London.' Selby was nodding, her dance partner for these few steps. 'I don't know her well, but I recognise her. One of those girls.'

From the blur of London nights, Casey thought. It sounded true, because it was, so nearly.

'You sure?'

'Used to go out with one of my mates. Jonathan. Does a bit of consultancy work, now and again. She's cool, I promise you.'

The gun was sliding down. Josh stared at them.

'I promise you,' Selby said again. 'She's fine.'

Selby, the gambler, who never glanced back. Who saw a way through, and ripped at the throat. Selby, the gambler, who needed her alive.

'Have you told anyone,' said Josh, 'that you're here?'

Flick of the coin, toss of the dice.

'No,' she said. 'You can trust us.'

Words are easy, like the wind.

'And how about everything else you've said?'

Faithful friends are hard to find.

'I promise you,' she said, and the words seemed to hang in the air like moths for a moment. 'Ed was just curious. He wanted it.'

And rest in peace, Milo, she thought. If you can.

There was a long pause, then he turned away. He gestured to the Tuareg: it's OK. Casey felt her limbs go limp with relief.

He walked towards his car, and every step was a gift.

'I had to check,' he said over his shoulder.

'Sure.'

27

Selby glanced back at them, as Josh climbed into the car, and gave the smallest of shrugs. She smiled at him, grateful in her anger. The Tuareg were walking to their cars. Casey tried to stop her hands shaking.

'Do you think he's a sociopath,' Ed asked conversationally, as the cars pulled away, 'or a psychopath, the person behind all this?'

She could hear the struggle to keep his voice even.

'I never know the difference,' said Casey, as he accelerated.

'As far as they know, psychopaths are born, and sociopaths are made. Psychopathy is nature, sociopathy is nurture. Sociopaths have hints of a conscience, but not much. Neither of them cares much for ethics and morality and all that. Psychopaths are manipulative, and good at gaining people's trust.'

'You learned a lot from your books, in Helmand.' Casey strangled the fear.

'Psychopaths can't form emotional attachments, and they would plan out every step of this in advance,' he paused. 'So which one do you think he is, the man who organised this?'

'I don't know.' Casey watched the desert fly past. 'I'm just trying to work out which one Ross is.'

It was almost a joke.

But she felt her nerves jolt back, as they approached the crossing at Tinkarine.

It was always the same in these places. Fight or flight. And then, for a certain type of person, the adrenalin drains away. The body identifies the new normal, and starts to make do. Any jolt after is an aftershock, raising more dust, but not a new terror. The key lay in surviving that first surge of terror.

Casey could file in a war zone, tapping out the words as she listened for the scream of the mortar. She could do this.

This was Tinkarine, where the Gaddafi family had crossed, terrified, into Algeria. Fleeing as their country collapsed behind them. The convoy of expensive cars held for hours at the border, with the rage of millions screaming at their heels. This was the only road, across the desert, the only way to a strange sort of safety. But even they were allowed through, grudgingly, in the end.

Josh was waved through with an ease that spoke of familiarity. He gestured to their car. Cash was passed over, casual as a greeting. The border guard wandered over, chewing khat, skinny, a man's uniform hanging off boy shoulders.

'Passaporte.' He was proud of his English.

The guard's AK was swinging over his arm. The safety was off, out of laziness, or arrogance. Casey had looked and then wished she hadn't. She handed over their passports, praying that Josh would stay in his car, wouldn't come over for one last check, and glance at their passports. Because if he did, it was inevitable.

How come your name's Cassandra? I thought you said Carrie. Then would come more suspicion. And the checking.

But Josh stayed in his car, and Casey managed to breathe. He'd decided. The guard stamped the passports, barely looking at their names. The Tuareg rolled through, too.

As the car pulled forward, Casey looked at the page. The Tinkarine stamp, so familiar from Milo's passport. Less than a year since he has passed through here. Following in a dead man's footsteps. And was it this guard who'd stamped his passport, with the same lazy indifference?

'It's only a couple more hours,' Josh shouted across. 'Stay close. And don't drive off the road. No one ever got round to marking the minefields.'

Now they were in Libya, lawless, beautiful Libya. This world was half sand, half sky, and they never got closer to the horizon.

They passed a scatter of shacks by a small oasis. There were car skeletons here and there, with the occasional twisted oil drum. Because that's what it's all about, really: the oil.

Casey and Ed smiled at each other, united by relief, and rolled down the windows, and roared across the desert.

Casey had travelled to Libya, before. Back in that summer, as the Gaddafis fled or died. That brief moment when the Arab Spring felt like the future. People firing tracer bullets in the air in celebration. In the night sky, they looked almost like fireworks.

And the cars screaming along the seafront. Racing. Because that turns out to be the thing that people do when the rule of law collapses: they go out and drive very fast.

One day, Casey was driving back to her hotel, with her fixer, after a long day. The car was held up by a crowd of people.

Let's get on, she almost snapped. Come on.

They had banners, home-made ones. They were chanting. The fixer stopped the car, almost in tears.

'This is the first demonstration in Libya. The first demonstration in almost forty years.'

He talked through the window to one of the women. A long stream of Arabic, and then turned to Casey.

'They want to know if they are doing it right, the demonstration. They are not sure how it is done.'

They all wanted to tell their stories, the Libyans. One man, blank eyes, told her how his son had beaten one of Gaddafi's sons at football. Just once.

'They fed him to their dogs. Alive. My son. They tore him apart. I loved him so much, and they fed him to their dogs. My son. My only son.'

But, even then, there were signs that the future might not be their dream. As Casey moved around the city, she came across different militias. One group would smile at her, chat to her, thrill over this new world. Another would mutter disapprovingly at a woman wandering so freely. The divide was there, even then. Soon the fast cars were in long queues, as the petrol ran out. Lines of people pushing their cars to the pumps, remembering what they had, once.

They ripped Gaddafi to pieces, out in the desert. His convoy bombed by a Predator from Vegas. And he was left to the mob – the death that haunts every dictator – and an unmarked grave. Not for Libya, forgiveness.

Once again, it was a war that the West had started, without thinking about the end. As if this were a fire that could ever burn out. The tribes resurrected, along those ancient fault lines. The Arabs and the Berbers. The Tuareg and the Toubou. Dozens of fiefdoms, and the Islamists moved fast, to fill the void left.

And now, Casey was here again, rolling through the desert and thinking about death.

Her eyes tangled with Ed's for a second.

'Burning our bridges as we go,' she said.

'We'll be OK, Casey.' He looked at her for a second. 'But if we're not, promise me you'll run. You've got to get out of here. You've got to make it back.'

'I'll try.'

She put her hand out, into the air between them. Carefully, without taking his eyes off the road, he took her hand and squeezed it.

28

Back in London, Dash couldn't sit down. He strode around the office, unable to concentrate.

Hessa had reported the conversation to him, faithfully, as soon as she put the phone down.

'Message me next time they call in,' he had snapped, knowing he wasn't being fair. 'I need to talk to them direct.'

Now Dash tried to concentrate on the news list chucked to him by Ross. That junior minister, Alexander Kingsley, was making some announcement about new investment in border guards. Ross was right. That man would be the next prime minister. Dash tried to focus on the minister's careful words; gave up.

He tuned into the news desk babble for a second. Ross was shouting down the phone at a photographer. 'I want you to shoot him outside his house, but from right down the street. I don't want him to even know you were fucking there.'

Dash walked away from the news desk in an odd swirl of emotions. He wanted them to get this story, more than almost anything. It would win awards, this one. But half of him felt protective. They had no brakes, those two. They wound each other up.

And they manipulated him, he knew, like they manipulated everyone else. Casey, wild little Casey, would lie through her teeth now she was out of his sight. Cool as a cucumber, every time. Beautiful, ruthless, his little street fighter. But she was vulnerable, underneath it all. Where Miranda's pouts concealed steel, he worried about Casey.

Dash had never asked Casey about her background. People never asked much, in a newsroom. But he'd seen her flinch, once, at a gesture from the education correspondent. Flinched in a way she shouldn't have, really. She'd looked around afterwards, found his eyes on her and glowered instinctively.

Casey had survived by manipulating, Dash realised, early on. And he'd harnessed that damaged behaviour, again and again. Give her a moving target, and make sure it wasn't him. Watch the moment of loss when the story was finished. A greyhound catching the mechanical hare.

She broke it down: the pain, the agony, the despair; and sent it back in neat black and white. For Casey, even more than the rest of them, he knew, the *Post* was her home; the only place where people had her back and it all made a strange sort of sense.

It was his fault, really, this Libyan madness. He'd let the investigations team get away with plausible deniability for so long that they'd become the paramilitary wing of the newsroom. Out of control, really.

'They've done what?' He would pacify the incensed cabinet minister. 'I must apologise. I'll have a word. I'm shocked. Talk me through it, so I've got my head round the whole thing.'

And then he would walk over to their office, where they were sitting waiting, knowing the call would come.

'He's admitted the conflict of interest, shouldn't have asked that question in Parliament about the road link. So keep pushing on that. But row back on the fraud point. He sounded convincing there.'

If anything happened to Miranda and Casey, out in the desert, he would be fired on the spot, of course. He would expect that, despite what he'd told them. But knowing that he had let them go, for his ambition – he would have to live with that, for ever.

By that sin fell the angels, he thought.

Dash had dealt with kidnap before. The long hours of negotiation, and the sweating terror of the handover. When all you could do was listen in, as the ex-SAS boys went about their business. And hope that they managed, with cool heads and cold hearts, to swap the reporter for a few hundred thousand dollars. Because if the money was enough, he could breathe.

But of course, now, it wasn't.

Journalists used to get a free pass. Back when everyone wanted to tell their story, and everyone needed a messenger. Then, one day, it was possible to get their message out, everywhere, in seconds. Exactly as they wanted, carefully packaged and perfectly scripted. They could cut out the middleman, and so that is what they did, quite literally.

Now the journalist is the story. So they shoot the messenger, in beautifully edited films. And if it was Casey screaming into the camera …

Dash paused by the picture desk. The picture editor was scrolling crossly through a set of photographs from one of the agencies.

'Don't know why Cromwells have even sent these through. I mean, fucking look at them. Totally unusable,' Stan moaned.

Dash peered closer. An explosion in a hospital, probably an air strike. Syrian children, blown to tatters. A horrifically burned baby. A doctor, still in his shredded white coat, looking, hazily, at where his arm had been.

'We'd have to pixelate everything,' grumbled the picture editor. 'Useless idiots. They should know what we need, by now.'

Their public didn't like war to look too real; they would complain. But the editors had to examine it all, in close-up, bowdlerising where others glorified, so who knew what was real?

Dash had found Stan's deputy crying in the stationery cupboard once. She'd spent hours on the aftermath of a bomb in Jakarta: dozens of immaculate shots of screaming and death. Later that afternoon, Isis had dropped a new video, a pilot in a cage, and a stream of petrol, and a flame. And she'd had to watch the whole thing, to be sure they weren't missing anything.

So she'd cried, very quietly, in a cupboard. Stan, poker-faced, had gone the other way.

Dash wanted to put the whole lot on the front page. This is what a three-year-old looks like after she's been hit with the payload of a Sukhoi fighter-bomber. This is her face when she realises that her whole family is dead, and nothing will ever be the same ever again. Look at it. Don't tell me you don't want to see it. Don't tell me it's a little bit upsetting. *Look at it.*

'You can use that one,' said Dash. 'Pixel out that leg, the one on the ground there. It'll do.'

Dash wandered on.

The editor was over by the designers, watching impassively as they laid out a page. Dash veered to the left. He was avoiding Salcombe now. Impossible to pretend you'd just forgotten that a couple of reporters were running around north Africa.

I counted them all out and I counted them all back . . .

Dash went into his tiny office and closed the door, and waited.

The message came through. I see him. He is moving. To the restaurant.

She lifted her head, lioness. This pack hunts together.

They'd worked well together, from the beginning. By now, they read minds and finished sentences. Flicked hand gestures as he glanced away.

Two was better, and braver. And if one said barely a word, she would be watching and listening and ready to jump in.

'I think what Carrie means is . . .'

'Anna, do you remember when . . .'

And it always helped, on the other side of the world, to be together. Upside-down clock, and upside-down mind.

Not to be alone.

She carried cash, quite a lot. She could never pull out a credit card, embossed with her name.

She checked again, now, from superstition.

Yes, enough. Plenty.

Restaurants never minded cash. They assumed it was an affair.

She could hesitate on her address. She could hesitate on her phone number. 'Silly of me. It's new . . . You know how it is . . .' She could even mishear her own name. But she could never hesitate on her date of birth. So she was one year younger, one month older.

It's never a simple joy, either. She learns that, one day, on the way home. Crying on the Tube, which she thought she would never do.

Because her best day is always his worst.

Somewhere he is humiliated, and ruined, his world crashing around. Somewhere he is seeing his wife, and seeing her tears. And seeing himself through her eyes for the very first time.

And always the fear that he will walk under the train, or jump off the bridge, or swallow all of the little white pills. Because it can happen. It does happen.

And so it is never perfectly happy. The sadness is embedded, in every success. Baked in.

She wrote stories, not fairy tales.

At least, this time, he would disappear.

Injured, they were dangerous.

They didn't always disappear. Once, afterwards, across a crowded room at a polite party, he froze. Wounded, but not destroyed.

She faded into the crowd, then. Hid behind a doleful waitress, handing out canapés like an upside down Oliver Twist. But finally, he'd cornered her. Brave, really.

You used me, he said. Like a puppet. Like your puppet.

But I'm a puppet too, she thought. There's always someone pulling the strings.

We're puppets, all of us.

And suddenly she saw everyone tied together, bound by long and delicate strings. An arm twitches and a shiver runs round the room.

I was his puppet, she thought, and he cut my strings.

And I fell, I fell, I am fallen.

29

They just hesitated in Ghat, the garrison town, with the Italian fortress on the hill. The old fortress, from the days when you could see the enemy coming, and all you needed were strong walls, decent supplies and the will to win.

Then the convoy drove on, through endless rocky plains. Miles floated past under the huge sky.

'You OK?' Ed said into a silence.

'Just thinking about Isa.' Casey twisted her face.

'That,' Ed said simply, 'was shit.'

'Yes,' said Casey. 'And Miranda won't be able to explain. Not really. It would be a risk.' She turned towards him. 'I know you wouldn't have done it. If I hadn't been there. I am sorry.'

'I wonder what they're talking about, Josh and Selby,' Ed changed the subject abruptly.

'We've got to stop calling him Selby,' said Casey, after a pause. 'Josh doesn't know that we know his surname. And it will seriously alarm him if we let slip that we do.'

'You're right. Sorry.'

When they pulled off the road, the cars barely slowed despite the corner. They hooked in a sharp right, towards a line of hills to the south. Casey felt her stomach knot.

'Remember, you've got to butterfly,' said Ed. 'Giggle. We're here for a laugh.'

'But how can they? How can they do this?'

'Later. Not now.'

They could see Josh's car bouncing, as it hit potholes on the long track up to the red hills. The Hilux grumbled, struggling with the pace.

And then, quite suddenly, the white marble palace appeared. It was vast, with long rows of Moorish arches mocking the desert, and golden domes above. There had once been a long row of cypress trees leading up to its gates, but the trees had faded to bleached skeletons, or been hacked down. Serried colonnades held up a massive portico that glittered with Arabic words.

As they drew closer, they could see the huge bronze statue of a fist snatching a US fighter jet out of the air.

'Dictator chic,' said Casey. 'You can get something very similar in Hampstead.'

The four cars pulled up, the Tuareg drawing away to the left. Josh, energised, jumped out of his car.

'Welcome,' he shouted. 'Welcome to Euzma!'

'It's stunning,' Casey enthused. 'What a place.'

'This is magnificent.' Ed spun out the syllables. 'How the hell did you find it?'

'Come in,' said Josh. 'It's worth seeing.'

They followed him up the marble stairs, to the huge golden doors. Confused by the dark of the entrance hall, Casey looked up at the roof of the portico. Underneath, its roof was painted with scarlet and vermilion swirls. She had the sudden sense of walking into the underworld, the last moment before crossing the Styx.

'Come on, Carrie.' Ed nudged her on.

The entrance hall was the size of a ballroom, the floor a mosaic of silver and emerald and indigo, stretching away like a dream. In the centre, a vast fountain was silenced. The white marble – a wedding cake of Carrara – shimmered in tiers.

A balcony ran the whole way round the hall, held up by gleaming columns. Down one length of the wall below it, an unknown soldier had unleashed a full magazine, a long line of bullet holes scarring the marble.

'This is fucking incredible.' Oliver dropped his bags and held up his arms. 'Look at this place.'

Casey twirled forward, laughing at the beauty of the room with him. For a second, Oliver caught her eye, and then he shrugged and smiled at her.

Josh was pleased at their enthusiasm.

'I'll show you to your rooms,' he said. 'The other guys are somewhere about.'

Casey's skin prickled at the mention of more people, unknown people. Every new person was an electrical surge of fear.

An elderly woman bustled out with a tray, carrying long, icy glasses filled with mint.

'Delicious.' Casey tried to smile, but the woman looked away.

Clutching their glasses, they followed Josh to their room, up some stairs, down a long corridor. Oliver was in a room a few doors away.

'Here,' Josh gestured. 'I'll leave you to it. We'll be out on the terrace, at the back.'

'It's so huge that we should scatter breadcrumbs,' said Casey. 'Like Hansel and Gretel and the gingerbread.'

The bed was frilled with pale pink lace, piled high with cushions, under a circus tent of mosquito nets. An awkward golden sofa sat beneath the window. It was shaped like a mermaid, petulant head at one end, the seat a swirling tail. A huge statue of an eagle was balanced in the corner, next to a dark oak side-board. The eagle was snatching at its prey, beak screaming wide.

'An odd sort of paradise,' said Casey, wondering which of the fallen Gaddafi princesses had chosen the clouds of lace. Maybe Aisha, who had given birth to a baby girl in Djanet just hours after crossing the frontier at Tinkarine, the baby a bargaining chip before she was even born, a card played to get over the border.

Humanitarian grounds, they said.

Or maybe it had been one of Gaddafi's buxom bodyguards who slept here, lolling on the satin coverlet and smiling in the huge gilt mirror.

Casey photographed the bed, snapping away like any other tourist. She fiddled with the mini-speakers she had brought, filling the air randomly with *Aida*.

On a coffee table lay a pile of magazines. An old *Vogue*, a battered *Tatler*. There were a few leaflets, in English and Arabic, that looked like they had been printed several decades ago, flaunting the region's sights.

'I don't mind sleeping on the floor,' said Ed quietly. 'I can sleep anywhere.'

'Don't worry,' whispered Casey. 'It would be miserable on the marble. The bed is absolutely enormous, and we don't want them walking in with you banished to the floor.'

They had agreed to say as little as possible in the bedroom because recorders were so tiny, so sensitive, so easy to use. The opera, pouring from the speakers, would blot out most of their conversation.

The windows were fifteen feet high. White linen curtains blew in the breeze, the desert plain spreading away to a horizon that shimmered like a mirage. They stepped out on to the balcony.

'It is magical.' Casey wondered, just for a second, what it would be like to be in this place with Ed alone. 'Just spectacular.'

She turned to him, and knew he was working out how they might escape. Could they climb out of this window? Yes, probably. How would they get to the car?

'Do we know where we are, relative to Salama?' she asked, trying to remember the satellite images.

'They didn't say. Oliver may have been getting a better guided tour.'

Casey had a shower in the huge bathroom, which had his and her jacuzzis. The towels were as white and fluffy as any at the Savoy.

She came out in a big dressing gown, to make Ed laugh, and slumped on the bed.

'I'm shattered,' she yawned.

'I know,' he said. 'We'll just go down for a while.'

Her nerves came flooding back as they left the safety of the bedroom. She pulled her hand away from Ed, not wanting him to feel her fear. Everything could be a trap. Everything. Every creak, every tap, every step.

A shadow fluttering in the corner of her eye had her spinning, but she forced herself to breathe, and swallow the sudden terrors. She stretched her face into a smile, because that was the easiest way to hide her thoughts, every time.

And so they made their way downstairs.

*

To give herself a precious few seconds, Casey poked her nose into some of the rooms. They were abandoned. Miss Havisham dust covered everything.

Just before they got to the terrace, she pressed record on her phone and put it in her pocket. Everything would be taped now, and sent back, as fast as possible. She didn't dare wire herself up, not here.

They found Josh and Oliver out on the terrace, under a blue and white parasol. Two men sat with them. As soon as she saw them, she felt her heart slow, and knew she would be all right, the actress on the stage managing that first line.

The men greeted Casey and Ed heartily, with the easy enthusiasm of all expats at cocktail hour. Evidently, Josh had made it clear that they were to be welcomed. Oliver treated Casey with pompous amiability, as if their conversation in Djanet had never happened.

All four men were drinking beers.

'Beer? Or gin and tonic for you, Carrie?' Josh gestured to a Tuareg man, standing in the corner.

The man disappeared, returning, a few minutes later, with a tray, ice clinking.

'Leo.' Josh nodded to one man, then the other. 'Rory.'

The four men half-stood as Casey sat down, oddly chivalrous. Ed sat down next to her, hand resting briefly on her knee.

The sun was drifting down, into orange sands and blue shadows. A huge swimming pool glistened like a sapphire, the gardens round it dried to dust. A rosemary hedge lined the terrace, wafting scent. It could have been any holiday. She could almost imagine the knock of a tennis ball, and a ripple of laughter in the distance.

Leo's voice could travel around the world in a sentence. Undertones of American, a hint of Australian and a faint touch of Cape Town that she caught on 'like' and 'yes'. But then Josh's South African accent was contagious. She wondered if that was where it came from, the slight twang in Leo's voice.

Leo was almost as tall as Josh, rugby-player solid. His nose had been broken, not just once, and a scar ran down his face, from temple to chin. There was a sparkle of dark humour in his eyes, and black hair that looked like he had cut it himself.

Rory was shorter, wiry, his hair clipped tight to his head. He said nothing as they arrived at the table. Hard eyes flicked over Casey and moved on restlessly. He was watchful, thought Casey. Behind the welcome, he was dangerous.

She wondered if they were Marakata Green, these two, sitting there in the gentle warmth of the evening, thousands of miles from their letterbox in that Caribbean haven.

Rory was staring at her, and she dropped her eyes, in a way that could have been shyness or fear, flirtation or submission.

'This view is incredible.' She hid her face by staring out across the plain. 'How on earth did you end up here?'

But Rory turned the questions back to her, again and again, keeping the conversation moving. She managed to speak easily, somehow, building a past, sentence by sentence. Then Rory asked Ed about the cave paintings. Ed – so fluent she almost applauded – told him the histories.

'Saw a leaflet in our room, too. We'll have to check that out.'

Ed had read book after book as a cover for the trip, he'd admitted almost shyly, as they drove across the desert. She'd laughed. I was good at exams, she'd said. Then forgot it all in a week. Even now she read her notes as she rushed to a meeting. But there on the terrace she listened to his conscientious words, so grateful.

Rory had his head on one side. He had a habit of staring for a little too long. He asked careful questions, and listened to every answer. She wondered, throat tightening, when she would run out of answers, and what would happen then.

But at least Ed was listening in, learning their story as she told it. Both of them laughed about the scruffy hotel in Djanet, and meandered on their imaginary journey across Africa. Casey bounded into anecdotes she'd told a million times. Because they were safely familiar, and filled up the air.

Storyteller, she thought. Liar. Every word could be the end.

But Ed rambled on, and two drinks in, it was Oliver who asked the question that Casey wanted to know: 'So how did you end up here?'

'We were down in Mali,' Leo began. 'A few years ago.'

'There was a bit of trouble down there.' Rory picked up the story. He was a Londoner, Casey thought, once long ago. 'So we were brought in to sort it out.'

Mercenaries, Casey translated. Working for the highest bidder, not unlike the Tuareg who had escorted them over the border. Men like these work all over the world, scattered along the spectrum between legitimate and assassin.

'After Mali was done, we were waiting around to see what would come up next,' Leo went on. 'So the three of us decided to drive up here, right across the Sahara.'

'We were just bombing down the roads, having a laugh,' Josh cut in. 'Mali'd got a bit messy, so we just wanted to chill out.'

Mali had got indeed got messy, Casey remembered. A sudden little coup, a few hundred dead.

She wondered what they had really been doing in Libya, these three. There had been so many rumours when the Gaddafis fled kingless, down the long road to Algeria. That the gold, all those pirate's ingots, had been shifted to Ubari, the desert town right down in the south. That the weapons abandoned in caches across the country were valuable, to the right buyer.

There were other stories, too, of course. That it hadn't been just the Libyans, at the end. That other shadows crowded in, at the last. Shadows there in order to be certain – completely and absolutely sure – that Gaddafi was gone, once and for all, and to send a message to all the despots: you won't get away, not without our help. You may need us, one day, no matter who you are.

'Anyway, we were on the way out to Ghat, when we saw this place, right up and away from the road.' Leo grinned at the memory. 'It looked pretty wild, so we headed up here.'

'It was booby-trapped,' said Josh. 'Careful which rooms you go into here, even now. Rory knows how to defuse them, but we haven't done them all.'

'I do them now and again.' Rory pulled a face. 'When I get a bit bored on a Sunday. Keeping my hand in. I think I've got most of them now, but maybe I haven't.'

'Gives us something to do,' said Josh. 'You've got to keep moving.'

'But don't go into a room if we haven't said it's OK,' said Rory, somewhere between a warning and a threat.

The sun was dropping fast now, the sudden Sahara night.

'So we found that this place was basically empty. Abayghur and his missus' – Leo nodded to the Tuareg who was sitting in the corner – 'were the only people here. They live in one of the outhouses round the back.'

'So we decided to hang out,' said Rory. 'Just for a bit, at first. We wanted a bit of downtime, after Mali.'

'The locals think it's cursed,' said Josh. 'They're very into witchcraft and that sort of shit out here. People die because they think they've had some spell put on them. It literally seems to kill them, believing it. Stupid.'

'They think Euzma had a spell put on it, so almost none of them will come up here,' said Rory. 'Some of the local talent came up, once, not long after we arrived, with some fancy ideas. They liked waving their AKs around. But we soon put a stop to that little plan.'

'We can' – Josh enjoyed saying it – 'look after ourselves.'

They spoke across each other in the way that old friends do. Oliver fitted easily into their little group. There was a plaster on his neck, Casey saw.

'We got used to living here.' Rory's diesel voice. 'Having a laugh. It'll be a bit hot for the next few months, but compared to winter in Europe, it's fucking nice.'

Casey felt Rory's eyes on her again, and didn't look up.

'Tell me about it,' Oliver interrupted. 'I can't stand London in January.'

'When you can't even remember how sunshine feels,' said Casey. 'It's just the worst.'

'Then the next job came in,' Leo carried on, and Casey wondered how it worked exactly, that network. 'Down in Nigeria, out on the Delta. One of the oil companies needed some of the locals kept an eye on. We knew it would be a couple of months, but we decided we wanted to come back here afterwards, when it was done.'

'So we pulled in some of those Tuareg guys you met earlier,' said Josh. 'They're from a settlement not too far away. They've got the whole area under their thumb, really, but, even so, they didn't want Euzma. We asked them to keep things going.'

'It's too far from the road for them, they say.' Rory raised an eyebrow. 'But I think even they believe in the curse. Mad, the lot of them.'

'They were cool with us being up here though,' said Leo. 'They've got their own operations, anyway. Moving stuff across the desert. It's amazing how much action there is round here, for such an empty dustbowl.'

'So now we come and go,' said Rory. 'A few months here, a few months there. Then we come back to Euzma, hang out a bit. The Tuareg keep an eye on it when we're away, and so does Abayghur.'

'We pay the Tuareg enough to make it worth us coming back,' said Leo. 'Alive.'

'There's a huge diesel generator in one of the outhouses, and we can tap a spur from the Great Manmade River for water,' Rory went on.

The Great Manmade River was one of Gaddafi's wilder dreams that came real. At a cost, of course. A huge series of pipes and a vast aquifer, plumbing the whole of Libya. They had passed the huge irrigation circles as they drove up, the enormous waterwheels dripping endlessly into the big green whorls. An ecological nightmare that would last until the aquifer ran dry.

Rory tugged the conversation on to Gaddafi, and his wilder plans. Casey sat and wondered how long it would be until she could circle the conversation. But then Oliver asked, and she didn't have to use up one of her cards: 'How much time do you spend out here?'

'It varies.' Rory ducked the question. 'We keep busy though.'

'And then the London operation got started.' Josh nodded at them. 'And that seems to be working well.'

It was so casual that Casey could hardly bear it. Ed stroked her hair, just for a moment.

'I think Tripoli has more or less forgotten this place exists,' said Josh. 'Gaddafi barely spent any time out here, once it was built. He was always having these mad plans, and then going on to the next thing.'

Casey had seen that despot's madness before, wandering around his palaces in Tripoli. She had spent long afternoons lost in the lunatic warrens beneath the palaces, and seen the endless nuclear bunkers hollowed out on the orders of a psychopath. There was a hospital down there, under the Tripoli pavements, and enough food and water to keep the Gaddafis going for years. Euzma was just a part of the madness.

'This part has always only ever been loosely controlled from Tripoli,' Rory went on. 'Gaddafi managed to dominate the tribes, more or less, but it was never completely under his rule.'

'They've got enough problems to keep them going up in Tripoli anyway, surely,' Oliver remarked. 'They've been trying to put together a government for the last few months, I think. Although they've been trying that for years now.'

Casey thought about the former defence minister, toiling to stick together a deal for Cormium, for all the Libyan oil.

'Exactly,' Leo nodded. 'It won't last for ever, us in this place. But it's here for now.'

'And we keep our cash safely out of this country, of course,' Rory added. 'No one would bring anything into Libya at the moment.'

'It must have been weird for the Gaddafis, driving past this place,' Casey thought out loud. 'Knowing all this was up here, just out of reach.'

'They could have defended this place for a while. There are some fortifications,' said Josh. 'But not for ever.'

'You can't defend anywhere for ever,' said Ed.

Casey thought about the Gaddafis, and their convoy racing past, not even pausing at their dream palace, the folly never used. Abayghur snapped her back into the room, bringing delicious food; lamb tagine, flatbreads, spice. He was deaf, Casey realised quite soon. At least partially. Helpful.

They ate for a while, before Casey and Ed yawned their excuses.

Josh walked with them as they headed back to their room. Just before they reached the huge entrance hall, he stepped into a large room off to one side. It was a vast suite, with two bedrooms leading off it.

'Our study,' he mocked. 'That's my bedroom there, and Rory's in there. If you need anything at night or whatever.'

The double doors to Rory's room were closed. Josh's room was huge. Casey could see a vast unmade bed on a dais under a lead crystal chandelier. Clothes were scattered, careless, on Chippendale chairs. A foxglove-purple chaise longue sat under the window, and a vast onyx lion crouched in a corner.

Josh tapped a laptop and then walked back to them, grimacing.

'There's going to be a bit of a dust storm kicking up tomorrow,' he said. 'It'll knacker the visibility. I was going to suggest that Oliver could go tomorrow and you the next day, but I think we'll have to push it back a day. Shooting distances with any sort of wind is a nightmare.'

'No worries.' Ed sounded like he was discussing a minor inconvenience. 'We can just hang out for the day.'

Ed was good at this, thought Casey. You never really knew beforehand.

'There's lots to do. I can take you up there, anyway,' Josh offered. 'So you can get the lie of the land. When was the last time you shot, anyway? You could have a practice.'

'Sounds ideal,' said Ed.

'And you wanted to see the cave art, didn't you, darling?' bubbled Casey.

'I don't know much about it,' nodded Josh, 'but we went up there once. I could draw you a map.'

'That would be really helpful,' Casey agreed.

'Is there anything else I can get you?'

'Think we just need to crash out,' said Ed. 'Been a long day.'

The moment they were back in their room, Casey stopped the recording. Their phones were encrypted, of course, but there wasn't enough signal for data out in the desert. Even though she couldn't be sure about the sophistication of the surveillance installed at Euzma, there was an almost primitive urge to file. She needed to get the story back to London if it killed her, where it couldn't be silenced.

Casey had brought a BGAN – the Broadband Global Area Network, as they were known more grandly – to send back footage. The size of a laptop, the only thing they needed was a direct line of sight to the satellite. She opened the windows wide, pointed the little transmitter at the sky. Silently, invisibly, the recording winged away, and, just for a moment, she felt free.

30

Hessa was waiting back in London. As soon as the file dropped, she sent Casey a quick answer: I am here, I hear you. Be safe. She saved the file, and made a backup copy, then tapped out a quick note to Miranda, waiting nervously in Djanet, and set to transcribing.

It was late now, and it wouldn't matter if she waited until tomorrow to decipher this conversation, but Hessa wanted it to be perfect, wanted the memo to be waiting for Dash when he came in first thing.

'Hessa,' Miranda had said, that day in Dash's office. 'I'm going to take you through a few things.'

They had paused then, for a few seconds, and Hessa had seen the quick glances between them.

'Hessa,' asked Dash too casually. 'Do you have any friends or family in Libya? Or Algeria?'

'No, boss. My family is from Bangladesh. Sylhet.'

Just a few thousand miles apart, and a completely different continent. It didn't annoy Hessa that sort of thing; not really. She had worked at the *Post* for just under a year, coming in on one of the diversity programmes that the paper ran, half-heartedly. A sticking plaster over the fact that the place was managed almost entirely by white men in their forties. But she'd seen the first step on the ladder, and didn't care why it was there. She had known, just as soon as she walked in, that the *Post* was the place for her. Even if the *Post* hadn't realised it yet.

Her father didn't like it, not at all. He didn't see why she needed to work in this place that took up all her time and left her too tired to help her mother. Her mother nodded along, baffled by her eldest daughter. Why couldn't she mind her auntie's shop, just down Brick Lane? It was right near their flat. A nice job, if she wanted one.

The family lived in a council flat, just off Chicksand Street, where the Bengalis were being edged out by people like Casey. Their flat – nice; too small for a family of six – was near the mosque that had been a synagogue that had been a church, once. At the weekend, Hessa looked out of the window, at the crowds on Brick Lane, and thought about stories, and dreamed.

She was shy around Miranda and Casey though – lots of the junior reporters were. But one day she heard them talking by the chocolate machine. Twixes for both, she knew without asking. They were trying to work out how to get in somewhere. They didn't say where out loud; they were always cautious, those two.

'You could wear the veil,' Hessa said quietly. 'The full niqab. You're invisible in that, you can go in anywhere. No one ever looks twice, not now. And they don't want to talk to you, so they don't stop you. I could pick you some up tomorrow morning, at the market on Whitechapel. If you wanted.'

She watched them startle at her voice, and then sharpen in on the idea.

'Interesting thought ...' Casey said.

'Hessa,' she filled in quickly.

'Hessa,' said Miranda.

They smiled vaguely, collected their Twixes and wandered off, heads together.

So Hessa was wobbling with excitement when they called her into Dash's office. She could feel the laser jealousy from the other junior journalists. She was going into the room of secrets.

The three of them had talked at her, rapidly, unemotionally, and then given her time to process, turning away to talk about flights and packing and dangers. It all sounded totally batshit, to Hessa. Then Miranda had turned back to her. 'You'll have to keep completely quiet about all this, Hessa. You understand that, don't you? It's absolutely critical.'

She felt Dash's eyes fix on her, fierce.

'I understand,' Hessa muttered. 'I promise.'

She listened now to the sound file that Casey had sent through from somewhere out in the desert, skin prickling. The other reporters moaned about transcribing, hating the tedium of going backwards and forwards over every word, but Hessa didn't mind. She liked listening to the senior reporters leading up to a question. Sometimes, when she finally heard the key bit of information, she would listen back, tracking the meandering path to the question that cracked open the nut.

And when it was a recording like this ...

The clock ticked round. Hessa had finished her memo now, checking it two, three, four times. It needed to be just right for Dash.

The other reporters had gone to the pub, the one opposite that the *Post* emptied into most nights. The Plumbers; all the best anecdotes started in the Plumbers.

'Two glasses of the white wine there and you wake up feeling like you've been hit round the head with a shovel,' the transport correspondent had warned her. 'It's eye-bleedingly awful.'

Hessa didn't drink.

The gaggle of reporters had lobbed her an invitation as they left, two hours ago, so casual and so precious.

Now Hessa shut down her computer, and geared herself up. She'd go for one drink, try to make friends, blend in.

They welcomed her as she walked over to their table, clutching a lemonade. They were four drinks in, and raucous.

'Go on, Hess,' said Eric. 'What are you working on?'

'Give us a clue,' they chorused.

Just for a second, she hesitated. She had known this was what they wanted, for that casual invitation. They'd seen her called in, a few days ago. They wanted to know. Journalists have to be the ones to know, and tell. The currency of knowledge is everything.

'Tell them you're superstitious about talking about stories,' Miranda had said. 'That's what I say. That you're worried it will fall apart if you say anything.'

'Not to sound melodramatic or anything,' she'd added. 'But it really is a matter of life and death. You could always say it's a very boring data project. That it'll take ages.'

In the pub, Hessa looked round the table. She wanted so badly to fit in with them, and their pints and their piercings.

'Tell us, Hess,' Eric persisted.

She opened her mouth, closed it again.

'It's a really boring data project,' she said. 'And it's going to take for ever.'

They grumbled, not quite sure if she was lying. But they were still friendly, and she felt herself breathe. The education correspondent pulled up a stool, told her a joke that made her blush, caught her up on the gossip.

There she sat, in the cosy circle of hacks, safe in the fustiness of the Plumbers, and thought about Casey, out in that wild desert darkness.

In the palatial en suite, Casey was taking as long as possible. She had packed and unpacked pyjamas back in her flat, settling on blue stripey cotton, boyish and invisible.

Ed was lying on the bed when she finally emerged. He had pushed a wedge under the door, the quickest way to change a flimsy door into a challenge.

Casey lay down on the bed.

'OK?' He didn't look up from his book. He was always reading. She remembered the Marines on the *Apollo* laughing about it, suspiciously.

The linen rustled.

'Night, Carrie.'

'Night.'

He switched off the light, and she felt him turn over, and away from her.

He seemed to fall asleep in seconds, and Casey lay in the dark, sleep unimaginable. It was so quiet, deathly quiet. The moonlight glowed through the curtains. She could feel Ed warm beside her. Just a few inches between them, and an endless emptiness. She thought of the refugees, out in the camp. Packed in a tent, surrounded by nothing. A baby crying in the dark. The smell of smoke. Unanswered prayers, like a curse.

Finally, hours later, she fell asleep.

*

The screaming seemed to fill the room, desperation flooding everywhere like lava. Terror blazed through Casey as she struggled awake.

Ed was rigid, shuddering, fear ripping through his body.

'Ed!' She edged towards him, trying to push away the horror. 'Ed!'

He half woke, rose, threw her away from him and pounced, hands to her neck, choking, suffocating, killing.

'Ed.' She fought for breath. 'It's me ... It's Casey.'

It seemed endless. Hands scrabbling and the darkness coming. He was so strong ... Too strong ...

'Ed,' the last gasp. 'It's me. Stop ... Please ...'

And she saw awareness flood his eyes, as he woke to a new nightmare. His hands fell and he flung himself away.

'Ed ...' She was gasping, breathless.

He was sitting at the edge of the bed, head in his hands.

'It's OK, Ed.'

He flinched as she put her hand on his shoulder. He was hot to the touch, still shaking.

'It's going to be all right.' Her voice echoed round the marble room.

'I'm so sorry.' He turned to her, eyes desperate in the moonlight. 'Did I hurt you? I am so sorry.'

'I'm fine.' Casey hoped that her neck would not bruise overnight. 'It was just a dream. It doesn't matter. It's OK.'

'No.' He was distraught. 'I hurt you ... Sorry ... I am so sorry ...' His voice trailed into silence.

'Lie down again.' Casey tried to pull him back to the bed.

'No. No.' He stood up, switched on a light. 'I can sleep on that sofa.'

She couldn't stop him, as he found a sheet and pillows in a cupboard.

'Not very comfortable there.' She looked at the thin velvet cushions of the mermaid sofa.

'It'll be fine.'

He lay down, feet curled up to fit.

'Ed ... It might help ... if you told me about it.'

But the light clicked off and the room sank into darkness, the distance unbridgeable.

The wind outside was beginning to keen, raising the dust that would block out the light. Casey almost smiled, just for a second, that she, the girl who could get any secret from anyone, had fallen for someone locked away, and so impossibly distant.

She was inspecting her throat the next morning when he followed her into the bathroom.

'I am so very sorry. It was unforgivable.'

'Please stop apologising.'

Her neck was bruised. She covered it with foundation, avoiding his eyes.

He came closer, framed behind her in the huge gold mirror.

'You said your real name last night,' he whispered.

'I know. I didn't have a whole lot of choice.' Their eyes met in the mirror. A smile. Better.

The dust was blowing wild djinns outside, reducing visibility to just a few hundred yards. The roiling dust confused the eyes and choked the throat.

They had let themselves sleep in, both exhausted. Oliver was already at breakfast, three places set at a table for twenty-four.

'Morning, you two,' he winked at them. 'Sleep well?'

'Blissful, thanks.' Casey took her place at the table.

They were crunching toast when Josh appeared.

'The visibility is buggered.' He poured a coffee. 'Hopefully, it should have blown through by this afternoon though. In the meantime, Ed, you and Carrie could head up to the caves? I drew you a map.' He pushed it along the table to them.

'Thanks, mate.' Ed took the map, studied it. It could help if these men were used to them heading off on random little expeditions.

'And I'll drive you up to Salama,' Josh went on, 'when you're back. It's only about twenty minutes up there. No harm in doing a recce.'

'I'd like to practise with the rifle.' Oliver spooned up yogurt. 'Even though the weather is a mess. Haven't shot for a few weeks. Don't want to get rusty.'

'Where did you learn?' Casey asked.

'There's a place out to the west in Wales,' said Oliver. 'Never stops bloody raining, but there's not a lot else out there, so you can practise shooting those long distances. There's another place up in the Highlands, and I went for a sort of crash course in Dubai, out in the desert there.'

'Sounds cool,' Casey nodded. She wondered if Dubai or Wales had pointed Oliver towards Libya.

'How about you, Ed?'

Casey felt herself tense. They had rehearsed this question, back in the car. She needed to be able to ask questions, and find out patterns. But that meant Ed needed to reciprocate, smoothly.

'Same sort of thing,' Ed said. 'But mainly up in Scotland, at my uncle's estate. They do a lot of stalking up there. Deer, of course. And I gradually upgraded to sniper rifles.'

'Rains even more up in bloody Scotland,' Oliver nodded. 'Do you shoot, Carrie?'

He had got into the habit of smirking at her, almost conspiratorial. She forced herself to grin back.

'No,' she said carelessly.

For a second, she caught Ed's eye, with a tiny smile. He had taught her to shoot, a little Sig Sauer off the back of the *Apollo*. The Marines had been having a training session, and Casey had been bored.

There was nothing for miles around, out in the Indian Ocean, so they shot off the flight deck, at paper humans, bullets splashing into the sea.

It had been more fun than Casey cared to admit.

'The great outdoors isn't Carrie's thing, exactly,' Ed chimed in, to cover her smile.

They finished breakfast and escaped, back along the *Marie Celeste* corridors. Then, clutching their leaflets, they headed out to the Hilux.

Halfway down the cypress avenue, a little road ran off to the left, winding its way up into the red hills. Josh had told them where to park.

'At the big rock that looks like a goat,' he'd said, pouring honey over some yogurt. 'I put a splash of blue paint on it, but keep an eye out, because that little road runs for miles out there. Comes out on the main road most of the way back to Ghat.'

They parked the car and started the climb, the path twisting up the hill. As they walked, Ed told Casey about Tadrart Acacus, the Acacus mountains.

Tiny drawings, dancing brave. Giraffe, camels, elephants decorated the cave walls in the mountains above Ghat. Casey liked listening to him speak.

At Tadrart Acacus, Ed went on, the art survived ten thousand years. And then met a very modern destruction. The Salafists arrived, armed here only with white spirit, and hammers. As determined, in their own way, as the Taliban at Bamiyan, or ISIS at Palmyra.

'Why does it shock us so much?' Casey asked. 'That urge to destroy?'

She was out of breath, and stopped to glory in the sun. They had reached the mouth of the cave, high up in the hills above Euzma. The desert plain stretched out before them, nothing but cobras and scorpions and a million ways to die.

She yawned, and turned to look back to the car. The path wound down, twisting through the rocks. Her eye followed it lazily.

And she saw it.

A flicker. A glint. A tiny movement, that shouldn't have been there. Only for a slice of a second. A gleam in her eye, and then gone.

It was enough. A shudder ran down her spine.

Rory. She knew, at once. Rory, who would take nothing on trust. Who would never tire, and never give up. And never believe his own eyes. Prowling in their wake, waiting and watching, and baiting and catching.

Breathe, she thought. Breathe.

The death zone. It kills you, just being up there.

And no one would ever know.

Her mind flurried. How would they look, to Rory ... The young pretty couple, locked in their world, smiling into the desert. Was this how it ended?

She turned to Ed, hugged him close. 'Careful.'

He understood at once. Took her hand, and led her towards the cave.

'Look at this' – and the calm of his voice steadied her, for a moment.

Beyond its mouth, the cave opened up to a huge cavity. The scale was surprising, like the backstage of a theatre. Fragments of light tumbled in. Casey tilted her head back, looking for bats. Here and there, tunnels ran away, disappearing into the dark.

Ed took a step, and wrapped her in his arms. As they wandered round the cave, she felt her heartbeat slow to his pace.

Breathe, Casey, breathe.

Ed made her concentrate. This cave had been ignored by the special madness of the twenty-first century, only scraps of graffiti here, a name chiselled in the rock there. Hands intertwined, they peered at the paintings, Ed pointing out one, then the next.

They glanced into the tunnels that narrowed away from the main cave.

All the time, Casey could feel Rory, hidden from sight. Watching her, hunting her, wanting her. She watched for shadows on the wall of the cave.

Who are you? Tell me who you are.

'You're OK,' Ed said, so firmly she almost believed him.

And she expected Rory to appear, any second, blotting out the light. The caves were bait, she realised suddenly. No coincidence, those leaflets on the coffee table. And ignoring the bait might have been enough for deadly suspicions.

Everything, a trap.

So slowly, Ed walked them back to the entrance, glanced around. Rory was nowhere to be seen. They stood in the sun, side by side. Ed pulled her to him, looking down into her eyes, and kissed her, quite suddenly, so that she lost all her thoughts. And then stopped and smiled again. 'You're OK.'

They hesitated. A small path ran towards the top of the cliff, high above the cave entrance, and Ed began to climb. Casey followed, slipping in her flip-flops. They climbed, pausing casually to look at the view. Rory could not follow them here, not without being seen.

Because maybe that was all he wanted. To be glimpsed in the corner of her eye.

You won't survive, if I don't believe. And there will be no mercy.

Be brave, she thought, and learn his mind.

At the top, they found the rocky lookout point. Ed sat down, back against the rock, and she curled herself into his side. A beautiful couple, on a strange sort of holiday. Believe what you see, Rory. Believe your eyes.

'It's stunning up here,' said Ed, in her ear. 'And yet, God, I can't wait to get away.'

'I know.' Casey tried too. 'So many beautiful places in the world, and when I think of them, I feel only fear.'

She ticked off war zones like a Japanese tourist with the *Mona Lisa*. But there was a strange sort of joy too, even now. I'm here, I'm really here. Even with Rory in the shadows.

'We've got almost everything we need, don't we?' Ed was whispering in her ear. 'We've got them on tape. We can get out of here soon, can't we?'

Casey let the silence drift. She could use this solitude. Needed it, even.

For a second, she saw their silhouettes through Rory's eyes.

'Ed,' she said. 'We aren't going to be able to run this story based on hearsay.'

He digested this.

'What do you mean?'

'I mean that we're not going to be able to do this story on the basis of a few guys chatting about something terrible. It's too easy for their lawyers to pull it apart, to say they were only joking, or fantasising, or spinning us a line. And we would never be able to prove that it wasn't a lie, especially with Milo dead.'

'But they've said ... They've said it over and over again.'

'I know,' she faltered, just for a second. 'But we need real evidence.'

'What do you mean?' His voice was hard. 'Real evidence?'

'I mean' – she steadied her voice – 'that we will have to go up there, to Salama, and see what they do.'

'See what they do ...' A long pause. 'You mean, see them shoot someone? We're actually going to watch Selby fire a gun into the camp?'

She felt him push her away. He stood up, took a few steps.

'Yes,' said Casey, so there was no going back. 'That is what I mean.'

A wild dust devil blew across the desert. She watched it twisting and twirling, spiralling and coiling.

Far below them, the cave gaped, and just for a second her mind lurched. You've got to go into the cave, to know. You go into the dark, to find the monsters. That's what they said. *That's what they said.*

'We can't watch that.' Ed broke through. 'We can't watch him kill someone, and say nothing. We can't not try to stop him.'

He was edging away from her.

'We have to.' Casey rose and followed him, with casual steps, her voice a whisper. 'That's what we're here to do. To see it, and write it down, and make it real. And then go home and tell everyone, and make it stop. It's what I do.'

'Someone will die.' Ed turned back to face her, his voice low and urgent. 'That's more important than any story. That's a human being, Casey. That's a life. That's somebody else's story.'

'I know,' said Casey. 'I know.'

She stepped away from him, pulled out her camera, took deliberate photographs of the view.

'And you knew all along.' He was angry now, only just hiding it. 'You and Miranda knew every single step of the way. And you let me believe ... You got me out here, to spring it on me like this, up by some cave, so I don't have a choice ... You played me like you play everyone else.'

The dust devil was fading now, dying against the blue of the sky.

'I'm sorry,' she said, pointless little words people use like a charm. 'I'm sorry.'

She stepped up to him, put her arms round his neck. He was rigid, almost pulling away from her.

'And you're even using Rory, aren't you?' He put his mouth right next to her ear. 'Because you know I can't walk away from you, not with him watching. I can't escape you, up here.'

'No,' meaning yes.

He arched his head away from her, watching her as if he had never known her at all.

'We can't do this.' Ed's words were abrupt. 'Tomorrow, Oliver will go up to those hills, and lie down on the ground. And then he will look through those sights and kill someone. And you know that, and you're not doing anything to stop it. We can't let it happen, Casey. We can't. It's wrong.'

She let him go, turned to the view, hating the feel of his eyes on her.

'They would do it whether we were here or not.' The wind whisked her words away. 'The only difference is that this time, we will be there to see it. To witness it. We can make this the very last time.'

With her back to him, she smiled as she spoke, an empty smile to satisfy Rory, wherever he was.

'But this person' – Ed was pleading now – 'whoever they are, is out there in that camp right now. This person we will never even meet. They're walking around the camp, smiling at friends, and wondering about tomorrow. We can save this one person.'

'Miranda went out to cover the last big famine,' said Casey, still smiling out at the desert. 'She was out in Kenya, as the people were pouring over the border from Somalia. They hadn't eaten for weeks, those people. Miranda told me how she watched a baby dying, and made damn sure the photographer got the shot. I saw that photograph. The tiny baby with the huge eyes and the huge stomach, and almost nothing else. That baby died right there, and then Miranda and the snapper went to get lunch. And people cried over that photograph, and sent millions to charity. But, out there, in the middle of nowhere in Kenya, Miranda had to eat her lunch. Because otherwise, she couldn't do the job. We're observers, Ed. That's what we do.'

'But we're not just observers, are we?' Ed's voice was quite cold. 'You go in and say things and do things and be things, and people respond. You and Miranda, you don't just watch, do you? It's not that simple.'

'No,' said Casey. 'It's never that simple.'

You're an agent provocateur, the office lech had said once, rubbing his hands. She flinched at the memory.

'We can't just watch this happen,' said Ed. 'No one can just watch this sort of thing. We can't be complicit. It isn't human.'

'It is, though,' said Casey 'isn't it? And we have no other way. I know this, Ed. You have to trust me.'

'How far can you walk in another man's shoes,' said Ed slowly, 'before you walk with his stride? And where does it end? When I hit Isa ... It changes you, every move, and I don't think I believe in your cause, Casey.'

They stood silently in the wind. I never wanted to hurt you, she thought. And you'll never believe that, now.

'We're not going to stop it, are we?'

'We are not going to stop it tomorrow. But afterwards ... Afterwards, we are going to stop it for ever. Or try, at least.'

'I can't let you do this,' he said. 'I can't be a part of this.'

He turned away.

She couldn't be sure that he would walk up there tomorrow. Walk alongside her, and soldier the horror. She didn't know.

He swung away from her, now, walking back down to the cave, and its tiny ancient drawings. Casey watched him go, still smiling calmly. Then she sat down, against the rock, and pulled out a novel.

She waited a long time, turning the pages in the sun, and at last he emerged from the cave. Walked up the hill to where she sat, and paused. He stood beside her, half turned away.

'Shall we head back to Euzma?' she asked.

He nodded.

There was no sign of Rory as they walked back down the track. At the mouth of the cave, so that it would look like a mistake, she dropped a scarf into a crevice in the rock, one she had bought in the souk in Djanet. It lay, caught between the rocks, white embroidered with blue.

One more glance at the desert, and they climbed down the hillside, back to the steady old Hilux. The wind was falling now, just the occasional drift of sand twirling across the landscape. The heat was stifling, and Casey's shirt was glued to her back.

They climbed into the car, and drove back to the white palace in silence.

31

Oliver and Josh were waiting for them next to the huge bronze fist.

'Hey,' Oliver waved. 'We're going up to the rocks. A recce to see the camp.'

Selby's eyes rested on her for a moment. There was no choice. They piled into Josh's pickup, and headed down the drive, back past the cypress skeletons. From nowhere, the Tuareg fell in behind, their secret shadows.

'On your left' – Josh put on a tour guide's tone – 'is the little track up to the cave. I trust you enjoyed your expedition, Ed and Carrie?'

'Five stars,' Casey somehow managed to joke. 'I would highly recommend it to other travellers.'

'We're thrilled you enjoyed your trip,' Josh laughed at her. 'And thank you for all the positive feedback.'

In another world, he would be attractive, thought Casey. With his big sudden smile and knowing eyes.

Ed was still silent, and Casey filled the silence with giggles.

The pickup purred expensively down the avenue, making nothing of the potholes. As they were pulling out on to the main road, an open-topped truck hurtled past, so many people on board that it was almost invisible. Sacks and bags were tied on like fenders. Men and women and children clung on as the truck shot down the road. With their faces wrapped in rags to protect them from the sun, Casey saw a blur, not people.

'There they go, another few dozen,' Josh waved. 'Off to make it out of Africa, or die trying. Most likely die.'

He turned on to the road, following the truck east.

'What happens to them?' asked Casey airily.

'Bad stuff,' said Josh. 'All the time. Last year, a couple of trucks headed off out of Arlit, in Niger. They got a hundred miles north, up towards Tamanrasset, right down the southern end of Algeria. Then one of the trucks conked out. So the second one turns round, heads back to Arlit, to get a spare part or something. That one gets forty miles back towards Arlit, before it flatlines too. They found them scattered about, over quite a wide area. A few under trees. Some out in the sun. Some had been eaten by jackals. They were in groups, mainly. But there were a few kids out there too, on their own. Ninety-two dead.'

'God.' Ed had forgotten himself. 'My God.'

'A few of them made it all the way back to Arlit,' Josh added. 'Which was fucking hardcore by them. Some of them even got as far as Tamanrasset, fuck knows how. And that lot got sent straight back to Niger anyway.'

The pickup had effortlessly caught up with the truck. A small girl, maybe seven years old, was clinging on at the back. She was wearing a purple vest and pink trousers, hair whipped to wildness by the wind. Hungry eyes, and skin, and bone.

Where am I? Why am I here?

The little girl waved at Casey, from some forgotten habit.

'Snakes and ladders.' Casey waved back.

'Mostly snakes out here,' said Josh. 'The West sees those pictures, of the boats in the Med, and they think that is the worst. But that's just the bit they see, and they don't see much of that. And it's not even the worst part of that journey. No one knows how many the Sahara takes.'

'Survival of the fittest,' said Oliver briskly.

'Quite.' Casey's laugh almost broke.

'Why do they go then?' Oliver asked, sounding cross. 'Why don't they just bloody stay where they started? Where they belong.'

'They can't really.' Josh waved at the dust still in the air. 'The Sahara gets bigger and bigger every year, nibbling away at the surroundings. Back in the sixties, there were two dust storms a year in Mauritania. Now there are eighty a year. Eighty. You can't grow a thing any more. There's nothing left down in these countries. They literally just have dust. The people have to leave. It's not a choice.'

His voice was practical.

Casey felt her heart skip as Josh skidded the car to the right, heading back towards the mountains. Here, the red sandstone rose up sharply, the track picking its way up through huge jagged rocks.

'The main entrance to Salama is further along the main road,' Josh explained. 'This is the back route up to the hills around the camp. Salama started in a sort of valley, with mountains on three sides, and then sprawled.'

He slowed to drive up a steep path. The wind had dropped now, dust settling. There was still a haze in the sky, a smear against the sun.

'There was an oasis here, which is probably why the camp started,' Josh went on. 'It must have been quite nice, once.'

'They've always based themselves round the oases, haven't they?' Ed was staring out of the window. 'The people of the Sahara.'

'You'd think the old caravan trails would be straight,' agreed Josh. 'From point A to point B, like the borders. But of course, they're not, because they had to go from one oasis to another. And if something went wrong with an oasis, and you were days and days from any other water, it was a disaster. The end, really. They used to fight to the death for control of an oasis.'

Casey thought of one oasis after another, strung out like pearls on a long and delicate necklace. The Bedouins risked it all to trade the ebony and the salt, the ivory and the ostrich plumes. People died to traffic ostrich plumes? Yes. Yes, they did. Gold for salt. And a little bit later, God made his way down the very same routes.

And slaves too, of course, millions and millions of them.

'Do you see the swallows?' she asked. 'In the spring and the autumn.'

'Sure.' Josh spun the wheel to avoid a rock. 'They fly hundreds of miles a day, the swallows, from one oasis to another. All the way from England to Africa in a couple of weeks. That's how the plants appear around the water in the first place, of course. Bird shit.'

They climbed and climbed, the pickup's engine churning. Finally, Josh slowed. He parked the car, and gestured for them to follow him.

It was a narrow track, barely used. They walked, kicking up dust, and dodging round boulders before, quite suddenly, Salama opened up beneath them. The ground fell away sharply from where they were standing, in almost a sheer drop. For a second, Casey felt like a kestrel, turning idle in the breeze, and searching for the kill.

From the rocks, hundreds of feet above, the camp looked almost endless. Rows of tents sprawled into the distance. Dwarfed by the cliffs, these tents were tattered now, bleached by the sun.

Down below them, larger buildings interspersed the tents. In among the maze of paths, people had built shacks of corrugated iron and wood, tarpaulin and anything. Pallets were everywhere. Because even pallets are precious, out here.

It was oddly colourful, the camp. Some people had run up shreds of flags, brave against the sky. Scraps of garden had been scratched from the dirt. The big blue United Nations logo blew in the wind.

A scruffy fence ran round the camp, a rambling barbed-wire barricade. Here and there, Casey could see a few tiny people. Some striding with purpose, others just sitting, staring. Children were playing a haphazard game that might be tag.

It always surprised her, the size of the tents. So small, for a family of seven or eight. The sleeping mats rolled up in the corner during the day, so neatly. And not always enough blankets, for the cold Sahara night.

Casey remembered an aid worker, at Zaatari, crying over a simple question from one of the Syrians.

'How?' a mother had asked. 'How do I decide which of my children to keep warm? Please tell me. How do I decide?'

I am Malak.

'It's about five hundred metres to the camp from here.' Josh was efficient. 'People gather around that building there at this time of day, can you see? The one with the big mural down the side.'

The distances would matter for the calculations. Casey concentrated on the mural, of a smiling Tuareg child holding a huge bunch of pink flowers. No one in this camp could ever have seen a bunch of pink tulips, not in real life.

'I see.' Oliver squinted in the light. 'No problem.'

He lay down on the ground.

'There are lots of possible viewpoints, because of the hills,' Josh waved round the shallow bowl. 'Lots of angles. We haven't been to this one for a while. We need to go for somewhere right at the edge of the camp, of course, because otherwise they'd hear the bang as the bullet went overhead. It creates a sort of supersonic crack, might arouse suspicions. But, as you can see, it's a big camp. There are plenty of places. We never go to the same place more than once a year, twice at the outside.'

'How many people have come out here?' Casey asked carefully. 'With you.'

'Thirty? Forty? Something like that.'

'And don't people notice the refugees being shot?' Casey made it a joke. 'The corpses lying around?'

'Sure they do. But there are guns all over this camp, so no one wonders too much about a stray bullet. They make a mess, the big-calibre bullets, but it's not like they're doing post-mortems out here. And what are they going to do about it? It's not like they can call in the cops anyway.'

'I didn't know they were allowed guns in the camps,' said Oliver.

'They're not. But they're moody fuckers in these camps, and properly tooled up, some of them. There's a lot of organised crime there, and the traffickers control the area, really. Just because they're refugees doesn't make them nice people, you know. They're fucking human. The NGOs started bringing in caravans, quite decent ones, down from the Gulf states. The aid worker in charge of assigning them, he needs an armed guard just to move around Salama. It's fucking dangerous in there. And there are riots all the time, over food and fuck knows what.'

From a kestrel distance, the camp looked peaceful.

They got back into the car, and drove along to the next point. This was where Ed would come a day after Oliver, and they went through the routine, again.

'It's just easier if you focus on a building they need to come to,' said Josh. 'You'd wait near a watering hole when you're hunting.'

'Sure,' agreed Ed.

'That's one of the big water tanks,' Josh gestured. 'People come here all day every day, with their big buckets. They pick up their bread from somewhere else.'

'Makes it straightforward,' said Oliver.

'What,' asked Casey, 'is the building with the big mural?'

'That one,' said Josh, 'is a school.'

32

They climbed back into the car, U-turned sharply and headed back down the hill. The Tuareg stamped out their cigarettes and followed.

'I see how you do it now,' said Casey.

'It's pretty straightforward,' Josh shrugged.

She gestured to the Tuareg.

'Don't they mind?'

'They don't give a shit,' Josh said. 'They're the most ruthless fuckers of the lot, those boys. Their gang has got a new trick, as they traffic people through Libya. They work out which of the refugees have friends or relatives in Europe. Because a lot of them do, you know. Then they grab them, force them to ring their family and torture them as they call. So all the family can hear is a lot of screaming and a power drill. And if it's your sister screaming, you wire through whatever the traffickers want.'

Casey winced.

'No,' Josh finished. 'That lot do not care what we get up to up at Salama. And that's what people vote for. Sending out the Navy to defend the Med. Sending them back to their deaths, while they tell themselves it's the right thing to do.'

He sounded almost angry. Oliver was quiet, looking out of the window, watching the shadows in the desert.

'How did you first come up with the idea?' Casey asked.

'The London operation came up with it.' Josh changed mood easily.

'And who,' Casey asked, 'is the London operation?'

He smiled at her, big hands steady on the wheel.

'The London operation is a lot jumpier than us,' he said. 'Paranoid, a bit. Stands to reason, though. I don't think Western police forces would appreciate us one little scrap.'

'But who ...' Casey persisted.

'They don't like us talking about them at all.' Josh shut her down. 'It's their one rule. Their only rule.'

Casey sighed loudly.

'I haven't even said you're out here,' Josh shrugged at her. 'London would go crazy.'

She would have to get it out of Oliver, when they got back to London. If they got back to London. Swap anonymity for secrets, it was always the way.

'So how did it all come about?'

'I've known our London buddy for a long time, one way and another. It was just a suggestion, came out of nowhere. I thought it was crazy, at first. Then a few days after we first spoke, me and Leo and Rory went down to Nigeria. You know, it was pretty dark what that company was getting up to out there. Sure, we're employed by a subsidiary of a subsidiary of a subsidiary, and we invoice for security, or whatever. But they know what we're doing. They know exactly what we're doing down there.'

'Which company?' Casey asked, almost in a reflex.

'She asks a lot of questions, your girl,' Josh said to Ed, still smiling. 'It doesn't matter which company. One of the biggest. So we went to Nigeria. Then the next job, that was a coltan mine, down in the DRC.'

'Right in the heart.'

'Exactly. Now coltan,' Josh went on, 'coltan's in everything electronic. Everything. But especially your mobile phone. And you do not want to know what we had to do to keep that mine ticking over. But we had to lay down a marker out there, so everyone, in all the little villages all around, knew: you do not go and fuck with that mine. I don't give a shit what else you get up to in the DRC, but you do not fuck with that mine. You leave it the fuck alone. Then we train up a few of the locals, to stay and guard. Teach them which way to point a gun. Although they all know from the cradle down there.'

Casey turned her phone over in her pocket, catching every word.

'Sounds a bit edgy.'

'It was.' Josh paused. 'Then next we went to keep an eye on a diamond mine, for a bit. Then bauxite, which they dig out and turn into aluminium. That mine was fucking horrendous.'

'They strip-mine those sites, don't they?' Casey said.

'Yeah, miles of earth ripped to shreds, everything gone, just for the top layer. So then the locals get even more fucked off, and now the company really needs us to come in and sort it out.'

They had reached the main road, now, turning left back towards Euzma. Algeria and safety lay hundreds of miles ahead of them, all the way down the long road.

'Sounds delightful,' said Casey.

She wondered if Oliver, Cormium's superstar, who bought and sold untold tons of bauxite every single day, was listening. He didn't seem to be. Oliver looked bored.

'So eventually, I got to thinking,' Josh went on, 'that basically everyone is doing this shit. Absolutely everyone. Every time they fill up their car, it's because of us kicking the shit out of some fucker out on the delta. When they take a call, they're using tantalum, which comes from coltan, which comes from some shithole out in the DRC. When they're down on their knee, proposing to some stupid bitch, they're using a blood diamond from God only knows where. And the girl's special dress is stitched together by some child in Bangladesh. And when they do their line of coke to celebrate, well, Christ knows what happens to get that to England. And, so I thought, fuck it. Fuck it. Everyone's doing it really; they just don't know it. So I called London, and they started sorting it out.'

'Cutting out the middleman.' Casey yawned, stretching.

'Exactly,' said Josh. 'Exactly. That, and I thought if I didn't do it, some other fucker would do it anyway.'

She could see the huge bronze fist now, in front of the palace, clutching ugly at the silver plane.

Josh waved at it.

'And that's just what these companies get up to when they're only using us. The UK was about to get everything started up again, in Libya, before it all went south once and for all. The whole country knew exactly what he got up to, Gaddafi. They just didn't give a shit. I can live with this. I'm OK.'

'I take your point,' Casey sparkled at him.

He jerked the car to a halt. As they climbed out, Oliver came alive.

'I can't believe I'm actually here. This is so fucking awesome. I can't wait.'

33

Almost before Casey was back in the bedroom, she was stopping the recording, sending it whirling back to London.

Hessa was waiting. She messaged Miranda: They're OK. Then she opened up the file, and started to transcribe.

In the *Post*'s offices, Hessa's desk was near the back bench, the row of desks where the subs pull together the copy, article by article. When the page layout is decided, the word counts are fixed. The subs go through each sentence, snipping every superfluous word.

Right now, the editor was standing by the back bench, tightening a headline.

There is an art to a good headline; the tabloids pride themselves on it especially. Up Yours, Delors. Gotcha. Freddie Starr Ate My Hamster.

As Hessa looked up, Dash was walking past. Hessa watched Salcombe watching Dash.

'Dash,' the editor called. 'We can't get the splash headline quite right.'

The splash headline sells the paper.

'By the way, where are Miranda and Casey at the moment?' The editor's voice was casual.

Hessa felt her head jerk, ever so slightly.

'They're just checking stuff for that big data project,' said Dash. 'And they're planning to take a couple of days off at the end of the week. Think they're a bit bored with that whole project, bloody divas.'

Hessa dropped her head, concentrating on her screen.

'Aaron,' the editor said to the sub. 'If you swap medical for health, we can do it in two lines.'

Dash turned away from the back bench.

'Dash,' Hessa said apologetically. 'There's a ...'

'Could you come into my office, Hessa?' Dash interrupted smoothly.

Back in Euzma, Ed took Casey in his arms, and held her, for a long time. It wasn't about sex, she knew. It was wanting to know that we're both here. If nothing else, I can touch you. We're real, you and I.

He wasn't agreeing over Salama, but they couldn't fight each other as well as everyone else. It was too much.

'You're doing that in case we die out here, aren't you?' he whispered. 'Sending back the recordings so they've got them, no matter what?'

'We're not going to die, Ed.' But she couldn't promise.

She put on the music again, sound pouring tinnily from the cheap speakers.

They lay on the bed, side by side.

'You start to believe it, don't you?' said Ed quietly. 'You listen to them talking and talking, and suddenly they start to make sense.'

'I was looking down at that camp,' said Casey. 'So many of those women, when they finally get to Europe, they're shoved into the worst brothels. Fed lies by the only people they trust. Trafficked across Europe and raped by a thousand men. Disappearing into that nightmare world, for ever. And they can't escape, or they'll be sent back here. You start to wonder whether someone might prefer just to die, out here. A quick bullet. Because we know where they're going. And maybe I'd rather be dead, than that.'

'It makes you insane, being out here,' said Ed. 'You would never think any of this at home.'

'I know.' Casey rolled over, face in the pillow. 'I know. It gets into your head, when you're living a lie. It always does somehow. You have to believe it, for it to be believable. And if you force yourself to believe for long enough, it starts being real.'

She jumped at a knock at the door.

'Who is it?' she called out. You never opened the door if you didn't know. Never went to the spyhole in a hotel either. Because someone could wait, gun ready, and fire when you blocked out the light.

'Bullet straight through the eye,' a former spook had told her, with a certain relish.

'It's Josh.'

Josh liked her, Casey thought, too much now. It was often a problem. You needed to be liked, flirted with and taken into the circle of trust. But that could so easily go too far.

'Take off your clothes,' she whispered to Ed. 'Go to the door, wrapped in a towel.'

He understood in a second, stripping off his clothes.

'All right, mate?' Ed opened the door, clutching a towel. 'We're ... A bit tied up.'

'Sure, buddy.' Casey could almost hear Josh wink. 'We'll be out on the terrace. Oliver wanted to do a bit of practice with the rifle. Thought you might too.'

'Awesome. Down in a bit.'

'Take your time.'

Ed turned back towards the bed, catching Casey admiring his chest. He raised an eyebrow at her, and she got the giggles. Laughing was almost unfamiliar.

'We've got to take our time now,' he said. 'I don't want them thinking I rush these things.'

Ed threw himself on the bed.

'This bed is amazing,' he said. 'Like sleeping on a cloud.'

They stared up at the ceiling together. The crystal chandelier sparkled dustily, sending flicks of light around the room.

'Fit for a princess,' said Casey. 'And not a pea to be seen. Sleep in it tonight. You can't be tired tomorrow, and I know you didn't sleep well on that sofa.'

'I'll try. And I am so sorry about all that, again.'

'Forget it.'

Ed chucked aside a pink satin cushion.

'It's such a weird contrast, isn't it? All this, just down the road from Salama.'

'That bit doesn't shock me any more,' said Casey. 'I used to find it bizarre. I remember interviewing migrants at Ventimiglia, down on the Mediterranean. This group of migrants stuck on the border between Italy and France, with nowhere to go. They were sleeping on the beach, under tarpaulins and driftwood and torn plastic bags. And I'd look up while we were speaking, and there was Monaco, just a few miles along the coast. The most expensive real estate in the world. And when you're out in

Mumbai, the slums run right up to the glitziest skyscrapers. Or there's Zaatari, where reporters aren't allowed to spend the night in the camp, so me and the snapper were staying in a five-star hotel in Amman. Even in London, we step over the homeless.'

'Juxtaposition,' said Ed. 'The ridiculously rich and the impossibly poor.'

'With smiling Jordanians bringing us breakfast in bed,' remembered Casey. 'You're looking at a gold tap in the bathroom – just a tap, with endless clean water – and thinking that would be the height of luxury, out in Zaatari. On our day off, the photographer and I would drive out to float in the Dead Sea for a bit, or climb up through Petra.'

'With the tourists all around.'

She'd flown back for a party, once. Straight from Tripoli to Cap Ferrat. Well, via Cairo and Stuttgart and Nice, because that was the quickest route. Body armour in her luggage.

'Why the body armour?' Suspicions at border control.

'Family wedding.' A smile and a shrug. They laughed and waved her through.

A taxi had taken her down the coast, heart stopping at every traffic light. Oh, not another checkpoint, every time the taxi braked. No, you're here, it's OK. You're safe in your borrowed dress. Dancing on the edge, and peering across the sea in the dawn. Dreaming, that night, that the corpses floated up and out and in.

'When you're laughing over a silly joke,' she said, 'it starts feeling wrong to laugh.'

She turned to him and hugged him, lying soft against his chest.

*

As they headed down to the terrace, the door to the suite was open. Casey paused.

'Don't, Casey.' Ed's hand was on her back, nudging her forward. 'Both of them ... Don't. It's too risky.'

'I won't be a second, Ed. Please. I have to. Wait round the corner. Shout, "Get a bloody move on, Carrie" if they're coming.'

'Casey ...' But he went.

Casey slipped into the room, with that surge of adrenalin that made every sense burn. She looked around the room carefully. No sign of a trap, she thought, but then nobody sees the best ambush.

She walked, spring-footed, to the desk. Her heart thudded.

Rory's desk was large, grand, topped in green leather. It didn't fit with the rest of the room; he must have dragged it from somewhere. A bust of a Roman emperor glowered down, incongruously disapproving.

Josh's room was chaos. But on his desk, Rory kept things neat.

Apart from a pile of magazines dedicated to motorbikes, this desk was almost empty.

On a shelf above the desk there was a stack of diaries – navy blue leather, year stamped in silver. Three years of them, a big page for every day. Far too many to photograph, page by page.

Casey opened one of the diaries at random, almost screaming in frustration. Rory wrote in code, she saw. Impossible to read the numbers.

155511. 451092.

She photographed a page, knowing it wasn't enough. Pages had been torn out too, she saw. She slid the diary back into place.

Breath shortening, she switched on his computer. In the big bedroom, the start-up rattle echoed loudly.

'Shit,' she muttered. 'Shit.'

The screen lit up impassively. 'Enter password.'

Casey thumped the desk in frustration.

'Get a bloody move on, Carrie,' Ed shouted, voice echoing down the hall.

Casey slammed the off button, praying it would shut down in time. She raced to the door, slipping for one terrifying second on the white marble.

'All OK?' Josh turned the corner, and Casey wasn't sure if he had seen her, diving out of the office.

On the wall beside the door to his office, a huge painting hung in a heavy gilt frame. Casey stared at Arab horses, racing over the desert, wild flourishes of joy.

'I love this,' she pointed. 'Most of the art in this place is hideous, but this is beautiful.'

'I don't know anything about art.' Josh was beside her now. He glanced past her, into the room. The computer might still be glowing, blind blue and deadly.

'Ed only knows about caves.' Casey was focusing all her attention on the painting. 'He's hopeless at all this. It does my head in sometimes.'

Josh looked at her sharply, and she smiled back, just a hint of promise.

'Maybe you should teach me,' Josh said.

'Maybe.'

They stared at each other, for a second.

'Ethan would have loved it here.' She broke the spell.

'He would have.' Josh stepped away as Ed appeared round the corner.

They walked to the terrace. It was blazingly hot. Rory was playing a game of solitaire and smoking a cigarette.

'We practise just over there.' Josh pointed at some red dots in the distance. 'Leo's just setting up the targets on that rise. They're the same distance as between the viewpoint and Salama.'

They watched Leo in the distance.

'Have you had interesting people out here?' Oliver asked the question Casey hadn't dared ask.

'All sorts.' Rory looked up with a grin. 'But we don't talk about them.'

'Oh, go on,' Oliver nudged. 'We'll never tell anyone.'

'Sorry.' Rory was unapologetic.

A few yards from the house, the gun case lay in the dirt. Josh clicked it open.

The gun lay there, ugly as death.

It was the M24 system. The military version of the Remington 700 rifle, with the telescopic sight spoiling the lines. It looked in good condition.

Kevlar, graphite and fibreglass. Used by armies right round the world. Fifteen thousand-odd built over the decades, so no one would ever notice if one went missing.

The Remington is bolt-action, Casey remembered from somewhere, which slows it down a bit, but not much. Not enough. Highly accurate, effortlessly so, for the distance from the rocks to the camp. Death delivered by a speck in the distance.

'It's loaded.' Josh nodded at the gun. 'Take it easy.'

'Do people ever miss?' Casey asked.

'Not really,' said Josh. 'Some people have to take two shots, which isn't ideal. London makes sure they can really shoot, before they come out here. This isn't a fucking practice effort. And they never back out.'

'We had one guy.' Rory laughed at the memory. 'The first time he missed so completely no one in the camp even noticed. There's a silencer on the gun and the bullet never went anywhere near them. Fuck knows where it went. Probably took out someone a couple of miles away. Then he took another shot, and got it perfectly.'

'You need to be pretty good.' Josh clapped Oliver on the shoulder. 'But it isn't a hard shot from up there.'

'Out in Afghanistan, the snipers have been putting people away from well over two clicks,' said Rory. 'For that sort of thing, you need to think about the curve of the earth. Control your heart rate and everything. A heartbeat is enough to shift the bullet over those distances. My favourite story was when one of the British snipers knocked out one of the Taliban, from a long way out. The Talib was wearing a suicide belt. He blew up and took ten of his fucking mates with him.'

As they spoke, Oliver was measuring the wind, reading the distance to the target. He took the gun out of the case, easily confident. Now Casey could see the ruthless alpha male, closing deals and crushing opposition. Eyes narrowed, every gesture purposeful.

Josh eyed him with satisfaction. 'You know what you're doing.'

Oliver lay down on the ground, the gun balanced on the bipod. He stared down the barrel, sighting the gun. There was a pause, just for a few seconds, then Casey saw his finger squeeze the trigger. Such a small movement.

The gun jumped. The air shuddered.

'Well done, mate.' Josh had binoculars out. 'You got it bang on.'

Casey applauded loudly. 'You're so good, Oliver. Brilliant.'

'Your go,' Josh said to Ed, and Casey heard the challenge in his voice.

Ed held the gun as if it were an extension of himself, every move instinctive. He dropped to the ground, tiger in the grass. The gun had fired almost before Casey was ready, and Ed was back on his feet before Josh had time to call it.

'Straight through the middle, buddy. I guess those Scottish stags never knew what hit them. Nice one.'

And, just for a second, Casey could see that Ed was thrilled with himself. He dropped the gun back into its case, took two steps towards her and kissed her, deep and hard.

34

'Fancy another go?' Josh asked Oliver.

They practised firing, Ed and Oliver barely missing, enjoying their skill.

'Why do you think,' Rory said to Casey, 'that Americans spend all their time on a shooting range? Do you think none of them ever think about the next step? Not ever?'

Casey laughed and clapped and coquetted.

'Dying for a drink,' Rory said to her, in the end. 'Shall we grab one?'

Casey followed him towards the blue and white umbrellas on the terrace.

He moved a book, Shakespeare, away from a chair with a flourish.

'Only book in the whole bloody place,' he said. 'Someone left it out here on a trip. Josh claims to have read *Macbeth*. It's his favourite, apparently. Took him about a month to read it.'

'"All is but toys",' she recited. '"Renown and grace is dead".'

'Indeed.'

In the distance, she could hear the crack of the rifle and the tangled bursts of laughter. She was thinking about ice and lemon, and blue and white umbrellas.

'Abayghur,' Rory shouted. 'Gin and tonic suit you, Carrie?'

'Please.' A big smile.

'So,' he said. 'Carrie ...'

He let his words fall away to a silence, and there was a sudden thud of fear. She looked up with a jolt and found his wolf-grey eyes upon her. The trapdoor yawned open. Rory was hunting.

Grey wolves hunt their prey for miles. They stalk and they chase and endure. They wait for that moment – just one moment – when their prey is alone. Isolated and panicked, just for a second.

Because it takes only a second.

There on the terrace, Casey felt the terror flood through her body, and saw the end. The unmarked grave, and that forgotten girl. She stood, a lazy, steady movement, and strolled over to the hedge of rosemary. But the others were too far away. Even if she ran, she could never outrun Rory. And she could never leave Ed to this fate.

She waved at Ed, just the same. He hesitated for a second, and then waved back. She forced herself to stretch, quite carelessly.

Hide the fear. Bury it deep. So deep that no one will know.

'I gather you knew Milo.' The voice was low. 'And Ethan.'

Casey stretched her face into a smile, and spun round to Rory.

'Did you know Ethan? I love hearing about him.'

Casey sounded thrilled, because fear can look like excitement, and he wouldn't be expecting delight.

'He was one of my oldest friends. Where did you—'

'He was such an incredible man. Where did you meet him?'

Her voice sounded forced. She clasped her hands to stop them shaking, and it was almost a prayer. Accelerate through the curve, it's the only way. Keep asking the questions, keep smiling and smiling and smiling.

'We met in Angola,' said Rory. 'Did he ever tell you about Angola?'

And because she'd read the few cuttings Hessa had found, and because Miranda had sent the notes of that brief conversation with his mother, and because there was no other choice, Casey was able to laugh.

'He was out there five years ago, wasn't he? It sounded pretty wild. God, I miss him so much. Did you meet him when he was doing maritime security?'

Because Josh, back in Djanet, had talked about the super-tankers. When they were on the same team as the Marines. Or at least fighting the same enemy, which is almost the same thing. She could use those stories.

'We did a couple of trips together,' Rory said. 'What did he tell you about it?'

'He said that you were on a ship going from Mumbai to Piraeus.' Casey let her eyes go soft. 'The crew picked up security in India because they'd been attacked on the way through the Red Sea, down towards Mumbai. The pirates had got right on to the deck, Ethan said. The crew had no guns at all, then. But they threw jam jars down, and there was shattered glass all over the deck, and the Somali were barefoot, so they had to give up.'

'That was a close one,' Rory nodded.

'So then they hired you guys for the next leg of the journey. But on the trip after yours, down to Dar es Salaam, the ship owners couldn't be bothered to pay for security,' Casey recited. 'So that time the ship did get snatched. The pirates called the owners, but they wouldn't pay the ransom. Those pirates held the ship for months, and then radioed the owners again. And the owners listened as the pirates cut off the captain's arm.'

Keep talking, she thought. He isn't sure, but he can't quite make this an interrogation.

'Those owners were cheap,' Rory shrugged. 'They never got their ship back. She sank somewhere off Eyl, in the end. He was a good guy though, that captain.'

Under her sad smile, Casey was scrambling through memories, and Hessa's careful research.

'It's Ethan's birthday next week,' she whispered. 'It's always so hard, thinking of him, locked up in that jail for his birthday. I don't know if he would even know the date any more.'

Rory was nodding. She wondered if she should cry. It would be so easy. And it might embarrass him too.

She heard the steps, running up towards the terrace, taking the stairs two at a time.

'Those look delicious.' It was Ed. 'I'm stealing one. Got bored of shooting. Didn't miss a thing.'

He grabbed her drink, and pulled her close with his other hand.

Thank you, she said with her eyes. Thank you. I'm sorry about all this.

I know, he smiled at her.

'Are you OK?' he asked loudly.

'Ethan,' she buried her head in his neck. 'Sorry.'

'It upsets her talking about him,' Ed said over her shoulder. 'We never speak about him.'

'Sure,' said Rory, looking away. 'Sure.'

35

The next morning, Casey woke up with dread in her bones. Ed had slept through the night.

'Morning, you.' He smiled at her, heavy with sleep.

It felt so right, waking up next to him, that Casey had to roll away, clear her throat, break the mood.

They dressed in silence. He was fiddling with his boots, head down, when she heard him take a breath.

'Casey, I can't.'

The word dropped, stone into water.

Automatically, she switched on the music.

'I'm sorry ... I can't go up there ... And watch that madman shoot into a school. It's wrong. You can't watch a man do that to another human being just because he wants to know how it feels. You can't be a part of it.'

'But we have to, Ed ...'

'You can't be a spectator.' He shuddered at the word. 'It's barbaric, and you know it.'

'I've watched people kill each other before,' she spat. 'I've gone out, with the Army, off in Helmand. And watched them shoot to kill, when we were pinned down in some awful canal.'

'That's different,' he said. 'They're retaliating when they've come under fire.'

'But it's not different for me,' she said. 'I'm going out there to watch someone kill another person, regardless. Deaths that would happen if I were there or not. And some days I choose to be there and watch. And some days I don't.'

'You don't know …' and his voice stumbled. 'You don't know …'

'What?' Casey was almost impatient.

'When I was in that field,' he said. 'When there wasn't any way out. There was another man. And he was so near … I shot him. Before he could shoot me. I could see his eyes, and he knew. He knew it was me or him, and I moved first. And it can't be undone, not ever. Everyone who's ever loved him, their lives will never be the same … Not ever. And I just turned and ran, and left him alone, out among the maize. And I can't go out today … With people who want to do that, just for fun. You don't know.'

He was sitting on the side of the bed, with his hands in his lap.

'Ed …'

'No,' he said. 'I thought the end justified the means out there, too. That's what we told ourselves every single day. And we were wrong. We were so very wrong.'

'This is different.'

'They're going to a *school*, Casey. They're going to kill a fucking child.'

'I know,' she said. 'Do you think I don't care?'

'But how can anyone do it?'

'He's a man,' Casey said slowly, 'who's always thought of people as numbers. Because that's how they learn to think, those men. Of people as employment figures and mortgage defaults, life expectancy and spending power. And, sure, a child is younger and prettier, and a little bit more innocent. But it all stopped being real, so long ago, when he started putting a price on it all. People are numbers now. So how is a child any worse? And what does it even matter?'

'And how,' asked Ed, 'are we any different? You're thinking of this child as the last in a line. This child is a number to you, too. But that child is out there right now, with a whole life ahead. And to you, it's just a better story.'

Casey's head jerked.

'That's not true, Ed. It's not.'

'Are you sure?'

'In the founding books of Christianity and Islam,' she said slowly, 'the word for martyr is almost identical to the word for witness. Someone who testifies about their beliefs. We bear witness, Ed. And no one makes it easy.'

'No one,' he said, 'would call you a fucking martyr, Casey. You're doing exactly what you bloody want.'

For a moment, Casey stepped away from him, staring out at the desert. Then she turned, heel to floor.

'I've got to go.'

'Please, Casey.'

'I am going, Ed. Even if I have to go up there on my own.' He went still.

'You can't go up there alone. It's insanity.'

'I can. I'll say you're ill or something. I don't care.' And now Casey's face was diamond-hard. 'I haven't come this far to turn away at the last.'

'I can't let you go up there on your own.'

'Well, make up your mind, Ed.' It was almost a taunt. 'You're in or you're out. And once we leave this room, you'll have to see it through. And you'll have to just watch up there. No heroics. Or we'll be killed too, you know. Left up on that cliff to die, with no one ever to know.'

'Casey ...' There was a long pause. The linen curtains fluttered in the breeze.

'Make up your mind, Ed.'

'We've got enough now, anyway,' said Ed.

'We don't have enough,' said Casey. 'The lawyers will never let us run this, unless we can absolutely prove that Selby shot someone up on that cliff.'

'And so the end justifies the means? Always?'

There was another long pause.

She would have to go on her own, she thought despairingly. Walk up there and be on her own for the worst. She turned, and made for the door, listening to the silence behind her.

'Wait ...'

She turned back. He was standing there. Shoulders slumped, but standing.

'Ed ...' She walked back to him, wrapped her arms around him. 'I am sorry ... I am so very sorry.'

And the useless words floated away in the silence.

Oliver gave them a thumbs-up as they walked into the dining room.

'Today's the day!'

He was juddering with excitement, knocking over a bottle of orange juice with a sudden movement.

'Steady on, dude,' Josh laughed at him.

They walked out to the car, and Rory appeared from no-where.

They climbed in, Oliver almost giggling. The road away from Euzma was familiar now. Casey recognised a distorted cypress here, ticked off a pile of rocks there. It was molten hot, even the sky shaded to yellow.

Another truck blazed past, with its desperate cargo.

'I was talking to one of the Tuareg last night.' Rory jerked his thumb. 'The traffickers have started forcing the women to take birth control. Injections, before they set off. Because some of them get raped at every truck stop.'

Casey shuddered.

'Out in the desert,' muttered Josh. 'Out in the desert.'

'They shoot horses,' said Rory. 'Don't they?'

Josh pointed out a black vulture in a twisted tree, hunched like death.

Next to Casey, Ed was staring at the horizon, eyes narrowed. And Casey realised abruptly that she didn't know this man. Not really. He could do anything, up here. It might be this that broke him.

She felt a flare of rage at Miranda for suggesting it. Miranda, who never cared.

The arrogance of it all. The stupid, wilful arrogance.

They stormed along the main road, and then the pickup swung left, and up. Up the track, and into the hills.

It was impossible, all of this. Casey felt like a child left alone in a car. Pressing buttons, and all at once it's moving. Faster and faster, and people are starting to scream. Or the acro-bat, in her glittering pink leotard, sparkling in the spotlight and flying from her trapeze. And, just for a second, she looks down, and sees that today is the day they forgot to put out the safety net.

The pickup's engine began to howl as they reached the steepest climb.

Maybe there never was a net after all.

36

It was as if she were watching from a distance. The car skidded to a halt. Five figures stepped out. One pointed, admiring the view. They had parked further down the hill, today, careful not to slam the doors.

Nothing grows, in these Sahara hills. The men picked their way through broken brown rocks.
    Oliver Selby, the forty-four-year-old chief executive of Cormium was excited. He had looked forward to this day for a long time ...

One of the men picked up the gun in its small coffin from the back of the car. He smiled back at the others, over his shoulder.

Oliver Selby, forty-four, chief executive of commodity traders Cormium, chatted as he walked up the path towards the view-point over the refugee camp. Salama, in the south of Libya, is ...

Then they turned, towards the narrow path that picked up the hill. It was a long walk to the top of the bluff.

*

At the age of forty-four, the Cormium boss had achieved almost everything on his bucket list. There was just one thing left …

The girl slipped. Falling to the ground with a cry, and scraping her arm. The rest of the group stopped. One of the men walked back, waited.

Casey looked up at Ed. Blood trickled from her cut, surprisingly bright. 'Come on, Carrie.' He pulled her to her feet, almost rough. 'Come on. We're here now.'

His eyes were blank. He turned, and walked to where the other three waited.

'Sorry, guys,' she found the words.

'No worries.' Josh turned up the path.

A spiny shrub tore at her shirt. The sun beat down, a too-bright inferno. A bird screamed in the sky, and she flinched. She could feel a thread of blood trickling down her arm.

On that scratchy path, Casey felt reality float away. It was impossible that she was here, on a dusty track in Libya. She should be in London, cosy in her flat. Door closed, and all so safe. Not here, with no rules and no sanctuary. It wasn't possible. Surely, something would come and stop it all. Surely, someone would see sense. It wasn't real, surely. Someone will die, the voices screamed in her head. Don't let this happen. And don't – *for God's sake, don't* – watch this happen.

Casey dug her fingers into the cut on her arm, shooting agony and smearing blood. The shriek of pain snapped her back to the hillside.

She felt Rory's eyes on her. He had turned back to her, a few steps up the path.

'They call it henhouse syndrome.' His voice was sing-song. 'But maybe that's the world now. There aren't many animals that kill for the hell of it, you know. Foxes and lynx, sometimes. And even then, it's freak behaviour. It doesn't make sense, you see, using up food when you don't need it. Animals kill to eat. Or occasionally for the practice. It's just us who do it for the hell,' he paused on the word, 'of it. Everything all right there, Carrie?'

'Fine.' She managed a twirl of the hair and that careless smile. 'I'm fine.'

'Only humans,' he hummed. 'We're only human.'

It seemed to take hours to reach the viewpoint, one step, then another, and another, remembering to breathe. Rory and Josh were chatting in desultory tones. Oliver had gone quiet.

Casey couldn't bear to turn to Ed, and see herself reflected. A sudden flood of shame, now, as Oliver strode ahead. It would brand them for ever, this. Be part of them, for ever.

Stop it, she thought. Stop it. You're Carrie now. It's not real. It's not you.

Asim and a little green toy car. No doors and no bonnet, but so very precious. Car noises, a giggle. And a tiny face, covered in chocolate. His mother rubbing him clean.

It is real.

It is.

It is you.

She couldn't remember why she was here, like a gap in her mind.

Was I not enough?
How could you leave me?

And finally, Josh signalled and the men dropped to the ground. They crawled the last few yards, and Salama spread out beneath them.

Casey hung behind. She had to find a place to watch. That was all that mattered, now. She needed her viewing spot.

The thought came from a distance, slow as Morse code.

Rory looked round again, and she managed, somehow, to force a smile. Her mouth felt unfamiliar.

Yara, screaming down the path, racing from the horror. Run, little girl, hide.

She touched her hand to the cut again, skin rough where it should have been smooth. The blood smeared, and when she moved her hand there was a metallic glint in the air. A fly buzzed inquisitive.

'I'll go up there.' She fumbled for the words, gesturing to a rock further back, slightly higher. 'I can see better from up there.'

But the four men barely heard her. Ed was moving more easily now. As if he had realised that there was no other choice. *The best way out is always through.* And, just for a second, Casey raged against him, too.

The chief executive of Cormium was arrested today, after the Post *revealed . . .*

Quite deliberately, Casey rammed her arm against the rock, reality flickering like a dying candle. Her arm left a sticky pattern of blood.

They had stopped just short of the cliff overlooking the camp. Josh unclipped the gun case, and Casey saw Ed's eyes flicker to the gun.

One last time, he turned and looked back at her, two, three, four seconds.

It is real. It is.

But she met his stare, somehow. Because every time he glanced across, she must find a way to hold on to him. Hold on. Everything depended on that.

I could save her.

Don't do it, Casey pleaded. Don't stop them. Let them kill this one last person. We'll die out here if you don't. And they'll carry on doing it for ever. Please don't. Please. Make it real.

And then her worst thought: Don't ruin it, Ed. Don't spoil it.

Let it happen.

Our last chance.

They'll kill us, you know. If you shift now.

Let them shoot.

And let them die.

Now Oliver's eyes were fixed on the target, sliding forward with the gun in his hand.

Josh was spotting Oliver, because looking down the sight of a sniper rifle is like looking at the horizon with a drinking straw. And someone needs to be searching around, always.

Ed looked away from Casey, down to the camp, and she felt her face crumple.

I can't watch, she screamed in her head. I can't bear it. It will be all I see when I close my eyes, for ever.

I can't.

And then the different voice: You must. You have to watch. You have to see every last second, and tell the world what they did.

It's the only reason for anything.

Bear witness.

I can't bear it.

You must.

Josh glanced at the wind-speed monitor. 'It's just very slight, from right behind us.'

'Perfect,' grunted Oliver.

From her rock, Casey could see straight over the four heads. Far below, Salama looked just as it had the day before, and the day before, and the day before.

The flags under a harsh blue sky. The beige of the tents faded into dust, with just the bright tarpaulins fluttering colour.

And there were a few small figures dotted around the school, the school with the huge mural of pink tulips.

Children.

Sure now that the men would not look back, Casey pointed her phone at them. It watched impassively. Her hand shook, and she steadied it with an effort of will. The four heads were completely focused on the faraway camp.

Oliver lined up the gun. He couldn't get it straight, at first, kept fiddling about. He seemed almost calm.

And then she realised. He was choosing. Far below, the children had formed a little circle. Ring-a-ring o' roses ...

'Pass me that rock, Ed,' Oliver whispered.

As Carey watched, Ed picked up a small chunk of rock and handed it across.

Oliver got the gun straight, balanced on the lump of sand-stone.

'Right.'

A daughter screaming and screaming, until her voice disappeared. God knows what happened to her.

Casey gazed on as Oliver stared down the sights. He was completely still under the blazing sun. She couldn't breathe.

Yara, dancing. Little green car.

Not the child. Not the child.

I am Malak.

The gun fired, and the tiny figure crumpled.

37

There were a few seconds of silence.

'You got her,' said Josh. 'Clean kill.'

'Holy shit,' said Oliver. 'Fuck.'

Leaving the gun on its tripod, he rolled on to his side, arms raised.

'Good shot.' Rory punched his shoulder. 'Nice.'

Casey jolted her camera out of sight, mechanical, frozen inside.

Ed was still staring at the tiny figure. She was sprawled on her side, all alone. The other children had fled, disappearing like smoke.

A murderous rage flooded Casey. She could kill Josh, kill Oliver, kill them all.

'What do you think?' Josh was grinning up at her. 'Pretty wild?'

'Pretty wild.' It was as if someone else was speaking. A pause and then the question she always asked: 'How are you feeling, Oliver?'

'I've always wanted to do it.' A huge grin split his face. 'And now I have. I've always wanted that experience. To know what it feels like.'

He lay on his back for a moment, staring up at the huge African sky.

Josh was looking down at the camp through his binoculars.

'They've all scarpered,' he said. 'That's why you'll have to come back tomorrow, Ed. You can't do two in a row. They'll all be hidden for the rest of the day now. Like rabbits when a hawk goes overhead.' He turned back to Oliver, hand on his shoulder.

But as Casey watched, a woman exploded on to the patch of dirt next to the school. She dived on to the small body, throwing herself across the child, distress in every line. They couldn't hear the screams. It was too far away. Another figure, a man, appeared. Frantic, running as fast as he could, limbs flailing with desperate speed. He stumbled to a halt as he saw them there. The woman had the child in her lap now, curled over the body, twisted in grief.

The man fell upon them, wrapped his body around both, holding the woman as she threw back her head, wailed up to the sky. Oliver and Rory were looking at Casey, while Josh fidgeted with the spotting scope.

'Sorry, missed what you were saying.' She had to snap back to attention. Had to, or it would be the end.

'You play *Call of Duty* or *Grand Theft Auto* or *Battlefield* all the time,' said Oliver. 'And suddenly it's real.'

And Casey smiled at him, somehow.

Ed was still frozen, still watching the little broken family, down by the school.

Casey slipped off her rock. She walked over to Ed, threw herself carelessly on the ground beside him.

'All right, darling?' She stared into his eyes. They were blank, empty, lost.

Come back to me, Ed.

She leaned forward, kissed him deliberately. He didn't respond.

Come back to me. She bit him hard, on the bottom lip, and saw the flash of pain in his eyes.

'Hey, baby.' She stroked his hair, hugging him close, just for a second.

The others were locked in congratulations, oblivious.

'Right,' Josh broke in at last. 'You ready to head back to Euzma?'

'Sure,' said Oliver.

Oliver didn't look back at the camp as he picked up the gun.

Behind him, the man and woman were still tangled together, hopelessly.

Oliver brushed himself down, reached for the water bottle. Then the five of them walked back to the pickup. Josh, coolly efficient, unloaded the gun. He checked it, and stowed it in the back of the car.

'Right,' he said. 'Ready?'

'Sure.'

Casey couldn't remember much of the drive back to Euzma.

There were figures at the edge of her sight now. Fading, as she twisted to see them. Small bodies, tiny ghosts. Yara, a bullet hole in her forehead. Malak, bleeding from her mouth. Eyes unseeing, lying sprawled.

Another truck hurtled past, and this time, she looked away. No more. I can't.

I won't.

The long drive up the avenue, and she waited, in silence.

The car stopped.

'I've got to have a shower,' Casey muttered.

'I'll come with you,' Ed managed.

They didn't speak as they walked back to the room.

Within seconds, Casey was sending the file back to London. Ed watched her. When she glanced up, he looked away. By the time she had finished, he had pulled a chair over to the balcony, and was watching the drifting sands.

Casey switched the music on, instinctively. She crouched down on the floor next to his chair, and stroked his hand.

'I'm sorry, Ed,' she whispered, although apologies could never be enough.

He stared at her for a long time, as if he could barely recognise her.

'Don't,' he said. 'Don't. You wanted to see it. You chose this, Casey.'

She stumbled away, into a corner of the room.

Finally he stood up, walked to her.

'It's done now,' he said at last. 'It's done and over.'

She leaned back against him, and almost without meaning to, his arms went round her waist.

'I'm sorry.' Her voice was sand blowing across the desert. 'I'm sorry.'

'I know.' He let her turn to him.

He let her hug him.

'I'm sorry,' she whispered again.

'We need to get out of here. Right now.'

She hid her head closer to his neck.

'Not yet,' murmured Casey. 'Please. Not quite yet.'

'What the hell do you mean, not yet?' He stiffened away from her. 'We've got everything we need.'

'Just a little bit longer, please.'

He pulled away from her. His hands on hers, unwinding them from his neck.

'I can't stand it,' Ed said. 'I can't bear these people. I want to ... I want to kill them. We've got to get out of here.'

'We need to get the diaries.' Casey kept her voice a whisper. 'In Rory's room. We've got to.'

'No, Ca— ... No.' It was almost a shout.

She made a gesture, fast, hushing him.

'I've got to, then.' Her voice was low. 'I'm not leaving without them.'

He stared at her for a long time, hard-eyed again.

'I knew you were manipulative, Casey.' He only just kept his voice low. 'But not like this. Not like this ...'

The curtains blew in the breeze, the desert sprawling golden in the setting sun. Hundreds of miles to the north, the Mediterranean lapped abandoned beaches.

'I am sorry, Ed. I never planned for it to be like this ...'

'You're mad,' he said. 'Completely mad. We've got it, the story. We can go home.'

'We need to know what the diaries say,' said Casey. 'And who's been out here. We'll never know otherwise. The minute the story runs, everything will be lost. All those people, who came here. They'll all get away with it.'

'You don't know what the diaries say.' Ed's hands clenched. 'It could be nothing.'

A message bleeped in, on her phone.

'Brilliant stuff.' It was Miranda. 'Outstanding. Now get the fuck out of there.'

Casey put the phone back in her pocket.

'Just a few more hours, Ed, I promise you. Then we'll be gone.'

'I'm not going back up to Salama.' There was panic in his eyes. 'Not tomorrow. I can't, Casey. I just can't.'

'We won't go back up to Salama,' Casey said. 'I promise you. That's over.'

'He sleeps in those rooms, you know,' said Ed. 'And he'll see as soon as those diaries are gone. He's sharp, Rory, and he'll kill us without thinking about it. They could be another ambush, for all you know. That's how his mind works.'

Everything a trap.

'I will work it out,' said Casey. 'I can do this.'

She went into the bathroom and locked the door behind her. She stared at herself in the mirror. Then she showered for a long time, turning the water as hot as she could bear, clouds of steam billowing round the huge bathroom.

'Always have clean knickers,' Miranda had said once. 'Sometimes clean knickers make all the difference.'

'Emergency knickers,' Casey had laughed.

But Miranda was right, and the shower steadied her.

When she came back into the bedroom, Ed was lying on the bed, staring up at the dusty chandelier.

'You don't need to come down,' she said. 'I can say you're ill ... Drank some of the water by mistake or something.'

'Casey.' His eyes were haunted. 'I'm not letting you go down there on your own.'

'Well' – she knew her voice sounded brutal – 'if you're coming down, you've got to focus.'

And she reached for her phone, pulling up Miranda's number.

38

In Djanet, Miranda was waiting for the dusk. She always hated the support role, the understudy waiting for her moment. But Casey was relying on her. And it was critical, this role. One person, a step back from the chaos, scanning the horizon for disaster, while the other focuses everything on the target. Miranda ran over her plans again. In the last few days, she'd walked a hundred miles round Djanet, pacing the alleys of the dusty town and watching the scraps of rubbish blowing in the breeze.

She ticked off the risks one by one. She was trained to focus on the small, tedious tasks. Because she couldn't afford to slip up; not for a second. It was the small things that mattered. From a safe distance, Miranda had watched Ed and Casey race down the road towards Libya. Then she went and bought Amina some new glasses and a beautiful bowl.

Amina had sulked, but a few minutes later she'd looked at the bowl, blue and white and delicate, and smiled. At least journalists know how to patch things up the morning after the night before.

Miranda implied that she and Casey had fallen out; Miranda a victim too. So the hotel was fine again, and she sat under the bougainvillea and drifted in the hammock.

She left money, but no explanation, at the Palais front desk, for Isa. She worked hard, in her hammock, focused on logistics, notepad in hand. She sent another message to Hessa. Within seconds, she had a detailed response. The young reporter had blossomed, working on this job. Hessa's shyness, Miranda discovered, masked an absolute determination to get the job done. She'd barely been home for days.

'Thanks, Hessa,' Miranda tapped. 'Great work.'

Now Miranda's phone bleeped again. A message from her husband, her lovely, kind husband.

'When will you be back?'

Tom and their snug home, that pretty house in Queen's Park, seemed implausible. He was used to her disappearing; he didn't like it.

'Not sure. Sorry. A few days.'

'You'll miss the Lyons' dinner party.'

'I know. Sorry. Tell them I am really sorry.'

'Are you safe?'

'Completely.' It was what she always said, no matter what. And sometimes, at breakfast a few days later, he would look up from the *Post* and say, 'You weren't safe, were you? Not really. Not at all.'

It was hard to hide when it was on the front page.

And she would smile and fiddle with the toaster and say, 'Well, I am fine now.'

And they would both pretend that was normal.

She knew he wanted children, to match that pretty house in Queen's Park. And to match his successful job as a corporate lawyer. In-house now, more money, better hours. Tom had married his beautiful girl, straight out of university, and he'd thought she would fit into his dream. Neither of them had realised that his wife would turn into a huntress, a Diana who lived for the chase.

Miranda struggled, now, at the barbecues. Hesitated when someone asked, 'And what are you up to now, Miranda?'

Because that couldn't be answered with: 'Well, this week I watched a toddler have his leg set, without anaesthetic, because – oh, you know how it is – they ran out of the stuff months ago.'

No, you couldn't say that when you were surrounded by three nice women and their coordinating husbands, all wearing school-gate smiles and last year's Boden. But those were the children that interested Miranda. And the children Tom wanted would put a stop to all this, for ever. And time was running out.

But she couldn't think about that today. Not today.

'Tell the Lyons I am really sorry,' she wrote. And then almost an afterthought: 'Love you.'

And remembered, with a stab, the days when it was all she knew. *I wish your dreams were enough.*

But what she had to do, right now, was plan for getting Ed and Casey back out of Libya.

She put her thoughts aside, like an old love letter, and went over her notes one more time.

They'd been lucky in some ways. Able to top up the fuel tanks of the Hilux here and there, at tiny stations along the road. They filled up the containers in the boot at the same time, making the car a mobile bomb, but it was better than being stranded miles from anywhere. And the Hilux could not outrun the black pickup. Miranda had seen that pickup as it shot past. The Hilux was at full stretch just to keep up.

And then, a few hours ago, Casey had casually mentioned the pickups full of Tuareg bodyguards. Miranda looked up at the desert stars and contemplated the very real possibility that they might not be able to get out.

'No story is worth dying for,' she had told Casey a few years ago.

'Some of them are,' Casey had said, which worried Miranda even then.

They had been talking about Marie Colvin, who died out in Homs, right in the heart of the battle for Syria. Refusing to leave the story even as her paper pleaded, knowing that this war was too close, far too close.

Miranda had last seen Marie just outside the Radisson Blu in Tripoli, a few months before she died. The battered Radisson, a broken link in the sleek chain of hotels that wrapped around the world. The lifts had stopped working, of course, and they were laughing, rolling their eyes before Miranda climbed the dozen storeys to her room. 'I'll get fit, at least.'

Miranda remembered looking up at the wreck of a hotel. They'd struggled with their BGANs out there, that time. The reporters had ransacked their rooms, to find a way of lining them up with the satellite to get the story out. So when they looked up there were ironing boards sticking out of every window. They'd found that funny, too.

In Syria, Marie must have known, as the mortar fire got closer, that this was the story that might kill her. She must have chosen the story over the escape, must have decided the story mattered more than anything else.

Miranda shook her head, concentrated. She had let Casey go in; there had to be a way out. Not Casey. It couldn't happen.

Although, of course, it could.

She worked out all the assets to hand. She'd hung out at Tiska, the shabby airport. She'd gossiped in cafés, finding out who could be hired, and what they could do. She'd gone over the maps, again and again. Because it was Casey, Miranda had done everything.

Her phone bleeped again and there was that sudden punch of joy. A message from Hessa. Casey had managed to send through the footage from Salama.

Horror, too, but Miranda pushed that aside for the thud of relief. Miranda picked up her phone, typed out the plan, messaged it to Casey.

39

Ed took Casey's hand as they walked down the stairs, feeling her tense as they got near Josh's rooms.

'Don't,' he whispered, holding her hand tightly. 'Please don't.'

'Oh, hey, you guys.' Josh was in the study, door ajar. 'Head on over to the terrace. I'll be out in a sec.'

They were watching the stars appear against velvet blue when Josh emerged, carrying a bottle of rum. Oliver was beside him.

'What an amazing day.'

Leo and Rory appeared as Josh opened the bottle.

'We found this rum in the basement, gallons of it.' Leo nodded happily. 'Old Gaddafi knew his stuff. There's literally everything you could ever want at Euzma. It's paradise.'

He lit a cigarette, breathed out contented smoke.

They drank together, watching a sliver of moon rise over the desert. The Milky Way stood out clearly. Starry path, peaceful glitter. Cassiopeia, Andromeda, Perseus: nightly familiar.

Although she could have drunk herself to oblivion, Casey drank slowly, with Ed waving the bottle away.

'Not too much before tomorrow,' he laughed. 'I won't know which way to hold the gun.'

'Go on.' Rory nudged the bottle closer. 'You can go in the afternoon. You're going to the water tank, aren't you? There are people there all day.'

The evening wore on. Abayghur went back and forwards from the kitchens, bringing olives, ice, crisps. Rory jumped up and down, pacing about, too energetic to sit for too long. Ed and Casey would be missed too quickly, far too quickly, if they stood up, made their excuses, escaped.

Oliver was going over the day, blow by blow, pulling apart every detail. Josh was drinking, angry, fast.

'Do you remember that stupid game, we played back in Djanet?' Oliver asked. 'Feels like a million years ago now.'

'But you have to keep this a secret,' warned Josh.

'I will,' said Oliver. 'I will, I promise. I'm in it too, don't forget.'

'How are you feeling now, Oliver?' Casey hated herself for the brightness in her voice. She could feel exhaustion slipping over her, like a tide.

'It's another thing ticked off the wish list,' Oliver grinned.

'No Ferrari sadness for you then,' said Leo.

'What's Ferrari sadness?' Ed managed.

'This one guy, who came out here,' said Rory. 'Said when he was younger, he'd always wanted a Ferrari. Worked like shit, you know. For years. He finally got this Ferrari, and then on the very first drive, it hit him: it's just a car. And he'd worked all that time, and sacrificed so much, and wasted so many years, and it was just a car. Just a lump of metal.'

'So he came out here?' Ed asked.

'And the same thing happened again,' said Leo. 'He thought he would be ecstatic, after all that. And he was just sitting in that chair right over there, saying, "But I just feel the same. Nothing's changed."'

'I,' said Oliver, 'don't feel like that at all.'

'He was having,' Leo laughed, 'one hell of a mid-life crisis.'

'And no one feels guilty afterwards?' Casey asked. 'No regrets?'

Rory's eyes were on her, crocodile at the watering hole.

'No,' said Rory. 'No regrets.'

'You ever been big-game hunting?' Josh asked Ed. 'Out on safari?'

'Never,' Ed said, 'and I suppose it will be spoiled for me after this.'

Josh was pouring more drinks, clumsier now.

'They're a different challenge, the big five. The rhino, the buffalo, the elephant ... You have to hunt them in particular ways.' Josh was drunk now, showing off. 'For the leopard, you have to bait them. You kill an impala or a warthog first, and then hang it, up in a tree. Out somewhere in the leopard's territory, so that slowly, slowly, he'll learn to come to you. You build a blind, and you wait, and you wait, and you wait. It can take days. You have to learn patience, to bag a leopard.'

He poured another glass of run, splashing the table.

'But leopards are so beautiful,' Casey managed eventually.

'They make lovely coats,' Josh teased, eyes glinting. 'That much is true. And it takes skill. Some of the parks, down in South Africa, they do canned shooting, for the lions.'

'What's canned shooting?' asked Ed.

'It's when they release the lions just to be shot,' said Josh. 'People fly down to Africa, with this big dream of killing a lion. They've always wanted to do it, you know. Be the man. Get the photograph. Have something to tell the neighbours. Trophy wives and trophy kills. But, often, there aren't enough wild lions in the area. So the operators catch them, breed them, let them out to die. In some places, they even drug them, so they can't get away.'

'You can always tell, though,' said Leo. 'If a lion has spent most of its life in a cage, it won't have the scarring the wild ones have. Or the fear, or the arrogance. The lions, they have to fight all the way through, just to survive.'

The candlelight ran down the long scar edging his face.

'Canned shooting is considered poor form,' Rory mocked. 'Sometimes, those lions even wander towards the tourist, because they think they're going to be fed.'

Leo poured them all more rum, and looked around for another bottle.

'I wonder,' Oliver said almost pensively, 'whether Salama would be considered canned shooting?'

They all laughed, Ed forcing a grin.

'The refugees have got their scars, man,' said Leo. 'They've had to fight all the way through.'

'The big six, dude.' Josh was shaking his head. 'It's the big six.'

40

They fell asleep, somehow, just for a few hours. Casey's alarm went off at 4.30 a.m., when the house was in its deepest sleep. They were bleary, just for a second.

'We should just go,' said Ed. 'Straight out the front door.'

'But I have to try,' Casey whispered.

They had packed a few things, the night before, in a couple of rucksacks. They were leaving enough clothes behind so that if someone glanced round the door, it would look like they were still there. Ed threw a towel over the mermaid corpse.

Now they pushed their way through the silence, down to the huge entrance hall. The silence felt as if it could shatter into a million pieces.

'Go.' Casey nudged Ed towards the front entrance.

She turned, alone. Step by step. At the wild Arab horses, outside the room, she hesitated, electric with fear. Anything; she'd do anything to stay outside.

The suite was quiet. No light showed under the door.

Very slowly, Casey turned the handle, feeling a burst of relief when the door gave, just slightly. They hadn't locked themselves in.

Bait over a pitfall.

She edged the door open, very carefully. It mustn't bang against the wall. Mustn't.

She crept into the room. It was very dark, the air heavy with sleep. The double doors to Rory's room were closed, but she could hear Josh breathing in his room.

It was fifteen feet to the desk.

Five more steps to the desk ...

Three ... Two ... And Josh half sat up, and muttered something.

Casey froze, ice down her spine.

But he settled back down, pushing a pillow away, grumbling. She crept on, quiet as snow, mind like a glass bridge that could shatter at any moment. The silence deafening.

Three diaries. Reaching up for them, feeling for them. For fuck's sake, don't drop one. Lifting them so very slowly, and waiting for the alarm to scream.

The silence echoed on.

She turned towards the door, a split second of dread that there would be someone standing there, a new silhouette.

But there wasn't and, step by step, she edged back towards the door. Now she was holding the diaries, there could be no excuse.

'I'll go in,' she had said to Ed. 'Just me. It has to be just me. Because if Josh wakes up, I can say ... I was looking for you ... I came to your room ...'

'You can't say that.'

'But I can,' she said. 'I can.'

Now she was inching back towards the door, a nightmare version of grandmother's footsteps, the diaries in her hand, so there could be no pretending.

Don't hurry. Don't rush. Don't snap.

I am Malak.

At last she was at the door, carefully putting the diaries down on the marble. Don't rush, Casey, you always rush.

She edged the door closed, flinching at the tiniest clunk as it slotted back into place.

Then she picked up the diaries and forced herself to walk slowly, slowly, down the long corridor.

She crossed that huge entrance hall like a dream.

Ed was waiting by the Hilux.

'Don't slam the doors,' he didn't need to say.

They'd parked as far from the palace as possible, but as the engine roared into life, the silence shattered like a mirror.

'Go,' Casey begged. 'Let's go.'

The sky was starting to lighten in the east, thin pinstripes of grey streaking the sky. Casey's nails bit her palms. The scream in her head.

Ed turned the car, edging gently towards the long drive. Euzma turned in the mirror behind, the ogre giving up its prize.

Maybe.

Ed shifted the gears.

Maybe.

The avenue of broken cypresses was endless. Casey ticked off the cypresses one by one, as they were caught in the headlights for a second. Faster, she thought, faster.

Maybe.

She had almost begun to believe in escape, and they had almost reached the main road, when two headlights pierced the air.

'Shit,' said Ed. 'Shit.'

'We'll be OK.' Casey tried to believe it. 'Let me do the talking.'

The pickup, a red one, got closer and closer. It stopped in the middle of the road, casually blocking their way. The blood thudded in Casey's ears.

'You guys OK?' It was Rory. Rory with the wolf-grey eyes, who would tear her apart in a blink. Casey's heart pounded so hard he might hear it.

'Bloody Ed couldn't sleep.' Casey stepped out of the car. 'Too excited about today. Kept on waking me. And then I remembered I'd dropped my scarf up at the caves, so we thought we'd go and see them in the dawn. It must be gorgeous up there in the morning.'

The words hung in the air, because there were too many for sense. She couldn't tell if Rory believed her.

Smile, Casey, smile.

Maybe.

'Why don't I follow you up to the caves?' said Rory, so friendly. 'I'm not tired yet.'

There was nothing to do except climb back into the Hilux.

They watched as Rory moved the red car so they could pass, before whirling in a cloud of dust to fall in behind.

Ed drove in silence. Casey watched Rory in the rear-view mirror.

'I'm sorry,' she tried, but Ed didn't reply.

At the rock with the splash of blue paint, he jerked to a halt. They stared up the hillside, as Rory slid to a standstill beside them. Above them the path wound up steeply towards the little plateau in front of the cave. To the left of the path there were dark fissures in the rock face, with cracks disappearing into the dark. To the right, large rocks had split away, crashing down and flattening everything. The boulders piled up at the bottom of the slope.

Rory glanced across at them, and Casey shuddered.

Smile, Casey, smile.

Not hurrying, the three of them started towards the caves. The sky brightened imperceptibly.

As they reached the first twist in the path, a flock of birds screamed overhead, making Casey jump.

'What are those birds?'

'No idea.' Rory peered at the sky.

They trudged on.

'What were you up to,' Casey asked at last, 'out on the road at this time in the morning?'

'Oh,' Rory shrugged. 'The others conked out, too much rum. I went out to where the Tuareg keep some of the women they traffic through …'

He let silence take over, unembarrassed, but seeing no need for detail.

They had been so close to escape, thought Casey. So near.

Now, they were almost at the cave. The mouth yawned open.

'Where do you think you dropped that scarf?'

Casey thought about hitting him, suddenly. Over the head, a piece of rock, one of the large ones. They could kill him, quite easily, out here. And would anyone ever know? Ever care?

But she knew Rory had survived more than most. Would fight for his life.

She looked around for the scarf, trying to remember where she'd dropped it.

'There it is.' She almost ran to the scrap of white and blue cotton just inside the cave, her relief easy this time. 'I thought it was just so pretty.'

'She got it in the souk.' Ed managed to roll his eyes at Rory. 'The worst negotiating you've ever seen. The trader couldn't believe his luck.'

'He gave me some very nice peppermint tea.' Casey tried to pout.

'Glad you found it,' said Rory.

'Shall we watch the sunrise?' Casey put her arms around Ed, locking out Rory.

Leave, she willed. Leave.

But Rory yawned, looking to the east, and sat down on a rock.

After a second, Casey and Ed broke apart. Casey leaned against the rock face, kicking out at a stone.

Although he was staring towards the sunrise, Casey sensed Rory knew their every move. She felt for Ed's hand, and squeezed it. After a long moment, he squeezed back.

Around them, the dawn was lifting. The gentle dark, with all its hiding places, was dissolving into the day. No safety out here, now, not for another day.

The colours grew brighter, minute by minute.

'It's so beautiful,' Casey said, and Rory glanced around.

He'll have a gun, she thought. Rory would carry a gun, always.

And then, all at once, the sun was up, and impossible to look at. The dawn mist faded in the light, and they felt the first flicker of heat.

'Right.' Rory stood up. 'Back to Euzma for breakfast.'

'I'm just going to show Carrie one more painting.' Ed's voice cut across Rory's. 'We'll catch you up.'

There was a pause, just for a moment.

'There's no rush.' Rory moved back to his rock. 'I'll wait.'

On the threshold, Casey hesitated. The cave gaped ahead of them. Behind them, in the burn of the day, Rory was settling down.

'Come on, Carrie,' Ed's hand tightened on hers, painfully.

'I don't want to' – a whisper.

'Come on' – a jerk.

They crossed the mouth of the cave, Casey tripping on a rock, clumsy. Almost carelessly, they wandered across the cave, pointing out the paintings, here and there.

At the back of the cave, Ed paused.

'There,' he pointed.

Round a corner, she saw the inky patches in the dark.

'Tunnels?' Casey whispered. 'Where do they go?'

'I don't know,' he said. 'I climbed some of the way down one, when I left you that time before. But I don't know.'

There were three tunnels reaching away, clumsy fingers into the rock. The chill folded around them like a witch's cape.

'We have to try,' Casey decided. 'There's no way past Rory.'

She flicked on the tiny torch on her phone, and stepped forwards. The three tunnels waited, impassive.

'Let's try the biggest,' Ed whispered.

Even in the largest, the roof of the tunnel dropped down sharply as it left the main cave. Casey felt her head brush against the rock. Ed had to crouch slightly.

'I'll go first,' Casey insisted.

She edged forwards, phone in one hand, reaching out with the other. Her hand grazed the side of the rocky tunnel, and she was aware of the millions of tons above her head. One tiny shift, and this little tunnel would disappear as if it had never been, the earth barely moving in the sun.

And no one would know.

She inched forward, the torch lighting a fragment of path. One step, and another, so painfully slow. Almost a surprise that it could be so hard.

You go into the dark, to find the monsters.

She tripped over a rock, and felt it bite like an animal. Behind her, Ed slipped, and she heard rock on bone, and a curse.

Inch by inch, step by step, and the little torch picked out only a few more feet of tunnel.

'Carrie?' She jumped as Rory's voice echoed down from above. 'Where are you?'

'Just exploring,' her laugh echoed back up the tunnel. 'It's so interesting.'

She was moving forward again. The roof lowered with every step, and finally she had to drop to the floor and crawl. Behind her, Ed was on his knees too, and she sensed the despair in his movements.

'Come on, Ed.'

She crept forward. It was awkward holding the torch while crawling, and so slow. She felt gravel under her hand, then a sudden softness that made her force down a scream.

'Are you OK?' Ed was just behind her.

'It's nothing' She pushed away the fear. 'Nothing.'

They inched forward again, turning another corner. Casey had lost any sense of time and space. It was very cold now. They might be a mile from the cave, and they might be fifty yards.

The roof of the tunnel bit down quite suddenly, and she swore and dropped the torch. When she scrabbled for it, and pointed it forward, the torch picked out only rock.

The tunnel had shrunk to nothing. There was a crack, a hand width only, but that was all. Frantic, Casey raked the light here and there. There must be something … Must be …

But the rock closed in all around. Smooth black rocks, indifferent as strangers, all the nightmares at once.

'What is it, Casey?' Ed's voice came from a long way away.

'Nothing.' Her throat was dry. 'Nothing. There isn't a way out, not this way.'

The torch flickered for a second, and she felt the blackness close in. She thought of the birds, the shriek up through the sky, and felt the scream building in her chest.

'We can go back.' Ed's voice cut through. 'We have to go back. Try another passage.'

It was a struggle to turn in the tightness of the tunnel. She scraped knees and elbows. The rock pressed down and down and down.

And the moment they turned, she was lost. Theseus, forgotten. Had there been only one tunnel? Or was this whole mountain honeycombed with paths, all leading to nothing?

They edged back upon bloody knees.

Casey breathed faster and faster, dust filling her mouth.

'We'll be all right,' she said into the dark. 'We're going to get out.'

Ed didn't reply.

But at last, the tunnel roof rose away from them, and finally they could stand. They scrambled along, almost in relief.

Ed slammed off the torch, pushing her hard back against the rock.

'Why ...' But his hand was over her mouth.

Then she saw it: the finger of light reaching into the tunnel. But it wasn't the daylight, shining down. This finger wriggled and twisted and reached.

A torch.

Rory.

'Carrie,' the voice curled down, almost seductive. 'Ed. Where are you, whoever you are?'

They froze, backs cold against rock.

Pretty little air hostess, face smashed to pulp.

'I'll find you, you know,' the voice came again. 'I'll find you. You can't get away.'

The torch was flickering, here and there. And any minute it would find them. And then ... And then ...

Casey felt for Ed's hand in the dark.

Rory must be up where the three tunnels split off, thought Casey. Uncertain over which one to pick.

He wouldn't be able to call the others, not down in the cave. He would have to retreat, to call in reinforcements.

Unless he had called them before. Before he came down. Because that meant he only had to wait ... Cutting off all escape ...

It seemed like Rory stood there for ever, the torch reaching down like a claw. Casey pressed her head back against the rock, and wished she knew how to pray. The minutes ticked past.

If Rory hadn't had the torch ... If they'd stumbled straight into him in the dark ... Waiting like a cobra in the black.

You go into the dark, to find the monsters.

But finally, the finger of light flickered out, and they heard his footsteps clamber away.

'Come on.'

They crept forwards. Because any moment, Rory could stop and turn, and listen for their stumbling steps. But there was no choice. They had to edge on through the darkness of tunnel. Finally, they reached the point where three tunnels split off.

'Which way?' asked Ed.

One chance. They could all be dead ends. All empty passages, tapering to nothing. And then nothing but that fatal choice: back to Rory, or lying down to die. Abandon hope, and wait for the tunnel to become a coffin.

I am Malak.

'This one.' Casey pointed for no reason. Spin of the coin, flip of the dice. 'It has to be this one.'

Same rocks, same boulders, same choking dust.

Please, Casey bargained in her head. *Please.*

But the roof began to slope down again.

To stop the panic, she calculated how long it would take for Rory to call the others, to send the alarm shooting round Euzma. Would he wait at the mouth of the cave? Or would he run to destroy their car, leaving them with no escape?

'Shit,' said Ed.

And all at once, she saw that her phone was beginning to fade, the tiny beam of light dying in the dark.

They hurried, steps stumbling. But the torch dimmed every step.

'I left mine in the car.' Ed's voice was apologetic.

'You weren't to know.'

Come on, she willed the tiny torch. We can't die down here in the dark. Not here. But bit by bit, the cave was closing in around them. One moment, the tiny flicker was there, and the next it was gone. A terrible blackness filled Casey's eyes.

'Come on' – she heard her voice, from somewhere – 'We have to keep going.'

She felt for Ed's hand, and reached for the tunnel wall.

Inch by inch by inch.

Treasure hunt, hide and seek. A murder in the dark.

Inch by inch by inch.

A step further, and her foot went into nothing, and she screamed as she pitched forward, hand torn away from Ed.

But it was only a few feet, and she hit the ground hard as she landed.

'Casey!'

'I'm all right,' she promised, pulling herself up. 'Keep going.'

They limped on.

The darkness was alive now, rocks like enemies. She held a hand across her face, in a pathetic attempt to protect her eyes. Every step was slower.

Treasure hunt, hide and seek. A murder in the dark.

She froze.

There was a flicker of light snapping their perfect darkness.

'It's Rory,' Ed whispered.

'But he can't have had time,' Casey began, and remembered her scream, as she fell into space. He must have called the others, and then come back down the tunnel. Rory, the hunter, who would never give in. He had heard her, and given chase. And with his torch, he could move so much faster.

'Hurry!' said Ed pointlessly.

They scrambled forward, but the light grew brighter. Rory was gaining on them.

She scrabbled.

Never give up.

Casey gasped.

Far ahead, there was a needle of daylight.

Now it was a race. Casey felt herself crunch into a boulder, and barely noticed.

Behind them, Rory was rushing too.

Casey and Ed dashed to the breach in the rock. It was a narrow gap, out into the sun.

'Go on!' Ed pushed her.

Rory's footsteps were getting closer. They could hear him breathing. It must be only the fear of ricochets that stopped him going for his gun. She felt like a skinful of blood that might burst any second.

'Casey, you fucking idiot. Get on with it.'

She pushed herself through the gap on her elbows. For a split second, she imagined Rory's hands on her legs, pulling her back. That visceral terror of being grabbed from behind. And then she was through, leaping to her feet.

'Ed!' she screamed.

For an agonising second, his shoulders caught in the gap, and then he was beside her.

The daylight shocked her, the light blinding. She looked around, squinting. They had emerged from one of the deep cracks above the blue-splashed rock. Far below, the two pick-ups sat oddly peaceful, side by side. There was no sign of Josh and Leo, not yet.

'Run!' shouted Ed. 'Run to the car.'

He pushed her hard and she took off like a hare, down the hillside towards the car.

As she ran, she felt in her pocket for Dash's penknife.

There was a crash as Ed forced a rock into the gap, and then he was beside her.

'It won't hold him for long,' he said. 'I shouted into the gap that if he tried to climb out, I would kill him, but ...'

They were almost at the car. Ed made for the Hilux.

'Wait ...'

Casey was stabbing at a wheel of the red pickup with the penknife. Three stabs, and she was round to the next wheel.

'It'll slow him down,' she gasped, scrambling into the Hilux.

Ed looked sideways at her with a smile.

'Let's head along the small road,' panted Casey. 'Josh said it linked up, somewhere nearly at Ghat, and we don't want to collide with the cavalry coming up to the caves.'

Ed was turning the car, spinning it round the wounded pickup.

'He's coming.' Ed glanced in the rear-view mirror. 'He's coming.'

'Hurry,' Casey shouted. 'Hurry!'

Ed accelerated, the Hilux powering away as Rory sprinted towards them.

41

The Hilux kicked up a trail of dust as it roared down the path, up and down the little rises. It was a rough path, and all around was sand – sand that the car could sink into and never escape.

Casey fretted, turning to look over her shoulder.

'Don't forget the minefields,' she said. 'Josh said they never marked them out here.'

She checked the rucksack. The diaries were still there, with their passports.

'We should have gone earlier in the night,' she muttered. 'I'm so sorry.'

'We could never have stayed on the road in the dark,' said Ed. 'And God knows who else is out on that road at night.'

'If Rory managed to wake the others, they won't be far behind,' said Casey. 'Minutes, maybe.'

'You never planned the escape, did you?' Ed murmured, almost to himself. 'The escape was never important, not to you.'

They accelerated along, too tense to talk, the Hilux doing its best. Casey reached for Ed's phone, sending a message to Miranda.

She couldn't bear to look back, couldn't bear to see the black pickup appear like a shadow, hunting her down.

Ahead of them, the little road snaked away to the west. There were hills ahead, the track winding upwards. Ed was gripping the wheel, coaxing every inch of speed out of the Hilux. He took the racing line through a curve and Casey flinched.

'The mines. Don't forget the mines.'

The sun was up in the sky now, bright and brutal, the heat of the day starting to burn.

The Hilux bounced as it hit a pothole, tyres spinning in the air before the thud, and Ed cursed. She put his hand over his, just for a second.

Just as Casey thought they might get away, might escape, Ed looked in the rear-view mirror.

'Fuck.'

Casey spun round. The black pickup was storming along like a nightmare, a few rises back. Small now, but it was faster, that car, so much faster than them.

'Oh God,' said Casey. 'Oh God.'

Behind the black pickup, the Tuareg bodyguards were following in their battered truck.

The Hilux was climbing now, the little road rising up yet another hill. To their right, the road fell away, almost a cliff, a sharp fall, studded with chunks of rock. The bluff curved away to the right, and the road followed along the ridge, until the Hilux was heading almost due north. But inch by inch, the pickup was gaining on them, bouncing effortlessly over the rough dirt track. The Hilux jarred, slowing at every crater in the road. As Ed tried to avoid the worst of the holes, the pickup seemed to leap forward.

'Hurry,' said Casey, pointlessly. 'Hurry.'

The Hilux smashed into a rut, and skewed sideways.

Ed flicked a glance at her. 'What do you think I am doing, exactly?'

It was only about forty miles to the border now, to where the lazy guard at Tinkarine was dreaming in the sun. Impossibly far. They would never make it.

This was how Aisha Gaddafi escaped, Casey thought, west to safety, with hell on her heels. She had made it.

The Hilux raced over the ground, bouncing, battling, engine screaming with the effort. The road kept climbing, the precipice falling away ever more sharply to the right.

'Come on,' Ed begged, foot to the floor. 'Come on.'

There was a huge bang. A rock shattered a few feet ahead of the Hilux.

'Fuck,' said Ed. 'Fuck, they've got the M24.'

Another huge bang. Then another, and the windscreen shattered.

Casey's phone went. Miranda.

'Miranda,' Casey screamed. 'Where are you?'

'To your right,' Miranda's voice was ice calm. 'We've got the sun behind us.'

Casey looked round, the sun blinding her. 'I can't see. I can't see ...'

'I know,' said Miranda. 'Don't try to see us, because it'll be too bright. But we're up here, Casey. We came in with the sun behind us. I promise I'm here.'

No one would ever be able to hear the clatter of the helicopter from that distance over the scream of the car engines.

Another huge bang. She could see them now, so close, too close. Josh was driving, Rory and Leo holding the guns, ruthless professionals, going for the kill.

'Oh God,' Casey said again.

'Casey.' Miranda's voice cut through her panic. 'You've got to find a way of getting ahead of them. We can't come in with the helicopter unless we've got time to land, grab you and go. The helicopter will be too much of a sitting duck.'

'I know,' said Casey. 'Don't come in unless it's safe. There's no point if ...'

One of the wing mirrors disintegrated, shattering into a million pieces.

'Casey!' She could hear the agony in Miranda's voice. 'Oh Christ, Casey.'

Another huge bang, and Ed screamed.

'Ed!' Casey cried. 'Ed.'

He had dropped the wheel, curled over, right hand reaching for his left arm.

The Hilux slowed.

Without thinking, Casey grabbed the wheel, spun right. The Hilux bounced off the road, paused for a split second and plunged over the edge of the bluff.

It was almost a sheer drop, splintering scree strewn with huge jagged rocks. The front end of the Hilux teetered and nosedived, a fairground ride jumping off the track. There was no point in trying to steer the car, but Casey desperately tried, dragging the wheel back and forth. The massive chunks of rock hurtled past, blurred, each one a threat of disaster.

'Casey.' She could hear Ed in the distance, but it was lost under the swirl of terror as the car smashed down the precipice. She felt as if she was being shaken to pieces. Her head hit the roof of the car, as it cracked down.

I am Malak.

And then somehow, the Hilux was slowing. Somehow it hadn't tipped over, crashed, disintegrated. They were reaching the bottom of the bluff, and slowing down again, straightening out.

The Hilux slid forward a few more yards and finally, almost apologetically, creaked to a halt. Silence fell.

Casey looked around, hazily.

'Casey.' A tinny shout. The phone was in her lap, somehow.

'Huh?' She found the phone, picked it up.

'OK, Casey. Well done.' Miranda didn't ask whether they were both alive. 'Can you drive the car a little bit further away?'

It seemed completely unimaginable to Casey right then. She looked across at Ed. His eyes were closed. There was blood on the window next to him.

'I can try,' she mumbled.

She clambered out of the car, ducking down, then peering up.

The pickup was parked up, high above, right at the top of the cliff. Just like at Salama, Casey thought dreamily. Just like at Salama.

Only it was Josh holding the gun now.

He would see her moving.

'Fuck,' Casey sharpened.

She ran round to Ed's side of the car, opened the door, heaved at him.

'Ed!' she screamed at him. 'Ed. You've got to move over. I can't drive unless you move over.'

A bullet hit the ground, a few feet away. They weren't following them down, not yet. They hadn't heard the helicopter. Didn't think they needed to chase. Thought they could cut them off, hunt them down long before they could reach the road. There might be time to get away.

Somehow, deep down, Ed heard her. He tried to move. She unclipped his seatbelt, pushed at him with all her strength. He fought to help her, leaning, collapsing, and somehow they got him halfway across the car.

Casey jumped in, slammed the door, tried the ignition, praying.

The Hilux started. Crossly, coughing, but it started.

Casey battled with the gears, put her foot down. The Hilux creaked forward, struggling like a tired horse in the sand.

'Come on, baby.' Casey was leaning forward, urging it on. 'Come on.'

They managed 400 yards, and then the Hilux stuck in the sand, tyres whirling impotently, sinking deeper. For a second, the engine raced, then stalled into silence.

The helicopter dived in, suddenly, wildly, and Miranda was jumping out, running across, ducking under the shrieking rotors before they had even stopped spinning.

'Miranda.' Casey could have hugged her, but there was no time. 'You came for us.'

'Of course I came.' Miranda was almost angry. 'I would never leave you, Casey.'

The pickup was still at the top of the cliff, just out of range. As Miranda spoke, a bullet cracked overhead. Aiming for the helicopter, the big, vulnerable target.

'Hurry,' screamed Casey.

Casey and Miranda dragged Ed out of the car, struggling with his weight. Casey grabbed her rucksack, abandoning everything else.

'Come on, Ed.' Miranda could barely be heard against the helicopter. 'You can do it.'

They heaved him into the back of the helicopter, and the pilot took off as soon as they were in, rotors racing, the helicopter tilting wildly as it spun away. It surged away from the black pickup, and only when they were far out of range of the M24 did it turn; turn and head for Algeria.

42

'Fucking hell.' It was Miranda's voice.

The three of them were lying in a sprawling heap in the back of the helicopter.

Casey looked around blurrily. It was a Bell 206, the workhorse used by everyone from police forces to television crews. She'd hired one once to buzz an MP in his Cotswolds mansion, a palace put on expenses. Lawns like green velvet and the taxpayers' swimming pool glittering in the sun.

This Bell was screaming over the Sahara, the rotor noise almost deafening.

'Ed.' Casey scrambled towards him.

He was half conscious, and Casey ripped apart his shirt, looking for the wound. He had been shot in the shoulder, blood smearing down his arm, across his chest.

'He'll be OK.' Miranda took over. 'It's nasty, but he'll be fine, I promise.'

Miranda reached for the first aid kit, sorted through it briskly and slapped the big field dressing over the bloody mess.

'Ed ...' Casey whispered.

'I promise you, Casey, he'll be all right.'

Miranda plunged a shot of morphine into his shoulder. 'Just a bit of it. It will help.'

They were racing over the desert now, staying low over the golden waves, trying to dodge the radar. The pickup could never track them at this speed.

'Are you OK?' Miranda peered at her. 'I don't know how you didn't flip that Hilux.'

'Me neither,' Casey said simply. 'I thought we were going to die. But they didn't factor in a helicopter. We'd never have got away without it.'

'Ahmed is flying the helicopter.' Miranda gestured at the pilot. 'He's furious with me, to be perfectly honest. I found him at Tiska airport and told him we were going just up to the border. And then when you said you were being chased, I told him we had to go over.'

'How did you make him?'

'He was all right, really. First I told him I had a gun, and would shoot him if he didn't keep going. But he still said he wouldn't fly over the border. Then I told him you were a friend, and I had to get you back, and he went for it. The truth works,' Miranda laughed. 'Who knew?'

'Thank you,' said Casey. 'Thank you.'

Thank you could never be enough.

'He said it would be fine flying into Libya, most probably' – Miranda waved her words away – 'but things might get a bit hairy when we try and fly back over the border into Algeria. Their air force might not take too kindly to this sort of thing. He says that the jets are supersonic, too, so we won't even hear them before we are blown to pieces.'

'Lovely,' said Casey. She smiled at the pilot, who ignored her.

'He figures that if we stay low enough, the radar might not pick us up for a bit,' said Miranda. 'But things might get a bit lively.'

'It worked for the Seals, going in after Osama,' said Casey. 'Let's just keep our fingers crossed.'

They were cruising west to Djanet. Ed was drifting back towards consciousness, still hazy from the morphine. Miranda constructed a sling for his shoulder, muttering to herself.

'Not sure I was paying quite enough attention during this part of the course,' she admitted. 'Think I was too busy flirting with that guy from Reuters.'

But Casey was staring out of the helicopter. The desert flowed beneath them, and far below, the road ribboned through the dunes.

She thought of the Gaddafis, racing down that road in those sleek cars. And the refugees, too, on that very same road, step by step by step. Same road, and a different journey.

She thought of them, walking and walking. Not knowing their destiny, but knowing only this: it must be better. Marching into a new beginning, in those long columns of hope: it will be better.

Those small incremental steps look like bravery, later. But it isn't bravery at the time. At the time, it is only a terrified scramble of decisions. Every time simply: what must I do to survive?

That scream: *I will not die here today.*

Maybe tomorrow, and who knows where. But not here. Not today. And not now.

You're so brave, they say after. *You don't know. And I don't have the words to explain.*

Casey gasped as the helicopter jolted sideways for a second, caught in the wind. And there was that flash in her mind. The flash that would be there for ever. A rip, always: a gun firing, a tiny figure crumpling.

A mother racing, so desperate. A father wailing up to the sky. And a little girl, eyes staring at nothing, clutched close for the very last time.

Casey shook her head and glanced across at Ed. He had bled through the bandage already, a strange, hopeful red. Half-sleeping, and twitching at each twist from the Bell.

'Which would you choose?' She almost missed Ed's words.

He was staring ahead, eyes hazy.

'What?'

'Would you choose the story, or everything else?'

His eyes were closing, and she waited a long minute to answer.

Then, the whisper. 'I don't know.'

Casey sat up again in her seat, her neck aching from the plunge down the scree. The cut on her arm was still raw, barely scabbed.

And so they flee.

Goodbye, and goodbye, and goodbye.

Miranda's phone went.

'What is it, Hessa?'

'Sorry.' Hessa sounded apologetic. 'I just thought you would want to know ... The Bombardier, it just landed in Djanet.'

'Shit,' said Miranda. 'It shouldn't be back for at least a couple of days. Where did it fly in from?'

'It was only just over in Nice,' said Hessa. 'It was a quick flight down.'

'Right. OK. Thanks for letting us know.'

Miranda leaned forward, spoke to Ahmed.

He cursed, and changed course rapidly to the north.

'We're going to head to Illizi,' said Miranda cheerfully. 'Refuel and then keep going. We should have just enough fuel, hopefully. Ahmed's got auxiliaries, and after that we can hop all the way up to Algiers.'

Ahmed muttered something in Arabic.

'He said' – Ed was cheering up – 'that you'd better be on the side of the angels. Roughly. And that it's a fucking long way to Algiers.'

'Convince him we are with the angels,' said Miranda. 'Mostly.'

'Could the Bombardier have been trying to cut us off?' Casey wondered aloud. 'God, I would love to know who is on board that plane right now.'

The mountains of the Tassili n'Ajjer rose up sharply as they crossed the border and left Libya behind. There was nothing to mark the border, just wilderness.

Grumbling to himself, Ahmed hugged the hills, the little Bell juddering in the crosswinds as it soared over the rocks.

The editor was walking past Hessa just as she called Miranda.

Salcombe paused briefly, then walked on towards Dash's office. He tapped on the doorframe.

'Dash,' he said. 'Where are Miranda and Casey at the moment?'

Dash looked up. 'Not absolutely sure right now, Andrew,' he said, with perfect honesty. 'Can I check in with them and get back to you?'

Salcombe stood at the door, waiting. Dash picked up the phone, dialled a wrong number and listened to the tone.

'No answer,' he said, dropping the receiver.

'Dash,' Salcombe said. 'I want you to have located them within the next five minutes. Is that clear?'

'Crystal,' said Dash. 'If you wait in your office, I'll come straight over.'

Salcombe walked to his office, closed the door, waited.

After seven minutes, the editor called his PA.

'Send in Hessa Khan, please.'

Dash spotted Hessa when it was too late, walking towards the editor's office. He jumped up, but there was no way to cut her off.

Hessa had never been in the editor's office before. She sat down nervously.

'Hessa,' said Salcombe, silky smooth. 'Where are Miranda and Casey right now?'

She looked at him, surprised he didn't already know. She'd kept the secret so carefully, from Eric and all the others.

But the editor was the editor, and he had to know, of course.

As they approached the Illizi airfield, Miranda held her breath, but the little helicopter radioed in and bumped down, casual as a milk round.

A man was waiting nearby, as the rotors slowed. Ahmed waved to him.

'This is my friend,' Ahmed said, choosing his words with a pilot's care. 'I called him on the radio. It would take too many hours to go to Algiers in the Bell. But he knows. He has a small plane, this man. He will take you there. He will fly you to Algiers.' Ahmed nodded at the man. 'I trust him.'

Without waiting, Ahmed sketched them a farewell. He turned and headed to the scruffy arrivals hall. They watched him go.

'Will he be OK?' said Casey.

'I don't know,' said Miranda, suddenly flat. 'I don't know what we're leaving him to.'

It was always like this. Journalists rely on the kindness, the generosity, the faith of so many, in one crazed part of the world, or another. And then, one day, the headlines end and the journalists walk away. They go back to their cosy homes in Hackney, and they rarely look back.

Ahmed had quite crossly saved their lives, and none of them knew the consequences he might face.

Better here than in Afghanistan. But ...

'I hope he'll be all right,' said Ed, watching him stamp off.

The new pilot nodded at them, sideways. He was supervising the refuelling of a little plane, a baby-blue Cessna. Averting his eyes from Ed's arm and the shredded, blood-soaked shirt, he went through all the careful checks. Then they all clambered on board, hurtled down the runway and raced into the sky.

43

Salcombe stared at Dash stony-faced. The only sign of anger came from his hand, clenched around a fountain pen.

When Dash ran out of words, Salcombe let the silence spread.

'I am the Editor of this paper.' Salcombe's voice was low. 'I have to sign off on undercover work before anyone goes anywhere. You know that, Dash. You know the rules. This isn't what we do any more.'

'I know, and I am sorry.' Dash put reason into his voice. 'I should have told you. But they're on their way back now. They're most of the way out already. I know it's been a crazy thing to do, but it's basically done already.'

'You knew I would say no,' said Salcombe. 'You deliberately went behind my back.'

'I wasn't sure,' Dash admitted.

'If you run this story, you know what will happen,' said Salcombe. 'This will just be publicity for that little operation down there. The people you've got so far will disappear into the ether, but others will spring up. It'll be a new thing to do. A craze like half the things in our wretched travel section. Casey's article will just be marketing material for these people.'

Dash ducked his head. It was possible, and he'd known that all along. 'We'll keep tabs on it, keep chasing and hunting these people down. We have to believe in sunlight as the best disinfectant, otherwise what are we all doing?'

Salcombe was tapping the fountain pen against the desk. The desk had been brought in especially. It crouched, huge and ugly in the room.

'Is that all, Dash?'

'For now.'

Salcombe nodded.

Dash walked out of the awkward silence, and over to Hessa's desk.

'Hessa.' He peered over her shoulder. 'What time is the last flight out of Algiers?'

Her eyes flicked up, and then back to her screen.

'Direct? There aren't many,' she said. 'Not since all the tourists stopped going.'

Away from Salcombe, he could feel the excitement seep back. He stretched his arms, and breathed deeply.

'There,' she pointed. 'The last flight is an Anglo Air one, leaving at 4 p.m. Takes three hours.'

Dash was looking at his watch. 'They're not going to make it to Algiers in time, not in that Cessna. Fuck it. Those bastards can just cruise north in that Bombardier. We're not leaving them in sodding Algeria for the night.'

'Let me think.' Hessa was tapping again.

'We don't have time. Henry!' Dash shouted. 'Get over here.'

The transport correspondent looked up. He was balding, generous around the middle. Henry had once aspired to greater things, but was now quite happy writing about the battle for the third runway.

'Dash?'

'Can you get Peter Collingwood on the phone in five minutes flat?'

Peter Collingwood, the boss of Anglo Air. A rotund chief executive, with deep dimples and calculating eyes.

'Sure.' Henry didn't ask questions. 'Got his mobile somewhere.'

Dash marched across to the editor's office, and spoke loudly and deliberately.

'I need you to do something,' he said. 'It's for Casey and Miranda. Henry is getting Peter Collingwood on the phone. You're going to tell him that the Anglo Air flight out of Algiers is going to wait on the runway for three people. I don't care what laws that breaks, it waits. Is that clear?'

'Why would he do that?' asked Salcombe.

'I don't care.' Dash suddenly lost his temper. 'Charm him. Beg him. Or offer him free advertising. We're still giving Ferrari free space after that fucking idiot in the driving section put one through a bus shelter on a test drive. We might as well get something useful out of it this time. Or just tell him that three *Post* journalists will die if that plane doesn't wait, and we will hang that round his neck for ever.'

'Poor sod,' muttered Henry.

The transport correspondent's mobile was ringing. Salcombe took Henry's phone and closed the glass door.

'Right.' Dash turned. 'Where have they got to now, Hessa?'

'I'm sorry,' she muttered, eyes fixed to the screen. 'I didn't know ...'

'You couldn't know,' said Dash. 'It's not your fault.'

'Miranda say's they need someone who can crack codes,' said Hessa. 'And another thing. That Bombardier just took off from Djanet and it's heading north.'

They never knew what Salcombe said to Collingwood, but the hulking Anglo Air plane was waiting patiently on the tarmac when the little Cessna bounced down and slewed to a halt. Anglo Air had even summoned one of the border guards, who stamped their passports impassively, never even glancing at the Tinkarine stamp on Ed's and Casey's passports.

Anglo, in a burst of generosity, had put them into the business section. To the surprise of the people already sitting in business, tidy with their briefcases.

An air hostess batted her eyelashes at Ed and wrapped a blanket around him.

They were asleep the moment the plane took off, Casey with the three diaries tucked inside her shirt. Trusting the air hostesses with her three shades of eyeshadow, and ignoring the ghost of another girl, who'd smiled the same way, in that blue-eyed long-ago photograph.

Just three hours later, they were shuffled through the upright seats and stowed trays and heavy grey safety belts that make not a bit of difference when a plane explodes into a million pieces. It seemed impossible that the madness of the Sahara was just three hours from Heathrow and safety, and those polite grids of houses far, far below the flight path.

She paused at the entrance to the restaurant, actress in the wings. Alone this time. And it is harder, avoiding the spotlight, when she is alone on the stage.

Bay trees, neat on either side of the door, and gold letters.

She straightened up, still bruised.

You have to behave differently when you are wearing a camera.

Humans react when interested, she realised early on. They shift in their seat. They lean forward. They gasp and nod, they gesture and sigh.

And the camera, that black pinhole eye, moved as she reacted. And as she moved, the tiny microphone picked up nothing but rustle.

So she learned to freeze, upright, at that moment. That moment when he said, 'I know I shouldn't be saying this, but ...'

It was amazing how often people said those words.

'The Daily Mail *would go mad if they knew ...'*

And every time she knew. She heard the words in 24-point headlines, typing across her mind. Even as his mouth moved.

But she stayed still as he said it. Still as a statue. Wired up like a suicide bomber, and holding his face in her frame.

And she would smile as he spoke, that big glowing smile. And the smile was the only thing her camera, unseeing and all-seeing, didn't catch. And, encouraged by that dazzling smile, he would talk on, and on, and on.

You have to behave differently when you are wearing a camera. You go where the camera needs to go. You turn when the camera wants to turn. And you are still, tripod still, when the camera demands to be still.

Even when you're scared.

Because sometimes, just sometimes, she is scared. Suddenly terrified. Because the oligarch's bodyguards are standing behind her, and she can't see what they are doing.

Because five of his friends have just turned up.

Or because she has drifted away from her car, the car she always has waiting, and now a door is swinging open and she's sliding out of control.

And she has done all the self-defence classes and all the training – hostile environment training, they call it, how to get out of a minefield using only a chicken skewer – but when it comes down to it, she is a woman.

And she knows – deep down, she knows – that she won't win in a fight.

And the lion will see that it's only a chair.

And if he finds her, wrapped in lace and wire, it will end in the nightmare.

But not this time. This time, he can't fight to the death. She has chosen these hunting grounds, for just that reason.

Last chance. All on black.

It's the very end of that long, swinging shot, snaking in and out of the scene. Dancing perfect, singing bold; smiling gritted teeth.

She thought it would get easier, out on these hunting grounds.

And in the end, it just gets harder.

Slowly, she has learned the human qualities, and sins and graces.

And how to twist them. Emotions as an anatomy lesson, for just too long.

The people who should never trust her believed every word. And the others began to worry.

Because what is friendship, when you forge it in a few seconds? And if no one can trust you, how do you trust yourself? And when you've learned how to outwit, how do you learn to be kind? And if a man can fall in love in a moment, how can you trust the old tales?

So she pauses on the steps of the restaurant, just for a second, glancing at the beautiful Georgian windows. Hesitates by the bay trees, just outside the entrance.

The starlet twirling to the end of the long tracking shot.

Steady, girl. Steady.

You have to behave differently when you're wearing a camera.

And one day, she realised the camera was wearing her.

44

It was raining when they landed, a summer rain and the smell of warm tarmac. After the sandpaper air of the Sahara, the rain-soft breeze was home.

Hessa had smoothed their passage as much as possible, with a wheelchair on standby and a smiling porter. Before landing, Ed scrambled to wash off most of the blood in the tiny airplane bathroom as Casey inspected her bruises from the cave.

At the airport, Casey followed Ed into the ambulance. He was still wrapped in the green-and-red Anglo Air blanket.

'Ed ...' The doctors were bustling around him, white-coat efficient. 'Ed, I am so sorry ...'

'Casey.' He managed to smile. 'We can't spend all our time apologising. I'll be fine ... I knew what we were doing. Now, go. Go. Go and see if those diaries were worth getting shot for.'

She smiled, light for a second, turned and jumped out of the ambulance.

But as it pulled away, blue lights flickering, she felt the sudden emptiness, a space where he had been.

I miss you, she realised, and the thought was like a punch. And I've hurt you. And I've tried to cue you into someone else's lines. But if you can give me another chance, I will try. I promise. I will try.

She watched until the ambulance turned a corner, and disappeared out of sight.

They threaded their way through the holidaymakers and businessmen and sad-hearted taxi drivers. Outside the airport, Salcombe's chauffeur, Vadim, was waiting, the big Mercedes purring. Salcombe had inherited Vadim from the last editor. The new relationship had started badly, when Janet, Salcombe's PA, called down to Vadim to tell him to drive the editor to lunch at the Ivy.

Vadim had sounded panic-stricken. It turned out he was moonlighting, whisking tourists back and forth from Heathrow in the plush Mercedes. The newsroom had found this so funny that Salcombe hadn't been able to sack Vadim on the spot.

Now Vadim, round and familiar, smiled at Miranda and Casey. His shirt strained over his stomach and he had abandoned the tie that Salcombe required.

'You OK, girls?' The Polish notes in his voice hadn't altered in a decade. 'Dash was worried. He say you get to the office as quickly as possible.'

'Dash,' grinned Miranda, 'always says that.'

'He serious this time,' Vadim said. 'He very worried. He say, drive fast and drive straight into the underground car park.'

The moment Vadim pulled away from the kerb, Casey was frowning at the diaries, head down, making notes.

'Can you work it out?' asked Miranda.

'No,' Casey scowled. 'It'll take us ages to work out this code.'

It was turning into a beautiful summer evening as they headed east towards London. The rain was clearing. Here and there the light sloped golden through the clouds, brilliant arrows of light, making sense of the old paintings of heaven.

As they drove into the city, the parks were glowing green. The roses were out, wafts of scent almost crushed by the traffic fumes. The buildings were knife sharp against the haze of the sky.

Vadim raced along the motorway. The sun was setting in neon ribbons of cloud, giving Gunnersbury an unlikely glamour. To the south, the tower blocks were like witches' teeth.

'Nearly there,' said Miranda, just as the windscreen disappeared, shards of glass exploding everywhere.

The Mercedes jerked sideways, safety airbags exploding like a punch.

'Miranda!' Casey screamed.

The car spun horribly, violently out of control, the traffic breaking into splinters, and crashing all around them. A huge truck, vast and articulated, was careering towards them. Horn blaring, driver frantic.

In the mayhem, Casey just heard the blast of the rifle.

Somehow, madly, the truck managed to hook right, just missing a head-on collision with the Mercedes. It ploughed into the central reservation, horn still blasting, as the front of the Mercedes buried itself into its side.

The stillness was almost as shocking, stabbed by screeches and smashes as the rest of the traffic came to a halt.

'Miranda,' Casey whispered.

There was a long pause.

'I'm here,' said Miranda.

Very slowly, they opened their eyes, disentangled themselves, breathed.

'I heard a gunshot,' said Casey. 'At least one.'

'Shit,' said Miranda. She had hit her eye; it was already puffing up.

'Here,' whispered Casey. 'They're coming for us here, in London.'

Someone was screaming in the distance.

They stared up at the huge truck, magically, miraculously, blocking the line of the sight to the huge towers just south of the M4.

'He must be up there,' said Casey. 'Somewhere. There isn't anywhere else he could have taken that shot.'

They both, simultaneously, registered the deathly silence from the front of the car.

'Vadim.' Casey scrambled forward.

He was gasping for breath, eyes nowhere, the blood pouring from his chest. Always a surprise, how much blood there is in a human body.

Miranda, hopelessly, grabbed his coat, held it against the gaping hole. The blood soaked through almost at once.

'Oh God.' Miranda was covered with sticky red. 'Oh God.'

'That's from a rifle,' Casey said tonelessly. 'The hole on the other side will be even worse. The London operation; that's what Josh called it. It's here. They're here.'

She crouched down.

'We've got to get out of here, Miranda. They're coming for us.'

'You go,' said Miranda. 'Take the diaries, get to the office. Start publishing. Light the fire. Go on, Casey. Go on.'

The truck driver was climbing out of his cabin.

'Holy shit.' It was a broad Cockney accent. 'I thought we were all goners there. Fucking hell. You all right?'

He caught sight of Vadim, turned pale.

'I can't leave you, Miranda,' Casey was fading. 'I can't leave you here.'

'The police will come,' Miranda said. 'And the paramedics. If there's any way of keeping Vadim alive, they'll find it. But I've got to stay with Vadim. And you need to be gone before the police get here. Run, Casey. Get out of here!'

Casey looked at Miranda, Vadim, the truck driver, his mouth agape.

'Right.' Casey forced herself out of the car, the danger all around. Her body hurt. *Ignore it.* She grabbed the rucksack, turned. 'Be careful, Miranda.'

'I will.'

And Casey sprinted, keeping the truck between her and the towers, racing down the slipway. The whole motorway had come to a halt now, so she skittered between cars, running as fast as she could.

When she reached the bottom of the ramp, the street traffic was already slowing around her. In the distance she could hear the howl of the sirens.

It had been a brilliant shot, Casey thought, on a fast-moving target. A different league from the shot into Salama.

She raced for the train.

The other passengers looked almost alien, as she prowled up and down the platform, unable to stand still, heart a thud in her throat. It felt impossible that she could blend in.

Looking down at the tracks, she remembered one of the Marines, back on the *Apollo*, talking about returning from one of their wars. 'This policeman pulled me over, said I had been going at fifty-five in a forty zone. I was looking at his mouth moving and thinking, do you really expect me to care? Do you know what I've seen, and do you still think I care about your stupid little rules?'

The train drew to the platform, sparks bursting from the rails. Too slow, too slow. Her jaw clenched as she thought of Miranda, battling to save Vadim under a cool sniper's eye. And a jolt, again, twisting to see: is somebody watching here?

Casey got on, unable to sit down, in this ordinary world. The doors slammed closed and she messaged Dash: I'm nearly there.

45

Dash couldn't sit still. Miranda had called him, filled him in on the chaos on the M4, warned him that Vadim was clinging precariously to life.

The crime correspondent was writing up the crash, with no mention, yet, of the *Post*'s involvement.

'Psycho shooter in London horror smash,' the tabloids had headlined it already. The *Post*'s managing director had been dispatched to track down Vadim's wife, to try and hold her together, somehow.

Dash winced at the photographs as they filtered through: ambulances and flashing lights and solid policemen unfurling yellow tape. Then he turned to the next thing.

'Get me the crossword guy,' he shouted.

There is one thing that every editor knows, the only cardinal rule in newspapers: don't fuck with the crossword. A newspaper can get almost everything else wrong, and no one will really care. But at a spelling mistake in the crossword, all hell breaks loose. A hundred furious letters will flood in. Subscriptions will be cancelled. A dozen times, the crossword will be returned, neatly filled in with unflattering descriptions of the editor.

Cruciverbalists do not like wasting their time. They don't even like it very much if the crossword is moved, just a few pages from its usual place in the paper.

Peregrine Courtenay had written the crossword for the *Post* for thirty years. A quiet eccentric who thought in riddles, he lunched with the obituaries editor and the paper's astrologer.

The astrologer was paid almost more than anyone else at the paper, because thousands of people bought the *Post* just to find out what disasters were scheduled to befall them this week.

'Baffling,' Ross growled once. 'Although to be honest, the astrologer is better at predicting the future than those jokers on the politics team.'

'You're a Pisces, aren't you?' the astrologer had retorted.

The cartoonist sometimes joined Peregrine for lunch too, sketching idly on yesterday's paper.

Today, Peregrine was wearing a grey cardigan, red corduroys and a turquoise tie. His eyebrows gave the fashion desk nightmares.

Dash eyed him dubiously. He suspected, quite rightly, that Peregrine regarded him as some sort of barbarian, dragging the *Post* like a virgin sacrifice into the twenty-first century.

'Peregrine,' Dash began sternly. 'The investigations team are coming in with some diaries, and they think they are written in code. It's imperative that we crack this code, as soon as possible. Do you understand?'

Whenever he spoke to Peregrine, Dash felt like a subaltern giving orders in the First World War.

'Of course, my dear fellow.' Peregrine was nodding distantly. 'Of course. But you know, one of the best people at this sort of thing on the paper is Toby.'

'Toby?'

'Yes, you know, your young reporter. Brilliant mind. Quite brilliant. Does my crosswords in minutes every day. Of course,' Peregrine preened, 'I could make them harder, dear boy. But the readers don't like it when I do. Ruins their breakfast.'

Dash beckoned Toby across the office.

'You're both up. And I need this code cracked by the morning.'

Peregrine sighed, and pottered off to cancel his table at Wiltons.

Casey burst through the doors of the *Post*. Dash was waiting for her, eyes almost sympathetic.

'You OK?' He wanted her to be, though he knew she wasn't. 'I should have been more careful. I thought you would be safe in London.'

'The whole world thinks it will stay over there,' said Casey. 'Right up until it comes over here.'

The *Post* had emptied out now. Hessa had the big conference room all ready. She had transcribed the tapes, all of them, and even ordered sandwiches from somewhere. Peregrine and Toby, the odd couple, were waiting patiently at one end of the long table, Peregrine shooting occasional disapproval at the sandwiches.

'Did you know,' Peregrine asked the sandwiches, 'that Herodotus was the first to describe a scalping? The Scythians and *aposkythizein*.'

As Casey walked in, they fell on the diaries.

Ross leaned against the wall. Robert, the chief reporter, had his feet up on the table, notepad ready, headline eyes. Dash set out the publication plan.

'We would have liked to delay running this story,' Dash began. 'To give ourselves some breathing space. But we probably can't now. The tabloids are going feral over the M4 shooter, so we have to move things up. The police aren't anywhere near making arrests yet, as far as Arthur can tell, but you never know. They're trying to work out where the shots came from. Peregrine and Toby, I need you to throw everything at breaking that code.'

Salcombe walked into the room and sat down at the table.

'Carry on, Dash,' Salcombe nodded.

'Right. If we get any new names overnight, we can try and front them up asap. I'll get the general reporters in early so they can head out to any possible doorsteps. The moment this story starts breaking, anyone involved will lawyer up, and potentially try and leave the country. We won't have long to jump them.'

'Seconds count?' asked Robert.

'Apart from everything else,' Dash pointed out, 'we've got to assume that at some point, whoever is behind this will start warning the people involved. And at that point we lose the advantage of surprise. They may have warned them already, which makes them potentially dangerous.'

'What,' Casey asked exhaustedly, 'is the timeline on all this?'

'We'll break it online tomorrow afternoon and then it can be in the paper the next day.' Dash was thinking aloud. 'We can break it down into day one, day two, usual stuff. Selby first, and then we'll toss Newbury to the sharks in the evening. I'm going to need two thousand words from you, Casey, for day one, about the manhunt out in the desert. Bung in all the colour, with a nice drop intro.'

'Fine.'

'I'll call someone in from the Business section to put together a profile on Selby. Cormium won't like it, but tough. Robert' – Dash nodded at the chief reporter, who pulled together yards of copy when a major story broke – 'will knock up the news story.'

'I'll pull in one of Foreign team to put together a thousand words on the politics of Libya. Alice can do a piece on refugees,' Dash added. 'And we'll start getting video to splice something together from Casey's footage from the camp.'

'What are the legal implications of all this?' Salcombe broke in.

'We're not sure yet,' said Dash. 'We're fine with Oliver Selby, I would say. Casey saw him shooting with her own eyes, and there's the recording. So we can run him on the first day, and take it from there.'

'And you can't libel a dead man anyway,' Ross pointed out.

'What?' Dash looked at him.

'From what you've said' – Ross shrugged – 'they're not fussed about killing, these guys, and I can't see that Josh character letting him back out of there. Selby will know all about their modus operandi, and they won't want him trundling back to London knowing how they do everything. Plus they'll be on the run, the three of them. It would be a hassle to get him back to Algeria, and why would they bother? It will be a shallow grave somewhere in Libya for Selby.'

'And Selby brought in the Trojan horse, which will piss them off even more.' Dash was nodding. 'You're right. They'll cut their losses there. Spot of summary justice.'

'Vigilante.' Ross's smile had no humour. 'Just not down a dark alley.'

They were so casual. Casey squeezed her nails into her palms. She thought about Selby, taken out and shot in the back of the head. Just the latest in the long line of deaths at Euzma. But this death was hers.

'I'm going to grab the lawyer.' Dash barrelled out of the room. 'And get graphics working on a decent map of Libya.'

'I've got to check today's front once more.' Ross followed him.

There was a brief silence after they'd left the room. Casey powered up a laptop that Hessa had provided, and glared at her mobile. Ed's phone had been abandoned in the Hilux, and the matron at St Thomas' said he couldn't be disturbed.

Robert was reading through the transcripts, eyebrows raised. Casey was typing like an automaton. After a few minutes, Robert began tapping away too, pausing occasionally to check a fact with the room. Hessa was putting together a timeline, running in and out of the conference room.

'I don't mean to interrupt, Casey' – Peregrine was staring at a grid of letters – 'but do you know any of the names we're looking for? It would be helpful. Work backwards.'

'Milo Newbury.' Casey felt the tears stinging her eyes suddenly. 'Oliver Selby.'

'Ah.' Peregrine was scribbling again. 'Yes. Jolly good.'

'We need more clues,' said Toby, in the end. 'We need more.'

Casey moved round the desk.

Toby was typing long rows of numbers into his laptop, churning algorithms.

Casey read the numbers out loud.

'511734, 12375, 11852.'

There was a long pause.

'What do they mean?' she said into the silence. 'What's the pattern?'

'We don't exactly know yet.' Peregrine spoke unwillingly.

'Are they all like that?'

'There are symbols too.' Toby gave her a sympathetic smile. 'You said the flights went in and out of Algeria, didn't you? It would be helpful if you could make a list of the dates, when you think it would be most likely that someone was out at Euzma. When was Milo Newbury there, for example?'

'October,' said Casey. 'And we left Oliver behind, out there. We can cross-ref the Djanet flights to the diaries.'

'OK.' Toby calculated. 'OK. In that case, I think this little arrow symbol probably indicates one of their visitors. And that makes ...'

He stood up, scribbled on a whiteboard.

Milo Newbury: 55364, 33204, 23463, 34754

Oliver Selby: 431055, 53153, 42426, 1223

'Always assuming' – Peregrine shook his head – 'that this Rory character didn't make any mistakes with his own codes. And amateurs always do.'

'Why isn't it all groups of five numbers?' Casey asked him.

'I don't know yet.' Toby was doodling smiley faces around the codes. 'I don't know.'

'Write all the numbers with that symbol up on the board, Toby,' said Robert. 'There has to be a pattern.'

'And we have to break it,' said Casey. 'It's the only way to find out who else was out there. There has to be a way.'

46

Dash came back into the conference room. It was nearly midnight.

'Time to bugger off, Casey,' he said.

'Where do I go?' She looked forlorn, standing under the strip lighting.

'Ah, well.' Dash rolled his eyes. 'Hessa had an idea.'

The *Post* had recently installed a prayer room – 'multi-faith,' HR said proudly – a few doors down from the conference room. The newsroom had only identified its location after someone from Commercial was caught in a compromising position with the art director. It was the heavily Muslim IT guy who had discovered them, unfortunately.

'At least she was on her knees,' said the head of HR wearily. 'You bunch of idiots.'

Somehow, although most of the shops had closed for the night, Hessa had got a mattress delivered to the prayer room.

Casey's eyes filled with tears as she took in the pillows and the pretty duvet cover. It looked almost cosy, despite the institutional grey carpet. Hessa had even managed pyjamas, and a toothbrush.

'It's so kind of you, Hessa. Thank you.'

'Hessa's pulled together some clothes for tomorrow.' Dash shook his head. 'God knows how at this time of night.'

'I mugged the fashion cupboard,' Hessa grinned. 'And swiped the beauty samples too. Cressida's going to be spitting tacks.'

'Miranda's going to stay in a hotel,' said Dash. 'I think she's probably much less of a focus for them – they may not even know she exists. But she's booked in under Hessa's name just in case. Vadim's clinging on, by the way.'

'Oh God, I hope he's all right.' Casey could barely stand. 'But I can't leave them working on the codes. We've got to keep going.'

'You're to call it a night and that's an order,' said Dash. 'Hessa's organised security for you too. I wouldn't have thought of it, but she was worried.'

A small, tough-looking man was standing next to Dash. Another ex-Army type, Casey thought. They were everywhere.

'I've just got a few more words to write,' Casey said, peering beyond him into the conference room.

'Polish it up in the morning,' said Dash. 'I mean it, Casey. Go to bed.'

She could see the slump in Peregrine's shoulders as she said goodnight.

'It could be a fairly simple transposition cipher, with an element of substitution,' Peregrine explained. 'With your Mr Joshua Charlton adding in a few little quirks of his own, too.'

He was trying, clumsily, to cheer her, Casey could see.

'We'll keep working at it,' promised Toby. 'We won't stop.'

He was writing endless formulae, barely looking up. His keyboard pattered like rain as she walked to the prayer room.

As Casey closed the door to her little sanctuary, she could barely remember her own bedroom. It seemed a thousand years since she had left London. She thought of Ed, tucked in his hospital bed. Take care of him, she almost prayed, in the little holy room at the heart of the paper.

And then, because she always would now, she thought of the refugees out in the nowhere. Praying that, one day, the world would care. Praying for the bombed-out schools and the burned-out hospitals, and the sons who never come home.

And one day, there is no tomorrow.

A mother and father leaving everything behind, only to face the worst. And a nameless lost girl, a girl she watched die for a story.

Casey lay down on the unfamiliar mattress, and pulled the unfamiliar duvet over her head, and tried to sleep.

Casey jumped awake in the night.

There weren't any windows in the prayer room. It felt like a tomb.

Something ... There was something on the edge of her consciousness ... Something ...

She climbed off the mattress, and scrambled back to the conference room.

'None of those number groups starts with a number above five,' she said.

They looked up, wearily.

'We know,' said Toby. 'And the second number is usually quite low too. But then it becomes more chaotic.'

'"Most still, most secret, and most grave",' quoted Casey. 'It's from *Hamlet*. Mostgrave. That was the name of the company they used for the jet. It must have been a sort of joke.'

'*Hamlet*?' Peregrine raised an eyebrow.

'There was only one book in the palace,' said Casey. 'Shakespeare. The plays. Five acts.'

Toby pushed himself back in his seat, eyes flicking from side to side. 'So the numbers ...'

'They would use Arabic or Roman numerals,' said Peregrine. 'Surely.'

'Rory might not,' said Casey. 'That might make it too obvious. It might be act, scene, line ...'

She trailed off, mind whirling.

'And then syllable,' tried Robert. 'Or word.'

'It might work,' Toby's head jerked up from the screen.

'Rory was laughing about it,' said Casey. 'Those plays, he said someone had left them there. It made him smile. It must have meant something.'

'And it was what he had to hand,' said Robert.

'We need a copy of Shakespeare.' Peregrine hurried off in the direction of the Books department. 'They'll have a copy over there, I'm quite sure of it ...'

'Or' – Toby rolled his eyes, and turned back to the laptop – 'we could just read it right here.'

It took him only a second to find the plays.

'Which one?' Toby was asking, as Peregrine puffed back into view.

'I don't know.' Casey's eyes clouded.

'Well, only thirty-seven to pick from,' said Peregrine. He was clutching the complete works. 'Depending on whether you include *The Two Noble Kinsmen*.'

'We absolutely should' – Robert suppressed his smile – 'include *The Two Noble Kinsmen*.'

'Rory was reading *Macbeth*,' said Casey. 'We could start with that.'

'Act five,' deciphered Peregrine, 'Scene five ... and then try line thirty-six.'

'"Within this three mile may you see it coming",' Robert got there first.

'Mile.' Casey felt that surge of relief. 'Mile ... The fourth word in the line.'

'Act three,' Peregrine went on. 'Scene three. Line twenty.'

'"Thou may'st",' Toby stumbled over the word. '"Revenge – O slave!"'

'He's counted "may'st" as one word,' Peregrine concluded. 'Mile-O. That's it. Milo.'

A quick smile of triumph, and they hustled on to the next word.

'Word three: "With a new Gorgon: do not bid me speak",' Toby got there first. 'Then fourth from "Those that we bury back, our monuments."'

'"Shall be the maws of kites",' agreed Peregrine. 'Newbury.'

Peregrine brought out a silver hip flask in triumph.

'What about Selby?' Casey tigered on.

They worked it out slowly.

'O. Liver. Sell. By.'

'Well done, Casey.' Peregrine put his hand on her shoulder. 'We weren't getting anywhere.'

Suddenly laughing, Casey felt the room blaze with excitement.

'We've got to do all of them,' she begged. 'We've got to get every last one.'

'We will,' Toby grinned at her. 'Give us a chance.'

They swallowed their coffee, went back to work.

'Act five,' read Casey. 'Scene one, line one seven three.'

They counted, swiftly.

'But that scene doesn't have a hundred and seventy-three lines,' said Peregrine.

'"Good night, good doctor",' read Toby. 'And then that's it. They exeunt.'

He rolled the word around his mouth.

'But it must be,' said Casey.

'He might,' Peregrine's mouth sagged, 'have used different plays at different times.'

'Fuck.' Toby's eyes widened. 'Fucking hell. This is going to take for ever.'

'I suppose it was a game too, for them,' said Peregrine. 'Not just an aide-memoire.'

Robert had his head in his hands.

'It never occurred to me,' he said, 'that these people might actually get bored out there.'

'People get bored everywhere,' said Casey drily. 'You'd be astonished how boring a war zone is, most of the time. And then a mortar lands.'

'Casey.' The chief reporter took charge. 'Go back to bed. You're shattered. And we need you to be awake tomorrow.'

'I can't.' But she was staggering.

'You can.' Robert pushed her to the door. 'Get on with it.'

'Before you go, did he have any other favourites?' Peregrine looked hopeful. 'Did any of them quote anything?'

'I'd focus' – Casey stumbled out of the room – 'on the tragedies.'

Instead of going back to his flat, Dash had slept on the small sofa in his office. He woke at dawn, with a crick in his neck. For once, in the early morning light, the offices looked positively rosy, the dawn light giving an odd magic to the grey desks.

Dash stood in the dawn and telephoned Arthur, not caring that it was before 6 a.m. There had been no developments in the hunt for the M4 shooter. The police had identified the flat from where the shot had been fired, and nothing else. The door to the flat had been kicked in, a window smashed. No fingerprints so far.

'What have we got?' Dash asked, marching into the conference room.

Peregrine and Toby looked serious, and shattered. The conference room was littered with Red Bull cans and coffee cups. Peregrine was still boycotting the sandwiches.

Briefly, they explained the code.

'We've got a list of some of the names,' said Toby. 'Casey cracked the cipher. But we're not sure of all of them. And some of the names aren't quite right, either. I don't think we'll get anywhere near a criminal standard of proof, not using these diaries.'

'Right,' Dash translated. 'You mean that we're going to have to get these names to cough to it, or we're not going to be able to run the story.'

'That,' said Toby, 'is exactly what I mean.'

Peregrine tugged worriedly at his eyebrows.

'Fine,' said Dash. 'Give me the list.'

They handed it over: nine names.

'I thought he told Casey that there were thirty or forty who had gone out there,' said Dash, reading down the list. He read one name, read it again, whistled.

'That's only so far,' explained Toby.

'There may have been more anyway,' said Peregrine. 'The diaries have several pages missing.'

'We haven't worked them all out yet. And, of course, we're only getting names and surnames,' Toby went on. 'No other information.'

John Smiths are almost impossible for newspapers to track down; Casey would have been able to find a Peregrine Courtenay within thirty seconds.

Dash looked up at them both. They were staring at him.

'You've seen who's on this list?'

They both nodded.

'Alexander King Slay,' Toby nodded. 'Sometimes, it's like that. Not completely clear. Rory used homophones half the time. Sometimes the last number seems to refer to a syllable, sometimes it's the whole word. We're having to guess the plays too, unless we can work out more of the pattern. We think *Hamlet* is the key for King Slay. So we assume he meant Kingsley.'

They looked at the list again.

'It's just a matter,' Peregrine said delicately, 'of which Alexander Kingsley he means.'

47

Casey woke to a tap on the prayer-room door. After six hours' sleep in her small sanctuary, she felt alive again.

She opened the door. Miranda was standing there with the bodyguard and a coffee.

'All the trimmings,' said Miranda. 'You're alive then.'

'Matthew.' The bodyguard introduced himself again. 'No problems last night. No problems at all.'

Behind Miranda the newsroom was warming up.

They hugged for a long time. As she pulled away, Casey forced a smile on to her face.

'You'll be OK,' said Miranda firmly. 'It will be all right, in the end.'

Casey nodded. Miranda had a huge black eye.

'That looks amazing.' Casey examined it.

'Isn't it great?' said Miranda. 'Tom will be terminally unimpressed. But the good news is that Vadim is clinging on, just about. It's incredible what they can do in these hospitals.'

'Unlike in Salama,' said Casey. 'But I'm so glad about Vadim.'

Gulping coffee, she scrambled down to the unlovely showers in the basement. Then she dressed hurriedly, barely noticing the clothes Hessa had raided from the fashion cupboard.

'Considerably more chic than usual,' Miranda whistled at her.

'That cupboard is only in extremis,' Dash warned. 'Cressida's the one person I am scared of.'

He had been waiting for them in the conference room, bouncing a tennis ball against the wall. Toby and Peregrine had gone to the hotel next door for a couple of hours' sleep. Janet had brought in some croissants.

'You need to eat something, love.'

Now Dash pushed the list of names towards them.

'We always knew they might be big names.' Miranda refused to be cowed. 'The sort of person who can drop six figures on a trip down to Libya – they were always going to be major players.'

'I know,' said Dash. 'But how the hell are we going to break Kingsley?'

They contemplated him for a moment.

Alexander Kingsley had followed the classic career path for an aspirant politician. Oxford – PPE, of course – and then a few years as a special adviser. After that, he had dropped out of politics, for a few years in the business world, so he could talk about real jobs and real people and real life.

Eton was the only blot on his copybook.

Kingsley had married smart; the pretty daughter of some minor aristocrat. Lucinda, Casey remembered. Sharper than she looked, in her Zara dresses and Jimmy Choo shoes. Lucinda worked for a clever pottery company, in the nexus of floral and knowing. The Kingsleys had two children, a boy and a girl: the perfect family. His mates call him Alex, his spokeswoman said again and again.

In his early thirties, Kingsley had run first in a cannon-fodder seat somewhere in the north. That was the traditional baptism of fire. Five years later, he slipped into an ultra-safe seat deep in the Home Counties. Only four years into his parliamentary career, and already he was being talked about as a future leader. Casey had heard him on the *Today* programme, often, defusing the presenter like an IED.

Kingsley was fast with a quote, every time. So the political editors came back to him, again and again. In Parliament, he sat first on a security select committee, an effective platform for a bright young MP. Soon he was a very junior minister. Then he joined the small team charged with coaching the Prime Minister before the weekly questions, when the party leader was hurled into the bear pit.

The Prime Minister was struggling more and more these days, and suddenly Kingsley was being whispered about for the leadership. Not much experience, sure, but a breath of fresh air. A break from the past. Did you see him on that trip to India, with the elephant? The party needs someone like that.

There had never been any gossip about Kingsley, Casey thought. No nannies or secretaries or pretty young aides. None of the bear traps laid for hopeful MPs. Occasionally, he was seen at the most exclusive members' clubs, or the newest restaurants, with the longest waiting lists. But that just burnished his appeal, made older MPs look ever more antiquated. Lucinda was often on Kingsley's arm, and always smiling.

Sitting in the conference room, Casey dropped her head in her hands. 'How do we get to Kingsley?'

'Archie.' Dash got the political editor on the line, put him on speakerphone. 'Where is Alexander Kingsley today?'

'He's appearing before the Home Affairs committee at eleven a.m.,' said Archie. 'They want to bollock him about immigration numbers or something. Not that there's a whole lot he could do about it, since the Treasury cut all the funding for the border agency, but there we go.'

They could all hear it in his voice: Archie liked the clever young minister.

Archie would have spent a lot of time with Kingsley, over the years. First as a special adviser, when Archie was a junior reporter. Back then they would get drunk at party conference, bawl karaoke in some dive in Soho and recover at the football on Saturday. Because Kingsley had picked a team and read up about it. He might even have picked Arsenal, like Archie, for convenience.

This is the price of a pint of milk, sir – wouldn't do to be caught out. A loaf of bread, and your team's score for last night.

As Kingsley rose up the ranks, he would be getting more and more useful to the *Post*'s political editor, tapped right into the centre. It was the tightest of cliques, that Westminster bubble. Miranda had worked in the lobby briefly, and hadn't liked it. You never knew whether your back was going to be scratched or stabbed.

'Any idea where Kingsley'll be going after that?' Miranda snapped.

'It's Thursday,' Archie pointed out. 'He'll be heading back to his constituency at some point. He'll probably have a surgery or something tomorrow. I can check.'

Surgeries, where MPs are forced to interact with an endless stream of their constituents, are probably the low point of their week. Many of them avoided them. Kingsley was reputed to be fairly assiduous. After the surgery, he and Lucinda would spend a weekend at their pretty, but understated, cottage in the constituency. The cottage had roses round the door and was bigger than it looked from the road.

'Don't check just yet,' said Dash, hanging up.

Casey was throwing Red Bull cans and coffee cups towards the wastepaper basket. She missed twice for every time she got one in. Miranda rolled her eyes.

Over the desks, Dash could see the editor arriving in his office, nodding at Janet, picking up his magazines.

Dash headed towards the editor's office.

'Morning, Dash.' Salcombe had evidently decided to suspend hostilities.

'I need you to organise lunch with Alexander Kingsley today.' Dash went straight in.

'Kingsley?' Salcombe's eyebrows rose. 'I saw him a few weeks ago. I can't arrange a lunch today, he'll be booked up.'

If the editor of a national newspaper needs the Prime Minister on the phone, it probably takes fifteen minutes to organise, at the outside. They drop round for kitchen suppers, godparent each other's children, sunbathe together in Tuscany.

'You can,' said Dash, 'and you will.'

'I don't have time for lunch today,' said Salcombe.

Dash came closer.

'Get Kingsley to lunch today. One o'clock at Russet. Parliament Square.'

'This is ludicrous.'

'No. It's not.'

For a second, Dash thought that Salcombe would refuse.

Then: 'Fine. I'll call Kingsley.'

Dash walked into the conference room, looked at the clock on the wall.

'We've got five hours,' he said, 'to crack this.'

48

Russet, almost next to the House of Commons, is where a political editor can guarantee himself an hour and a half of a cabinet minister's time with delectable food as bait. Casey had worked there before.

Now she hesitated by the bay trees just outside the entrance. The maître d' hurried towards her.

'The Editor likes to sit beside the window,' Janet had insisted earlier. 'He requires it. It's important.'

'Of course, madam,' they agreed, in hushed tones.

Casey looked across. The beautiful Georgian windows dominated the room, the view out over the cold stone grey of the Treasury.

Casey smiled sweetly.

'I'd love to sit beside the window,' she said to the waiter. 'The sun is so gorgeous at this time of year, don't you think?'

The waiter hesitated. There was already a figure at the table for two beside the window. Next to the other window was a large round table for six, the only table for six in the room. Dash had reserved that table and would cancel in exactly five minutes.

'I'm so sorry, madam,' said the waiter. 'Would the one along from that gentleman be suitable?'

'Perfectly,' she said.

She smiled around her as she sat down on the brown leather banquette, straightened her black dress. Alexander Kingsley, sitting next to the window, smiled back; politicians are charming to anyone who might, some day, vote for them.

Casey looked around the room, and fiddled with her pearls. In one corner, the *Sun*'s political editor was bending the ear of the shadow chancellor; barely letting him get a word in edgeways over the crab cakes. In another, the *Sunday Times*'s political editor was coquetting with a pollster.

Casey turned away; they both knew her slightly.

Kingsley's phone bleeped. 'Sorry, running fifteen minutes late,' breezed Salcombe.

Kingsley folded his arms, and scowled on to Great George Street.

A moment later, the waiter rushed over to Casey's table with a bottle of champagne.

'Mr Lough sends his apologies, madam, but he will be a few minutes late.'

'Oh, that is simply too irritating,' Casey frowned. 'He is utterly hopeless.'

She sighed, as the waiter poured a glass of champagne. Kingsley smiled back at her.

'Do have one too.' She smiled at Kingsley. 'Please. He'll be hours now, and if I drink this bottle all by myself, it'll be a catastrophe.'

He hesitated only for a second.

'I don't normally drink at lunch,' he said. 'But why not?'

They chatted about nothing much, at first. So irritating how some people just don't care about being on time. I can't bear it.

It's so rude, isn't? Isn't that fireplace just beautiful? I love it here. It's very convenient. The turbot is absolute heaven.

Kingsley's phone bleeped again. Another fifteen minutes' delay.

'It's just too bad,' he said. 'I've got so much to be getting on with.'

'Have another glass of champagne,' Casey suggested help-fully.

They chatted on. Casey was getting a sense of Kingsley, now.

Who are you?

Tell me who you are.

For a while, she moaned about the elusive Mr Lough. He's a bit wild, but I think he will settle down, don't you? I mean, boys do, don't they?

Another glass of champagne.

'Of course he will.' Kingsley was genial.

'And who are you waiting for?' Casey asked.

'Andrew Salcombe,' Kingsley namedropped. 'You know, the Editor of the *Post*.'

'Of course,' said Casey. 'And I know that I recognise you from somewhere. I am just completely hopeless with names.'

'Alexander Kingsley,' he said. 'I'm the MP for Throwleigh South.'

Time to attack.

'Of course,' said Casey, then dropped her voice slightly. 'You know Josh Charlton.'

Kingsley went still. 'Josh?'

'Out in Libya,' Casey said. 'In Salama.'

His face registered no emotion. Casey's eyes never left his. He glanced away.

'I don't know what you mean,' said Kingsley, but there was a quiver somewhere.

'You went out to Salama.' Casey had dropped the charm now, like shedding a coat. 'You went shooting out there.'

He hadn't moved. It would look as if they were having a cordial chat, in the midst of the polite Georgian beauty.

'You're talking nonsense,' said Kingsley. 'I don't mean to be rude, but ...'

'I know that you went out to Salama.' Casey was going for the kill.

'If you're trying to blackmail me somehow,' said Kingsley. 'It isn't going to work.'

The MP's eyes flickered to the political editor of the *Sun*, the political editor of the *Sunday Times*. He wouldn't storm out, they had guessed beforehand. Those two political editors, apex predators, would smell blood in the water. They had thought about summoning Archie there too, to add to the crowd. Kingsley would do almost anything to avoid a scene in Russet.

He wouldn't know who she was, or what she knew.

'You see, we have the dates of your trip,' said Casey, barely changing her tone. 'To Tunisia. I spoke to Paul Heyworth this morning. He remembered that you'd been on one of those parliamentary fact-finding trips not long after you'd joined Parliament. He said it was a funny thing, but you'd taken off on your own afterwards. You didn't get the flight back from Tunis. He thought it was especially odd, because the MPs were all booked in first class. I gather you said you were going to meet your wife over in Morocco, for a romantic weekend down in Essaouira. Escape the kids, you said. First time in ages. Heyworth remembered it very clearly.'

'He must have been confused,' said Kingsley, a shade too swiftly.

'I'm not sure the MP for Murchington gets confused that easily,' said Casey, with cobra eyes. 'Heyworth keeps meticulous diaries, you know. Very detailed. I think he plans to retire on them quite soon.'

'I'll talk to him,' said Kingsley. He was sweating now.

'So after that chat,' Casey went on, 'our lovely fashion editor, Cressida, rang up your wife. They've talked lots over the years, haven't they? Lucinda's always so helpful with the press, isn't she? She really understands the value of publicity.'

And now he knew she was from the *Post*, and she saw the jaw push forward.

'I don't see why you would approach my wife.' Kingsley tried to sound outraged. 'How dare you?'

'Cressida said she was doing a Morocco-themed piece,' said Casey. 'Asking stylish celebrities about their memories of Morocco. You know the sort of thing. Lucinda said she'd love to, simply love to, but she'd never been to Morocco.'

'She must have forgotten,' said Kingsley. 'Or maybe she just didn't want to talk about it. She's entitled to her privacy.'

'Cressida really pushed her on it,' said Casey. 'Said Lucinda's own PR had suggested it. Said she'd mentioned something about a weekend down in Essaouira three years ago. A romantic break. But Lucinda really didn't know what she was talking about. Said that you'd talked about going but never quite got round to it. And, you know, sometimes you can just tell when someone is telling the truth. She really didn't know.'

'She's been very busy recently. It's harassment.'

'She was busy herself that weekend you were abroad, it turned out. But not with you. We know that she wasn't in Morocco that weekend.'

It had taken hours to locate her, that weekend. Toby had watched an entire tennis match on slow motion, freezing it at every wide shot of the crowd. Not there. Then they had widened out to her friends, all of them. And finally, there she was, at the races, smiling, betting slip in hand.

'Must have been a mistake.'

'We can prove it,' Casey shrugged. 'And anyway, do you think all those people will forget Lucinda was there that day? And do you think they'll lie for you, when they know the truth? And your passport, that will have a stamp.'

'I lost my passport a few months ago.' Kingsley blocked the shot. 'Annoying, but what can you do? My secretary organised a new one.'

'And then, of course, there was the Bombardier.' Casey would not be deflected. 'Paul Heyworth's secretary dug out the flight times, when you were supposed to fly back from Tunis. Two hours after that flight took off, we can see the Bombardier leaving Tunis for Djanet. And then, a few days later, it flew to Geneva. So, of course, that threw us. Why would you be flying to Geneva? Then we did some more research, and it so happens that you were attending a meeting at the UN that day.'

'My travel arrangements are none of your goddamn business,' Kingsley lashed out.

'But aren't you starting to wonder,' Casey taunted, 'how I know so much? Because who do you think is talking? And who do you think snapped?'

His eyes stayed on her face.

'Was it Josh?' Casey sing-songed. 'Was it Leo? Or was it that ruthless shit, Rory? And do they have photographs? And what did they say? Because I've been there, Mr Kingsley. I've driven down that avenue, and up into those hills. I've looked down at Salama, just like you. And I've watched those children play.'

There was a silence.

You see my outside, but you know my heart.

'I'll deny it,' Kingsley said. 'I'll deny every single word. You can't prove a thing.'

'Don't.' Casey's eyes were blazing. 'Don't you dare lie to me.'

Kingsley fell silent; shattering under her eyes. He seemed to get smaller, just sitting there.

The political editors chatted on in their corners. And a minute later, a pretty waitress came across.

'Can I get you anything, madam? Or you, sir? While you're waiting.'

I am Malak.

'Just the bill,' Casey said crisply. 'Just the bill.'

49

'He doesn't' – Dash paused the video – 'actually confirm it.'

Kingsley froze mid-grimace on the screen in Dash's office.

'Miranda would have nailed it,' Casey grinned. 'If she didn't look like …'

'Shut up.' Miranda threw some Post-it notes at her.

'Let's start publishing,' decided Dash. 'Get the Selby stuff out there. That'll ramp up the pressure on Kingsley. I think this recording is enough, personally, but we'll see.' He stopped. 'We could always shake down the wife; imply that her husband was in Marrakesh with someone else.'

'Let's run the Selby story now,' said Miranda, 'and then go to Kingsley's party HQ first thing tomorrow morning. Their director of comms is quite sharp. If he thinks Kingsley's involved in anything like this, he'll hold his feet to the flames for us.'

'And then,' Casey said, 'they'll throw him under the bus.'

'Put a reporter on Kingsley's doorstep,' Dash said to Ross. 'In London and in Throwleigh. Bump up the pressure on him. Get the family jumpy.'

'Right,' said Ross.

Casey looked back at the screen, at Kingsley frozen against the elegant backdrop of Russet.

The videos are the worst thing about undercover journalism, Miranda had said to her once.

Not just a crook, but a fool too. Walking into the ambush, with your idiocy immortalised. A twenty-first-century stocks, with clicks instead of eggs.

Casey looked at Kingsley, trapped for ever in the pixels, and shuddered.

They were gathered around the digital desk, the subs looking on impassively. Dash, the ringmaster, glanced at his watch.

'Send it live.'

The *Post* website changed abruptly, the banner headline taking up a third of the screen.

'Human safari,' it screamed.

There was a ripple of applause around the newsroom.

The video dominated the homepage, cut together with a map and white-on-black writing. Alice's voice, calmly talking the viewer through the nightmare. Casey's footage was wobbly, but the sound was clear.

'You got her.' Josh's voice. 'Clean kill.'

'Holy bleep. Bleep.'

The video ended with Oliver Selby's face, grinning, proud. And Casey knew it was with her for ever.

As she sat at her desk, she saw the other papers startle, focus and steal.

Within minutes, the story was exploding across every outlet, with even the *Financial Times* screaming: 'Cormium shares in freefall after boss named in Africa scandal.'

Casey thought of Josh, Leo, Rory. They would know by now, even if they were still at Euzma. They would know the net was beginning to close.

They might still get away, she thought, and disappear into the desert like so many had before. They were survivors, those men. No matter what happened, they'd probably seen worse. She had photographed all three of them though, quite carefully and quite ruthlessly, just to make that escape that little bit harder.

In the conference room the chief reporter was pulling together reaction for a long read-through in the paper. The justice secretary was already appalled, demanding an inquiry. The shadow justice minister was even more appalled. Heathrow had sequestrated the Bombardier.

On the big television screens, the former defence minister was being pursued down the street. 'Everything I did in Tripoli for Cormium was carried out in good faith,' he mumbled. 'The British government support and encourage UK companies as they invest overseas ...'

'Wanker,' Ross summarised, as the politician's face was lost in a flurry of camera flashes.

Alphavivo was rumoured to be launching a takeover bid for Cormium.

A text popped up on Casey's phone.

'Y'all can come and celebrate at Gigi's any time – drinks on me.'

'Thanks, Jasper,' she messaged back. 'You were the key.'

There was a loud cheer as a crate of champagne was delivered, with compliments on a cyan-blue card.

Miranda and Casey found cards in their pigeonholes, Victorian bunches of sweet peas in pink and blue vases.

'On Monday, the answer for three down will be "trium-phant",' Casey read. 'Peregrine.'

'Nine across will be "magnificent",' smiled Miranda.

'We never do it alone, do we?' said Casey.

And she wondered if they would know, out in Salama, in those little tents in the heart of the desert. Would it be better for that mother to know? Or would it be worse to know that her child had died only for some foreigner's entertainment?

Worse, probably.

And then the thud, that would always be.

You chose this.

It wasn't a choice.

Yes. Yes, it was.

As the paper went off stone, they put the Milo Newbury story up online.

Son of the legendary art dealer. Well-known Chelsea figure. Mystery surrounds death.

Casey stared at the photograph of Milo on the front page. They'd used the picture of him out in the desert. Smiling, in his birthday shirt, the golden sea behind.

'Copyright vests in the photographer,' Ross recited cheer-fully. 'Good luck coming along with an infringement grumble on that one.'

Inside the paper, Milo was smooth in a publicity shot for the gallery. In another, he was at the races with Bella, almost losing an eye to an alarming violet fascinator. There was a photograph, too, of the flat in Pimlico, where his mother was happy, once.

The other journalists were coming over to Casey and Miranda – good job, brilliant work, fucking fantastic – while Casey tried not to think about Lady Newbury. Lady Newbury and her endless grief. And through the congratulations, the thought nagged like a sore tooth.

It was late on a Friday night, but for once no one had made it as far as the Plumbers.

Casey and Miranda were calm now. It was often like this, during the biggest stories. The newsroom was powering along, quietly efficient. People knew what to do. A Cormium PR was fighting a rearguard battle with the news desk lawyer, and losing.

'No,' the lawyer was saying, 'the Editor is very clear, we're not taking Cormium out of the headline … No, of course it's relevant.'

Miranda and Casey were in their office, her bodyguard, Matthew, sitting like a shadow, just a few feet away.

'The eye of the storm,' said Miranda.

'Best' – Casey looked at her bruised face thoughtfully – 'not to mention eyes right now.'

'Shut up,' Miranda said, then focused. 'That's odd.'

'What?' yawned Casey. She padded round to Miranda's screen.

'There,' Miranda pointed.

'*Lovely work, though you know I hate to admit it. Great story. Just brilliant. Always better when these things come completely out of the blue too,*' Casey read out loud. '*At least it stops my news editor bollocking me quite so much. Catch up soon, Jess.*'

News editors will sulk for days over missed scoops and spend hours deconstructing how a story was missed. They analyse possible sources and send shirty emails to their reporters. In turn, journalists will dismiss rivals' stories: 'They got a tip, a ring-in. Nothing we can do about that, really … Just luck.'

Like when the Prime Minister forgot his daughter in the pub, and a helpful regular rang up the *Sun*.

'Nothing we can bloody do about that, Ross,' the journalists would chorus. 'Sorry. We can't have a reporter in every pub.'

'Can't we?' Ross had snarled. 'You all seem to spend enough time in the pub.'

Now Miranda and Casey read the *Argus* journalist's email again.

'Jess Miller is assuming the whole Salama story is based on a tip,' Miranda interpreted. 'But we thought that she went out to talk to Adam Jefferson, in Geneva.'

'She might be covering herself?' Casey suggested. 'They'd be fucking furious over there if they thought she'd missed it.'

'I don't think she'd bother telling me that though,' said Miranda. 'Where's the win?'

Miranda was typing. Thought you were on the case too? One of our sources said they'd spoken to you. Hope all well with you.

They waited; an email popped in within seconds.

'*No sodding chance,*' Miranda read out loud. '*I've been up a tree outside Heathrow, being papped by your useless snapper. Never stopped bloody raining. If I'd had even a sniff of this, I'd have been out of that flaming treehouse like …*'

'She didn't know,' said Casey. 'So who the hell spoke to Adam?'

Dash was passing; Miranda beckoned him in.

'We need to start working on the London operation,' said Casey.

'Jesus, you two,' said Dash. 'We've got at least another dozen names so far from that list. Let's get round those first.'

The reporters had fanned out across the country, to appear like Banquo's ghost. One chance to get it right.

'Remember to make it seem like you know it's them,' the reporters were told. 'You're checking a couple of minor details rather than confirming the whole thing.'

'But the London operation is the key to the whole thing,' said Casey.

'And, more importantly,' Miranda pointed out, 'whoever it was put in quite a spirited effort to kill us yesterday, and we'd rather stay alive, all things considered.'

'We can't keep moving from hotel to hotel,' said Casey. 'That prayer room will drive me mad.'

Dash sat down, rubbed his face with his hands.

'OK,' he said. 'What do we know?'

'Almost nothing,' said Miranda. 'We know that Josh knew not to talk about the London end of things. He was relatively chatty about other stuff, probably because he felt safe out in Euzma. So by extension I think we can assume that London must have hammered the need for secrecy into him. And they were tough enough for Josh to listen.'

'Josh owned ten shares in Mapledene, the company that owned the Bombardier,' said Casey. 'The other ninety were owned by Marakata Green, which could have been Leo and Rory, but probably wasn't. The three in Euzma seemed to be equals, and Josh did most of the work, trekking backwards and forwards to Djanet. It wouldn't make sense if the two of them got a bigger split.'

'So it's reasonable to assume that Marakata Green is the London operation,' said Dash slowly.

'The Bombardier was on a lease,' said Hessa, who had slipped into the office, 'and the lease was nearly up. I think that's why they weren't too fussed about abandoning it at Heathrow. The actual owners of the Bombardier are spitting tacks, but they don't seem to have much on payment details either. Just a bank account somewhere in the BVI.'

'And it was only used occasionally to fly in and out of Djanet,' said Miranda. 'It was doing something else the rest of the time.'

'We've got a list of everywhere that Bombardier went,' said Dash. 'Could we cross-reference that against something? Or can we get the passenger lists from somewhere?'

'I wouldn't be surprised if they've done something pretty sharp with any passenger lists,' said Miranda.

Dash sighed. The day was fading outside and he was getting tired. The sofa in his room had odd angles sticking out of it, it had emerged last night.

'I think we call it for tonight,' he said. 'Miranda, go and stay in a hotel, a different one from last night, and we'll take it from here tomorrow.'

They wouldn't sleep, he knew that. But it was worth trying.

'I've booked you into a nice hotel,' Hessa told Miranda.

Hessa had organised a car to pick Miranda up from the underground car park. Casey walked down to the car park, to stretch her legs. The bodyguard hovered a few paces behind.

Miranda climbed in, then peered out of the blacked-out windows. 'Do you think this is what it's like being a rock star?' she asked.

'No,' sighed Casey. 'I feel trapped.'

'Hunted,' said Miranda. 'I feel hunted.'

50

They published the story about Alexander Kingsley the next morning.

The *Post*'s lawyer, Anthony, fought them every step.

'Never publish what you can't prove, word for bloody word. You know that, Dash.'

'Kingsley knew about Euzma.'

'So what? His lawyers will say that he's a Libya expert, so of course he'd know the region. Kingsley sits on the parliamentary group for Tunisia, for heaven's sake. He's been down there on the taxpayers' dime. His team will say that he heard a rumour about it, or something. And I can't see how we would fight that.'

The lawyer was used to winning fights against journalists, over what gets published. The journalists always want to say more, but they cost too much, the big libel trials. Even with the best arguments and the strongest facts, a jury can still go rogue. No editor ever wants to roll the dice with his newspaper.

'Let Kingsley sue.' Dash defied the lawyer. 'We'll see him in court.'

'You can't call a wife to give evidence,' the lawyer said desperately. 'You can never force Lucinda Kingsley to testify that her husband lied about Morocco.'

'I don't care,' said Dash. 'We'll find a way.'

The lawyer paused, and mopped his face with a handkerchief. He lunched well, the lawyer.

'Where's Anthony?' Ross would bellow, often. Only to discover Anthony was in the Ivy, the Ledbury, Le Gavroche and the rest.

Casey had infuriated Anthony once, by getting the *Post* slammed with an emergency injunction, with an incensed judge hauled out of bed in the middle of the night.

'I was halfway through the cod at Nobu,' Anthony had bawled. 'Do you realise ...'

'Just shove in a few allegedlies,' Ross would rage, but Anthony would shake his head.

Now Anthony tangled his fingers.

'I really must advise ...'

'It's my call,' Dash interrupted. 'And we're publishing.'

A few minutes later, Archie went hard to Kingsley's director of communications, setting out the case, blow by blow.

The director of communications listened impassively.

'I see,' he said, without a flicker. 'I'll get back to you.'

They waited on tenterhooks as the clock ticked down to the deadline. It passed, and they published.

There was no denial from Kingsley, and no impassioned outburst on a doorstep as he reached for the sword of truth.

An hour later, the Prime Minister gracefully accepted a resignation that had not been tendered.

And Casey's flat burned down.

51

She was sitting in her office when Dash had to tell her. It was early on Sunday morning, and she had spent another night in the prayer room.

'My flat?' she said, just once, and then went silent.

Dash wanted to hug her, but didn't know how.

He gestured to Miranda, who descended on Casey.

'Oh God, darling, I am so sorry. I am so very sorry. We'll get him, I promise. We will hunt him down.'

But Casey's head was full of flames, flickering through her rooms.

A small red toy car. A doll, balding slightly. A music box, with lavender italics.

Most loved objects, one by one. Memories catching and blazing, and gone. The bookmark, that photograph, just ash amidst ash. Three children laughing, three children burning.

Goodbye and goodbye and goodbye.

Casey shook her head, pushing it away.

'They're getting closer, Miranda. My flat ...'

Dash looked at Casey's slumped shoulders.

'Everything is gone,' she said. 'Everything that wasn't in the house was back in the Hilux. I haven't got anything left.'

'Stay where I can see you,' was the best that Dash could manage. 'I'm sorry, Casey, really I am.'

He increased the security around her. Miranda's husband was sent on an all-inclusive holiday to Biarritz, rustled up by the travel editor.

'Biarritz?' asked Tom. 'Biarritz? But I can't ... I've got a job, darling. And we said we'd go away together ... We never go ...'

'Please, Tom. Please. Just go.'

A security team moved into the pretty house in Queen's Park. Miranda's cousin, they nodded to the neighbours over the fence. Staying for a few days. Yes, lovely weather.

The police had interviewed both Casey and Miranda earlier, gently chiding Casey for running from the M4 crash. With the fire, they redoubled their efforts. But the detective constable had pulled a face at Arthur, 'Honestly, mate, we've not got much so far. No one saw a thing in the blocks near Brentford.'

The other papers had picked up the motorway accident, and the connection to the *Post*, but for now they were too busy shredding Kingsley. He had fled to the pretty cottage in Wiltshire, with the pink roses around the door. Now the cottage was ringed with reporters.

Robert and Alice were in the office early on Sunday too. They were turning out piece after piece; Rob updating the online copy with every new revelation.

'Where does the name come from?' Rob asked Alice, as they wandered back from getting a coffee. 'The name Salama?'

Alice thought, frowned.

'I'd guess it would be an anglicised version of an Arabic word,' she said. 'The Arabic word for safety.'

*

At eleven, Dash called them all into the conference room.

Casey sat at the back, eyes red, very quiet. Archie looked like he hadn't slept since Thursday.

'We need to crack this,' said Dash. 'We need to get to the bottom of who is coordinating all this. They are ruthless bastards and I am not having them attack my journalists like this.'

They went backwards and forwards, over the same ground again and again.

The reporters rang in. Some of the men on the list had buckled under the pressure, confessed in tears. Some had denied it with a rage that might be real. None of the reporters had been able to get a name for the person behind the operation.

'Fuck it,' Miranda snapped, in the end. 'They're not going to get away with this. They can't.'

They stared into the silence.

'I could try Kingsley.' Archie sounded uncertain.

'Kingsley?' Dash raised an eyebrow.

'You never know,' said Archie. 'He's had forty-eight hours to think about it. I know Alexander. He'll be starting to calculate by now.'

They all stared at him, unconvinced.

'There's no way back for him now,' said Miranda. 'Surely?'

'The thing is,' Ross shrugged, 'that right now no one is going in or out of that cottage. But at some point, eventually, even if it is weeks from now, that pack will be called back. And then, if you're Kingsley, you've got to start worrying about who is going to turn up next. Milo Newbury is dead. Oliver Selby has not been heard from. It's starting to look a lot like a pattern, and I wouldn't fancy my chances, if I were Mr Kingsley.'

'Won't the police come and arrest him?' asked Miranda.

Arthur laughed, a harsh sound. 'There are jurisdictional issues, it turns out,' he said. 'Kingsley hasn't actually, so far as they have worked out, committed a crime in this country.'

'You're fucking joking?' Ross was on his feet.

'It's good for us.' Dash damped him down. 'It means that Kingsley's there, in the cottage. Fuck it, Archie, it's worth a shot. You know Kingsley, and he's going to talk to someone, in the end. It might as well be us. And you've known him for a long time.'

'It is a long fucking long shot,' Archie warned.

'It's all,' Miranda said, 'about long shots.'

Kingsley answered the fifth time Archie rang. The political editor walked out of the conference room, looping the office, rambling in big circles as he spoke. They heard odd words as he passed.

Your side of the story ... Whistleblower, really ... We've known each other so long ... Worried you're in danger. And your family, of course. Lucinda. The children.

Archie wore a huge smile as he walked back into the conference room.

'Archie.' Even Miranda was awed. 'I don't know how you managed that.'

'You're worth every one of those fucking lunches.' It was as close to a compliment as Ross got.

'We've got to drive down to Wiltshire right now,' said Archie. 'Miranda, come with me. You know the story, all the details.'

'Casey, you stay here,' said Dash. 'I don't want you leaving this office.'

52

From the front gate, the Kingsleys' house looked idyllic. The path to the front door was lined with clouds of lavender, and the last of the roses drifted in the breeze.

Lucinda Kingsley hid behind the door as she opened it, the cameras clicking like castanets. She had been crying, they could see. In her brave red dress, she looked like a poppy, battered down by the rain.

'I don't know why he's letting you, of all people,' she spat, 'into this house.'

Miranda and Archie blinked in the sudden gloom, peering around a large hall. Lucinda pointed towards a door, then disappeared towards the stairs.

'I can't even bear to look at him.' Lucinda glanced back. Her eyes were full of contempt.

Two small children were peering over the banisters. The little boy was crying. All the curtains at the front of the cottage were closed, a house in mourning.

The drawing room led off the hall, and they found Kingsley sitting beside an unlit fire. It was a beautiful room, soft pastels and exquisite furniture. An oil painting of the Kingsleys, just married, at their most hopeful, hung near the door.

The French windows were open on to a ravishing garden, with a striped lawn running down to the weed-clogged river. Red rhododendrons sprawled along the riverbanks, the beeches curtsying down to the water in their summer ball gowns. Swallows dived to and fro, pouncing on flies.

'The noble reporters from the *Post*.' He waved a glass of brandy. 'The heroes of the hour. Welcome.'

'Alexander,' said Archie, and Miranda could see the genuine sympathy in his face. 'I hope you are ... As well as can be.'

Kingsley stared at the pile of pine cones in the fireplace.

'Been better, old boy.' Kingsley was enunciating carefully. 'Been better. I thought I'd talk to you, Archie. Of all of them. Because we've been friends, haven't we? We've been friends. I didn't want to speak to those vultures.'

'Why?' Archie's voice caught in his throat. 'Why did you do it?'

Kingsley wandered over to the windows, rubbed at a smear. One of the beeches by the river had died; it stood out skeletal against the summer sky.

'You know, I've never been quite sure,' Kingsley said almost wonderingly. 'I suppose I've always thought about what it would feel like. But hasn't everyone? Now and again? Wondered what it would be like ... But I never thought I would have ... the opportunity. And then when the opportunity arose ...' He paused. 'You see, it's all so perfect, all of this ...'

He waved carelessly at a pale blue OKA armchair and a Rockingham china dog. The brandy slopped on to the Aubusson rug.

'I've always known what I wanted,' Kingsley went on. 'Since before school, even. I knew, absolutely, that I wanted to be an MP. But it means you have to be so careful, all of the time. You're always watching for cameras, right the way through. Always thinking about how it might look. And then only thinking about how it might look. And it gets worse all the time, all that.'

'But it's what you chose,' said Archie. 'It was what you wanted.'

'I know,' said Kingsley. 'I chose everything. I wanted it and I got it. And then I married Lucinda. And I love her, you know. Really, I do ... But it was all just so perfect.'

He spat out the last word, slamming the brandy glass back on the table.

'You look around and it's all so perfect that you just want to ...' he paused. 'No, you have to ... You have to break something. Smash it. Smash anything. Scream and shout and crush it all. I used to look at pictures of us. Me and Lucinda. Lucinda and the kids. And we were the perfect family. It all looked so idyllic. And inside, I just wanted to hurt someone ... I wanted ... I wanted to smash something.'

He stopped, as if almost shocked by his own words, then went on more quietly.

'And so when it came up, I almost laughed at first. And then ... then I couldn't stop thinking about it. Some of my friends go to hookers, you know. They want something secret and selfish. Dirty, even. Dangerous. Something that's all their own and nobody else's. I never did that. But this, I just couldn't get out of my head.'

'How?' Miranda broke in. 'How did it come about?'

A small smile played across Kingsley's face.

'She'll kill me, you know,' he said almost conversationally. 'I am quite sure she'll kill me. When you warned me about that earlier, Archie, I thought, well, I don't care any more. It's all over. The bitch can do what she wants.'

'She?' Miranda asked. 'She?'

'Emerald,' said Kingsley. 'Emerald.'

'Emerald?' Archie prompted.

'Where did you meet her?' Miranda sharpened in.

'She saw me first,' said Kingsley. 'I was at that members' bar, you know, the one in South Ken. I looked up, and she was staring at me. Just staring. I get that a bit, you know' – and even now, Kingsley couldn't resist running a hand through his hair, straightening up just slightly. 'But with Emerald, it was different. She thought I was someone else, can't remember who. We laughed about that, and then we chatted, for a while. She was so funny, so quick and perceptive. She laughed all the time. And then quite suddenly she said she had to go. I asked ... I asked if I could see her again. And she just smiled and said she was sure we would bump into each other again.'

'And you did,' said Miranda.

'We did,' said Kingsley. 'We did. I was walking along the river, my route home from the House of Commons, and suddenly there she was, sitting on a bench, watching the river. We talked again, laughed. She stopped everything feeling so perfect, while making it even better. I don't know ...'

'How often did you meet up with her?'

'Lots of times,' said Kingsley. 'I couldn't count.'

'And were you sleeping with her?'

'I ..' So they knew that he had.

'And how did the whole idea come about?'

'It just came up.' Kingsley screwed up his face in concentration. 'I can't remember how it started ...'

Emerald had brought it up, thought Miranda. Every time he wasn't sure, it was Emerald.

'Anyway,' Kingsley went on, 'the whole idea turned into something we talked about. And one day she said, almost casually, that she could make it happen. And I remember being shocked. I do, really. I would never have ... Before I could say anything, she was talking about something else. But you know, I kept thinking about it.'

'The seed planted,' nodded Archie.

'Exactly,' said Kingsley. 'Exactly. And gradually – I'm not even quite sure how – it became something I was going to do. Something I was excited about. Something I was looking forward to. We went up to the Highlands together, for a weekend. She taught me to shoot, up on the moors, miles from anywhere.'

'She taught you to shoot?' Miranda asked.

'She's a brilliant shot, you know. I had to practise a lot too,' said Kingsley. 'Here and there. I'd never even held a gun before all this, oddly.'

'It must have taken a long time,' said Miranda.

'It became a hobby,' said Kingsley. 'Lucinda used to laugh and say it got me out of the house, at least. When I got a new gun, she got a new handbag. You know what I mean. And this hobby was more interesting than golf. The comms people for the party didn't like it, they didn't want a photograph of me out there, holding a gun. Lucky' – he almost laughed – 'that they insisted on that now.'

'So you went out to Libya?' asked Miranda.

'The parliamentary trip came up,' said Kingsley. 'And it seemed like the perfect timing. I was watching the other MPs, as we went round the factories and the souks and the God-knows-what-else in Tunisia. It was so dull. So bloody boring. And I had this glorious secret, which no one would ever guess.'

'And you travelled up to Euzma?' Miranda thought about him making that journey, the dusty long road.

'I thought Euzma was magical,' said Kingsley. 'That white marble palace. We went up to the camp, and I felt like a god, looking down on all those people. And afterwards I felt alive, completely and utterly alive.'

'And you didn't go back?' Miranda asked.

'Never,' said Kingsley. 'It was always going to be a one-off. I promised myself that much. I can see, you know, how people get hooked on it. Addicted even. Serial killers, I suppose. But it was always going to be just once, for me. So that when I was sitting there in one of those endless bloody meetings or stuck in a traffic jam or something, it would be this precious little memory I could bring out and polish. And then tuck away again. *I won.*'

'And how did she know them, the men in the desert?'

'I think Charlton had been her bodyguard somewhere. On a trip. Something like that anyway.'

'And where' – Miranda disguised her repulsion – 'where is Emerald right now?'

'I have no idea,' said Kingsley. 'She could be anywhere. I never knew where she was, even when ...'

'Do you know where she lived? Anything?'

'I just don't know, I'm afraid. We always met in hotels.'

'So you stopped seeing her,' suggested Miranda. 'After you'd been out to Libya?'

'She drifted away from me.' Kingsley's face sagged. 'I was hypnotised by her, in an odd sort of way. I haven't seen her for a long time now.'

'Do you have her number?' Miranda asked, thinking, I'll hack that phone. I don't give a shit. I'll hack that phone in a second.

'It went dead ages ago,' said Kingsley. 'Must have been a burner. And she just chucked it …'

There was almost self-pity in his voice.

'Look at my face.' Miranda had covered up most of the black eye with concealer, but the bruise still showed through. 'She's lethal, and she can't be allowed to carry on. Are you sure you have no idea where she is?'

Kingsley's eyes met hers almost gently.

'None whatsoever,' he answered, and Miranda didn't know if he was lying or not.

They talked on, until Miranda couldn't bear it any more.

'We've got to go,' she said. 'Archie will call you if we have any more questions, Mr Kingsley.'

She bustled Archie towards the door, but he pulled away for a second.

'Alexander …' Even now Archie was hopeful. 'Don't you … Don't you have anything to say?'

'What?' Alexander looked up. 'Oh. Yes. Of course. I am very sorry for it all. I apologise unreservedly.'

Even Archie could see he didn't mean it. Miranda didn't bother to say goodbye. She opened the door into the hallway.

Lucinda was slumped against the wall, next to the door. Miranda wondered how long she had been listening there.

'I thought I loved him,' Lucinda whispered. 'But I never knew him, did I? I never knew him at all.'

53

Casey was pacing up and down the office. Past Business and Pictures and Sport, spin, and back again. Back and forth, back and forth; bored tiger at the zoo.

'Do stop.' Janet waved some biscuits at her. 'You're exhausting me.'

Casey prowled into the conference room. They had pinned up photographs now: Milo smiling, Selby stern.

'Some cultures believe that a camera steals a piece of your soul,' commented Peregrine. 'With every photograph.'

'Maybe' – Casey turned away – 'it's the person taking the photograph, instead.'

Her phone went, and she fell on it.

'Is that Cassandra Benedict?' It was a Scottish voice.

'Yes,' she grumbled.

'I'm calling from St Thomas',' said the woman. 'Ed Fitzgerald is awake, and he's asking for you.'

'He's asking for me?' Delight flooded Casey. 'I'll be there as soon as possible.'

She bounded over to Dash.

'I've got to go, Dash.'

'Wait a second,' said Dash. He was marking up a proof, red pen flying. 'We haven't got a driver at the moment. Or a car for that matter.'

Vadim's hold on life was still precarious, but the doctors were starting to look more hopeful.

'I can take a taxi.' Casey felt her temper rise. 'I feel like I'm being held to ransom. It's Ed. I've got to go to him ...'

'Casey,' Dash growled. 'We're just trying to keep you alive.'

'Dash,' Ross shouted. 'The PM's going to make his first statement since Kingsley, any sec.'

Distracted, Dash walked towards the news desk. The grey face filled all the television screens. Robert was transcribing in neat shorthand. Casey hovered for a minute, then slipped towards the door. Without looking back, she hurried out of the entrance and paused in the fresh air, enjoying the sudden sunlight after the office air-conditioning. The hospital was just over the bridge from Parliament; she could be there in minutes.

There was a movement on Casey's left and she jumped like a startled deer.

It was Lady Newbury. She looked even older now, frail, and leaning on a stick. Casey knew somehow that Lady Newbury had been waiting for a long time, outside the *Post*'s offices.

'Lady Newbury,' said Casey, and then couldn't say anything more.

'You came to my house,' said Lady Newbury. 'And asked to see his passport.'

'Yes,' said Casey hopelessly.

'And that photograph, of Milo in the desert. You took that from the flat. And you put it on your front page.'

We only know snapshots.

'I did.'

'I said to you,' Lady Newbury went on, almost dreamily, 'that the worst thing was not knowing. Not knowing what happened to him.'

'I remember,' said Casey quietly.

'It's not the worst thing, it would seem,' said Lady Newbury. 'There are always worse things, it turns out. Far, far worse. I asked you to tell me if you found out what happened to my son, I remember. I suppose you did that much.'

'I am sorry,' said Casey. 'I am so sorry for everything.'

'I trusted you,' she said, and the rage bubbled up. 'I let you into my house. My home. My husband ... Conrad can barely speak. I have never seen a man so despairing. Milo was already dead, for heaven's sake. Couldn't you let him rest in peace?'

'I am terribly sorry for your family,' said Casey. 'It must be awful.'

The words sounded so trivial.

'You have ruined my family to sell a few newspapers,' said Lady Newbury. 'You have destroyed all our memories, and we can never make new ones. It was all we had left, the memories.'

'It wasn't to ...' But Casey couldn't explain; there was too much to explain. 'Milo did—'

'But he is still my son.' Lady Newbury raised her head. 'And I will never stop loving him. I wanted you to know that. There is nothing that any of you can do to make me stop loving him.'

She turned stiffly towards a navy blue Mercedes. Bella Monroe was sitting in the driving seat. She stepped out to help Lady Newbury into the car.

Bella was wearing old jeans, her hair scraped back.

'We all loved him, you know.' Bella looked older, as if she had grown-up in the last few days. 'I know you think I'm a fool, and I have been silly. But I loved him, you know. He used to be different. Before. We never knew what had happened to make him change so much.'

'I know,' said Casey.

Bella closed the car door on Lady Newbury.

'At least now I understand some of what happened.' Bella looked straight at Casey. 'They will never forgive you, but I think that maybe I would rather know. No more false dreams now.'

Casey watched as the blue Mercedes pulled away. Her phone snapped her back.

Miranda. She would get in a taxi towards St Thomas', then call her back.

Casey hailed a taxi, jumped in.

'It's a woman,' said Miranda. 'She's called Emerald.' She talked through the rest of the interview with Kingsley. 'Where are you right now, Casey?'

'In the office.' Easy came the lie. 'But they called from the hospital. I want to go and see Ed.'

'Casey.' Miranda sounded impatient. 'You mustn't leave the office. It isn't safe right now.'

'Ed's woken up!' said Casey. 'He wants to see me. And I feel like a caged animal.'

'For fuck's sake, Casey, this is not a game. Dash is trying to keep you alive.'

'I'll speak to you later,' snapped Casey. She was tired of being told what to do.

She shut the phone off, and thought of Milo. Milo, the man she would only ever know from the photographs. The photographs and the paintings, and the memories of people who never really knew him at all. She thought of Lady Newbury, back in the flat, as the memories and curtains faded.

The traffic was immobilised on Victoria Street. Sitting next to the red-and-white candy stripes of the cathedral, Casey shivered.

Vadim smiling. The windscreen shattering. A scream as the traffic broke like a wave.

She should get out. It wasn't far to Parliament, especially through the back streets, and then she was nearly at St Thomas'.

The taxi driver's radio babbled.

'There's something about a bomb scare over at Lambeth Bridge,' said the taxi driver. 'Happening all the time, they are now. Bloody nuisance.'

Casey paid him off, and started hurrying through Westminster. She always enjoyed Parliament Square. Big Ben, Westminster Abbey, a wave at Winston Churchill. She ducked through the tourists and thought about seeing Ed, with that quick smile on his face.

She bounded on to the bridge, smiling at the Lion, the Witch and the Wardrobe lamp posts. Casey loved the Thames, that salty ribbon reaching right into the heart of London. There was County Hall, which Casey loved, because anywhere else in the world, it would be *the* building, and in London it's just a coffee shop. There was the London Eye, turning as slow as time.

Casey ran her hand along the parapet, the green of the benches in the House of Commons, and smiled.

'Don't move, Casey.'

A beautiful woman was blocking her path. She was wearing a long black coat, almost a cape, that flowed in the breeze.

'Come over to the edge of the bridge, Casey. Come and stand with me for a while.'

There was something familiar about the woman, and yet Casey felt only the menace, the echo of a nightmare dreamed before. For a second, she couldn't take it in.

'What do you want?' Casey battled to keep her voice steady.

'A car will come for us in a moment,' and Casey heard the woman breathe a laugh. 'It's been held up by the bomb scare.'

'And it's your bomb scare.' Casey's mind raced. 'The traffic ...' Lambeth was the only other bridge over to St Thomas.

'Maybe,' the woman said, in a Scottish accent. The nurse.

Stupid. So stupid. Casey's anger almost blotted out the fear, for a moment.

'I should have known,' said Casey.

'You should have known.' It was almost reproving. 'I think it's your heart that's the problem.'

Casey glanced across at her profile again. The quick glance, the flicker of a smile. Those emerald eyes, oddly familiar.

'You're Amelie.' It flooded back. 'That night in Gigi's. You were there.'

'So quick,' she smiled. 'I knew you'd remember.'

The tourists were ambling past, red from the sun, and laughing at the human statue who never blinked. Someone was playing the bagpipes, badly, over by Westminster tube.

The best ambush never looks like one.

'I won't get into the car,' said Casey. 'I'll never get into that car.'

'I think you will,' Emerald's eyes drifted up the river. 'Because there's a rifle, of course.'

54

Dash was watching the Prime Minister speak down the barrel of the television camera.

Appalled about these allegations surrounding Alexander Kingsley. Only allegations at this point. But horrified by the idea, of course. Accepted his resignation. International development always been of crucial importance to this government.

He trailed off slightly at that point, almost embarrassed, but gathered himself.

The reshuffle of the Home Office ministers will be completed shortly. We'll all be working together, as a cabinet, through any challenge.

The Prime Minister spun away from the camera, leaving the political correspondents to pick over his words.

Ross punched the sky. 'This story!' he gloated. 'This fucking story!'

'You like it,' Dash said slowly. 'You love watching them die.'

'Just giving the public what they want,' said Ross. 'Roll up, roll up. And dance for the crowd.'

Dash's phone went, and it was Miranda, giving him the read-out of the Kingsley meeting, almost dissolving with rage.

The editor hesitated by the news desk. Dash glanced up, impatient.

'You were right.' The editor forced out the words.

Dash gestured: it was nothing.

'Extraordinary, though.'

'Yes.' Dash turned back to the list.

'We never think ...' Salcombe went on. 'We never thought what it is like, from the other side. When these women are ... They can make you say anything. And do anything. And be anything.'

Dash glanced up. You understand them, Dash thought. You understand the killers. 'That's not the point, and you know it. They were doing it already, these people. You know that.'

'Maybe,' Salcombe said. 'Maybe.'

'If they could wave a wand, and make none of this exist, do you think they would?' Salcombe asked. 'Casey and Miranda. They wanted it all to be true, every step of the way.'

'They didn't,' said Dash, knowing it was a lie.

Salcombe almost smiled. 'We'd have burned them all for witches, a few centuries ago.'

When the battle's lost and won, thought Dash. And they burned for a rumour, not for a truth. He stared down at his list and a few seconds later Salcombe walked away.

Ross was moaning about the layout of page five when Miranda walked in.

'Where's Casey?'

'Don't know.' Ross looked around vaguely.

'Where the fuck is she?'

Dash walked over to the investigations room. There was no one there.

'Has anyone seen Casey?' He tried to keep the panic out his voice.

'She got a call from the hospital.' Arthur looked up. 'Remember?'

Miranda was gone, racing across the newsroom, and crashing out the door.

55

'Because there's a rifle, of course.'

Casey ducked instinctively.

'Stand up,' Amelie ordered almost gently. 'Come and stand next to me.'

Somehow Casey made it to the edge of the bridge, next to a green and gold lamp post with shields at her feet. They leaned against the parapet, looking down at the House of Commons. They would look so normal, the two of them, watching the evening river, with the tourists chattering all around.

Casey imagined the sights trained on her body, and felt her heart stumble.

'"The river glideth at his own sweet will",' whispered Emerald.

'What do you want?' Casey interrupted.

'We didn't guess each other's game that night in Gigi's.' Amelie almost smiled. 'I asked Jasper about a Callie a couple of times. Said I'd really enjoyed meeting you. But he couldn't place a Callie, even though I'd seen you chatting to him. I should have guessed. We both should have guessed, I suppose. I saw you stumble into the table, knew you hadn't broken your shoe. I thought it was deft, that arrival. I might borrow it one day.'

Emerald. Amelie. Once, a long time ago, this girl must have been named Emily or Amabel, Emilia or Emmeline. That first syllable; enough to turn her head.

'So you heard Adam talking?' guessed Casey. 'That night.'

Emerald inclined her head. 'Just by chance, really. Just like you. I'd just met Selby, back then.'

'So you went after Milo?'

'I couldn't have him talking.' Amelie shrugged. 'I went to that flat of his, in Pimlico, the day after that night in Gigi's. He was all over the place, towards the end. The guilt had broken him. It can happen, one gathers.'

'So you told him to throw himself out of the window?'

'I pointed out the incongruity,' explained Emerald gently. 'That he was telling his friends, and yet terrified that people would become aware. It emerged that he was horrified by the thought of his parents' knowing. I may have mentioned that there was a way' – Amelie paused – 'a way that his parents need never know. I said I could ensure it, in fact, if he gave me a list of the people he had told. It wasn't a long list, in the end. I think he had only told a couple of people when he was drunk, and then felt even more terrified. He wasn't making much sense at that point anyway, too much drink, too many drugs ...'

Milo had jumped to protect his parents, Casey thought. And then Casey had forced the knowledge on them anyway.

'And after that you went after Adam, to Geneva.'

'You and I started at different ends, but I could work backwards, don't forget,' said Emerald, 'But then, when I spoke to him in Geneva, Adam didn't talk about Milo. Even when I pushed him quite hard. So I let him ...'

Amelia paused delicately. Casey thought of Adam and Lulu in Geneva, oblivious. The bullet had passed so close.

'And you took the painting from the flat? The little Renoir?'

'Oh no,' said Amelie. 'He gave me that in return for his journey, oh, ages ago now. I love beautiful things.'

She looked at her watch, a silver Cartier. Her face was exquisite in the fading gold of the light.

'The car won't be long now,' she said.

'Is that why you do it?' asked Casey. 'For the beautiful things?'

'I suppose that is a part of it.' Emerald stared up the river. 'It's certainly a part. But there's something else about it too. When a man is dancing absolutely to your tune, and yet still believes he is leading every step. You know that feeling, Casey, don't you?'

One of the big ferry boats was passing under the bridge and Casey thought about jumping. But the sniper would be there, somewhere.

'I'm nothing like you,' said Casey. 'Nothing.'

'Maybe, maybe not.' Amelie glanced up as a seagull shrieked down the Thames. 'I've been thinking about you, Casey. Wondering. I spoke to Josh, you know. He's so angry. You made a fool of him, didn't you? And men never like that. They hate it, even. You've disrupted so much, Casey. All that work.'

'A nice little business, was it? And you never even had to see them die.'

'It's all in our heads though, isn't it? For us.' Emerald ran her fingers along the bridge. 'I've researched you, and your friend Miranda, over the last few days. You know exactly how it is, don't you? When you're playing that game of chess, and you can't even acknowledge the board.'

'I don't know what you're talking about.'

'I could always tell the ones who wanted the kill.' Amelie was almost talking to herself. 'Sometimes, you just know, don't you think? Across a room. Although they didn't even know it themselves.'

'You're mad.' Casey felt the anger surge.

'They all want it, Casey. The kill. Somewhere deep down. Because isn't that why you love your soldier boy? Just a bit?'

'No,' said Casey. 'No. Never.'

A Chinese bride was posing for photographs just a few feet away, stiff in satin. Smiling for the camera as her new husband clutched her hand apprehensively.

'You can't kill me up here,' said Casey, not sure if she believed it. 'You'd never make it off this bridge.'

It seemed impossible that this could happen, right in the shadow of Parliament, in the centre of the city. A cyclist swept past, too close to a taxi.

'Oh, I can.' Emerald was quite confident. 'And I will, if I need to. Rory just wanted to talk to you first. Say goodbye, I suppose.'

I'm going to die, Casey thought sadly. This is how it ends.

The traffic was starting to move again. The police had evidently found nothing in their hunt of Lambeth Bridge. Any moment, a car would draw up, and Casey would disappear into the darkness for ever.

She looked across at the block ugliness of St Thomas'. Ed was up there, somewhere, hurt but alive.

I love you, Casey thought. I never told you, but I do. I love you.

A few yards beyond Amelie, a blonde figure walked up and leaned against the parapet, almost invisible in the crowds.

She looked towards Casey, eyes fixed on hers.

I'm here, she seemed to say.

It will be all right.

I'm here.

And she never looked away.

'Why Milo?' asked Casey.

'Milo ...' Emerald was looking at Parliament, eyes drifting along the crenellations. 'He had everything, didn't he? The looks, the charm and that beautiful girl – Bella, I think it was. But it was never enough, any of it. I first saw Milo at one of their private views, up on Dover Street. My old hunting grounds.' Amelie smiled. 'Milo was talking about something, I can't even remember what now, and his father dismissed him, just like that, in front of everyone. I think Milo wanted to conquer someone. Anyone, really. Just crush them. Instead of always being flattened. I knew I could use that rage. But then ...' She paused. 'Then it broke him instead.'

A ferry boat was cruising up the river towards them, dozens of cameras clicking at the honey glory of Parliament. It had passed under Lambeth Bridge, the red of the House of Lords' benches, and now it steered left to ogle the Commons. Emerald watched it idly. It was high tide, the water lapping the terrace where the MPs were drinking away the day.

Casey's glanced at Miranda, leaning against the parapet.

'But that's not all,' said Casey. 'It's not just about the beautiful things, and the control, is it? There's something else.'

'I knew you would ask.' Amelie's eyes were appreciative. 'You, Casey, would have to know. You couldn't bear not to know. And you need there to be something more. You can't let me just be the bitch. And I wondered ...'

Casey let the silence grow. Emerald flicked a smile at her.

'Revenge, I suppose.' Amelie stared south down the river, over the silver towers. 'Maybe.'

Casey heard the scream in the wind. Almost knew what had driven Emerald to take her revenge on those men, and seize back her strange sort of power.

'Now I make them dance as I wish.' Amelie's eyes searched out Casey. 'I have the power, now. My toys.'

'Toys ...'

'Is this the power of the confession?' Emerald threw away a smile. 'You know it too well, Casey.'

At that moment, Casey realised she could never believe a word that came from Amelie's mouth.

'But why refugees?' she asked. 'Why refugees, of all people?'

'Ah,' Emerald shrugged. 'Everyone else uses them, so why shouldn't I? Does anyone care at all? The world lets them die on their mountainside, and so what is the difference? I'm just streamlining.'

'You offered the clean kill,' said Casey. 'With no messiness. You dehumanised death.'

'It's where we want them though, isn't it?' said Amelie. 'Not on our home front. Refugees, and death. Photogenic, and at a safe distance. We don't want them here, do we?'

'But why?' asked Casey, that question she'd asked so many times. 'Who needs that?'

'Who needs any of it?' Emerald's glance floated up the river. 'Who needs strawberries in winter and roses in autumn? Who needs cheap little dresses and fast little cars? And why ever do they bring me diamonds? I take it because I want it. I take it because it's fun. I take it' – she paused – 'because I can.'

The ferry boat was nearing Westminster Bridge now.

'Watch the hand,' Amelie fluttered her fingers high. 'Watch the hand.'

The tourists waved back.

The crack of the rifle deafened the Thames.

Miranda sprinted the last few strides, hurling Casey to the ground.

'Wait …' gasped Casey.

And Emerald jumped straight off the bridge, down on to the ferry boat.

56

'The police marksmen really didn't like firing straight into a hospital,' Arthur was laughing. 'You can sort of see their point.'

It had been Josh, up in one of the small hospital rooms. Lying with the rifle arrowed towards the bridge, his world narrowed to that tiny circle.

He'd been rushed just a few floors down to emergency, the doctors ignoring the M24 on the floor, and battling to save him despite it all. He died, just the same.

'He was in a coma patient's room?' Ross asked. 'Bit of a waste of that view.'

'Miranda ran all the way to Parliament.' Hessa bounced on her toes. 'She realised you'd gone, Casey, and worked it all out.'

They were back in the *Post*'s offices, drinking endless instant coffees.

'Miranda was shouting at me to call the police as she ran out of the office,' said Arthur. 'She phoned me as she was running down the road to Westminster Bridge. She'd worked it out. He was good, that detective, the one who came and interviewed you both. He put me straight through to the team up on the House of Commons. They didn't believe me at first, of course.'

'I sent through a photograph of you, Casey,' said Hessa. 'One of them spotted you out on the bridge.'

'Why didn't they just shoot Amelie?' asked Miranda.

'They couldn't be sure,' said Arthur. 'I mean, she could have been anyone. Some bird that Casey'd just decided to meet up on the bridge for some reason. Or Casey could have bumped into an old friend, just by chance. You can imagine, if the police gunned down some girl ...'

'So they started looking for the gunman?' asked Casey.

'They started looking for something. Some of the best marksmen in the world, up on the roof of the House of Commons.' Arthur was almost boasting. 'That gunman could have been almost anywhere, I suppose. But they figured he would be on the west side of the bridge, the side you'd walk across. And maybe the hospital just made sense.'

'I suppose,' Miranda realised, 'they meant to kill Ed too, once Casey was accounted for. That would have been easy, for Josh.'

Casey felt her heart shudder, again.

'Miranda walked out on the bridge,' said Hessa, with pride. 'The police were there, down by the statue of Boadicea, arguing about whether to empty the bridge or not. They told her not to, ordered her really, but she just walked out.'

Miranda ducked her head.

'Thank you,' Casey said to her. 'It made ... a difference.'

'They haven't caught her yet,' said Arthur. 'She hijacked that tourist boat, cool as you like. Jumped down like a cat on to the deck.'

'Wild leap,' said Ross. 'She was lucky with the tide.'

Not lucky, thought Casey. And not controlling the tides. But knowing, and using, and that meant the same, really.

'All the tourists were screaming their heads off,' Arthur went on. 'She had a gun to the captain's head. Poor sod, he steered it straight into the pier at the London Eye, and Emerald disappeared into the yelling herd stampeding off the boat.'

'The police are a shade embarrassed about that bit,' Arthur said. 'She dumped that long black coat, ducked the cameras, and they just missed her somehow.'

But they didn't know her, Casey thought now. The ruthless player who would never be in check, just because she'd lost her knight. The police would never catch Amelie. She would know the police had a photograph of her, and be long gone, by now. Probably abroad, slipping out of the country like a ghost.

But they wouldn't catch her, the police. Casey knew that much.

'So, Josh was up in the hospital,' said Miranda. 'Does that leave Rory and Leo driving the car?'

The police hadn't found the car either. It must have stayed hidden in the traffic chaos and then slipped away as London gradually began to unfurl.

'I bumped into Lady Newbury,' Casey remembered suddenly. 'She was waiting outside the office. I felt so sad for her. It was awful.'

'Isn't that,' Ross said, 'like a shark feeling sorry for its lunch?'

'It's stopped it though, hasn't it?' Casey was reading the headlines scrolling along the television screen. 'This will end them, won't it? It has to.'

'You do it to change things, don't you?' said Miranda. 'And I do it for the story.'

'I don't know,' said Casey. 'I watched a child die. I sat up there and I never did a thing to stop it. Not many people get the chance to be a hero.'

And then walk away.

She turned towards the news desk. All around them, the room was fizzing. The huge television screens were alternating between the taped-off Westminster Bridge, lights flickering in the darkness, and Salcombe, filmed hours earlier, praising his reporters with the *Post* logo huge behind him.

'Sensational traffic online,' Ross said happily.

The Sunday papers had just dropped: 'Gunman horror in the heart of London'.

'Your "My gun siege nightmare" piece can wait for tomorrow, Casey,' Ross said generously. 'We can put that out whenever works for you, really.'

'Too kind,' said Miranda.

She and Archie had driven back up from Wiltshire, Miranda breaking speed limits all the way. She took off a wing mirror turning into the car park, Archie whispered, still haunted.

'Stay in a hotel for a few more nights,' said Dash. 'I'm sure Emerald will have left the country, but we won't know for certain.'

Casey thought of a lifetime of glancing over her shoulder.

'I will,' said Casey. 'But first, I am going to see Ed.'

'Be careful,' said Miranda, automatically.

'I will be.'

Dash watched Casey as she left. Matthew had been super-seded by a small squad of men, who trailed her like a comet's tail.

As Casey reached the doors, Miranda caught up with her, softening suddenly as she did sometimes. Dash watched them hug and smile. Tomorrow, said Miranda's gesture, tomorrow.

It's always about tomorrow in a newspaper.

And Dash walked back towards the news desk, because there's always something at the news desk. There's always the race, the race for tomorrow.

ACKNOWLEDGEMENTS

It seems odd that two friends – one couple – were so central to the creation of this book, but that is how it turned out. Ages ago, one slightly disastrous year after I had left university, I met up with my friend Collette Lyons.

'I don't know what to do with my life,' I moaned, quite a few drinks into proceedings.

'I'm doing work experience on the *Style* section of the *Sunday Times* this month,' she said cheerfully. 'Come in with me. We can break in through the turnstiles together! No one will ever notice there's two of us.'

So we did. The *Sunday Times* did eventually notice, but failed in their various attempts to get rid of me, and that was the start of my career in journalism.

A few years later, Collette very wisely married the lovely Paul Vlitos, a novelist and senior lecturer in creative writing at the University of Surrey.

At about 2 o'clock one morning, after yet more drinks, I admitted: 'Trynawriteabook.'

'Send it to me tomorrow,' he said, with immense generosity.

And then, a few days later: 'You have to finish this.'

Given that Collette was responsible for my journalism career, and Paul was responsible for my book – and I am not quite sure where I would be otherwise – I promise I will be the very best godmother to the gorgeous Buffy.

An especially huge thank you to all my amazing friends who took the time to read *To The Lions* and advise on in its early drafts. In particular – Alex Marrache, Alice Ross, Alice Wood, Amelia Hill, Claire Apps, David Pegg, Felicity Fitzgerald, Francesca Hornak, Jasmine Miller, Kate Kingsley, Laura Roberts, Michou Burckett St Laurent, Presiley Baxendale, Richard Fitzgerald, Romilly Holland, Sarah Mahmud, Tabbin Almond and Victoria Naylor-Leyland.

During my ludicrous career in journalism, I have had some of the best fun with some of the most brilliant people. In particular, Robert Winnett and Claire Newell, you, um, inspired me.

My fantastic agent – Andrew Gordon at David Higham – was vital in turning *To The Lions* into a recognisable book. The moment I met Alison Hennessey from Raven Books, I knew she had to be the person to publish it – and everyone else at Bloomsbury has been incredibly kind and brilliantly inspirational.

My family were heroic throughout every stage of *To The Lions*. Nicky and Simon, James and Cressy, your advice was invaluable and your support irreplaceable. Thank you.

And finally, darling Jonny, I am so happy that you wandered back into my life.

NOTE ON THE TYPE

The text of this book is set in Minion, a digital typeface designed by Robert Slimbach in 1990 for Adobe Systems. The name comes from the traditional naming system for type sizes, in which minion is between nonpareil and brevier. It is inspired by late Renaissance-era type.

THE DEAD LINE

A Bangladeshi camp. A British ambassador. A Harley Street doctor.

Investigative journalist Casey Benedict is used to working on stories that will take her from the bottom to the top of society – stories with a huge human cost. And her latest case is no different.

A frantic message is found hidden in clothes manufactured abroad for the British high street. *They take the girls...*

Casey and her team at the *Post* know they are on the brink of a major exposé but identifying the factories in which the clothes have been made is one challenge, following the trail of those taken is another.

Their attempts to find the girls will take Casey from her London newsroom across the world and into the very heart of families who will be destroyed if what she uncovers is ever revealed.

PRE-ORDER YOUR COPY:

BY PHONE: +44 (0) 1256 302 699; **BY EMAIL:** DIRECT@MACMILLAN.CO.UK

DELIVERY IS USUALLY 3–5 WORKING DAYS. FREE POSTAGE AND PACKAGING FOR ORDERS OVER £20.

ONLINE: WWW.BLOOMSBURY.COM/BOOKSHOP

PRICES AND AVAILABILITY SUBJECT TO CHANGE WITHOUT NOTICE.

WWW.BLOOMSBURY.COM/AUTHOR/HOLLY-WATT

BLOOMSBURY